DREAM KING

Realm of Night
Book One

Copyright © 2021 Elise Knight
ISBN: 978-1-989997-54-3
Enchanted Quill Press

This book is a work of fiction
Any resemblance to actual persons is purely coincidental

Contact the author at www.eliseknight.com
Cover by Jesh Art
Interior Formatting by Enchanted Quill Press
Editing by Rose Lipscomb

Realm of Night

- Dark Court
- Dream Court
- Nightmare Court

Prologue
1 year ago

Seven days and seven nights.

That's how long the world slept.

Every single person fell asleep at the exact same moment, no matter the time of day. Those already sleeping were the luckiest; they were in their beds when it happened, blissfully unaware. But the people who walked around in broad daylight weren't so lucky. Pilots fell asleep at their aircraft controls, nurses passed out while administering medicine, kids' heads slumped to their school desks. Fire-fighters battling a blaze dropped to the floor peacefully, leaving the fire to rage out of control and consume them. Cars crashed, planes fell out of the sky, boats hit rocks and sank. People the world over died, and still, no one woke. Not until the seventh day...

CHAPTER ONE
One year later

The heavy cream envelope sat on my dresser, mocking me. Downright sending me into a murderous rage, if truth be told. It offset the lovely pile of bills with the red ink of OVERDUE stamped all over them. Cream and red. Like blood and bandages. And I was pretty sure there would be both if I actually opened the damn thing. A fucking massacre!

Trying to ignore it, I slurped back a cup of coffee for the caffeine hit and attempted to pull my long white-blonde hair into something managing a ponytail.

The envelope stared at me. I stared back with narrowed eyes before giving into temptation, snatching up the envelope, and ripping it open savagely. Sucking in a deep breath, I pulled the invitation out. It was beautiful. Thick monogrammed cardstock with a hand-drawn picture of a bride and groom surrounded by embossed hearts. It was elegant but also vaguely sickening. I swallowed thickly before opening the card.

Mr. and Mrs. Johnson request the presence of Miss Anastasia Lowell at the wedding of their daughter Sophie Louise Johnson to Mr. David Smith on...

The words blurred. I didn't read any further. After five years of dating the dipshit, he hadn't even bothered to give his in-laws-to-be my correct name. I was Anasazi Lowell, not Anastasia, though most everyone called me Ana. I slapped the invitation down on the dresser and slammed my half-full coffee cup down on top, staining the card with a tidal wave of murky brown liquid. I'd braced myself ever since I saw the perfect calligraphy on the card, but the pain still stole the breath from my lungs. It wasn't the murderous rage I wanted to feel, but a squeezing of my heart that was fucking pathetic. The card was a shot to my already well-pummelled heart. And now I was facing a wall of grief like I'd not felt since my mother had come down with the sleep curse that was still affecting people. And it was worse because my mother hadn't chosen to leave me. Not like David, gorgeous asshole David, who had made the choice, just as my father had done when I was too young to remember. At least, David and I hadn't gotten around to having kids yet. That would have made this whole shitshow so much worse.

Picking up my brightest lipstick, I painted my lips, smacking them at myself in the mirror. Grey eyes stared back at me. "You're still hot!" I pointed at myself and clicked my tongue before sighing. Picking the soggy invite out from under my coffee cup, I threw it, embossed envelope and all, into the trashcan beside my bed. The one that still held condom wrappers and the used condoms that David had left behind, together with the crippling debt and mortgage on the apartment. The apartment he'd shared with me until three months ago when the bastard announced he was marrying someone else as calmly as he might ask what was for dinner.

Yes, it was disgusting, and yes, I really should have taken out the trash by now, but grief has a way of hammering at your soul and leaving you bereft—debilitated. Mundane shit like cleaning seems less important when your whole future's been flushed down the toilet.

My phone chirruped in my pocket, and for the briefest of seconds, my stupid, ridiculous, treacherous heart hoped to see the fucker's name. But it wasn't him. I pressed the call answer button.

"Hey, Chris." I flopped back onto my unmade bed and closed my eyes.

"Bitch!"

"I love you too." I pulled my spare hand to my forehead, already knowing what he was going to say. If I had an invitation to the wedding, Chris would too. David had always hated my best friend, but he liked to show off. Rubbing Chris's face in his posh expensive wedding was the perfect way to do it.

Chris audibly sighed down the phone. "You know I'm not talking about you. I can't believe the audacity. The whole thing is a disgusting sham. Please tell me you aren't going."

Thank fuck for Chris. The one person still on my side. I shook my head then moaned at the pain that was beginning to creep through my temples. Downing the last of my tequila last night had not been my finest moment. "Nope."

"Good," Chris enthused. "The whole thing is such a cliché. Marrying the boss's daughter. What a loser. We're obviously not going. We should go on a shopping spree that day, then paint the town red. What do you say?"

I didn't have the heart to tell him that I couldn't even afford enough paint to cover the questionable black stain on my bedroom ceiling, let alone splashing it all over town. The shopping spree was equally unlikely for the same reason.

I murmured something incoherent, hoping he'd understand.

"You know what they say," Chris sing-songed. "The best way to get over a man is to get under another one." I could almost see the mischievous grin on his face to accompany the words. And while getting under, or indeed on top of, behind or in any other position with men was something Chris liked to do on a nightly basis, I wasn't planning on dating another man ever again. Though I did appreciate his enthusiasm.

"Will you stop gossiping on my time. Tell her she's needed." The cranky tones of Gerald McGee, my prick of a boss, had me sitting up straight.

Chris came back on the line. "Oh, yeah. You have to come in. Alexis has got an emergency spa appointment, so we're understaffed. See you soon. Love ya."

He hung up before I had the chance to respond. Before my eyes, my room began to spin, my headache turning into something epic. At the last minute, I managed to lunge over the side of the bed and puke in the overflowing waste paper basket.

Feeling slightly better, I fished the dripping invite from the trash and memorized the address before writing it on one of the clean, padded envelopes I kept in case

I needed one. The old condom doused in tequila, and stomach acid came next. Writing a little note telling Mr. and Mrs. Johnson that I was sorry, but I wouldn't be able to make it to the upcoming nuptials, but here was a gift for the bride and groom, I put the whole stinking lot in the envelope and attached my last few stamps.

Gazing wistfully at it, I placed it in my bag. Petty and juvenile, I knew, but so was leaving your long-time girlfriend saddled with debt to marry some rich bitch at the office.

This certainly wasn't my finest moment, but with my tequila headache threatening to take over my entire brain and my stomach still planning a rebellion, I didn't much care. My only wish was that I could be at the wedding, if only to see the looks on the guest's faces as David and his bimbo bride pulled out the vomit-splattered condom.

Caught between groaning and giggling, I picked up the waste paper basket I'd not emptied for three months, threw the contents into a bin bag, and put the lot outside. After my shift tonight, I'd start on the rest of David's crap that he'd left behind. Not that he'd left me with much. The bank accounts he'd emptied. He'd even taken the engagement ring he'd given to me. Cheap bastard had told me he was going to get it cleaned for me, and like a fool, I'd believed him. There was no doubt in my mind that the only diamond I'd ever owned was now sitting on the finger of Sophie fucking Johnson.

Apart from the used condoms (he took the unused ones with him), he'd left me with three socks, half a bottle of aftershave his nana had bought him three Christmases ago that smelled like bleach gone bad, a chipped mug, and his Game of Thrones DVDs. Like an idiot, I'd kept hold of the lot, hoping that he'd come back for them, come back to me. But not anymore. I was sick of simpering after the useless, cheating, bastard, sleazeball. I was going to throw away everything he'd ever touched...If my hangover didn't kill me first.

***

Fuck Vancouver traffic and fuck Vancouver weather right along with it! I cursed under my breath.

Today was supposed to be my night off. I wouldn't have consumed half a bottle of tequila had I known that Alexis was going to flounce off to some spa. But I should have known. It wasn't the first time. Being the boss's daughter came with perks, and she used them to her advantage as much as she could. But who goes to a spa at night? Urgh. My version of a spa was a hot shower, a luxury ever since I'd forgotten to pay the electric bill.

"You're late," McGee roared as I tramped through the door, soaking wet from my dash across the parking lot. McGee was as round as he was tall, fat off the millions he was currently making from owning The Vancouver Sleep Clinic. When I'd started, we'd been lucky to have more than a dozen clients a month, but since the Big Sleep, business had boomed, and we were booked out months in advance, commanding the highest rates. His bushy, once auburn but now mostly white moustache took up most of his face, though his beady, piggy eyes peering out over the top were equally unnerving.

"I wasn't meant to be in today," I reminded him grumpily, pulling off my soggy coat and hanging it up on a coat hanger. "It was supposed to be Alexis's night, remember?" I added spitefully. At eighteen, McGee's daughter was nine years younger than me and already earning more, despite knowing absolutely nothing about anything and having more spa days than I was currently having hot dinners.

McGee's moustache twitched. I knew there was no comeback to that. His daughter was a lazy bitch and we all knew it. "Yes, well, Chris is already here and setting up tonight's subjects. Take care of them. They're paying handsomely. I'm going. I have a golf game this evening."

I gave him a wry nod, then headed down the low-lit corridor into the sleep chamber where Chris was carefully hooking the subjects up to the monitors.

The sleep chamber had been built to accommodate two beds, but cheapskate McGee somehow managed to squeeze twelve in there. It reminded me of the hospital ward my mother was in, but more cramped. I had to turn sideways to get between the beds. The people we took nowadays were mega-wealthy, but very few complained about their lack of privacy or cramped accommodations for the night. Their lives were more important to them than luxury.

As far as I could see, Chris had done eleven of the twelve already. I moved to the last bed and read the chart. Mr. Collins. He was an old chap who looked to be in his mid-seventies. He gave me a doleful smile as I attached wires to his chest then to his temples. I wondered how he'd made his money. It was a game I liked to play. Was he rich to begin with, or had he been saving up for a year for this? The cost for one night alone would pay for a luxury cruise to the Bahamas or two weeks in the Maldives. Instead, they spent their money being watched sleeping by me and Chris.
Utter fucking insanity!

"These won't hurt," I assured him, reading his expression, "but they'll restrict your movement a little it's best to sleep on your back and try not to move too much. It will provide us with better readings."

He nodded in understanding. "Thank you, my dear. I'll do my best to." I liked the guy immediately. He had a sad kind of compliance to him that I had a feeling had nothing to do with the wires or machines I was hooking him up to.

When I saw that everyone was attached to the machines, I made my usual announcement to the group of faces peering at me. The one I'd memorized once the customers had started pouring in after The Big Sleep.

"I know this is a strange environment, but please do everything you can to get a good night's sleep. Chris and I will be watching through the mirror there." I pointed to the long mirror, taking up almost one wall of the room. "It's a one-way mirror, and we can see you at all times. The doors will be locked once we leave and will remain so all night. If, however you wish to use the bathroom, there is a button on the side of your bed. It will be silent to you, but we'll hear it and open the door for you. The toilets are just along the corridor, which will be kept lit throughout the night. The button can also be used if there is an emergency, but we ask that you don't press it for any other reason. Any disturbances in the room affect the readings, so we like to keep everything as peaceful as possible. The time is ten p.m. We'll open the doors at six a.m., and once we've collated the data, we'll send you your reports. It usually takes twenty-four hours. The lights will be dimmed but not turned off completely to allow us to monitor you throughout the night. If you need one, a sleep mask has been provided for you on the nightstand beside your bed. Does anyone have any questions?" I waited for the inevitable questions, but none came. I left the room and joined Chris in the observation room for another long, boring, pointless eight hours of watching old people with more money than sense snore and fart their way through the night.

CHAPTER TWO

"You didn't!" Chris snorted, his eyes sparking with mirth. Mock indignation followed by a huge grin covered his face when I told him about my 'gift' to the happy couple which I'd posted on the way to work. He ran his hands through his perfect red hair, only ruffling it slightly.

"I did," I admitted, feeling shitty about the whole thing. "I shouldn't have. It was petty, not to mention disgusting."

"It was a triumph. A masterpiece of villainy. I think you're my new hero." He clutched his hands to his chest in his theatrical manner, eyelashes fluttering over deep blue eyes. Of course, he'd think it funny. He despised David almost as much as David had despised him. They were like chalk and cheese. David with his gym-going body and conservative attitude, who thought that anyone not like him was weird, and Chris who was camp and fun and silly and generous. Pretty much everything that David was not. It was no wonder they hated each other.

I picked up my coffee and took a swig. It was almost as bitter as I was. "I'm not sure."

Chris leaned forward and covered my hand with his. I noted he'd painted his fingernails orange today. That meant he was in a good mood. I always could tell how he was feeling by the color of his nails. Orange was happy, Blue was horny, Pink was angry, and black was deep despair, or so he told me the very first day we'd met on the job. "Darling. He completely screwed you over. I think a little petty revenge is exactly what is needed. It's good for the soul."

It didn't feel good for my soul. It felt like I was dragging myself down to David's level. The level that was lower than an ant's testicles. My soul felt well and truly wretched.

"Yesterday, you said Rege-Jean Page was good for the soul," I sighed, wishing I didn't feel so bad about the whole thing. Up until this evening, I'd prided myself on my maturity. However much I wanted to throw a brick through David's car window, I'd refrained. Now, I didn't even have that to console myself with. I was single, broke, and acting like a fucking child.Chris sighed melodramatically and stared off into space with a sickly sweet look on his face. "Rene-Jean is God himself."

"He's an actor in a Netflix series," I reminded him. "I'm not sure God would deign to be in a historical romance TV show."

Chris turned his eyes to me, narrowing them. "Bitch, please. You've not even watched it. Don't talk shit about what you do not know."

I ignored him and looked at the sleep subjects who were now all asleep or at least close to it. I didn't want to admit I couldn't even afford Netflix anymore.

***

"I swear to god. I saw a guy."

I swirled the dregs of my coffee around in my paper cup and leveled my gaze at Chris. He raised both perfectly coiffed eyebrows, waiting for me to shoot his weird theory down. The weird theory that he'd seen some kind of hot guy in the sleep chamber in the two minutes it had taken me to use the bathroom. I didn't even bother to shoot a glance through the one-way glass. I already knew who was in there, and not a single one of them could be described as hot. Rich, old, maybe too much in the way of cosmetic surgery in the case of one of them, but nothing remotely resembling hot.

"Wishful thinking much?" I finally said. Chris liked to regale me with his sexual escapades, which were both extensive and mostly gross, but imagining a hot guy was a bit much for him, even if he was going through, in his words, 'a dry spell.'

A dry spell for him was two nights without sex. My own version of a dry spell was akin to the center of the Sahara Desert in the middle of summer.

"Jealousy doesn't become you, Ana," Chris replied, quirking his lips into a frown. "He was super hot. You know the type. Brooding. Sexy. Dangerous." His eyes misted over temporarily as he remembered the scene. The scene that he had most definitely imagined in that torrid mind of his.

"Uh-huh. Did he look like Rege-Jean Page by any chance?"

Chris examined his nails before batting his hand at me. "If only! No, this guy was pale. Freakishly so. Still smoking hot, though."

"Freakishly pale is not on my top ten wants in a

man."

Inside the sleep chamber, twelve people dozed, each tethered to machines that checked their heart rate, their breathing, and what stage of REM sleep they were in. Taking a quick look through the one-way window, I saw that all was quiet apart from the odd snore from the participants.

"Fine, don't believe me," Chris huffed, standing up from his chair and pouting. "I'm going to get us some real coffee; that stuff you drink is dogshit."

He wasn't wrong. Despite the sleep clinic being packed out for months with a waiting list so long, it would keep us above capacity for years, the boss, Gerald McGee, was still a cheapskate, which meant our only source of coffee was a drinks dispenser in the main part of the clinic which dispensed what could only be described as watered down witch-piss.

"Go to the place on the corner," I called after Chris as he left the small viewing room. "It's open until two and has the good stuff. I'll take an espresso."

"Good luck with that, bitch," Chris called, throwing me a cheeky wink as he closed the door behind him, leaving only me in the small observation room. I extended my middle finger, but he'd already gone. The lights were off, but the low blue glow from the sleep chamber plus the light from my monitors were enough to see by. A glance at the clock told me it was close to two AM. Only four hours to go, plus the hour needed to print up the reports, and I could go home and actually get some fucking sleep.

The low hum of the computers was the only sound. The speakers connected to microphones in the sleep chamber were all turned off as they usually were. No point in spending eight hours listening to chronic snorers. I finally cast my gaze through the one way mirror to the sleep chamber. There was no way that Chris saw a guy in there, not beyond the eight that were currently sleeping. Nor could he have mistaken any of the women for one. All twelve subjects were deeply asleep. The computer monitors reflected that. But...it wasn't like Chris to see things. Crazy and over the top though he could sometimes be, irrationality was not one of his traits. He must have seen something in the few minutes I'd nipped out to use the toilet, but what? The door had been locked at ten pm, just as it was every night. No one without a key card could open it, and the only four people with a key card were McGee, Chris, Alexis, and me. However much Alexis hated me, she wouldn't pull a prank and mess up her father's income, which was also her only source of income. Plus, she wasn't a hot guy.

And, of course, there was no way on this earth McGee could be described as sexy, even to a sex-starved, cranky, sleep-deprived guy like Chris.

Still, I looked anyway. Twelve people. All sleeping peacefully. Most were lying on their backs which was how we'd told them to try to stay, but a few had curled up into their favorite sleeping positions. The guy on the end had kicked his thin blue blanket to the floor, where it lay in a heap of low shadows. Nothing unusual. I pushed the button to turn on the speakers to make sure and heard exactly what I expected to hear. Some light snoring, punctuated by the loud snore of the blanket kicker on the end. A year ago, we'd have diagnosed him with sleep apnoea and sent him on his way. But that was a year ago before the big sleep. No one cared about sleep apnoea anymore. Not since the day when the whole world fell asleep only to wake up seven days later.

I moved to turn the speakers off again when something pricked my ears up. Footsteps. Barely noticeable above the snoring, but definitely there. Another quick look in the chamber. Again, no one was out of bed. Turning the sound level up, I heard the sound again.

"Chris?" I called out, wondering if he was already back and the speakers were picking up ambient noise from the rest of the clinic. They weren't supposed to, but there was no other explanation for the sound.

When he didn't appear, I decided to go into the sleep chamber to check on everyone. Strictly speaking, Chris and I weren't supposed to go in there unless there was an emergency. Just our presence in the room could affect the readings, but the footsteps were intriguing me. I needed to know what the sound really was. A faulty machine, probably.

Just my fucking luck!

A faulty machine meant having to start everything again, which in turn meant leaving late. Something I really didn't want to do.

Opening the door to the observation room, I headed out into the corridor and took the few steps to the entrance to the sleep chamber. The corridor was painted white to make it feel clinical and sterile, but in the low glow of lights, it just came across as creepy. A quick tap of my key card and the automatic door opened silently. It felt weird and wrong to be going into the room even though I'd just spent the last four hours watching these strangers sleep. Going into the room with them felt more intimate somehow. I mentally berated myself. They'd signed up for this. They'd paid a lot of money to be checked out, and they were told we'd have access to the room. Still, my heart rate increased slightly as I took a step inside and let the door close behind me.

I couldn't hear the footsteps anymore. Whatever it was had stopped. *Thank fuck!* I picked up the blanket and gently placed it over Mr. Collins, careful not to touch any of the wires attached to him. Wires I'd placed on him mere hours ago.

I was almost back out the door when I heard a sound. Turning quickly, my heart nearly seized completely when I saw him. A man. He wasn't there seconds before. I'd have seen him. But he was here now. My mouth fell open as I tried to process this creature in front of me.

Well fuck! Chris wasn't joking. He'd just failed to clearly articulate just how breathtakingly beautiful the man was. Beautiful: check, brooding: check, dangerous: double check. He should come with a warning label. I was momentarily paralyzed by him, both by his breathtaking beauty and partly by the fact he wasn't supposed to be here and hadn't been here just a moment earlier.

Long black hair cascaded over his shoulders, partially hiding tattoos down his arm and his muscular chest, which I could see because he was only half-dressed. On his bottom half he wore tight black pants and no shoes, and on his head sat a golden crown. An actual freaking crown! The dim light cast him in all shadows and highlights. But it was his eyes that drew me in. So dark that I couldn't see where the pupil ended, and the iris began, cold calculation in his gaze. He was so fucking beautiful, it was all I could do to breathe. And then I couldn't...

A bird of some kind (a raven maybe?) flew over my head, and a wave of pleasure washed over me, making my whole body tremble so hard that I had to grab the bed of the old man at the end to stop from keeling right over with the brutal force of it.

What the fuck was happening?

I took a deep breath to push through it, struggling to keep my eyes open as the strange man turned his eyes to me.

His eyes widened as he took me in, not that I could pay much attention. I was too busy trying to breathe through the ripples of pleasure as they finally began to wane. I was barely breathing with the force of what just happened to me, and I had to take a moment to find my equilibrium.

His black eyes met mine. The moment of surprise he'd shown earlier had already faded from his face to be replaced by something else? Revulsion maybe?

As I stood staring at him, wondering what the hell I was supposed to do, he jumped onto the nearest bed. Right onto one of our clients, a local widow by the name of Mrs Rose who just happened to own half of Vancouver.

I screeched out a strangled noise as he landed right on her middle, but the second his feet touched her blanket, he'd gone. Completely disappeared into thin air.

My brain struggled to understand what I'd just witnessed, and my heart was pounding so loudly that I was sure the microphones were going to pick up on it

I took a deep breath and ran to Mrs. Rose, expecting her to be injured, if not dead, but she was asleep, breathing deeply. As I watched, her lips curled up into an indulgent grin, and her eyes moved rapidly under her paper-thin eyelids. She was dreaming. A doozy of a dream going by the expression on her face.

A flap of wings wafted my hair, taking my

attention from her face. The raven! I'd almost forgotten about it, what with everything going on. It flew toward Mrs. Rose's middle, right where the mysterious man had disappeared.

"Oh, no, you don't," I hissed, grabbing out quickly, squeezing my hand into a fist. The raven, its leg caught in my hand, began to squawk in desperation to get away. There was no way I was letting it go. It came with him. And I was sure that I'd finally done what months and months of sleep studies had failed to do. I'd finally found the cause of the sickness, and it wasn't a what. It was a who.

CHAPTER THREE

"Get back into the clinic now, Lowell!" Mr. McGee roared at me down the phone almost an hour later. I cradled my cell phone between my ear and shoulder as I wrestled the raven into a cage that once belonged to a guinea pig of my neighbor's seven-year-old daughter. (Rest in peace, Mr. Snuggles) He must have been seriously pissed to use my last name.

The raven flapped its wings furiously, causing the stack of bills to fall onto the floor.

Shit! I had them piled up in the order I was going to pay them. Not that I could actually afford to pay any of them, but the electricity bill was on the top of my wish list.

"I can't right now, Mr. McGee," I panted down the phone. "Sorry. I've got a lot on my hands."

Literally. The pet bird of the most beautiful man I ever encountered and who, more than likely was a figment of my over-active imagination, squawked, and I almost let the little shit go.

"Well, get it off your hands," he grumbled. "I've got twelve angry customers, and Mrs. Rose is refusing to pay."

The raven took that moment to nip at my finger.

"Sonofa..!" Blood dripped onto the stack of bills adding to the already too much red as I shut the cage door trapping the little beast inside.

"Ana," Mr. McGee practically shouted down the phone, bringing me back to the conversation. "I was called into the clinic at some ungodly hour to find feathers all over the sleep chamber, the machines all going haywire, and Chris blubbering in a corner. I suggest you haul your ass back here right now if you want to keep your job."

I opened my mouth to apologize but found myself saying sorry to a hung-up tone.

"You can stay there!" I grumbled to the raven while pulling my blonde waves into a messy bun. "I might think about buying you some birdseed if I don't get my ass fired first!"

The raven gave me a withering look and stuck its beak up in the air as though it understood exactly what I was saying to it.

Get a grip, Ana. It's a bird, Not an omen... Probably.

However much I hated watching rich people sleep for a living, I needed the job. It was easy, and I was not qualified for anything else. And however little McGee paid me, it was still more than I'd earn doing some shitty waitressing job, which was exactly what I was doing before coming to work at the clinic.

I picked up the keys to my crappy old Audi and headed out of my apartment. The stink of old cabbage filled the air as I walked down the corridor to the entrance reminding me it was Thursday. Tomorrow the corridor would smell like fish, and Saturday, it would smell like curry. I'd not needed a calendar since moving into the shithole apartment block, thanks to my neighbor, Mrs. Amos's unwavering cooking schedule.

I pressed the button on my keys to unlock Lucy, my ten-year-old car. It was held together with rust and wishes, but it was reliable and got me from A to B. Or, in this case, Apartment to Boring job.

I made it back to the clinic in record time, thanks to the earliness of the hour. Anytime after six am, Vancouver was gridlocked, but at four, it was a pleasure to drive.

Chris ran out to meet me in the parking lot, his red hair unusually messy as though he'd been running his hands through it.

"What did you run off for?" he pouted, falling into step with me. "You left me right in the shit."

"Sorry, Chris. I didn't mean to."

The truth was, seeing that guy with the startling black eyes and having the weird heat wash over me had set me completely on edge in a way I couldn't explain. I wasn't accustomed to having what was basically an orgasm in public for no reason, and I certainly wasn't accustomed to watching the hottest man I'd ever laid eyes on jump into another person without even waking her up. Not that I could say any of that to Chris. He'd think I was having another breakdown.

"I had a panic attack," I half lied. "I had to go home to take a breather."

Chris stared at me. He'd known me long enough to know when I was holding something back, but he kept his lips pursed.

"McGee said that the machines have all gone haywire," I continued when he didn't speak. Chris usually never shut up, so to have him so quiet was enough to tell me he was really pissed with me. Deservedly so.

He grabbed my arm. "No shit. I came back from Starbucks to find you zooming off in your car, the machines showing readouts like nothing I've ever seen, and all the subjects awake and angry. Not to mention black feathers all over the place. What the hell happened?"

"A raven!" I said, trying to come up with something slightly more plausible than what had actually happened. At least that part was true.

"A raven?" Chris arched one of his perfectly manicured eyebrows. "Seriously, if you're in trouble of some kind, tell me." Chris looked at me with worry in his eyes, and I hated it. He'd been a rock to me when David had left and taken basically everything I owned, including my sanity, with him. I couldn't blame Chris for worrying, but I didn't need it.

"I'm not in trouble."

Chris shook his head and folded his arms. "You need to know when to let people help you."

"This isn't about me," I mumbled, wishing I wasn't having this conversation. I sucked in a breath and tried to think of a way to flesh out the lie that didn't sound too implausible. "I told you it was a bird. It somehow got into the sleep chamber. I had to go in and get it out. I guess it must have set the machines haywire."

Chris narrowed his eyes at me and pursed his lips again. "The door to the sleeping chamber was closed when I left to get coffee, and I think I'd have noticed a bloody big blackbird flying around in there."

"Raven," I reminded him like it mattered. Not that I knew what the difference was. They were both big, black birds.

Chris clenched his hands into fists by his side. "I don't give a flying fuck if it was a peacock dancing the can-can; it wasn't there when I went to get coffee."

Maybe I should have told him the truth. I already had told him half of it, and he did see the weird guy too. If I was crazy, then so was he...but then I thought of my mother asleep in a hospital wing in Winnipeg and decided against it. My mother was one of the people that had never woken up after The Big Sleep. She was the reason I needed to find out who the strange guy and his pet bird were before I was confined to the loony bin.

"I guess a gust of wind must have blown it open somehow," I said as I pushed the clinic door open. "You thought you saw a hot guy, remember? Who knows what you could and couldn't see." Urgh. I knew I was being a bitch, and none of this was Chris's fault, but I was irritated and confused by the whole thing, and I just wanted it all over with so I could go back home, go to sleep, and try to figure out what the fuck to do next.

He still didn't believe me. Not that I needed him to. It was Mr. McGee I had to convince. He was the one that paid me.

I found him sitting with his head in his hands as I entered the main office. With bare white walls and pale gray carpet, the place lacked any kind of interesting atmosphere, and the only concession he had made to decoration was a lone, framed photo of his wife and teenage kids that I knew for a fact he only kept there because his wife made him. He waited until I sat down before he began to speak.

His moustache twitched with anger, and a vein throbbed in his forehead, but he just about managed to keep his voice in check. "Do you want to tell me what it was that cost me the best part of thirty-six thousand dollars tonight?"

"There was a bird," I began, feeling foolish. "It somehow got into the sleep room. I had to go in and get it out."

"A bird?" His moustache twitched again as he steepled his fingers and leaned forward in his seat. He was close to losing his shit, and his face was so red that I could practically feel the heat radiating from it.

I nodded, trying to keep my own cheeks from reddening. I never was any good at lying. Lady Gaga's 'Poker Face' was most definitely not an ode to Anasazi Lowell.

Gritting his teeth, he almost growled. "I checked the door log, and once the door was shut at ten pm last night, the only one in there tonight was you. Do you mean to tell me that a bird managed to clone one of our key cards and figure out how to use it to get in?"

He twisted a pen between his fingers as he spoke, his knuckles white on chubby red fingers.

I swallowed thickly, feeling myself falling deeper and deeper into the lie and glad that we didn't use security cameras in the sleep room. "Maybe one of the clients took it in, hidden in a pocket?" Even to my own ears, it sounded like a pile of shit.

He tapped the pen on his desk a couple of times and licked his lips. "Come with me."

I followed him to the observation room to find reams and reams of paper from the printer in a pile on the floor. He picked up the end and practically slammed it in my face, only coming to a stop three inches from my eyeballs. "The Polysomnography tests are all over the place. A bird could not have done this."

I looked at the lines on the paper. Pretty normal stuff until 1:58 am. Turning, I sat at my desk and wiggled the mouse to wake up my monitor. The same thing... for all the subjects. Normal sleep, everything within the realms of normal sleep patterns, and then just as I'd entered the sleep room, all but one of the subjects simultaneously began to experience sleep problems. If you could call my swearing at a raven then running out of the door in a panic with said raven a sleep problem.

One of the subjects had started with the strange brain waves a few minutes earlier. I thought back to what had happened minutes before everything had gone to hell. I'd gone to the toilet, and Chris had seen the guy in black. Him.

Mrs. Rose! I typed in her name and brought up her results. Just like the others, her results were wacky, but hers went haywire thirty seconds before anyone else's—the exact same time the guy jumped on her. She had felt him after all...in her dreams.

"I don't know what to tell you," I said, shutting the screen back off. "A bird got in. I went in after it, and I must have woken everyone up. Sorry."

McGee massaged his temples and gritted his teeth as I held my breath. I couldn't afford to lose this job. It paid for my shitty apartment, and my shitty apartment was only one up from living on the streets or begging Chris to let me sleep on his sofa. And I knew what Chris did on his sofa...regularly.

"I need you to call all today's subjects and apologize to them," McGee grumbled. Do. Not. Mention. A. Bird." He said each word slowly and deliberately as though he thought I'd either gone deaf or lost my mind. I wasn't altogether sure I hadn't.

"Yes, sir."

He pointed a pen at me. "Tell them that you were PMSing or something. Then call tonight's subjects and reschedule them too."

I resisted the urge to grab the pen and shove it up his fat nose. Instead, I plastered on my best eat-shit smile and said "yes sir" again, almost following it up with a salute.

I spent the morning placating annoyed rich people and promising them ten percent off their sleep trial. Not that they needed it. Anyone that could afford three thousand dollars to be watched sleeping for a night by Chris and me wasn't the type of person that needed a discount.

It was only the thought of my unpaid bills that got me through the next few hours, but I did get through it and set out, three hours after my shift would normally end.

The raven was still there when I finally got home. I was not quite sure why I expected it not to be. It eyed me beadily as I pulled my coat off and threw it on the table.

"Sorry, bird. I forgot the birdseed. It was your fault, though. No time to hit the pet store because I had to clean up the mess you and your owner left behind. I'll get you some tomorrow."

It ruffled its feathers and turned its back on me.

Fuck you too!

It looked like a normal bird. A bit haughty maybe, if haughty was a word that could be used to describe a bird.

I was totally losing it. It was not haughty. It was a bloody bird, that was all, not some harbinger of doom, not some kind of grim from Harry Potter, and most certainly not the bringer of mysterious orgasms. I grabbed a bread roll from my kitchen and broke a bit off for the bird. It pulled it through the cage and swallowed it down before turning its back to me again. *Rude fucker.*

After slapping a couple of slices of out-of-date ham in what was left of the bread roll and eating it, I pulled my clothes off, dragged on my ratty old nightgown, and hopped into bed. Despite the exhaustion I felt, sleep was a long time coming. The irony of my insomnia never escaped me, doing the job I did. I could do with a sleep trial myself, but I'd never be able to afford the price. Not that I really needed it. Insomnia was insomnia. No mystery there. I finally felt my senses begin to dull and my mind wander as the first tendrils of sleep crept in. I gave myself up to it, letting myself drift...

I was back in the sleep clinic, but the edges of my vision were out of focus. The beds in the sleep chamber were empty, but the printer in the observation room was going crazy. My heart pounded as I tried to make sense of it. I could hear McGee screaming at me from outside, banging on the door trying to get in. But I couldn't let him in because then he'd know that I was not doing my job properly. And then, in the sleep chamber, red stamped envelopes flew around. There was nothing I could do. They were through the one-way mirror, and I couldn't get to them without passing McGee. My heart was pounding, and there was not a fucking thing I could do to stop it. To stop any of it. I struggled to catch my breath as the envelopes turned into black feathers that swirled around slowly.

The man appeared again, but this time, he was looking right at the mirror. Except he knew it was a one-way mirror, and he was looking right at me through it as though it was not even there.

I suddenly felt calm. The panic fell away as I drank him in. I couldn't take my eyes from him. His hair floated in the air as though he was underwater, but he was bone dry. It meant I could see more of his chest and his tattoos. They'd moved since I last saw them. I reached out to him, but my fingers touched glass, the window to the sleep chamber. The moment of calm was gone, and once again, I was fighting for breath.

I opened my eyes. I was wide awake, my heart hammering like thunder in my chest and sweat pouring down my face.

It was a dream. I was at home in my own bed. The peeling paint and familiar cracks in my ceiling were enough to tell me where I was.

I sucked in a deep breath and tried to calm down. My bedsheets were soaked in sweat, and I had somehow managed to coil them around myself. I untangled myself from them and swung my legs out of bed. Turning my eyes to my alarm clock, I recoiled in horror.

He was here! At the end of my bed. Really, this time. This was no dream. Chills swept through me as I took him in. His black eyes looked upon me with intrigue as though I was the weird interloper in this scenario. His long blue-black hair fell over his shoulders, covering his muscular chest and the weird armor he wore, not to mention the tattoos. Atop his head sat the crown I'd seen him in before. And below it, a face with cheekbones that could cut glass, perfect lips, and eyelashes that should be illegal on a man. By god, he was beautiful.

Insanely, overwhelmingly so.

And a fucking, weirdo stalker dude that somehow had not only found out where I lived but also broken into my apartment. I wanted to look to see if he'd broken my window and gotten in that way, but I didn't dare take my eyes from him.

The forceful feeling washed over me again. Rushes of intense waves of pleasure. I crushed my lips together, but it wasn't enough to stop the moan from escaping my lips.

What the actual...

He'd done this to me twice now. Or at least his bird had. I wasn't sure which one of them had given me more pleasure than any man I'd ever been with, not that the bar was set that high, but the guy hadn't even laid a finger on me. He hadn't even taken a step toward me. He waited until I was finished, and then with indifference in his voice, he spoke.

"You have my bird."

His voice was deep, almost guttural, with an accent I couldn't place. It was also sexy as all hell which only added to my embarrassment of moaning like an overpaid hooker in front of him.

"You messed up my sleep trial," I retorted, pulling the straps of my nightgown back up over my shoulder before the girls fell out. Might as well try and have a little dignity.

He didn't speak again. I watched as he turned and opened the small cage door where I'd put the bird.

He struggled to get the bird out owing to the fact the cage was made for a guinea pig, not a freaking raven.

I had no idea who this guy was, but he wasn't human. Ok, like, what the fuck was I thinking? He had to be human...but he wasn't. No human looked that perfect.

I'd seen with my own eyes him somehow jumping into Mrs. Rose. I wondered for a second if he was a demon? Only I could get myself involved in some other level exorcist shit.

"You possessed Mrs. Rose. Did you take her soul? Are you a demon?"

Even to my own ears, I sounded like a lunatic, but what other explanation was there? He stroked the back of the raven then looked upon me with disdain in his eyes. His anger at me was palpable. Another feeling came upon me as his gaze pierced me. This time, it wasn't pleasure I felt. It was a frisson of fear.

"To you, I am the devil himself." His voice sent a shiver down my spine more than the words themselves, although they were damning enough.

He jumped again, just as he had in the sleep chamber at work, but this time instead of jumping into a body, he jumped toward a red door. A red door that was most definitely not there when I had gone to sleep. I leaped out of bed and reached out to him. Devil or not, I was not going to let him go. My hand almost connected with his arm, but I was too slow. He was already through the door. I leapt fully off the bed and dived through after him. I closed my eyes as my whole body was squeezed through what felt like a tube of toothpaste.

When I felt ground beneath me, I opened my eyes. A dark forest floor covered in shadowy gray leaves and dirt spread out in all directions. Two long parallel rows of identical grey doors cut through the forest as far as the eye could see, one row to my left running into the distance both in front and behind me and one to the right. Doors, door frames, but no walls. The doors were not attached to anything and went nowhere. Between the frames, I could only see more of the dark forest.

Behind me was the door I'd just come through, above me, stars twinkled in the night sky, giving this part of the forest at least a little light.

"Where the fuck am I?" I murmured, wondering if I'd lost it completely. Behind me, the red door shut with a bang, almost making me jump three feet into the air.

I barely had time to check out my surroundings as Mr. elusive-as-fuck was already almost through one of the gray doors. I hauled myself up from the forest floor and hot-footed it after him, but it was too late. He was already through the door. And if the last five minutes hadn't been weird enough, he didn't come out through the other side. Not only that, but the row of doors all began to move in unison, shifting one spot toward and then beyond the red door.

The forest was eerily quiet and devoid of color. The tree trunks were gray, the leaves different shades of gray. The silence was foreboding. There was nothing living in it—no creatures scurrying through the undergrowth, no birds in the branches above my head. If I hadn't been completely sober, I'd have wondered if I hadn't fallen into some drug-induced haze.

I was alone. Fuck knew where in a forest that smelled of flowers and summer rain but looked like death. The smart thing would be to turn right back around and go right back home through the red door before it too decided it didn't like where it was and went on a vacation around the vicinity. Thing is, I'd never been smart. Smartass maybe, but not smart. Instead, I put my hand on the grey door handle nearest to me, opened the door, and stepped inside.

CHAPTER FOUR

I already knew it wouldn't open to the forest, even though that was all that was behind it, but I was still surprised to see myself in a room that seemed to form out of the darkness itself. Large floor-to-ceiling windows with thick drapes took up the whole wall in front of me, and to the side, a huge mantelpiece over a real working fireplace held framed photos, all of which were blurry. The view from the window I recognized. My breath hitched in my throat as I saw that I was still in Vancouver. Somehow, seeing the mountains made me feel less alone. Because I was alone. Wherever he was, it was not here. I swore I saw him walk through this door, but then again, the doors had moved, and I was still disconcerted when they had. It wasn't against the realm of possibility that I'd picked the wrong door. My heart did a race around my ribcage as another door opened, and a man walked in and only calmed when I saw it wasn't Sexy-Freakshow. I recognized him immediately.

I'd seen him last night at the sleep trial. He was the man that had kicked the blanket from his bed. I scrabbled around my fuddled brain for his name.

"Mr. Collins?"

I waved my hand in front of his face, but he looked right through me with no response. It was like I was a ghost to him. Almost like I was not there at all. As if I'd died and fallen into the pits of hell. All that was missing was the hellfire, though why Mr. Collins would be here was beyond me.

He picked up one of the photographs from the mantelpiece and began to sob. As tears splattered on the glass frame, the picture in it cleared. It was of a woman. She was smiling at someone just out of frame.

I watched as Mr. Collins closed his eyes and began to sway. He was no longer crying. The picture began to shimmer, then grow and change shape until it was the woman.

Of course, it was. Nothing weird about that. No, perfectly normal. Nothing to see here.

It took all the willpower I had not to dash back out through the gray door, but I was transfixed. The woman was wearing a red dress just as she had been in the photo. The pair of them danced together as I tried to figure out at what point I'd been slipped a fucking hallucinogenic because there was no fucking way I was sober right now.

I closed my eyes and rubbed my hands over my face. It felt like flesh and blood. I felt alive, but what the hell did I know? In the past twenty-four hours, I'd watched a man in armor jump into the body of a woman, walk through not one but two doors to fuck knows where, and had an orgasm without being touched—Twice. A woman coming to life from a photo was becoming par for the course.

The room began to dim, and the ground rumbled beneath my feet. The couple was still dancing as though nothing weird was happening. Everything began to fold into itself. I dashed out through the door as the scene faded completely to black. The door slammed shut behind me, almost knocking me to the forest floor. Then, because my life wasn't fucking weird enough, the entire row of doors on one side moved again. The door I'd just been through passed the red door, and I found myself face to face with another one.

The door behind me began to open. Instinctively, I knew it was him. With a reflex action, I scooted around it before he had a chance to see me. I was not ready for him to know I was still here. Not until I figured out exactly where 'here' was. I ducked behind the nearest tree and watched him. Only part of him was visible from where I was standing, owing to the angle of the door he'd just walked through. I could see enough to know he was perplexed about something, and I wondered if he knew what I had done and that I was still here.

I held my breath and ducked back behind a nearby tree as he slowly pivoted on the spot. If I didn't calm the fuck down, I was going to give myself away by my thundering heartbeat. I took a deep breath and tried to relax. Not easy when the self-described devil standing six feet from me could and probably would crush me if he knew I was still here.

He finally turned and walked through the door I'd been face to face with moments before. His raven followed, and I let out a long slow breath and fell to the forest floor. The darkness was all-pervading, sending a shudder down my spine. A pale blue light flooded the place, though the moon or whatever it was that was providing it was nowhere to be seen. Below me, blue-gray leaves crunched beneath my fingers. Dead leaves, although the live leaves in the trees had the same color to them. My own tanned skin looked washed out in the eerie light. The silence around me was palpable. No wind rocked the trees, and no animals skittered along the forest floor. In fact, the only thing I could hear was the sound of my own breathing. The whole place was damn freaky, unnatural. The red door was right there, not ten feet from where I was sitting. It would be so easy to stand up and walk back through it, leaving this place. I could go back to wasting my life being miserable about my shitty ex and not being able to afford to eat like normal people. So easy, and yet I couldn't. While I'd found myself in a kind of living hell, or actual hell—I wasn't sure at this point—it held answers. The answers the whole world had been looking for, for a year. The answer to why my once perfectly healthy and active mother had been asleep for a whole year for no discernible reason.

I was so caught up in the memory of the doctor telling me that my mother had succumbed to the sleep sickness that I didn't notice that he'd come back through the door. He was around the doors and almost on me before I could react, and he looked pissed. Face as dark as night, full-on, bat-shit insane rage. And coming at me the way he was, with his eyes blazing fire, he was terrifying. Jumping to my feet, I turned away from the tree that had done a very poor job of hiding me and raced into the darkness of the forest.

Dead leaves and fallen branches cracked beneath my feet as I ran through the darkness, my breathing ragged with the unexpected rush of adrenaline. He was on me before I knew it. Of course, he was. He was built like an athlete, and my version of exercise was going to the fridge for another beer when I could afford such a luxury. Still, it hurt as he grappled me, and we both fell to the ground, him right on top of me.

I went down with an 'oof' as his weight knocked the breath from my lungs. I had literally no chance of escape. The motherfucker was huge and ripped and currently pinning me to the forest floor, face down. I spat out the dead leaves I'd managed to almost inhale as I'd crashed to the forest floor. I was not going to make it easy for him. I clawed my way forward, trying to wriggle out from under him. I managed it slightly, but then my flimsy nightshirt ripped, and I had to add flashing the demon my boobs to my list of problems. At least it would be as soon as I stood up. Currently, I was only flashing him a bit of my back. The question rolled around in my mind. Do I keep trying to pull away and possibly lose my nightshirt entirely, or do I lie still and see what happens?

It took me half a second to weigh up my possibilities and make a decision. I grabbed what was left of my nightshirt, scooping up half an armful of dead leaves along with it, and shimmied around until I was facing him. Then with as much strength as I could muster, I kicked upwards in a move I'd learned from my one and only self defense class. At the time, I'd thought it was a waste of money and not gone back. Turns out it was worth every penny because the swift knee in the family jewels was enough to take his attention from me and enable me to pull myself out from beneath him.

I resisted the urge to shout 'girl power' like some teenage Spice Girls fan in the nineties and instead concentrated on running away and holding what was left of my nightdress up.

Twenty seconds later and I was eating dirt again. This time he wasn't going to let me go. His legs pinned mine down, and his hands clasped my wrists to the ground. I turned my head to the side to be able to breathe as my brain flashed images of my soon-to-be violent and frenzied death. His hot breath warmed my cheek, sending shivers of fear down my spine. I was well and truly fucked.

Hate shone in his eyes as I tried to claw myself out of this mess. It was a pointless endeavor. He dragged me to my feet and grabbed me by the throat, pushing me against a tree. His fingers were strong as steel, pinning me to the rough bark of the tree at my back. It was only then that I grasped just how tall he was. The way he held me, pinned me to the tree with one hand at my neck, had my feet at tiptoes, and still, he towered over me.

My nightdress was now around my waist, and everything above it was on show, but that was the least of my problems. I was pretty sure the guy was going to kill me. If I wasn't already in hell with the devil, I soon would be heading there. The way he looked at me, his eyes flashing with anger, his teeth bared, almost feral, left me in no doubt I was lucky to still be alive. Whether I'd still be by the end of the night was anybody's guess.

"How dare you come into my world."

There was that voice again. Deep, sensual. I really hated that my mind was thinking that instead of something more sensible like 'Oh fuck, he's going to choke me to death.'

"You shouldn't have been in my sleep study," I choked out, although it sounded more like youshntbnimasleestuy. My vision began to go cloudy at the edges, but this was no dream. I was on the verge of passing out due to oxygen deprivation.

He lessened his grip on my neck a little allowing me to take a deep breath.

His face darkened, and his eyes flashed with anger. He deliberated for a second what to do with me, and all I could do was stand and wait until he decided if he was going to kill me or not. All he had to do was squeeze a little harder, and I was a goner. I tried to appear tough, as though him pinning me to a tree didn't bother me in the slightest, but the shivers in my arms were enough to give me away. My body betrayed me, shaking like one of the leaves above us. He was so much stronger than me. No amount of self defense classes could have prepared me for the nightmare I'd fallen into. His muscular arm flexed as he tensed up, and I knew I'd taken things too far as was my way. My mother had always told me that my smart mouth was going to be the death of me, and it stuck in my throat that her premonition, no matter how flippantly she'd said it was going to be proved right.

I can't die. Not here. Not now. Yes, my life is as shitty as it gets, but that doesn't mean I want it to be over. I can't die when I'm literally at my lowest point.

His breath came hot on my cheek, and I was all too aware of my naked breasts, inches from his chest. I'd gotten myself into some ridiculous situations in my time, but this was some real fucked up shit, even for me. I was a lamb to the slaughter, and he knew it. I tried breathing evenly as he deliberated what to do with me. With his free hand, he grabbed one of my wrists and spun me around so that my arm was twisted up my back and my face scraping the rough bark of the tree. Now, I was sure this was another move that they taught me how to get out of in self defense class, but my brain was so foggy that I forgot what I was supposed to do. I knew that you were supposed to shout fire instead of rape because no one shows up if you shout rape, but I didn't think that was applicable here for two reasons. The first being that I was naked from the waist up with my nightdress hanging on only because of my broad hips, and he had barely batted an eye at me below my chin. The second being there was no one to hear me yell out anyway. Not apart from the bird, but I'd not brought it the birdseed I promised earlier, so it was hardly going to side with me.

He leaned in close, his hot breath on my ear. "I should rip the flesh from your bones and feed you to the insects, human filth."

Human filth? Rude! "And mess up this lovely place you have here?" I clapped back, waiting for punishment for my smart mouth. I couldn't seem to keep the bloody thing closed, even when my life was on the line.

"All this time, and it turns out you are not worth it."

What the fuck was that supposed to mean?

He half-dragged, half-pushed me back to the rows of doors. We slipped between two door frames to the red door. With his bare foot, he kicked it open, and without so much as a 'goodbye, it was nice knowing you,' he roughly kicked me through it.

CHAPTER FIVE

I turned around to find the door being slammed in my face, and seconds later, it was gone as though it had never been there at all.

I fell to my bedroom floor, my breath ragged, my nerves surging with electricity. Nothing in my whole life had prepared me for what had just happened, and yet a quick look around my bedroom told me that nothing had changed. The bed was exactly how I'd left it, unmade with a book I'd been reading before I'd fallen asleep a couple of nights ago laid out on the cover. The walls still had the forlorn shabby, flowered wallpaper that I'd been meaning to pull off since the day I'd moved in with David three years ago but hadn't managed to get around to. In the last few months, it had been money rather than time that had been the excuse for me not decorating. The excuse for me not changing the dresser that I'd bought from a thrift store with the intention of renovating it, though it had accumulated even more chips in the wood that no one could get away with calling shabby chic. Maybe I could invent shitty-chic and get rid of it that way.

Everything was exactly the same, but it wasn't. I now knew why my mother was sick. Why the world had come to a halt a year ago. All the doctors and epidemiologists in the world hadn't come close to figuring it out, but I had. I'd had one chance to find out why, and I'd blown it. The door to wherever it was had vanished, and it was the only way I knew to get there. I fell onto my bed and screamed in frustration. The light outside told me it was still daytime. My senses were off-kilter thanks to spending the last half hour in the dark, but a swift check of my clock told me it was dinner time. Stroking my neck, which felt bruised thanks to Asshat, I headed to my kitchen and put a cheap meal in the microwave. It was my last one. While it cooked, I picked up a garbage bag and threw everything I had left of David's into it. I'd started pulling off the wallpaper in the bedroom when the ting of the microwave alerted me to my last meal. The depressing mess looked about as appetizing as the cardboard box it came in, but beggars can't be choosers. It was better than I would eat tomorrow. My cupboards were bare. Only some old crackers remained. Wolfing down the meager portion, I then cleaned the guinea pig cage out, ready to give back to my neighbor, and headed out the door for my next shift at work.

It was with apprehension that I pulled up in the parking lot after last night's disaster. McGee would be there again, no doubt all pissed at me. I didn't even have Chris to help me get through the night shift, not unless Alexis was having another spa appointment or she'd broken a nail or some other dire emergency.

So it was a surprise to see his car in the parking lot. For a second, I wondered if my luck was changing, but then Alexis pulled in, in her brand new Ferrari, courtesy of daddy.

My stomach twisted as I knew what was about to come. Alexis was a first-class bitch who didn't miss any opportunity to remind me that she was above me in every way.

"I heard about last night," she drawled, her pearly white teeth grinning at me in almost a snarl. She was the cat, and I was the mouse, and I fucking hated her for it. She had more money than I would see in a lifetime, and she did nothing to help anyone with it. "Shame I wasn't there to see it."

"If you didn't need so many spa days, you would have," I spat back. "I mean, how ugly do you have to be to need to see a beautician once a week."

Once upon a time, she might have started crying and gone running to daddy, but in the six months she'd worked here, she'd learned better ways to hurt me, and she'd gotten good at it too.

"At least I can afford to go to a spa. Maybe if you went to one once in a while, your fiancé wouldn't be fucking some other woman."

Fuck shit fuck!

How did she know? I'd deliberately not told her because I knew it would be just one more thing for her to lord over me. One more pile of shit for me to deal with.

She waltzed past me, opening the door of the clinic with fiery red talons, fake just like her boobs, hair, nose, and personality. She slammed it shut behind her just so I'd have to open it again. McGee greeted me with a scowl in the reception area and practically dragged me into his office past his grinning bitch daughter.

"Chris has kindly volunteered to come in tonight," he said gruffly, perching his hands on his desk. "I don't want a repeat of last night. Do you understand me?"

I bit back a scathing retort. It was two days until payday, and I couldn't afford to give him more reason to fire me. "Yes, sir."

He narrowed his beady eyes, waiting for some smart ass quip, but I buttoned my lip. When he saw that I wasn't going to add anything, he visibly loosened up.

"Good. Treat the subjects like royalty tonight. I can't afford any bad reviews."

Like it mattered. He could have a thousand one-star reviews saying he was a quack and the sleep study was a phony crock of shit, and still, people would be queuing up around the block to get a place.

"I'm leaving Alexis in charge. One false move, and she'll let me know, so do a good job."

The 'or you're fired' was implied. I opened my mouth, outrage spilling through every pore. I'd worked here for three years. If anyone should be left in charge, it should be me. In the six months Alexis had been here, she'd done nothing but look at her fingernails and post Instagram pictures. The girl didn't have the first clue how to interpret the readings, and there was no way on this earth she would deign to touch any of the subjects long enough to connect them to the machines.

I knew I should have kept my mouth shut. If there was any trouble to be found, my smart mouth had a way of getting me in it, but I couldn't help myself. Frustration bubbled up inside me. "I've worked here the longest. I'm the one who knows how all the machines work. Don't you think I should be in charge?"

A low grumble emitted from McGee's mouth. "You are lucky to still have a job after what happened last night. Now get out of my sight before I change my mind."

With gritted teeth and my blood boiling, I left his office and stormed down to the sleeping chamber where Chris was already hooking everyone up to the machines. Alexis was nowhere in sight. No doubt, she was watching us do all the hard work from the comfort of the observation room while filing her nails or bitching to her social media followers.

I ignored the mirror and concentrated on my job, attaching the wires to Mr. Collins.

He gave me a bolstering smile. "I'm sorry that last night's observation wasn't a success, but I have to admit to being secretly happy to come back. I'm quite lonely since my wife died, you see."

His wife. The lady in the picture with the red dress. "The two of you must have been very happy together."

His eyes crinkled up at the edges, and I got the feeling that he had no one to talk about her. "Oh, we were. Forty-three years we were together."

"You danced with her," I remarked absentmindedly.

He gave me a curious look, then continued. "We most certainly did. Edith loved to dance. She was a beautiful dancer. Every man in the place wanted to be with her, but she wanted me."

I gave him a smile. "It sounds like you were lucky to

have each other."

I'd seen his dream, how it kept his memory of her alive. I'd been scared when I'd been there, not understanding, but now I knew. Earlier I'd seen right into Mr. Collins' dream during his daytime nap, and it had been beautiful.

Looking up, I saw that Mrs. Rose was the only one left. Chris gave me a withering look as I sidled up next to him.

"I'll do Mrs. Rose. You go and set up the monitors," I said breezily as though I had no ulterior motive.

"I can do it," he argued, clearly still pissed at me.

I picked up the wires and gave him a smile. "It's ok. After last night, I think I should be doing this."

He mumbled something incoherent then left me to finish wiring up Mrs. Rose.

"I hear it was your fault that I have to be back here," she sniffed, pulling her covers right up to her neck as I attached the wires to her temples.

"Yes, sorry. I was...PMSing." God, I really hated myself, echoing McGee's excuse to her. If I was really PSMing I'd have rammed his pen down his throat.

"Hmmm," she said, her eyes narrowing. "We didn't do that in my day and age. We were taught to respect our elders."

I plastered on a fake smile, wishing I'd not insisted on wiring her up. "I'm awfully sorry. I promise tonight will run smoothly... I was wondering. Did you have any dreams last night? About a man with long dark hair?"

Her eyes narrowed further with suspicion, and I wondered if I'd gone too far.

"Whatever are you talking about, girl?" she snapped as I wrestled the covers down to be able to attach the heart rate monitor to her chest.

"I just wondered."

She gave me a nasty smile. "Actually, I did dream last night as it happens, but not of a man with long black hair. I dreamed of my vacation in the Caribbean that I'm going on next week and..." she pulled me closer and whispered, "the very nice young waiters that see to my every whim."

Her cheeks grew rosy with the admission, and her expression softened. I couldn't help the grin that crept onto my face. The woman was eighty if she was a day. No wonder she had smiled at the dream of some hunky, young, Caribbean waiters.

"And none of them had long black hair?" I questioned her again at this change in mood.

She shook her head and pulled her blanket back up now that I'd finished affixing her to the monitors. "All of them have black hair, but short hair. Except for Lars. He's Swedish. Blond, you know. It was his first year last year. I hope he's there again this year."

I smirked and left her to her thoughts of Caribbean bliss. After another apology and the usual speech, I lowered the lights and headed out of the room.

"What were you two chatting about?" Chris asked as soon as I walked into the observation room. "I saw you having a very nice chinwag with Mrs. Rose. You even got her to smile. What did you do? Tell her the night was free?"

It was good to see that Chris had forgiven me for leaving him the lurch.

"She was telling me about some hot Caribbean studs, actually," I said, sitting in my chair and turning my monitor on. Usually, I'd give it a perfunctory glance to check it was all set up, but after the disaster last night, I double-checked everything carefully to make sure was working properly.

"Lucky lady." Chris mused. "Do you know where Alexis is? McGee said she would be coming in tonight."

I turned to him. "I thought she'd be in here with you, to be honest. I saw her in the parking lot where she decided to remind me how rich she was and how poor I am, then told me it was no wonder David left me for someone else."

Chris picked up the waste paper basket and mimed puking. "She's probably in the ladies, plastering on her make-up."

"Probably," I agreed. "McGee told me she is in charge of us tonight, so no messing about and no stories about your love life."

Chris's eyes widened as he put the waste paper basket down. "He didn't? What an asshole!" Everyone knows you could run this place with your eyes closed. She can barely find the entrance to the observation room. It wouldn't surprise me if she was outside in the corridor now trying to figure out where to go."

I laughed as the door opened, and Alexis waltzed in. She eyed the two of us suspiciously. "What are you two laughing about?"

"Nothing," we chorused like a couple of schoolgirls. Chris caught my eye and smirked as Alexis took her seat next to his and pulled out a fashion magazine.

"I'm not sticking around tonight," she announced from behind the pages. "Once Daddy goes, I'm going out on a date. I expect neither of you to tell him." She lowered the magazine and stared directly at me, daring me to go against her.

Out of the corner of my eye, I saw Chris about to pipe up, so I rested my hand on his arm to stop him. "We wouldn't dream of it, would we, Chris?" Chris gave me a questioning look but answered in the negative.

Alexis broadened her red lip-sticked smile and disappeared once again behind her magazine. With any luck, she'd be out of here by ten-thirty, and I wouldn't have to put up with her scathing remarks and bitchy attitude.

"Why?" Chris mouthed at me, giving Alexis the side-eye.

I shrugged my shoulders. The truth was, I had a plan. A plan that I knew Chris wouldn't like, and I needed Alexis out of the way to do it.

***

The clock struck one-thirty, and Alexis and McGee had both been gone for hours. I doubted I'd see either of them before dawn which was fine with me. I'd spent the last hour listening to Chris wax rhapsodic about some guy he was seeing and watching the second hand tick round on the clock. I had a theory. Last night, the freak show had jumped into Mrs. Rose. Later, when I followed him, I somehow managed to go into Mr. Collins' dream. He'd gone in from the outside, I'd gone in from the inside, but both of us had ended up in a similar place. Mrs. Rose had dreamed about her hunky waiters, but I had no doubt freakshow was there, just as I had been in Mr. Collins' dream. He'd not seen me, only his dead wife. If I was right and he was going into people's dreams, there was a chance he'd do it again. It was the longest of long shots, but it was the only shot I had. That's why I'd been making hmmming noises to appear interested in Chris's tawdry conversation while watching both the clock and the readouts.

With each tick of the clock, my heart pounded. The waiting for something to happen was excruciating. And yet, despite all my wishing and waiting, the readouts appeared normal. At one-fifty, I turned the speakers on. The sounds of heavy breathing and the occasional snore filled my ears.

"Sorry if my story isn't good enough for you," Chris sniffed. "Is my boyfriend not hot enough for your ears to hear about?"

I turned to my oldest friend and shot back with the truth. "You've slept with him twice. You can't remember his name, and you've been waffling on about him for over an hour."

"And your problem with that is?" Chris huffed back, folding his arms in a petulant manner.

I shrugged my shoulders nonchalantly. "And my problem is, I just thought I'd see how they are doing in there."

Chris narrowed his eyes and sat forward in his chair. "You want to go back in there! Something did happen last night. I knew it! It wasn't just a bird, was it? Oh.Em.Gee, please tell me that the hot guy is your secret boyfriend and had come for a hookup but got the wrong room." His grin almost reached his ears.

I shot him a withering look. "Hardly."

David had been gorgeous, but not even he could touch the splendor or the dangerous sex appeal of the Freakshow. I paused, wondering if I should tell Chris the truth. He was the only person I could talk to, and if I couldn't tell him about Freakshow, who could I tell?

I glanced to the door to make sure we were alone. Alexis probably wouldn't be back for hours, but I didn't want to take the chance that she would come back suddenly and overhear. When I was sure that the door was well and truly closed, I took a deep breath and began my story. "I saw the man you are talking about. The one you saw last night."

Chris bounced up and down in his seat and clapped his hands together. "I knew it, I knew it!"

"I'm not sleeping with him. I don't even know him," I cautioned before Chris rocketed off his chair in excitement. "I went in to see what he was doing. He had a bird with him. The raven I told you about."

I thought back to the night before. How confused I'd felt, but how excited I'd been too.

Chris calmed down a little. "Oooh, mysterious. So who was he?"

I hesitated, knowing how ridiculous it was going to sound. "He disappeared. Just like that." I clicked my fingers. "I took his bird and hot-footed it out of there."

I looked Chris in the eye, waiting to see what his response would be. If he'd just told me the same thing, it would be an invite to mockery. As it was, I had to hope he was a better friend to me than I was to him.

He stared at me open-mouthed with a hint of confusion. "He disappeared? Where? You mean he ran past you into the corridor?"

I shook my head, almost bemused by Chris's shocked expression. "No. He just disappeared. Right into Mrs. Rose's chest." I pointed through the window to where Mrs. Rose was sleeping. My voice was full of an emotion I didn't think I possessed. I needed Chris to believe me so I could believe it myself and know I wasn't crazy.

Chris was saved having to answer by my computer beeping. Turning quickly on the swivel chair, I saw one of the patient's readouts running riot. He was either having a heart attack, or the freakshow was in him. It looked just like Mrs. Rose's weird readout from last night. A quick look told me all was quiet in the sleep chamber. I scanned the beds until I found the man with the weird reading. He looked perfectly normal.

"What's going on?" Chris asked, peering at the readout over my shoulder. "That's not right."

"No, it isn't." I leapt up and raced past Chris, pulling my door pass from my pocket. Seconds later, I was in the sleep chamber with Chris pulling up behind me.

Nothing was out of place. Nothing was wrong. From here, I couldn't hear the sounds of the computer beeping wildly, but I knew it was. By some miracle, our dash into the room hadn't disturbed anyone.

The man in question was asleep. As far as I could tell, his breathing was normal. Nothing was out of place. Chris grabbed my arm, fear in his eyes. He didn't know what was going on any more than I did.

"Let's get out of here," Chris whispered, pulling urgently at my sleeve.

I pulled back sharply. This was my one chance. I'd seen freakshow do it. "Tell McGee I'm sorry," I whispered to Chris, and with a leap, I jumped right into the middle of the sleeping man.

Expectation had led me to believe I'd somehow magically appear in the dark forest again. What I hadn't expected, and probably should have, was the man to open his eyes and let out a roaring bellow.

"What in the blazes do you think you are doing?" He gripped his midriff and groaned as Chris dragged me from the bed. All around me, the subjects were waking up. Someone screamed, more than likely Mrs. Rose. And I couldn't blame them. The enormity of my mistake hit me like a truck. I'd fucked up. Fucked up so badly. My job was gone after this. McGee wouldn't hesitate to show me the door. And the man I'd jumped on. He would sue for sure. That was if I hadn't killed him. His red face glared at me as he shouted more cuss words than even I knew, so he'd probably live, but that was little consolation.

"I'm sorry," I babbled, feeling sick to my stomach. What a complete and utter fuck up.

I gasped for breath as Chris spun me around. I'd never forget the pity in his eyes as I looked at him then. All I could hope for now was that McGee didn't fire Chris too in a fit of spite. I was about to say as much when two arms grabbed me forcefully from behind and pulled me back.

The same sensation of being squeezed happened again, and when it stopped, I found myself back in the dark forest. And there, looking down at me, was Freakshow. And he didn't look happy. In fact, he looked like he wanted to devour my soul and rip my body to pieces with his teeth.

Oh, fuckety-fuck!

CHAPTER SIX

"You dare come into my realm again!"

It wasn't a question. A cleverer person might not have taken it so and known when to keep their mouth shut. Unfortunately for me, I'd never been that person, and even though I knew my smart mouth was going to get me into trouble, I couldn't help myself.

"You dragged me here this time."

His hand clasped around my bruised throat, almost but not quite cutting off my oxygen while flames of anger danced in his endless black eyes. While I struggled to fill my lungs, he glared at me, not disguising the contempt he felt for me. The pain was indescribable, exacerbated as it was by the bruising he'd already caused me hours earlier.

"Despite my better judgment I allowed you to live, but you tried to get back in here. I killed the last human that set foot in this realm," he growled. "Tell me why I should treat you any differently."

If he was waiting for me to be impressed with his macho bullshit, he was going to be waiting a long time. Plus, there was the fact I couldn't talk now if I wanted to. Instead, I used what little oxygen I had left to keep my head up and my eyes on him. If he wanted to kill me, so be it. I felt the onset of darkness creeping into my peripheral vision, and I knew it was nothing to do with the dark scenery but with the lack of blood getting to my brain. I was going to pass out if he didn't let me go soon, and I had no way to stop it. He was a brute of a man, and his strength far outweighed mine. He was a beautiful monster.

I choked out a word, but it was undecipherable even to me. It was my death knell, but nothing more. The darkness closed in until there was but a pinprick of light, and then it was gone entirely.

***

I awoke to find myself tied in a sitting position against the tree I'd hidden behind the first time I'd been there. The bastard was nowhere to be seen, but his bird was nearby, keeping its beady eyes on me. Close enough to see but not close enough to kick the little fucker.

I soon learned that struggling against my ropes was impossible, not because they were tied tightly, but because the asshole had tied me up using something I'd never seen before. It glowed with a deep purple light and moved as though it was alive with tiny sparks of purple light emanating from it and fizzling out into nothing.

The raven squawked when it saw I was awake and flew up to a nearby tree branch, settling about ten feet away and six or seven feet up.

"What kind of loopy shit did your boss give me?" I asked it because there was no way I could really be here, tied up with whatever this purple bullshit was. I was probably drugged at the last one of Chris's parties and taken to one of his perverted friends' sex dungeons. That might explain it. Unlikely, but a damn sight more likely than what I was seeing with my own eyes.

The raven turned its back and ruffled its feathers as though talking to me was beneath it. Not that it could talk...probably.

I craned my neck to look at the doors. From this angle, all I could see was the back of one row and parts of the other row through the gaps. To my relief, the red door was still there, exactly where it had been before. Of all the doors, that one was the only one that didn't seem to move. It represented freedom, my way home. The whole place was surreal. Surreal and silent, just as it had been before. The only sound was my breathing which sounded louder to my ears than it ever had, owing to the lack of sound elsewhere. Every movement I made rustled the crisp dead leaves under my ass and legs.

At least this time, I was dressed, and though I wouldn't say it was cold, the black jeans and boots I wore protected me against the sharp edges of any branches that might have fallen. My arms were firmly strapped to my side, but my legs were free to move. I made circles with my feet to keep the blood flowing to them.

I had no idea how long I'd been unconscious. The blue light of twilight looked exactly the same as it had when the bastard had brought me here, but I had a feeling that it was always that way. Wherever I was, if I wasn't drugged by some psycho party boy and in his basement, it was perpetual night. Or at least the hour before night when the sky isn't quite black. The only color I could see was the purple of the weird rope-thing moving around me, giving my arms a purple glow. In front of me were the ashes of a long-dead fire and a pile of small bones. Scary as shit, but at least they were not human.

Wherever I was, it was clear that I had to plot an escape because whatever the bastard—yes, I'd upgraded his name from Freakshow—had in store for me, it wasn't going to be good. He'd hinted that he was going to kill me, but that hadn't happened...yet. Something told me that was only because he had other plans for me. Other plans that would no doubt be worse than a quick, painless death. I didn't have to wait for long because one of the gray doors opened and out he came.

CHAPTER SEVEN

I sucked in a breath as the doors moved one space along as they had before. The gap between two doors allowed me to get a good look at him. He was painfully beautiful, majestic, even though there was a roughness to him. Despite his pale skin that glowed almost blue under the strange twilit sky, he had a darkness about him that was beautiful and strange. I closed my eyes to admonish myself for thinking him anything other than dangerous, but that made it all the worse. The prick was going to kill me. The fact he had muscles cut like a god and hair I could run my fingers through shouldn't matter. Then the doors moved, and I couldn't see his face anymore. A sliver of disappointment rushed over me until I reminded myself it was a good thing. I heard a door slam, and just like that, I was alone again. He'd not looked my way once.

And so it continued throughout the day if I could

call it a day. The light didn't change once. The misty black and blue with the added purple of my bindings reminded me of a bruise which made it all the more grotesque, and yet when I closed my eyes, the scent of the place reminded me of a flower garden, and though there was no breeze, the air was fresh and clean. Every five to ten minutes, he would exit one of the doors, wait for them to move, and then enter another, ignoring me completely, just as his bird was doing.

My arms ached with lack of movement, and my body felt bruised and battered, even though, as far as I could tell, he hadn't touched it anywhere apart from my neck. I wouldn't have been surprised if it had a purple hand mark on it. My stomach grumbled, and my throat felt like a desert, not to mention I'd needed to pee for quite a while. Hours of struggling against the purple bindings had not given me any advantage at all. I could move no more after hours of struggling than I could when I first woke up. Maybe that was his plan to kill me. Tie me to a tree and pretend I didn't exist until I died of thirst. It was easier than any other option and would leave less literal blood on his hands.

I thought of my mother, asleep in a hospital bed in Winnipeg where she'd been since the Big Sleep along with so many others. And the numbers were growing all the time. Literally everyone on earth had fallen asleep at the same time, and most had woken up seven days later. Those that had survived. My mother being one of them. She and hundreds of thousands of others had never woken up, despite being healthy in all other areas. That was only the start. Millions had since succumbed to the sleep sickness. It was unrelenting as it raged through the earth's population. There was no telling who would get it next. Young, old, rich, poor, black, white, healthy, sick. Nothing mattered. You either got it, or you didn't. Unlike normal sicknesses, this thing didn't seem to transmit person to person. Nor was it airborne or waterborne. In fact, the leading scientists the world over had spent a year researching the cause and transmission of it and were no closer to finding results. Governments were spending billions of dollars only for scientists to shrug their shoulders and shake their heads. That's why people were so scared. No one knew how it was caught, and so, no one knew what to do to shield themselves from it. Many people had been driven crazy by not letting themselves sleep. That was also why McGee was raking in the cash. He was a snake oil merchant. He had no idea what caused the sleep sickness any more than any other person, nor did he say he did. He was cleverer than that. He marketed the Vancouver Sleep Clinic as an overall sleep health center and alluded to the fact that we could detect the sleep sickness. That's why so many people had come through the clinic and spent so much money on a report that told them little to nothing. The day would come when one of our subjects succumbed to the sleep sickness. It was only a matter of time, something I'd pointed out to McGee, but he was taking his chances and spending his money on fast cars and tropical vacations while he had it.

  I turned my thoughts to tropical vacations. If I closed my eyes, I could pretend I was on a Hawaiian beach somewhere, and someone was about to bring me a cocktail. The fragrant forest made it easier to believe. And if I wasn't in so much pain and so desperate for the toilet, I might have believed it.

  I crossed my legs, trying to think of anything but the fact my bladder was about to burst. I cursed myself for all the coffee I'd drank the night before. The way I saw it, I had two options. Either shout to the bastard the next time he emerged from one of the doors and hope he had a better nature to appeal to or sit in my own piss for however long. Deciding that wetting my only pair of jeans was probably not the best idea, I did the unthinkable. The next time one of the doors opened, I called out to him.

"Hey, Fucker. I need to pee!"

He didn't turn his eyes my way as he slipped through another door.

Fuck!

"Hey, Raven, Can you get your boss and tell him it's urgent?" The raven actually deigned to look my way, but I swear to all that is holy, the little bastard shook its head. "You can understand what I'm saying. I knew it! Tell your asshole of a boss he needs to let me go soon unless he wants his home, or whatever this shithole is, stinking of piss."

It didn't answer because, of course, it didn't talk, but it did flap its wings and take off into the sky. I watched as it circled a few times then landed on the frame of one of the doors. There it stayed until the bastard came out, and then it hopped onto his shoulder. I liked to imagine that it was telling him about my current predicament, but it was an absurd thought.

Still, he strode over to me, the raven still on his shoulder.

"What?" The way he spoke was all venom and anger. Here was a man that didn't like to be taken from his job.

"I need to pee," I said, trying not to bounce up and down on my ass too much.

He narrowed his eyes and folded his arms. "So urinate.

I do not see anyone stopping you."

Bastard!

"I'm not going to pee in my pants. I gave that up when I was a baby. I need a toilet."

Frustration driven by a heavy bladder had me spitting out my words. I couldn't believe he was going to make me piss myself.

He remained unflustered. What did he care whether I was wet or not? "There are no toilets. This is a forest."

No shit, Sherlock. He really was a freakshow. Pleading to his better side wasn't going to work. It was obvious the guy didn't have one, so I spun it so he'd want to let me go.

"It smells beautiful here. You wouldn't want to spoil that, would you?" And it seemed that this was his home. The trees were thinner here than in any other direction, and the remains of the campfire in the center of the clearing told me that he liked to sit here when he wasn't going through doors.

He sucked in a breath through clenched teeth then held his hand out to me. At first, I thought he was going to grab my throat again, but when the purple light bindings sputtered out, I saw that he was giving in to my request. I was free.

My legs were like jelly after hours of not using them as I tried to stand. As the blood began to circulate, tingles began to flow through my fingers, then arms, as the feeling came back to them. In seconds the tingles became great stabbing pains, and my legs gave out beneath me.

Freakshow was beside me in a flash. He grabbed my arm, stopping me before I completely crumpled to the ground. I'd hoped, rather stupidly, that he would help me walk to wherever he wanted me to pee, but instead he dragged me along the forest floor by my arm. Dead leaves raked at my face, and my ears were filled with the sound of them crunching beneath his feet. When he finally stopped about five minutes later, the crunching noise was replaced by something else. The sound of running water. A stream!

He let me go, and I fell completely to the ground, face down in the dead vegetation.

"Empty your bladder here," he said simply.

It was clear he wasn't going to turn around nor give me any privacy, but I was too bursting to care. I fumbled with my jean buttons before ripping them down along with my panties and hovering over the stream. The relief was heavenly, even taking my mind from all my other problems and pains for a second.

When I looked up, he was staring at me.

"Not seen anyone taking a leak before?" I asked sarcastically, pulling my jeans up and buttoning them.

"Only in dreams," he replied.

"Fucking pervert," I mumbled under my breath, trying to look as badass as I could when I'd just had a stranger watching me pee. He'd confirmed my theory, though. The doors led to people's dreams. To the inside of people's minds. Wherever I was, it wasn't normal, and it wasn't anywhere on earth. The thought that I'd wandered so far away from home terrified me, but it intrigued me too. I was in a place that no one knew existed. A realm that, until a night ago, I couldn't have even imagined because this was where all of humanity converged, even though I was the only human here. If each of those doors represented a person, this is where we all came to dream.

"Your words do not hurt me, girl, though I find it amusing you think they can."

The fucker heard me! He must have supernatural hearing along with all the other supernatural crap he had going on.

I ignored him and turned back to the stream. It sparkled and shimmered in the blue light, but it was black, like ink. I'd never seen anything like it.

I dipped my hand in then pulled it out again. The black water dripped off, leaving no stain.

My throat rasped at the sight of the water, but my brain told me not to drink it. And yet, I was parched. My throat felt like I'd swallowed sandpaper. Who knew when or if he'd let me go again. I clasped my hands together into a bowl shape and plunged them into the cool darkness. Bringing the ladled water to my face, I lowered my head to drink. Before the inky substance touched my lips, my hands were batted away, knocking all the water from them.

"I need to drink," I rasped as he hauled me to my feet. This time I was more steady and able to stay upright as he dragged me back through the forest. As was becoming usual, he ignored me.

"I'll die if I don't drink soon."

With a completely unperturbed look, he pushed me roughly against the tree and waved his hands. The slithering rope of purple magic or whatever it was appeared again, binding my arms and body to the dark gray tree trunk. He turned on his heel and squeezed between two of the door frames. I heard the click of a door being closed, and once again, he was gone.

I closed my eyes and tried to sleep. Anything to take my mind off the burning in my throat and the empty rumbling of my belly.

When I awoke some time later, he was still nowhere to be seen, but there was a bowl of clear water next to me. With me being unable to pick it up as my hands were bonded to my sides, I had to shuffle the best I could to lower my head and drink from the bowl the way a cat would drink milk, by lapping it up with my tongue.

It was only after my thirst was sated that I realized I could have pulled my phone from my pocket when I was free. I had no way of knowing if this place would get a signal, nor if it would connect to the normal world, but I was going to make it my mission to find out. If I could find a way to get other people here, they would be able to overpower the bastard and wake people up. Wake my mother up. With that in mind, I smiled sweetly up at the raven as I concocted my plan.

CHAPTER EIGHT

Eventually, he came to me and sat in the clearing. The raven flew down and landed on his shoulder as he whipped up a fire from nothing. The light bonds around my arms were one thing, but watching him conjure up fire was just fucking weird.

"What are you going to do with me?" I demanded.

He didn't even bother to look up at me, and I wondered if he even knew. He'd pulled me back in his world for a reason. I needed to know why.

"Hey, Dipshit. Care to tell me what I'm doing here?"

He flicked his eyes upward to me, then lowered them again and pulled out a knife from his boot. Boots that I'd not seen before. He'd been barefoot in the real world. I sucked in a breath as his eyes once more traveled up to mine. They reflected the orange glow of the firelight reminding me of Lucifer himself. Yet again, I wondered if I'd actually died, and this was my own personal hell. If I was dead, then a knife couldn't kill me, I reasoned, though the sight of it was enough for my heart to quicken with anxiety.

I let out a breath as he picked up a stick that had fallen from one of the trees and began to whittle at it.

"You don't want me here!" I shouted out, wondering if he could hear me at all above the crackling of the fire. He was certainly acting as though he didn't. "Oy. I'm talking to you."

"So you are. It's tiresome, and I am already out of patience with it."

"Well, fuck you too," I managed, wondering why I was even trying with this guy. He didn't care what I said, nor that I didn't know anything. He was probably getting off on having me tied up at his mercy. This whole charade was probably one big turn-on for the jerk.

I wanted to see what he was carving, but the flames were too high for me to see as low as his hands. Instead, I watched him as he worked, an intense look about him. The firelight danced on his face, creating an orange glow, making him appear more human than he normally looked. It occurred to me I'd never seen him in daylight. The first time I'd seen him was in the dim light of the sleep clinic. I'd then seen him in my bedroom, where the curtains had been closed so I could block out the daylight and sleep. And here, in this perpetual twilight where he looked pale and otherworldly. I still didn't know what he was. The devil himself had run through my thoughts more than once, but in no part of my imagination could I conjure up the thought of the devil whittling. Whittling human flesh from bones possibly, but not carving something from a stick.

"You can't just keep me here," I said, hoping to sound at least authoritative because the truth was he could keep me here. Could and was doing. "I have friends who could kill you without batting an eyelid. They'll come looking for me."

He was up and over the fire before I could blink, and now, the knife was at my throat.

"Didn't I tell you to shut your infernal jabbering?"

"Actually, you said you'd lost patience with me. You didn't actually tell me to stop."

"So stop. I'm telling you now," he growled, his face full of menace.

God help me; I should have stopped. The feel of the blade on my flesh should have been warning enough, but it wouldn't be me if I did the sensible thing.

"Tell me why I'm here."

He threw his knife down where it landed blade down in the dirt beside me. His eyes searched mine as though he was the one looking for answers. A cruel darkness descended over his features. One I'd seen before when he'd first brought me here. "I don't have to answer to you. You don't have any friends to come looking for you. Your one friend would balk at killing an insect. And just like an insect, I could crush him with my bare hands."

As though he needed me to understand, he grabbed the fleshy part of my arm and squeezed it tightly, all the while looking directly into my eyes. I death-stared him back, trying not to linger on his beauty. This was not the time to be ogling a man who was trying to maim me, if not kill me.

"Fuck you," I spat out, causing him to tighten his grip until I cried out in pain. He let go, and I thought that was it, but he was merely freeing his hand to grab my neck, this time at the back. He pulled me down and forward, contorting my body into an unnatural position until my face was once again in the dirt

"You are here because I have not killed you yet. You

are alive, not because of my mercy, but because I have yet to decide the depths of hell I want to send you to and then test the pain limits your body will allow until it breaks." He pushed down until my face was so far into the ground that I could no longer breathe. At that point, he whispered in my ear, his voice chillingly cold. "Remember that it was your choice to come looking for your worst nightmare. Well, now you've found me."

Only then did he let go, satisfied that I'd gotten the point. I was silent for the rest of the night.

CHAPTER NINE

The next day, or night—It was impossible to tell which—followed a similar theme. He left me for hours to do his job, whatever that consisted of. I'd figured out he was going into people's dreams, but what he did in there was anybody's guess. Probably jerked off to people's subconscious desires, the sick fuck. I wanted to not care, to ignore him as he ignored me, but it was difficult when he was literally the only thing in this whole forest to look at. After his warning last night, I daren't take my eyes off him. Every ten minutes or so, he'd come out of one door then go in through the next, never stopping, never taking a break. I only caught glimpses of him through the gaps in the doors. I'd not seen him eat once in the whole time I'd been here. Nor had I seen him pee or do anything vaguely human. I calculated as best I could how many hours I'd spent in the forest. The constant darkness made it difficult, but it felt like I'd slept a good amount. He'd taken me in the early hours of a Tuesday morning.

I was pretty sure I'd had at least one more night here, so it was probably around Thursday morning. I thought back to the sad packet of dry crackers in my kitchen cupboard and wished I'd have thought to bring them with me. Not that I could have foreseen being tied up for two nights without food. My stomach grumbled painfully every time I thought about food which was pretty much all the time. When I was sleeping, my bowl had mysteriously refilled with water, so I wasn't going to die of dehydration any time soon. Plus, he'd taken me to the stream a couple of times, so my bladder was no longer a problem.

"I'm hungry," I grumbled to the raven, who ignored me. It was a trait he'd probably learned from his boss. The two of them suited one another.

The raven squawked and took off into the sky. It came back a few minutes later and dropped a couple of worms into my lap.

My stomach lurched at the sight of the fat wriggling monsters in my lap.

"Take them away!" I hissed, jumping my legs about in an attempt to throw them off. The raven picked them both up, then threw its head up and swallowed them both down whole. If I'd had any food left in my stomach to lose, I would have lost it.

"Thanks," I whimpered. At least it was trying. That was more than its boss was doing. It ruffled its feathers and took off back to its favored branch. Then it turned its back on me.

The doors moved, and I saw Asshat stepping from one door to the next.

"I'm hungry," I shouted out, temporarily forgetting my self-mandated plan to never utter a word to the bastard ever again.

I thought he was ignoring me again, but then he appeared in the gaps between the doorframes.

"I need to eat, or I'll die."

He narrowed his eyes and tapped his feet impatiently, clearly annoyed that I was interrupting him. "What do I care? Starve then."

He was a wily asshole.

"You obviously brought me here for a reason," I pointed out. "The first time I followed you, but the second time you pulled me back in. I doubt that reason was to watch me die, tied to a tree, even if you are a sick bastard."

He grimaced, then turned away from me and headed to the red door. With one swift movement, he was through it, slamming it shut behind him. The sound rattled the frame and reverberated through the forest.

It was the first time I'd seen him use that door since the first time he'd brought me here. Then it had led to my bedroom. I wondered where it led now. I didn't have too long to wait to find out.

The door opened again. I was sure I heard someone screaming on the other side of it, but then it was once again slammed shut.

"Here," he said, throwing a fast-food pizza box at my feet. I recognized the brand straight away. It was one of the worldwide pizza brands. The smell of it almost took me to heaven. Only one problem. I couldn't reach it. I raised my eyebrows at him.

He huffed then raised his hand. The purple bonds holding me to the tree evaporated. I lunged for the box, throwing it open. In my food-starved mind, this was a trick, and the box would be empty, but when I opened it, I saw the most delicious-looking pepperoni pizza. I grabbed a slice and shoved it in my mouth, letting t molten cheese drip down my chin.

"Mmm, thssgggd," I mumbled.

Asshole took a step forward and sat opposite me, with the ashes of last night's campfire between us. "Am I supposed to understand that?"

I waited until I'd swallowed the last of the slice before gracing him with an answer.

"I said, it's so good. Want some?"

He curled his mouth down at the edges the way I was certain I'd done when the raven had brought me worms. His loss. I picked up a second slice and took a bite.

He watched me as I ate with the same curiosity he showed when I went to pee. It was like basic human needs were weird and foreign to him. Maybe they were.

"Why don't you eat?" I asked between mouthfuls. "Or sleep, or pee?"

"Just because you don't see me do any of those things does not mean I don't do them. I just choose not to share them with you."

Haughty bastard. "So you're shy then?" I knew I was stepping on thin ice, but I couldn't help myself. There was something about the arrogance of this guy that triggered my smart mouth.

"Why did you come here?"

Not the answer I was expecting. It wasn't even an answer at all, but I'd roll with it because this was the first conversation we'd had, and color me curious; I wanted to know more about this strange world.

"You brought me here," I reminded him a second time.

"You followed me here, then you tried to find me when I threw you out. Why?"

The first time I'd followed him without really thinking. He'd been in my room, and I'd chased him. The second time was because I needed to find out about my mother. Not that I was going to give him the satisfaction of knowing that.

"I like to travel," I smart-mouthed back at him.

He snarled and stood up. "You are not what I thought you were. In fact, you are a disappointment."

Yeah, and I love you too, Dickwad.

At least I managed to keep that thought in my mind rather than on my tongue.

With one swift movement, he raised his arm and conjured the purple ropes that bound me to the tree. At least this time, my arms were free. He turned and went back to his job of invading people's dreams.

I mused his words as I chomped down on the pizza. If I was a disappointment, then he'd been expecting me. But why? I hadn't even known he existed before he showed up in the sleep clinic.

It was another conundrum left for me to ponder.

How the fuck did he know me, and what exactly was he expecting that made me such a disappointment?

Fuck only knew, but I was going to find out.

CHAPTER TEN

It became depressingly obvious that the Pizza was a one-time offering. I should have saved some. Hell, I already knew that starving me wasn't a problem for him, but I'd been hungry, and my stomach had over-ridden any sensible thoughts I might have had on the subject.

I stared down at the pile of leaves and berries that he'd obviously plucked from some bushes nearby.

"I can't eat this."

"So don't," He shrugged and turned to walk away as he always did.

Bastard! He knew I needed to eat. He'd kept me waiting for another full day and night. He also knew he needed to be near me when I did eat because there was no way he was going to untie me when he wasn't around to supervise.

"Fine," I capitulated. "I'll eat it."

He huffed in irritation.

"Make up your mind. I don't have time to be dealing

He sat down in his usual place and brought out his knife to whittle again after magically making my bonds disappear.

I picked up a leaf and sniffed it. It didn't seem likely that he'd poison me. If he wanted me dead, I was an easy target, but I could totally get that he'd pick any old leaves without knowing if they were poisonous or not. The guy didn't seem to give a shit about my welfare anyway.

"They are safe," he said without even looking up, then went back to his whittling.

I chewed on the leaf while watching him. It was no pizza and stuck in my throat, but it was better than nothing, which, at this point, was my only alternative. Without the fire, I could see exactly what it was he was carving. It was a person. A woman. I was too far away to see the features on it, but it looked like a beautiful woman.

"Who is she?" I asked, hazarding his wrath. It did not come.

"None of your business."

"An old girlfriend?"

"None of your business."

"Nice weather we're having," I said, trying a different tack. He was no company at all, but it was better than talking to the raven that was unable to answer me.

He looked up from his carving. "Why do you speak so much? Your incessant chatter gives me a headache."

"It's not like I have anyone else to talk to. I'm bored. You obviously don't want me here, and as you've no plans to kill, I may as well go back home."

He looked at me with curiosity in his eyes. "What makes you think I have no plans to kill you?"

I shrugged and threw a handful of berries into my mouth. They were surprisingly sweet. "You've had plenty of opportunity. If you were going to kill me, you'd have done it already."

He leapt up and held his knife to my throat. "I wouldn't get comfortable in that thought if I were you. Just because I haven't killed you yet, doesn't mean I'm not going to. His eyes were ablaze with fury, but there was hesitation in them. "Let me make something crystal clear to you. You are never ever going back through that red door. Do you understand me?" He bared his teeth, and the muscles in his hand tautened.

"Actually, I don't understand," I said pushing at his chest. "I'm obviously a burden to you, and you have shown no interest in killing me except for a few empty threats, so why not let me go so I can leave you to go back to jerking off over other people's dreams?"

It was like something snapped in him. I had that way with people. He roared, pulling me up by the front of my shirt. The leaves and berries that had been sitting on my lap scattered everywhere.

HIs strength was unbelievable. He held me up with one hand, his arm extended vertically. With his other hand, he waved magic from nothing, and before I knew it, I was hanging from a branch of the tree above me, tethered by my wrists.

His face was as black as thunder, his voice harsh. "Do. Not. Question. Me. Again!" He stormed off through a gap in the door frames and through one of the doors, slamming the door shut with a bang that echoed through the forest. Looking up, Raven gave me a look as if to say that my situation was all of my own doing. I couldn't disagree with him.

CHAPTER ELEVEN

The days that followed could only be described as a living hell. Pain became a constant companion. My wrists were chafed raw from the magical ropes, and my shoulders screamed in burning agony from being held in such an unnatural position. He'd made it very clear that he didn't give a monkey's toss about me at all, but I'd pushed it and pushed it because I couldn't keep my mouth shut. In all the days I'd been here, many emotions had crossed through my mind, but this was the first time I'd felt real fear. Sure, the adrenaline had been surging as he'd squeezed my throat and held a knife to me, but this was a thousand times worse. It was slow and drawn out, only made worse by the fact that asshat had decided I didn't exist again. Each time he came out through one of the doors, I hoped my torment would cease when he saw the raw agony in my face, but he never looked my way. The only times he bothered to acknowledge me at all were the few times he let me drink at the water bowl.

When it became too painful to move my head, he gripped my chin, pulling my head up and dribbling the water into my mouth.

"I'm going to die!" I mumbled hoarsely as the dirty water dribbled down my chin. "Why bother with the water?" Agony rippled through me at the effort. Death would be a welcome path at this juncture—anything but the torment of this...nightmare. I couldn't feel anything but pain, and my clothes were full of my own filth. Death would be a relief.

He held my chin up so he could look me in the eyes. The prick probably wanted to see the living daylights drain from me. Another perverted kick for him. Close up, his eyes were unnerving, cold and dark, just like his fucking soul.

"You aren't going to die. That would be too easy." He turned as if to move away, then hesitated and turned back. "Why did you come here?"

This again. "Fuck you!" I spat at him, though missed by a wide margin, thanks to my neck being weaker than a newborn giraffe's.

"It seems to me that you like the pain. Otherwise, why do you ask for it?"

This time when he turned, he left.

I was asleep or passed out unconscious when he eventually let me down by untethering my wrists and letting me drop to the ground in a heap. I was too sore, too exhausted, and too utterly pissed off to complain.

"Drink this," he said, holding the bowl of water to my lips. Part of me wanted to throw the bowl right back at him, but he'd broken me. I was too tired and too thirsty to do anything other than bend my head to drink, and even that was an effort of Herculean proportions. I uttered a moan of pain as I supped at the luke-warm water. My wrists had felt like fire after ten minutes of being strung up by them, so I hadn't noticed how much my neck hurt, and oh, fuck, it did.

He brought me berries again, but I didn't have the will or the energy to bother to eat them. Instead, I closed my eyes and let myself fall into blissful oblivion away from the pain.

The next morning, my wrists felt, if it was possible, worse than they had the night before. I glanced down and saw that the skin around where the magic had grated against it was now mottled and bruised, with shreds ripped out of it, the blood congealed in a thick black band. A quick look around told me that Asshat was back at work in one of the dreams. I expected that the doors would move at any minute. I also noticed that my hands had been left untied. I was no longer tethered to a tree or anything else.

Why had the fucker done that? Surely the sick fuck wasn't about to let me go?

And then it became apparent that, no, he wasn't about to let me go. I stood up, or at least, tried to. My legs wobbled beneath me, unable to hold my weight, and the forest swirled in a kaleidoscope of darkness. I collapsed to the ground, emptying my almost empty stomach of bile to the ground next to me. This was worse than the night I'd gotten pissed at one of David's work parties and puked in a hydrangea bush. At least I'd had the fun part before the hangover. This wasn't even a result of drunkenness. If only. I was weak from lack of food, from being strung up, from my body clock being so messed up with lack of light that I didn't know anymore what day it was or what time of day it was.

Asshat was upon me in seconds. I gave him a cold look as he pulled me up into a sitting position and put a fresh pile of berries on my lap. They were the same as before. Small, dark berries. He watched as I ate them, and I was sure saw satisfaction in his eyes as he saw the immense pain picking up each one caused me. I knew better than to ask him for help. He was enjoying this way too much to actually help me, so I had to weigh up the pain in my wrists against the pain in my empty belly. Neither was a great option, but not eating would kill me, so I gritted my teeth and ate as many as I could before it got too much. When he saw I couldn't eat any more, he bound me again to the tree and left to go back to his work. Stringing me up hadn't been the end of my life as I had predicted, merely an interlude of anguish in his symphony of torture.

And so the days went by and by and by. I lost count of how many.

When he wasn't in the dreams, he was close by, never leaving my line of sight. He didn't sleep, rest, eat or drink, or at least he didn't do any of those things in my waking hours. He just worked none stop like a machine. I tried to make conversation, he stood up and left or ignored me completely. Not that I cared much. What was the point? My only saving grace was that he hadn't tried to kill me again, but it was little consolation. At first, I thought I might die of infection in my wounds, but as they cleared up, turning from black and blue to faded brown, I realized his plan was to have me die of boredom. At least in the beginning, when he'd held a knife to my throat, it was exciting. Not the kind of excitement I usually went for, but anything was better than the endless days of solitude and silence.

For my part, I spent the days and nights making a plan. He watched me like a hawk when my arms were unbound, but one of the times he'd taken me to the stream, I'd managed to pull my phone from my pocket and check it while he was distracted. It had still had a bit of battery left. I'd turned it off to conserve its meager charge and slipped it back in my pocket.

It was just a matter of time until I'd slip away from his reach. He couldn't watch me forever.

My plan was simple. Wait until he was distracted, then run into the forest. It was a weird place with darkness everywhere. There were plenty of hiding places. Once hidden, I was going to try to phone someone. Not Chris. He'd think I was pranking him or be so worried he'd have a spasm. Wonderful as he was, he was not good in a crisis. It only left my sister, who hated me. On reflection, I should probably have gotten myself more friends, but the matter was moot. My sister was the only one who would keep her head and know what to do, just like she always did. Whether she'd believe me or not, that was another matter.

I'd noticed the raven coming with us a couple of times as we made our twice-daily toilet trip. Maybe it wanted to stretch its wings, or maybe it was a pervert too. Who knew. If I managed to do something to the bird, it might keep Freakshow distracted long enough for me to get away.

The days struggled by, each one feeling like an eternity.

My body clock was so screwed up from the perpetual nightfall that I couldn't even hazard a guess at how long I'd been Freakshow's prisoner, but it had to have been at least a week, probably closer to two. I felt disgusting. My clothes stank, and my hair was clumping up into a birds' nest. Basic hygiene was not a priority for asshat, although he always looked and smelled good. I didn't know how he did it. Magic probably. Magic that was not afforded to me. What did he care if I looked like shit and smelled like shit? It wasn't as though he had to come too close to me. I'd tried washing out the shit and piss from my pants in the stream, but I'd ended up naked from the waist down while they dried. Plus, interesting as the black stream water was, it did little to freshen up shitty pants. The raven kept a doleful watch on me when its master was weaving in and out of the doors. I looked up at it. I wasn't a bird expert, but it looked sad to me, like it was missing out on adventure. Perhaps it was. The first time I'd come here, it was because I'd bird-napped it. Now it didn't travel anywhere with Freakshow. It was my guard and my only companion. I had a feeling it resented me for the job it was now required to do.

"Why don't you come for a walk with us?" I asked it nonchalantly after waiting days for it to come up with the idea itself. As it usually did, it ignored me, but when Freakshow came to untie me, I noticed with some satisfaction that the raven followed, flying above us in the dusky treetops.

No longer did Freakshow pull me along to the stream, but he walked close by, enough to grab me if I attempted to run.

"Nice weather," I said. It had become a routine. I'd make conversation, he'd grunt, or, like he was doing today, remain silent. Since the day he'd hung me from the tree, I'd kept mostly quiet, but today I needed him to have his guard down. I needed his mind occupied with banality and not focus on whether I would run or not. So I chatted away about the weather. It was always the same. I asked him questions. He never answered. But everything I said was calculated. I knew he wasn't going to answer me when I asked him things. He never had up to now. Nor did I care about the weather or rather lack of it. I just needed him to think I was comfortable here or at least used to my situation. Not once had he told me why he kept me here, and he'd not been forthcoming as to what he was going to do with me.

We got to the stream, and he rested against a tree trunk. I made a mental note of where the raven came to rest above him on a branch. I did what I had to do then, and after buttoning myself back up, I dipped my hands into the stream. I felt around on the bed of the stream for a suitably sized stone. Then with as much strength as I could muster, I turned and took aim. I already knew throwing it at Freakshow himself was pointless. He was stronger than any human I'd ever met and had armor covering part of him. A stone would just bounce off him, but the raven. The raven was a smaller target but much more likely to fall. The stone flew through the air, arcing between us below the foliage of the trees. As if in slow motion, the raven saw the danger and began to take off, spreading its great black wings out. For a second, I thought the stone was going to miss, but it clipped the raven's wing, sending it spiraling to the ground. My stomach felt heavy as I watched it fall to the forest floor, landing right next to its master. I'd never hurt an animal before, and I hated what I'd done, but it was my only way to escape. Terror flooded me as I saw the coldness in Freakshow's eyes at what I'd done to his bird. I didn't stay around to watch further. Instead, I leapt over the stream and took off into the forest.

Bushes whipped around my face as I raced through the darkness. Only slivers of light peeping through the trees allowed me to see where I was going. Just like the parts of the forest I'd already seen, the darkness was endless. The dark trees faded into black in the distance in every direction. It was like driving on a pitch-black night with only the car's headlights to show me where to go, revealing one part at a time.

I zigged and zagged my way through the undergrowth, not keeping to a straight line. The farther I got from Freakshow, the better. The hardness of my phone felt securely pressed against me in my pocket, my only comfort in the terrifying forest. Branches whipped out across my face, coming as if from nowhere, stinging me and slowing me down. The only sound I heard was my own ragged breathing and the crunch of dead leaves beneath my feet. Asshat was either much quieter than I at running through forests of crunchy leaves, or I'd lost him. I stopped to catch my breath and really listen. Complete silence made the forest even eerier. Living in Vancouver had accustomed me to noise all day and night. Living in a city meant that silence was not something I was used to. Not like this. Despite the trees all around me, the darkness and lack of sound had me feeling like I might lift off into space at any moment and spend my days floating, untethered to anything.

Pulling my phone out from my pocket, I turned it on. Only one bar remained. Nothing came through. No signal, just the glow from the smiling photo of David and me. I'd forgotten to change my background.

"Damnit!" I hissed, holding the phone higher to try to get a signal to no avail. Closing my eyes, I fell

back against a tree trunk and looked at the picture. It had been taken during happier times. Way before Sophie had entered the picture. Fuck, I'd even call Sophie if it meant she could get me out of this hell hole. Turning to the tree, I grabbed a branch and hauled myself up to give myself a higher platform from which to get a signal. With each branch I stepped up on, the fruitlessness of the endeavor became more apparent, and the higher I went, the more hopelessness seeped in. Up in the canopy of the trees, I'd never felt more alone as the signal bar showed nothing, and the battery life bar got increasingly lower, almost as if it was connected to my mood. In any normal forest, I'd have been able to use my height in the tree as a vantage point, but in the endless darkness, all I could see were more trees, more branches, more leaves that were black enough to appear dead, but surprisingly weren't. I shook the phone, applying the age-old tactic of shaking to get a better signal. It didn't work. In fact, all it accomplished was a loud crack in the branch beneath me. I grabbed out for a branch above, anything to get purchase, before the phone fell out of my hand, tumbling twenty feet to the ground, with me following very quickly behind it.

Thanks to all the branches I hit on the way down, my arms and legs hurt like hell, but it slowed my fall, meaning that I didn't die when I hit the ground. The leaves cushioned my fall, winding me but not sending me unconscious. I sucked in a breath as pain wracked my body, making me wonder how I'd managed to simultaneously land on every single part of my body because literally everywhere hurt.

"Are you alright? I saw you fall."

I was momentarily taken out of my own pain by the strange being in front of me. She was like nothing I'd ever seen before in my life. She was tall and slim, with skin a tone of which I didn't think possible. Like a blackboard that someone had covered in white chalk and then unsuccessfully attempted to rub off. A pale matte grey, I supposed I'd call it. She had bright violet eyes, long lilac hair that hung over her shoulder in a braided ponytail with two pointed ears peeking through. There was no way she was human, and yet, I sensed no danger from her. There was only worry in those mesmerizing eyes of hers, giving me the sense that she wasn't about to eat me or strangle me like Freakshow had. A raven flew above her head, this one different from Asshole's raven. This one had a hint of green and pink coloring coating the black of its feathers.

"I think so," I finally said when my brain finally kicked into gear, and I realized she'd asked me a question. "I don't think anything is broken, at least."

She held out a slender hand to me. It was thinner than any adult human hand, with long elongated fingers that tapered to shaped black nails. "Aethelu, and this is Tourmaline or Tour for short. she's my companion." She pointed to her bird. I let her help me into a standing position, and it was only when I was upright that I finally realized how tall she was. Just like Freakshow, she was exceptionally tall. Maybe six feet four or five. She wore a long, deep purple dress that brought out the color in her eyes—the only color I'd seen around here since I'd come apart from the red door. It made a refreshing change. She was undeniably beautiful. Strangely so. Otherworldly, which I supposed she was, but stunning nonetheless.

I felt like a dump truck next to her. She recoiled a little and wrinkled her nose as I stood up. Not really a surprise as my current aroma du jour was eau de shit. It didn't stop the look of worry in her eyes. In fact, it only increased it. I was like a stinky puppy that someone had thrown out of a car to her.

"I don't know you," she said, her voice almost as strange and beautiful as she was. Melodic and light but with strength to it. There was an undercurrent to it, a duality as though she wasn't the only one speaking.

"I'm not from around here," I replied, feeling foolish and gross next to her perfection. It was obvious I wasn't from around here. I wasn't some kind of gorgeous, giant weirdo for a start.

She laughed. "I can see that, but..." she cocked her head to the side. "You look strange to me."

I raised my eyebrows. She was some kind of tall freaky grey angel, and she was telling me I looked strange?

"I'm from the world...you know...the world. Earth. Canada. Err." I was mumbling, such was the strangeness of the situation and the awe in which I regarded her. I needed to pull myself together.

The confused expression remained on her face. "I'm sorry. I don't know of this Worldearthcanada place. Is it part of the Dream Court or Nightmare Court? I thought

I knew all the places but..." a look of horror appeared on her face. "You're not from the Court of the Dark? Your hair..."

I shook my head, wondering if I'd banged my head more than I thought when I tumbled down from the trees. "I'm from the...er...human court."

Shock painted her face, taking over from the horror she'd just shown. In the tree behind her, Tour squawked and ruffled its feathers.

"You're human?" Her demeanor changed instantly. Her mouth became taut, and her pupils widened. "You aren't supposed to be here. Humans aren't allowed in the Night Realm. How did you get in?"

I opened my mouth to tell her the whole sordid story when something occurred to me. "If you've never met a human before, how come you are speaking English. Rather convenient, don't you think?"

It was a trick. It had to be. Freakshow had done this. He'd seen and heard humans through the billions of dreams he'd seen. His speaking English wasn't entirely strange, but to someone who had never set foot in the human world, how would they be able to speak any language in it? Especially the one I happened to speak.

"I'm not speaking English. I've never heard of that dialect. Everyone in the Realm of Night is a...polyglot."

"A polywhat?"

She cast her eyes to the side and held a finger to her lips. "A multilingual. A speaker of many languages."

Uh-huh. "Ok, I understand that, but how can you speak a language you've never heard of, let alone learned?"

Her face loosened up a little. "I don't need to learn a language. I hear your words. I don't understand them, but then they change into words I can understand in my mind. When I speak, the same thing happens, but the other way around. I think polyglot isn't the exact translation for what I am, but I don't know of a literal word for it in your language. You hear the translated words, so to you, it sounds like I am speaking English. Were you to speak Ravenish or Elvish, those languages are what you'd hear me speak. For example, I can speak to Tour here and understand when she speaks back to me."

Tour let out a caw in response. It didn't sound like it meant anything, but what did I know?

It sounded plausible. Or at least it sounded as plausible as anything else in this fucked up place. It explained the duality of her voice. I'd heard her real voice with the translation over the top. At least I wasn't going completely batshit insane.

"I think this talk of language is not really the most important thing here. The most important thing is getting you back home. This place is not for humans." She darted her eyes to the side as though just being in my presence would cause danger to her. Perhaps it would. Freakshow had almost murdered me about fifteen times in the last couple of weeks. Maybe one day he'd just do it. I couldn't imagine he'd thank this woman for helping me.

"Thank you. I'm lost," I blurted out, thankful for her help. She was the first kind face I'd seen since stepping into this hell hole.

"I'll say," she said, a wry smile on her face as we both started the long walk back toward the red door. "You still haven't told me how you came to be here. I can't help you unless you tell me how you got in. The last human that managed it didn't...er."

"Survive?" I vaguely remembered Asshole mentioning

something about killing someone.

"Yeah. This really isn't a place for humans. I wouldn't want you to get eaten."

"Eaten?" *What now?* "By what?"

She carried on her long strides through the forest with me practically running to keep up with her. "There are many creatures that roam this forest. Most will kill you as soon as look at you. You've done well to survive at all, especially with you being so...forgive me...fragrant."

She must have seen a sickly look on my face because she took my hand and continued. "Don't worry. You will come to no harm with me by your side, but pray tell me where we are going? I cannot help you return to the human realm if I don't know where it is."

"It's through a red door. This way, I think."

I carried on walking but was yanked back by her hand holding mine. She'd stopped suddenly.

"A red door? The King brought you here?"

King?

"No. Some fucked up weirdo with a... a crown."

She eyed me with both amusement and trepidation. "That would be the Dream King, Dream. "

Dream? That was his name? Freakshow suited him better, but I wasn't about to quibble. "He didn't exactly bring me here. Well, maybe. I followed him the first time, but then the second time, he pulled me through with him."

Her hand shot up to her mouth in surprise. "Oh, my. Why would he do that? What did you do?"

"Nothing," I said, shrugging my shoulders. "I might have kidnapped his bird."

Her eyes widened as she took in my reply. "You really are in the shit, girl, aren't you?"

She didn't seem the type to say words like 'shit.' She looked far too elegant for such words, but she wasn't wrong. Maybe there wasn't a literal translation for the word she wanted to use. A word that was more elegant.

"Not if you help me get home."

She shook her head, her hand at her heart. "Do you know who Dream is? I mean, really know?"

I shrugged. "I know he's an asshole with a grudge who thinks it's fun to tie up women."

She blinked then looked about her as if looking to see if anyone was overhearing me. She lowered her voice so that I had to lean in to hear her. "Asshole he may be, but don't let him hear you calling him that."

I snorted. "I've called him worse to his face, and I can't see that I'd stop now. He *is* an asshole."

She brought her hand up to her forehead as though I was giving her a migraine. I probably was.

"I'll hand it to you. You are lucky to be alive. I've known the king for a long time. I wouldn't say we are friends. He's the king of these parts, and I'm not even a noble, but he knows me. I can't take you to the red door. It is not my place. I can only take you to the king and plead your case with him."

The familiar sensation of dread descended on me. "I can't go back to him. He's the reason I'm out here in the woods. I'm running away from him. He's kept me tied to a tree for ages. I've not changed my clothes for weeks."

For some unfathomable reason, she didn't seem in the remotest bit surprised at this tidbit of news. I guess my stink gave me away.

"He hung me from a tree for days," I added, holding out my wrists where the thin bands of bruising were still visible.

Her brow furrowed. "I can see by your expression that you are telling me the truth, but it doesn't sound like him. He doesn't like...people. He really doesn't like humans. I cannot see any reason why he would keep you. He is not the type to play games."

Right. No one said any of this was a game. "Yeah, well, you said you don't know him that well. Maybe he's exactly like that."

"Maybe." she didn't sound convinced. "Maybe he has good reason, although I can't think of one. The whole thing is very strange."

No shit! "He's a stark raving lunatic. I don't think he needs any other reason than that. That's why I need you to help me get away." I pleaded with her. When I'd first gotten here, I'd been scared of him, but now that I knew what he was capable of, my fear had turned to something much deeper. I didn't fear him killing me. For some reason, I didn't think he would, despite all his promises to, but causing me pain came easily to him. He got a kick out of it, and I knew that there was a lot more where that had come from.

She gulped then pulled herself up tall. "That may be, but he'll find you no matter what I do. If he knows I'm with you and then let you go... "

"You're going to force me to go back with you?" I asked incredulously. What was it with people around here? Was there seriously so little in the way of entertainment that kidnap was the only option?

She gave me a wry smile. "I'm not going to force you to do anything, but if you run away through these woods alone, you won't last the day. Going back to the king is your only option if you want to survive. I'll leave it up to you if you want me to come with you. I wouldn't want leaving you out here alone on my conscience, but I'm not your captor. The choice is yours."

Fucking great. Either I get eaten by some monster in the woods or go back to the monster I knew was waiting for me at the doors. Maybe this woman was right when she said that she could talk sense into him. Maybe he'd let me go if she was the one to ask.

She looked badass enough to whip out some really cool weapon from the backpack she wore and help me in a daring escape, but I guessed it wasn't to be. If I was going to escape, I was going to have to do it alone. It was then that I realized I'd left my phone behind. My one connection to the real world was under a tree somewhere in a pile of fucking leaves.

CHAPTER TWELVE

Dream looked up as we entered the clearing. "Aethelu. I see you've found my..."

"Captive," I cut in before he could finish his sentence. Aethelu had brought me back to the rows of doors, and I'd let her. My phone was gone - probably lost for good, and her pleading with Dream was more than likely my best bet out of here. She bowed slightly to him when he noticed our arrival. He was sitting pretty much where he usually did, whittling next to the ashes of the fire. The bastard hadn't even bothered to run after me. He smiled at me, and I swear my heart jumped. He'd only ever shown me torture and disdain. I wondered if there was something between the beautiful Aethelu and Dream. I also wondered why a spike of jealousy hit me when I thought of it.

Christ, my mind was a torrid mess.

"I was going to say guest, but yes, captive works."

I rolled my eyes. Since when did guests need to be tied up? Knowing this guy, he probably thought it was the height of good manners. He was being awfully civilized around Aethelu...Almost like a normal person. Who knew he was capable of it?

He turned to Aethelu. "Sorry to drag you into this mess."

Her eyebrows quirked. "Mess, Your Majesty? I was under the impression you brought her here on purpose. I have to say I'm dying to know exactly what that purpose is. It doesn't seem prudent to be bringing humans into our world after... ahem...what happened last time."

He narrowed his eyes and then flicked them my way. Heat scorched me at the way he looked at me; the intensity of his stare was overwhelming and full of loathing. The mask of indifference was well and truly off. Neither he nor Aethelu had hold of me. I was free to run through the red door. It was less than ten feet away, but I was bolted to the ground, held in his stare. Running back into the forest was a no-no. I'd already seen how easy it was to get lost in, and if Aethelu was telling the truth about all the things that would find me tasty in there, then the red door was my only way out. It would be so easy. A few steps. Open the door and jump through. Dream wouldn't be able to get me then. Sure, he could follow me through, but there were people there. Chris or even McGee or Alexis. And yet my brain was saying 'and then what?' What if I did escape through the door? My mother, and so many like her, would stay in their state of sleep. However much I loathed Dream for what he had done to me, I needed him. I needed him to make my mother wake up, and I fucking hated him for it.

A frisson of energy traveled up my spine as neither of us broke the stare. There was something about him that rendered me powerless to move. To do anything that would make the situation I was in any easier.

Aethelu coughed, and finally, Dream looked away. A hit of adrenaline hit me, and I had to suppress a smile. I'd won. Ok, it was a staring contest, but I'd take it. A win was a win, even a small one against a psychopath.

"I know it's not my place, but don't you think it might be a good idea to take her home?" Aethelu's eyes shifted to the red door.

"It's not as easy as that," Dream replied, his voice gruff.

"Does *she* know?" Aethelu pressed.

The way she said it made me think the 'she' in question was not me, but some other she.

Dream pursed his lips. "No, my mother does not know and I'd like to keep it that way. I thank you for bringing her back to me, but unless you need anything else, don't let me keep you. I know how busy you must be."

It was kind of nice to see he didn't direct all his rudeness to me. He was just a rude bastard in general.

Aethelu was having none of it. "Dream,...Your Majesty, this is not the place for a human. You cannot keep her tied up. I understand that there may be things that I don't understand about the situation, but I cannot in all good conscience let you keep her tied to a tree."

He grabbed her arm. Without thinking, I jumped between them.

"Don't hurt her. If you want to take this out on me, so be it. Tie me to a tree again if you must. She was only trying to help. She was the one who said I should come back here. Please don't hurt her."

Dream's eyes looked at me questioningly. For a split

second, there was no hate in them. Confusion maybe, but not hate.

"I was not planning to hurt Aethelu. I merely need to speak to her without you listening in to our private conversation."

He pulled Aethelu away from me and dragged her out of earshot to just below where Tour was sitting on a tree branch. The door was there. So close. My one chance at freedom. Maybe there was a way to wake my mother up without Dream's help. It wasn't like he'd shown any compulsion to help me so far. He'd barely said a word to me in all the time I'd been here, preferring as he did to sit and let me waffle on without making comment.

My insides churned as I contemplated my options. Whatever Dream and Aethelu were arguing about, they were doing it in heated whispers, and neither was looking my way. I had a clear run. My mother's face flashed up in my mind. I started to walk, almost mindlessly, toward the red door.

I was almost at it, my hand already extended to open it when Dream caught my arm and dragged me back to the clearing. Aethelu was already making her way back to wherever it was that she had come from, her lilac dress disappearing from view as she walked away into the darkness of the forest as Tour flew overhead.

"Sit," he commanded, the second Aethelu disappeared completely.

"What were you and Aethelu talking about?" I asked, ignoring his command completely.

He curled his lip, clearly antagonized by me not doing what he wanted at a moment's notice. Not that I cared. Something was happening. Something I didn't know about, and it was pissing me off. I hated not knowing things. It was my biggest fault. I had to know what's going on at all times, or I felt lost, and quite frankly, I couldn't feel any more lost than I did here.

"Sit down, human. You are not here to ask questions." Surprise, surprise. He didn't want to talk to me again. I should be happy. Him ignoring me was better than the alternative of him hurting me, but as usual, I didn't let it lie.

"So why am I here? You still haven't told me, but you obviously have a reason. " I couldn't help myself. He rolled his eyes and let out a breath of frustration but didn't answer my question. Figuring that we were in a stalemate situation, I gave in and sat down, crisscrossing my legs. It wasn't great, but it was a damn sight better than being tied to a tree.

He leaned forward, his steely eyes boring into mine and a grimace on his lips. "I don't know why you are here. So far, despite all your chattering, you've failed to tell me."

I crossed my arms. He wasn't the only one with secrets. Yes, I'd followed him in, but he'd dragged me back here. If he wasn't going to tell me why, I sure as shit wasn't going to enlighten him as to why I'd followed in the first place. I didn't trust him. If I mentioned my mother, he'd probably do something worse than just having her sleep. I couldn't let that happen. To give him that small part of me would be to give up any power I had, which was barely any. He held all the cards, and he knew it. It dawned on me that the only reason he'd been keeping me alive all this time was that I knew something he didn't. If that was the only thing standing between me and death, I'd hold onto it.

When he saw that I wasn't going to speak, he waved his hand, and a small flame ignited between us. In any other situation, I would have panicked by magical flames heading my way, but I was getting used to this guy's peculiarities. The flame hit the ground between us and became a fire like the ones we'd had camping when I was a child. Except, of course, this one was fuelled by magic rather than wood. It occurred to me then that I was becoming immune to his weirdness. I barely batted an eyelid at the use of magic. In all honesty, a magical fire was lame compared to all the other stuff I'd seen over the last couple of weeks or so.

Dream sat, his back against a tree, one leg out flat, the other bent a little. His face lit by the orange flames gave him a little color, making him appear more human.

If that's even possible.

The fire crackled as a normal one would, despite its apparent lack of kindling. My mind buzzed with questions that I knew he wouldn't answer, but the silence between the two of us was deafening. If only there were other sights and sounds for me to concentrate on, but in the forest of silence and blackness, the only stimulus I had was him and his bloody raven, which seemed to be absent.

"Where is the raven?" I felt like a total shit for hitting it with a stone. I hadn't really wanted to hurt it, only startle it.

He didn't look up. "He is flying. He will be back when I call him."

"Yeah, I'm sorry about that. I didn't mean to hurt him. Maybe I could do something for him. Dig up some worms or something."

Dream looked at me with curiosity. "You are scared of worms. Why would you do that?"

I cringed. Being scared of worms was as irrational

as it got, but they were gross and wriggly. Snakes I was totally fine with, but worms. They were disgusting creatures. "I hurt him. I want to make it better. Make him feel better. I want to say sorry to him and tell him I'll never hurt him again."

Dream licked his lips and regarded me with curiosity. "You want to apologize to a bird? Not many humans would lower themselves."

I shrugged. "I guess I'm not many humans."

"So I'm beginning to see."

Something about his answer embarrassed me though I couldn't say why. Maybe it was because he wasn't threatening me or barking orders. This might be the first time he was talking to me normally. It was weird.

He's a psychopathic murderer. Nothing more. Don't read anything into nice words of his. That's how they get you!

"I've never seen you relax before," I changed the subject, deciding to go with a statement rather than a question.

"This isn't relaxation," he muttered. "This is me making sure you don't try to escape again."

I could see it on him. The way he was posed, to anyone else, would look like prime relaxation, but there was a tell in the way his fingers moved slightly. The thumb rubbing against his forefinger. His toe tapping ever so slightly on the floor. I cast my eyes around the darkness, wondering what it was he was thinking, what he was afraid of, because it sure as hell wasn't me.

"So... What do you do for fun around here?" It was hardly the question I wanted to ask. I needed to know who he was, what he did, and why he was keeping me prisoner. I wanted to know what he was talking about with Aethelu and who the mysterious 'she' was, but I knew from experience that questions like those would get me shut down quicker than a rat in a burger joint.

His eyes remained on the fire, and I noticed how beautifully it reflected in them.

"I am not here to have fun. This is my job," he said simply, and for the first time, I detected some emotion in him. Some emotion other than psychopathic rage. He was resigned to the fact that his job was to perv on other people's dreams because that's what it looked like to me. He spent every hour of every day and night walking in those doors and seeing people's inner psyche. The doors were currently still. It was the longest I'd seen them go without moving, which told me his movements controlled them, not the other way around. I looked back at him and felt something other than fear or hate for him. I was sorry for him. Stuck alone, seeing people all the time but not able to communicate with them. No wonder he had kept me here.

"What exactly is your job?" I expected him to ignore me again. It was his way, so I was surprised when he spoke.

"Do you not dream?"

Why did I get the feeling this was a trick question. He knew I did. He must have seen inside my head, just like everyone else's. The thought made me feel vulnerable in a way I'd not felt before.

"You tell me," I challenged.

He finally took his eyes from the fire and cast them my way, eliciting a shiver down my spine.

"You are wearing a white dress in a big building with strange edifices. Weird creatures made out of stone. Everyone is looking at you and smiling. Except you.

You are crying. Flowers begin to fall around you."

Oh shit. Shitty shit, fuck shit. He's talking about my wedding. The one I never had. I knew exactly what he was talking about because I'd had this dream over and over again since David left. The building was the Fairmont in downtown Vancouver, and the stone creatures were the gargoyles that decorated the upper parts of the outside. In my dreams, I'd been so happy until I realized I was standing there all alone. David wasn't with me. He'd stood me up, and yet no one else in my dream had noticed. They were throwing petals at me and taking photos, full of joy as my heart tore in two.

"Bastard!" I said, standing up and turning away from him so he wouldn't see the tears in my eyes. I stomped away from him though I had nowhere to go. If he'd seen that dream, he'd seen what came next. To my utter shame, the wedding dream always changed after that point. Another woman came out of the building behind me. Sophie. She stood hand in hand with David, both of them perfect and smiling as the crowd of people carried on throwing petals. And I, to my utter horror, had walked over and slammed Sophie's head against the ground until there was nothing but blood and brain matter and petals and smiles.

Bile rose in my throat at the thought of the dream that had possessed me for the past three months. Even before I knew what Sophie looked like, I'd had the same dream, and every morning I'd woken up feeling ill at what my inner psyche really thought. Yeah, I was angry. I hated Sophie, and I hated David for what they had done to me. A less benevolent me might even have given her a good slap for what she'd put me through, but not once in any waking thought I'd ever had, had I thought about murdering her in such a vile way, nor in any way. In all the waking thoughts I'd had about revenge, most were petty and downright pathetic, like sending them a glitter bomb or keying her car. Not once had I thought about hurting her physically. Not to the point of blood anyway. And yet, the deepest darkest part of my mind was obviously a nightmare of horror. Sick and twisted and vile. I choked a little, unsure of what to do, now that I'd been uncovered as the disgusting creature I was.

"You aren't the only one."

"What do you mean?" I asked, turning around and trying to keep my face impassive. He'd seen my biggest weakness already. I wasn't about to allow him to see that it bothered me so much. He stood up and bridged the distance between us. I was so close to him that looking into his eyes was like looking into eternity.

"Death, destruction, pain. I see it all the time. I see people who enjoy it. I don't think you do." He held out his hand to me and swiped a stray lock of hair from my face. My breath caught in my throat at the gesture. It was too intimate. Too nice. Not the kind of gesture a man who wanted to kill a person might make. Confusion abounded in my mind. There was literally no reason for him to suddenly be nice to me, and yet he was being. At least he wasn't trying to hurt me or murder me. I wasn't sure I liked this new side of him. The filthy hot murdering psycho I hated, but I understood it. This scared me even more, if possible, because when he was being nice to me, I might just fall for what was obviously a trick.

"You don't know me at all," I whispered, swallowing back the lump in my throat. "Maybe I do enjoy it. Maybe that's what keeps me going."

I took a deep breath and stared at him, challenging him. He leaned forward, and for a scarily thrilling second, I thought he was going to kiss me, but he didn't. His breath caught on my neck as he whispered into my ear. "I know you better than you think I do. I don't think you would hurt her. Your thoughts and your actions do not always equate. I find you an enigma."

God, I hated him. I hated how he had the upper hand in all things. I couldn't even be on my own in my own mind.

My lips curled downward as I contemplated spitting in his overbearing face just to prove he was wrong. The bastard had my mother and hundreds of thousands of others like her locked in sleep. Where did he get off telling me I didn't enjoy hurting others? I was going to prove the bastard wrong. Even if it took me a month to figure out how, I was going to get that knife of his and slit his motherfucking throat.

CHAPTER THIRTEEN

I dozed fitfully, occasionally waking to the sound of the fire crackling and my body once again tied to the tree. Dream had gone back to work, flitting in and out of the doors along with his raven. It turned out the fire burned just as well without him paying close attention to it, and it was a welcome addition to the bleak nights I'd spent alone since coming here. Not because of the warmth. The forest was always temperate, but because of the color and life it brought to the otherwise lifeless forest. I could almost believe there were other people with me with the dancing shadows, and I wasn't completely alone with a psycho.

Any hopes that Aethelu would come back for me evaporated pretty quickly. I closed my eyes again, trying to find a comfortable position against my restraints. My arms hurt like hell, bound as they were to the tree. If I'd thought Dream was going to show me more mercy after our little chat last night, I was sorely mistaken. Sorely being the operative word, because every part of my body hurt like a bitch. I stretched my legs out and tried to get some blood pumping in them. At the rate I was going, I was going to end up with bedsores from staying in one position for too long.

It didn't need much thinking to know I was in a worse position than I had been the day before. At least then, I'd had a plan. A stupid, reckless one, but a plan nonetheless. Then I had the chance to get home. To go through the red door and leave all this behind. And I'd made the decision to stay, or at least, my indecision had made my decision. My head felt groggy with the lack of good sleep and the pain rearing its ugly head throughout my body. Ten feet away from me, Dream left one door, and the whole lot moved before he went through another. The sound of the doors moving—a quiet whoosh sound had become so familiar that I barely noticed it anymore. I only noticed when the quiet rhythm stopped. Not that it ever did for very long. I concentrated on the sound, whoosh, quiet, more quiet, whoosh, quiet...

"Get up!"

I woke up to find Dream pulling me to my feet, urgency in his voice and panic in his eyes. I'd never seen him panic about anything before, so to see it brought a shiver down my spine.

"What is it? "I asked, trying to get to my feet. The now-familiar tingles of the blood rushing to my extremities after being tied up began. Pain echoed through my body, stabbing me with thousands of pins and needles. My legs gave way beneath me.

"Come on. We don't have time for questions." Frustration over my frail human weakness had always been apparent with him, but never more so than it was now as he tried to keep me upright.

"I can't. The blood has been restricted from my arms and legs because of your magical ropes. It take a while for it to come back enough for me to walk." I rubbed my legs, willing the pain away. "And it fucking hurts, thanks for asking."

"I didn't ask," he responded, lifting me clear of the ground and hoisting me over his shoulder.

"What the fuck! Put me down."

Without giving me an answer, surprise surprise, he took off through the trees, with me on his shoulder. My indignance was soon replaced with terror as the reason behind his actions became apparent. The forest was no longer silent. Something was chasing us, something that growled and screamed. More than one something. Lifting my head up, I peered into the darkness behind me. Trees flew past at a breakneck speed as the pair of us careened through the woods. Not that I could see where I was going. I only hoped Dream could. I still couldn't see whatever it was that was making the bloodcurdling noises as everything was swallowed up in the darkness almost as soon as we'd passed it. Above and behind me, Raven cawed, splitting the night in two and still, the terrifying sound followed us.

Part of me, the more insane part, obviously wanted to see what it was that was making Dream run so fast, but the more rational part of my mind wanted whatever it was to stop and go away.

"What are they?" I mustered. "Wolves?"

"Not wolves," Dream huffed back. We'd been running, or at least, he'd been running for ages now. He must have been feeling it in his muscles, and yet his pace never slowed. "Beasts like wolves. You don't get them in your human realm. There is nothing I can compare them to that you would understand."

"Try me?" I spat back. If I was going to get eaten or mauled by some scary night creatures, I at least wanted to know what they were and what they were capable of.

"Nightwalkers."

"Nightwalkers?" Images of zombies filled my mind. Mindless humans out for brains. Except in no TV show or zombie movie I'd ever watched, did zombies sound the way these things did. "What the fuck is a Nightwalker?"

And then I didn't need him to tell me. Two giant reptilian, horned wolves leapt out of the darkness, their teeth bared, drool dripping from their jowls. They were like nothing I'd ever seen before and nothing I ever wanted to see again. Two pairs of yellow eyes fixated on me as they inched ever closer.

"Faster!" I yelled pointlessly. We were already zooming through the forest at an incredible pace. A pace that no human would be able to manage. And yet, it wasn't fast enough. On their four legs, both were faster than Dream, and neither had the added burden of carrying a human on their back.

Seconds raced by, and with each step they made, the gap closed further still.

"Can't you use your magic?" I screamed out as the pair got dangerously close. Their heavy breathing, almost snorting, filled the night air, echoing through the trees.

I had no idea what magic Dream had beyond the conjuring of fire and ropes from thin air, but either would be useful in this situation. It seemed that running from them wasn't working, and it was inevitable that we were going to end up as breakfast, lunch, dinner, and a midnight snack for these two.

Raven cawed in warning as the first one struck. It leapt, its two giant paws leaving the ground, its ferocious teeth bared and ready for action.

Dream turned on the spot. Momentum and the change in his direction sent me flying through the air backwards, over his head, as he was hit with the full weight of the vicious creature on top of him. I fell with a bump to the ground, the dead leaves cushioning my fall. Dream was completely under the giant beast, easily the size of a small horse. There was nothing I could do for him. I had no weapon or anything to fight it off. The first beast wasn't my major problem. Now it had gotten a snack, the second was eager to have one too, and its beady eyes, the color of saffron fixed on me. Unlike the first that had lunged at Dream, this one had come to a stop just feet away from me. It looked like he liked to play with his food before devouring it whole without so much as a drink of water to wash it down.

Raven cawed again. I cast my glance upwards, taking my eyes from the beast for a second. The same second it decided that maybe it didn't want to play with me after all, just eat me. But Raven wasn't cawing in distress or warning. He was giving me a way out of this.

Just above my head was a sturdy branch from one of the nearby trees. I leapt up and swung my body up onto it, using muscles I hadn't used since fifth-grade gymnastics class. The strain on my muscles hurt like hell, but it was nothing to the pain that having my body torn limb from limb would be The nightwalker pounced upward, dragging its claws down my legs, tattering my only pair of jeans and the skin beneath them. I stifled a yell and kicked out, landing my bare foot on its forehead.

"Fuck!" I yelled out as bone crunched on its reptilian-plated armor. There was no way I was going to win this fight. Blood dripped down my leg, adding insult to injury of the no doubt broken foot. The only way to survive was up. I hauled myself up to a higher branch, not putting any weight on my bad foot. From there, I could only watch as Dream was being mauled by the first Nightwalker. I could barely see him under the mass of the wolf-thing. He made no sound. No yelling or screaming, and I wondered if he was already dead. Raven settled on a branch next to me and cawed in my ear.

"What do you want me to do? Look at them. They'd eat me whole without chewing."

Raven cawed again, making me feel fucking awful. For all the bullshit I'd had to put up with from Dream, I didn't want to sit here and do nothing while he died an agonizing death just ten feet below me. I had to begrudgingly concede that the bastard had saved my life. He could have left me tied to the tree, but what was I supposed to do? Raven jumped up and down on its branch as if urging me to do something... anything.

"Ok." Fucker! Why did I let a bloody bird talk me into doing its bidding? It wasn't the first time. The only thing at my disposal were trees and leaves. Maybe if I'd done survival training or watched Hunger Games all the way through, I'd have known how to fashion a weapon from a nearby broken branch. As it was, David had started feeling me up in the back row of the movie theater before Jennifer Lawrence had volunteered to be a tribute, and I'd missed the rest of the movie. I knew I should have read the books. Grabbing the broken branch, I pulled at it, twisting the wood until it creaked and snapped with my weight pulling at it. The branch wasn't that thick, and because of damage it had already sustained, broke off quite easily.

Now what? From where I was, ten feet up in the tree, the leafy end of the branch could reach the Nightwalkers, but I wasn't strong enough to deliver a blow to either of them. The best I would manage if I tried was to tickle them with the leaves at the end.

"I don't know what to do!" I screamed at Raven, who was frantically jumping up and down on my shoulder, willing me to do something. I could have done with that polyglot thing Aethelu had talked about, and maybe I'd understand a bloody word Raven said. As it was, All I heard was his cawing, though I understood very well the urgency in it.

"Fuck this!" I shouted, hurling the thicker end of the branch downward with all my might. It fell, landing directly on beast number's two's head. The sound it made echoed through the forest. A clang-like wood on bone, which is essentially what it was. The strange horned exoskeleton of the creature protected it from too much damage, even from a huge branch dropping on its head. It had startled it, though, and that was my chance. My one chance to do something. Something ridiculously stupid. Something that, if I'd put any thought into it, I would most surely have not done. But I didn't have time for thought, only action. I launched myself from the safety of my branch and landed squarely on the back of the monster with a thump. The wind was knocked out of me by the force with which I fell and the hardness of the beast's body. It was like falling on an armor-plated rhino or a tank. Except this tank had two soft spots. His eyes were the only place of vulnerableness on the whole thing, and this was where I aimed. A thumb in each eye, pushing until I used enough force, for each one to pop with a splatter in my hand. Bile filled my throat as the beast yelled a blood-curdling yelp and tried to buck me off. It was now blind and in pain, which meant, for a change, I held the advantage. The branch I'd thrown earlier had come to a standstill propped against the nearby tree trunk. While the beast was roaring, with one hand, I snapped one of the smaller end branches from it. It was thin, reedy almost, and inflexible, but when I shoved it as hard as I could, broken end first into the eye socket, I'd already burst; it did what I meant it to do. The creature howled as I jammed the stick, this time with both hands, as far as I could into its brain. The roaring became silent, and the creature fell to the ground with a boom, taking me with it. I yelled an agonized scream as the full weight of it landed on my already, torn to shreds leg, trapping it beneath him. I pushed against its lifeless body, trying to get it away from me so I could once again jump up to the safety of the tree. Too late, though, as the first nightwalker had momentarily forgotten the prey it was playing with after the loud boom and turned its sights on me.

My breath quickened as terror filled my lungs, leaving me unable to do anything but stare at its angry face. I was in no position to kill this one as I had its brother. I was pinned to the ground, a sitting duck. All I could see of Dream was the bottom of one leg sticking out from under the monster. He wasn't moving, and there was no way to see if there was any blood. Adrenaline completely took over, corrupting my mind to think I was capable of more than I was. I was going to die one way or another, so I might as well go down in a blaze of glory, inflicting as much damage as I could rather than lie back and take it. Fear vanished, leaving me in the moment. Just me and the beast that was three times bigger and infinitely stronger. Staring into death didn't bother me as much as I'd ever thought it would. There were no flashbacks to happier times, no swift memories of things I'd done, or regret for things I hadn't yet accomplished. It was just me and the creature, its jagged teeth bared and ready to rip my body in two. In a swift movement, I leaned over and pulled Dream's boot off. The knife he used to whittle fell to the ground. I snatched it as the beast lunged. With as much strength as I could muster, I rammed the blade deep into the soft flesh at the front of its neck. Its eyes went wide as I twisted the blade for maximum damage into the only part of it I could see with no boned armor. This one fell soundlessly without a screech like its brother had. As it fell onto me, the blade was pushed further into its neck, ensuring its swift death. The forest was once again silent save for Raven cawing somewhere above me and the heaviness of my breathing. The heavy weight of my actions was only outweighed by the weight of one nightwalker crushing my leg and the head of the other pinning me to the ground. Its blood was surprisingly cold as it gathered on my belly, pooling on my shirt, and then when it was saturated, dripping down my sides to the forest floor beneath me

The last thing I saw before I passed out was Raven flying down from his branch and settling by the side of my head.

CHAPTER FOURTEEN

Pain ripped through my body as the tightness of darkness lost its grip on me. I was alive. The agony sweeping through my body was enough to tell me that. I groaned with the effort of just thinking, which lead me to another realization. A noise I'd not heard before in the forest—the lapping of waves. For one brief delirious second, I imagined I was on a beach in the Bahamas somewhere, and this had all been some kind of horrible dream.

Dream! I sat up, sending another jolt of pain screaming through my body. The world was dark, just as it always had been, but movement caught my attention—waves. Small ones, but definitely waves of inky violet lapped a shore of black sand. I was completely alone, but someone had brought me here. I'd passed out in the middle of the forest. The forest, I could still see about twenty feet behind me. In front of me, a lake stretched out into the distance ending at the base of a majestic mountain range covered at the peaks with snow. For the first time, I saw the source of the soft blue light here, shielded as it usually was by a canopy of trees. The moon, or at least what I took to be a moon, shone brightly, glinting off the small cresting waves like diamonds. The wide-open space filled me with awe and reminded me of all the open spaces near Vancouver. The mountain trails and parks with views that stretched on for miles. A pang of homesickness hit me as I took in the sight and the millions of stars in the sky. A quick look around told me that wherever my savior was, he or she had left me. They had left me naked, or at least half-naked. My blood-soaked bra was still in place, but my shirt had been taken off to use as a bandage for my leg. It was difficult to tell if the blood on it belonged to me or to the nightwalkers that I'd killed. Probably a little bit from column A and a little bit from column B. I let out a soft moan as I touched it lightly. The blood was dry, at least, which meant I was no longer bleeding so profusely. It hurt to fuckery, though, with the slightest pressure. I gritted my teeth and jammed my lips together, letting my breath out through my nose as I eased myself into a sitting position. My jeans had been taken off too, but they were nowhere to be seen. The last I'd seen of them was when they were torn to shreds by the claws of the nightwalker.

There was no way to tell how long I'd been out. In the real world, I'd have been able to check the position of the stars or the sun. But as there was no sun, the moon was nothing like any moon I knew, and none of the constellations were ones I recognized. Knowing the time of day was impossible. It felt like an eternity, but with the weird, dreamless sleep I seemed to have here, counting the hours was virtually impossible. If only I wore a watch, but I hadn't worn a watch since the day I got my first smartphone and no longer needed one to tell the time.

The knowledge I was completely alone, injured, unknowing of where I was or if I was in danger from more nightwalkers or other such creatures sat like a weight in my stomach. It had never occurred to me that there were worse things than Dream to be scared of in this world. He was monstrous enough without adding mental stress to that particular thought. Dream. A wave of sorrow hit me unexpectedly, though I didn't know why. He was a vile piece of shit. Worse even than the nightwalkers. At least their intentions had been clear. They only wanted what any other bloodthirsty monster wanted. To stave off their hunger. Dream had never once let slip what his intentions were with me. I wasn't even sure if he knew himself what he kept me for. Not for his own monstrous pleasure, that was for sure. In the short time I'd known him, I'd caused him nothing but annoyance and strife. And yet, he'd done everything he could to save me. He could have left me tied to that tree. An easy snack for the two nightwalkers, but he hadn't. He'd run with me for hours through that forest to keep me alive. At any point, he could have, quite literally, thrown me to the wolves, but he hadn't. He'd shouldered the burden of carrying me, eventually paying for it with his life.

A whistling sound caught me off guard. It was

the whistle of a merry tune coming closer from the edge of the forest. I narrowed my eyes, peering into the darkness between the trees, waiting to see who it was that had saved my life. Another person to thank in this weird world. My first thought ran to Aethelu because she was the only person I'd met in this place apart from Dream. But if there was one person, it stood to reason that there would be more. Maybe not human, but human-like and not intent on killing me like every other thing in this shithole.

I don't know who was the most surprised when Dream walked out of the forest.

"You are supposed to be resting with your leg elevated," he said, dropping the cheerful tune and reverting back to his miserable, bastard self.

"And you are supposed to be dead," I countered, shooting him an annoyed glance, ignoring the warmth spreading through me at the sight of him. He had saved my life, after all, and I should be grateful, though I wasn't going to give him the satisfaction of gratitude. He'd also stripped me down to my underwear. That thought was something I was going to have to unpick later.

"Someone saved my life," he said, taking a seat next to me on the sand. "I think it was you."

"Fighting off murderous bastards has become a theme in this place," I replied airily as he untied my shirt from my leg. "Oh, motherfucking fucker!" I yelled out as air hit the skin, sending searing pains up my leg.

"Why do you feel the need to use that word quite so often?" he chastised as he prodded the skin around the tears.

"Fuck?" I questioned, hissing as more pain shot through me. "It's my favorite word. I use it all the time when someone thinks it's alright to prod my obviously ripped to shreds leg. Don't you have any painkillers here?"

He shook his head, giving me a wry look. "No pharmacists, no, but you have me. I'm not prodding; I'm checking to see if it's infected. I don't think so yet, but it's a long way from healing. I'll need to keep an eye on it."

"Great," I huffed, sarcasm dripping almost as heavily as the blood that poured onto the grey-black sand below, making it even darker than it already was.

"I'll need to re-tie this shirt to stem the bleeding. It's not ideal, but it's all I have."

I extended my hand to gesture that he should go ahead. Maybe I'd die here on this beach from some disgusting infection. I lay back and watched the stars as he ministered to my leg.

"What exactly does it mean?"

"Hmm?" I took a deep breath to stave off the dizziness that was threatening to engulf me.

"Fuck? I thought it was a word used to describe intercourse, but you use it in strange ways."

A giggle erupted from my mouth at the absurdity of it all. "Fuck is a wonderfully versatile word," I mused aloud. "You can use it in pretty much any sentence in any way without messing up the sentence."

"How so?" He tightened the shirt roughly, causing another hiss to escape my lips.

I propped myself up on my elbows. "Say something. Anything. Just say a sentence."

He narrowed his brows. "How are you doing today, Ana?"

"How the fuck are you fucking doing today, Ana? That's

the first fucking time you've fucking used my fucking name too."

He cocked his head to one side as though thinking the sentence through.

"It means the same thing, though. Using Fuck, doesn't change the literal meaning of the sentence at all."

"Doesn't need to." I shrugged. "Just makes it more beautiful."

He didn't appear convinced

"You can fucking put fucking 'fuck' pretty fucking much fucking anywhere in a fucking sentence and fucking still fucking be grammatically fucking correct."

"I don't see the point."

"You wouldn't," I said, turning onto my side to get more comfortable. The sand beneath me was like a balm to my soul.

He stood and walked to the lake edge only ten feet or so from where I lay. Cupping his hands, he dipped them in the water and brought them over to me. I drank the strange violet-black liquid greedily right from his hands, only just then realizing how dry and scratchy my throat was. It tasted exactly like normal water, despite its dark glittery appearance.

"More!" I croaked, enjoying the coolness and freshness of it. Like drinking a pool of heaven itself.

He made four trips before my thirst was sated, and yet, I let him go back for more. I hated to admit how much I was enjoying the feel of his fingers against my lips. It had been a long time since I'd enjoyed human contact, and though he wasn't exactly human, the touch of his skin against mine brought back feelings I'd forgotten existed.

He was tender with me in a way David never had been. Not that I'd ever had to kill horned psycho wolf creatures for David, but I had cooked for him, cleaned up after him, And washed his goddamned underwear. Killing murderous beasts suddenly felt more important in comparison, even if it was to stop the killing of the psycho who had held me captive for weeks.

Fuck. What was I thinking? He'd shown me nothing but pain and disdain, and after one moment of tenderness, I was getting all soft and sentimental. He'd saved my life, but I'd saved his too.

We were even, the way I saw it.

"This going to kill me?" I asked as he lay in the sand next to me.

He raked his hand through the sand, then shook his head. "This water here is safe. It will help you heal."

I raised my eyebrows. Not that it should have shocked me. Why wouldn't glittery black magic water help me heal?

These questions whizzed through my mind, but none took precedence over the most important one.

"Are there any more of those things in the forest? The Nightwalkers?"

He shuffled onto his side, resting his head on his hand. His long hair dipped into the sand. In better lighting and on a normal beach, I might have mistaken him for an underwear model on a photoshoot. If it wasn't for the crown that permanently sat atop his head. Not even an attack by a mauling machine was enough to knock it off.

"Nightwalker is an umbrella term for all the creatures that inhabit the forest that come from... another place. Those particular ones were wolveries, and there might be more of them. They aren't the worst things that could have come for us, not by a long shot. They shouldn't be here in my forest, but obviously, they've wandered away from their homeland."

I turned this new snippet of information over in my mind. I knew nothing about this place. Dream was hardly forthcoming in the sharing info department. When I'd first got here, it had felt like a small world of just forest and darkness, but I was starting to learn it was more than that. It was a whole world, and I'd only seen a small part of it. It had creatures I knew nothing about and races of people I'd never heard of.

I shifted my weight, trying to lessen the pain in my leg, and mirrored his position, my elbow in the sand, my head on my hand. "What made them come this time?" I had an inkling I knew the answer already, but I needed to hear him say it.

"Fresh meat."

"Me, you mean?" I asked, seriously affronted by his assessment of me.

He nodded. "I think you had something to do with it. Not that the woveries coming to attack worries me too much. It's what their sudden appearance means that concerns me."

I eyed him warily. The way he spoke of our mutual near-death experience was what concerned me most. How could anyone not be worried by the sudden appearance of supernatural killing machines? And what the fuck was so bad that made the wolveries something not to worry about? One of the bastard things dam near ripped my leg off and the other. The other had been completely on top of Dream. I still hadn't figured out how he'd managed to get out of that one unscathed.

Because he was unscathed. At least the parts of him I could see, which was pretty much everything from the waist up and the ankles down. I remembered then that I'd pulled one of his boots off in the fight. Maybe he'd taken the other off and left it in the woods as it was nowhere in sight. I

raked my gaze up and down his chest, looking for any blemish in his skin whatsoever. He was perfect, annoyingly so. How was it my body had practically been savaged to pieces, and he'd come out of it looking even more perfect than he'd gone into it? Life sure as shit wasn't fair.

"The wolveries are not from my court and are not under my influence."

"Under your influence. They looked like wild creatures out for blood to me."

He gazed at me, but his attention was elsewhere as though he was looking through me.

"This is the Dream Court. Something is happening that I do not like. I suspect you are part of it, though I cannot be sure. I will endeavor to find out."

CHAPTER FIFTEEN

A steady silence descended between us, leaving me unsure of what to do or say next.

My body hurt in places I didn't even know I had body parts, but my leg that had been mauled by the wolveries was what pained me the most. Every movement I made, even small ones, sent shooting pains up from my calf, through my thigh, and then radiated out everywhere.

I shifted again on the sand and tried to make eye contact with Dream. He was whittling something with his knife. The knife I'd used to kill those creatures.

"So you are a king?" I said, finally growing bored of the silence. I needed something to take my mind off my own body that was threatening to consume me with pain.

He reached up and touched his crown in answer, then went back to whittling.

"Who are your subjects if the wolveries aren't?"

"Why must you continue to make conversation? It is like you are incapable of keeping that mouth of yours shut for a second."

I shot him a stare and huffed.

"Maybe if everything didn't hurt so much, I wouldn't have to make conversation. Maybe if you would tell me anything about what is going on, I wouldn't have to ask so many questions."

He placed the figure he was carving down next to him, and I saw for the first time it was Raven. He was doing a good job with it. I noticed that the real Raven was sitting in the tree above him.

"Having answers will not keep you safe; therefore, you don't need them."

Right. "So what will keep me safe then?"

He held his hands out as though it was obvious. "Are you not still alive?"

God, he was so infuriating and completely up himself.

"Let me get one thing straight. I'm alive because I killed two monsters. Not you. You are also alive for the same reason, so you don't get to tell me that I'm here and safe because of you. If it wasn't for you, I'd be home watching TV, not bleeding half to death on a black sand beach with you and your bird."

"The wolveries would not have killed me. You saved yourself."

I snorted. "Right, because it didn't look like that when one of them was sitting right on top of you trying to eat you."

He shook his head as though I was talking garbage. Then he ran the knife down the flesh on his forearm.

My mouth fell open as blood began to pour from the wound, dripping onto the sand just as mine had earlier.

Unlike mine, it soon stopped. The line of flesh knitted back together until all that was left was a smear of blood that was already beginning to dry.

"Satisfied now?"

"No," I grumbled. "Not in the slightest. So you have healing magic. Bully for you. It only makes what I did all the more amazing because I jumped onto that wolvery's back, knowing full well I might die. I'd say that my bravery far outshined yours!"

He licked his lips slightly. "I didn't believe this was a talk about bravery. I never said that you weren't brave. Indeed, what you did impressed me immensely. I thought we were talking about you still being alive and breathing. You are; therefore, you need not ask any more questions."

I scrunched my fist. "Your logic is bullshit. I'm tired, I'm hungry, I stink, and my leg feels like it has been ripped from my body, which it practically has. If you don't want to tell me about your petty little secrets, then don't, but don't give me any more bullcrap about me not needing to know. This isn't about me. It's you and your pathetic attempt to come across as all mysterious, when in fact, you are just a loner. The crown is probably made of plastic."

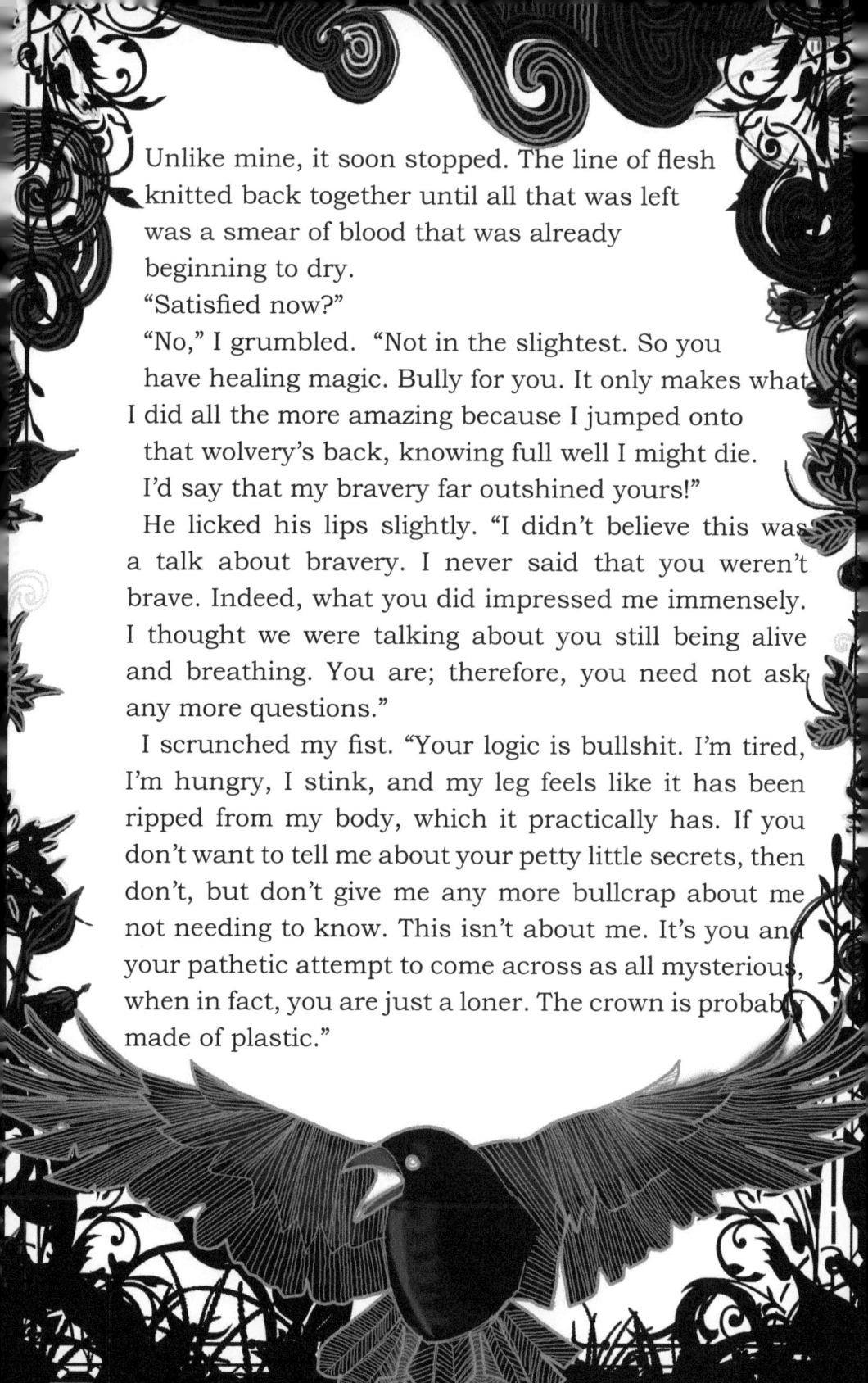

It wasn't. I could see it was gold, but I was pissed off and not going to give him the satisfaction of admitting it. Anger tugged at his lips. He threw the knife down where it landed blade down in the sand, then stood up and crossed the short distance between us. His face was dark as thunder. As he bent down to pick me up, I thought that I'd finally pushed him too far, and he was going to end the job the wolveries started.

He grabbed at my bra and tore it off. Literally ripped it from my body. Cheap, shitty material. Next came my knickers, gone, just like the bra, until I was completely naked save for my shirt tied around my leg.

"Oh, no, you don't, you fucker!" I screamed as he picked me up and hauled me over his shoulder. This time, there were no wolveries chasing us. It was just the two of us on the beach save for Raven.

I rained blows down on his back, punching him as hard as I could. I'd have kicked him if my leg didn't hurt too much to bend. The pain shooting through me was unbearable, and yet, it was better than what this monster had in store for me. It was keeping me alive, awake. And if he laid one hand on me, I was going to fight him so hard that he'd wish death would come to him when he got injuries.

I didn't see which direction he was taking me until I felt the cool chill of water on my toes. He splashed into the water until he was up to his waist, then he gently pulled me from his shoulder and lowered me down, tearing the threats right from my throat.

The water was unlike anything I'd ever felt before. An inch below the surface, I couldn't see my own body, only the glittering water around it that moved with my movements. But the feel of it soothed me in a way that normal water would never be able to do.

Now that I'd stopped thrashing, I let him lower me in until I was up to my neck, floating just below the surface. He was still standing on the sandy lake floor, so I could only see above his waist.

I closed my eyes and laid back, letting myself float on the surface. If heaven were a thing, this would be close. The pain, though still there, was almost sucked out of my body so that it was barely an ache. The parts of me that hadn't hurt before, now tingled pleasantly.

"You were right." Dream grumbled, breaking me from my moment of pure heaven as he carefully undid the blood-soaked shirt from my leg. "You did stink. Plus, you were probably going to get an infection in that leg. The water will help you keep infection at bay."

I splashed around a little while I decided what to say next. Sorry seemed like the most opportune word, but it didn't seem enough. What I'd thought he was going to do to me was a far cry from the path he'd actually chosen. He was helping me. Ok, he was doing it for his own benefit. He was probably sick of sitting so close to someone who hadn't bathed in forever, and he was definitely sick of listening to me; he'd made that clear. But he hadn't been about to rape me nor injure me further, and those were the two things that had sprung to mind when he'd ripped my clothes off and carted me over his shoulder.

I peeked at him through my eyelashes. He stood in the water up to his waist, looking for all intents and purposes like a naked Greek god, but he wasn't enjoying it the same way I was. His eyes were narrowed, scanning the shoreline, the same expression of seriousness he always wore on his face.

"I'm sorry I hit you," I finally said, deciding to be the bigger person. "I thought..."

"I know what you thought. That's why I didn't throw you in here and drown you. It crossed my mind, believe me."

Lovely!

I'm so glad I decided to be the bigger person!

I turned on my stomach and started to swim. My leg still pained me as I took deep strokes through the water, but it was a hell of a lot better than it had been. A rush of excitement hit me as I cut through the water. Swimming in the ocean in the summer was one of my few joys. Partially because it was free and I couldn't afford to do much else, but partially because of the freedom it gave me. Even back in Vancouver, when I wasn't being held captive by some supernatural asshole, I still liked how free I felt when I swam through the water. As though I could keep swimming forever. I swam toward the center of the lake, away from the shore. Every so often, I checked over my shoulder to see if he was following me, but his gaze was turned from me toward the tree line. Maybe this was my chance. I was a strong swimmer. Sure the lake went on for miles, but there was every chance I could turn left or right and swim to another shore.

He'd never find me. But more wolveries might. Not to mention the other nightwalkers that were apparently worse than armored wolf killing machines.

Plus, there was the small matter of my nakedness. It didn't matter when I was in the water. The blackness of it swallowed me whole, but I'd have to get out sooner or later, whether I tried to escape or not.

Which meant that going back to him would mean he'd see me naked. Really see me. I didn't think he was paying much attention to me when he'd ripped my bra off, despite my first thoughts on it. He'd been too intent on getting me in the lake. I should probably be offended at that thought, now that I came to think about it.

I had no other clothes. I'd been wearing the same outfit for weeks, doing my best to wash it in the stream when I could. No wonder he threw me in the lake. If he hadn't done it, my clothes might have got up themselves and voluntarily thrown themselves in. Not that any of that helped me. My grotty bra was now in pieces, my knickers ripped in two, and goodness only knew what had happened to my pants. They'd disappeared at some point between the wolvery ripping them to shreds and me waking up on the beach.

I swam in a small circle, debating which would be the worst death. Eaten by a supernatural monster in the woods or the complete mortification of walking back to the doors completely naked with Dream by my side. It was a difficult decision. One only decided by the fact that if I did die in the woods, my mother would surely die too.

I turned back toward Dream with the intention of swimming back to him and hoping he was good at walking with his eyes closed when I saw that he was no longer there. Panic filled me as I traced my eyes along the coast. The magical fire was now gone, but the pile of my discarded clothes was still just about visible on the sand. Where was he?

I swam quickly, taking broad strokes back to where I'd last seen him. The water was smooth, as was the sand below it. If he'd drowned, he'd have had to be extremely unlucky or extremely stupid. The water wasn't even up to my breasts, and he was much taller than me. I stood in the spot, spinning in circles, feeling below the water line, frantically trying to feel for him. Now that I was closer to the shore, it was clear he wasn't there. I'd only taken my eyes off him for a minute, surely not enough time for him to wade back to the beach and run into the woods, even at his speed. And why would he? He wouldn't. No reason to bring me here to heal me, then leave me here. What was the point? If he wanted me dead, he could have left me with the bodies of the wolveries.

So the logical conclusion was that he was under the water somewhere, and if he was, unless he had some water magic or was half merman (because why the fuck would that not be a thing), he would be drowning. I took a deep breath and ducked under the water. In the pitch black of the water, I couldn't see anything, so I was swimming blind. I dove to the sandy bottom and then back up again in wider and wider circles, coming up occasionally to take another breath. With each dive, my pulse increased as the panic at not finding him amplified. A human couldn't stay underwater for more than a couple of minutes. Even a professional diver couldn't go more than five minutes or so. Dream had to have been under the water longer than that.

I hated that he had me so worried. Ten minutes ago, I'd been thinking of running—or swimming away from him, and now, here I was filled with anxiety about him dying. Could he survive? He survived the wolvery attack without a mark on him, but being underwater for so long was a different beast altogether. Why did I even care? He had made it abundantly obvious that he didn't care about me. I tried telling myself that it was because he was my ticket home. I didn't know my way back to the doors. And whatever I'd thought earlier, I was safer going through the forest with him by my side.

I thrashed about until my own oxygen ran out, at which point I ascended to the surface with the knowledge I'd not found him.

He stood watching me at the shoreline.

Not in the water at all. Not drowned. Not dead. I let out a long breath as relief flooded me, though, in my addled mind, I had no idea why.

"You complete and utter fucking asshole!" I croaked out as I took another shaky breath and started walking back to him.

"What?" he asked innocently.

"How long have you been standing there watching me thrashing around in the water? I thought you'd drowned!"

He cocked his head to one side. "Why would I have drowned? It was three feet of water at most."

I gritted my teeth. "Because you weren't there! What did you think I was doing swimming in circles?"

"How should I know why you do anything? All your human exploits have so far confounded me. Why should this be any different?"

I rolled my eyes and waded back to the shore, covering myself as best I could with my hands. The water was brilliant at hiding anything below the surface, but it dripped clear once I was out of it, not leaving any black residue at all. Not so great for covering oneself.

I was almost upon him when he handed me something.

"Where did you get a towel?" I asked suspiciously as I took the fabric from his hand and wrapped it around me.

I shouldn't look a gift horse in the mouth. A towel was excellent. I was in no mood for him to be ogling my lady goods, but it was hardly as though there was a towel and soft fabric store anywhere nearby.

"Does it matter?" he snapped. "I've gotten you some clothing too. It would be nice for you to thank me once in a while rather than question everything I do. It's becoming quite irksome."

I gritted my teeth again, swallowing a clap back. Why did he have to be so infuriating?

The pile of clothes sat neatly near to where we'd been sitting half an hour before. I plonked myself down next to them and began to towel myself dry.

Dream came close and began to pull the towel away from my legs. This time I didn't jump to any conclusions, just let him do what he was doing. He took my foot in his hand and turned my leg slightly.

"It's looking a lot better," he announced, running a finger down my leg near where the flesh was still sore.

My body shivered at his touch. He was so gentle with me in every way but in his words. I let him gently pat the bloody mess with the towel. The water had healed some of it, but it wasn't a miracle cure. I was still in pain. Still bleeding. He picked up something then began to unravel it. Gauze.

"This will help stem the bleeding," he said, carefully wrapping it around my calf. "The lake water should stave off any infection."

I nodded slowly as he missed my knee, allowing it to bend, then carried on wrapping up my thigh. Winding the gauze around. The pain was manageable now, but the way his fingers grazed over my thigh with every wind had me holding my breath. The towel was parted almost right up to the top of my thigh. If he went any further, everything would be on show. My body reacted to his touch in the most embarrassing way. I was turned on. It had been a long time since anyone had touched me between my thighs and certainly not in such a way. I let out a breath when he stopped and tied the gauze off.

"You should get dressed," he said, pointing to the pile of clothes.

Disappointment flooded me when he turned around and picked up the wooden raven he'd been whittling half an hour ago.

I'd felt something when he'd touched me. He obviously hadn't. I was such an idiot. The guy hated me. I hated him. Why did my body not know that? I'd have to keep myself in check from now on. I turned and picked up the clothes. They were like nothing I'd ever worn before. For a start, there was no bra. Just a long dress similar to the one I'd seen Aethelu in, only much less pretty, and a pair of long underwear I could only describe as bloomers. I'd be winning no fashion awards, that was for sure.

The dress was a dull beige color, but it fit perfectly, and at least it covered me. Not once did Dream look my way as I put it all on.

"What now?" I finally asked once I was dressed. I was fed up and grumpy. "We go back to the doors?" I didn't want to. The doors were in the forest, which was in perpetual darkness. This place was dark too, but at least here, I could see the stars, the glittering lake, the white snow on the distant mountains.

He mused on it for a couple of seconds. "I don't think your leg is up to it yet, and I don't want to carry you. We'll spend the night here and see how you are feeling tomorrow."

I was surprised. In all the time I'd known him, he'd barely left those doors. He worked all the time, barely stopping to rest. He had no meal breaks, no pee breaks. He worked tirelessly, and here he was announcing that we could stay away another day.

"Are people able to dream without you?" I asked. "I mean, doesn't the whole world collapse if you don't go through the doors?"

"I will go back to the doors while you sleep."

"What?" I sat up in a panic. "What if the nightwalkers come back?"

He glanced up to the tree above my head. I followed his gaze.

"Raven? You expect Raven to save me if they come back?"

He shrugged his shoulders as though my fear wasn't his problem. "You pointed out earlier that it was you that killed the last two. I have every faith that you can do it again if need be."

I gritted my teeth. "Are you fucking serious?"

"You don't need to worry. There won't be more wolveries tonight. Are you hungry?" he asked, changing the subject.

I wanted to ask him how he knew that the wolveries wouldn't be back, but what was the point? I wouldn't get a straight answer. I was hungry, though. I really was. I couldn't remember the last time I'd eaten. Easily twenty-four hours ago. In all the pain with the leg and the stress of the wolveries, I'd not thought about food until he'd brought it up.

"I'm starving," I admitted.

He nodded and got to his feet. "Do not move. I will be back shortly with dinner."

He took off in the woods, and once again, the darkness swallowed him whole. At least I had Raven for comfort.

"Is he always like this?" I asked. Raven hopped down from the trees and landed close to me on the beach. He didn't caw, but he let me stroke him for the first time. I took that to mean that yes, his boss or companion or whatever he was, was always an insufferable ass and also that he had forgiven me for throwing a stone at him. It felt like the two of us might become friends, after all.

I lay down on the sand, my bad leg out straight, and gazed up at the stars. Right above me, a shooting star flashed across the sky then puttered out.

I closed my eyes and made a wish. Superstition and wishes had never been my thing, not even when I was a kid. I was the only kid I knew not to make a wish when blowing out birthday candles or throwing money into a wishing well. I figured someone would be down there stealing all the money. I was a cynical little git as a child, a trait that had never quite left me. And yet, wishing on a star seemed more appropriate right here. I'd seen real magic, so why not wishes? I started small, wishing for a plate of chili cheese fries. You had to start somewhere, right? And fries covered in gravy and cheese curds was only about as insane as anything else in this place.

I laughed when he came back with a dead animal that looked like a cross between a squirrel and a monkey, with a long furry tail and big rounded ears.

Dream pulled his knife from his boot and began to skin the animal.

"What is so amusing?" he asked, catching my grin.

"I was expecting something a little different." I shrugged. "A four-course Sunday dinner, perhaps. A plate of cheese on toast. A can of cold spaghetti sauce. Some berries and leaves?"

"I can't get to the doors without walking a couple of hours; therefore, I can't bring you the food you expect. Human food. This will taste good enough." He fashioned a spit out of some branches and put the skinned animal on the fire.

The meal was meager but delicious. I groaned in pleasure as the warm fat dribbled down my chin. I mopped it up with the towel.

"You should sleep now," he insisted after we'd eaten. It was the first time I'd seen him eat anything at all. "Sleep is the best healer of all."

I hated to admit just how tired I was. The pain in my leg had dulled to a low ache, but it had taken it out of me, as had the swim and then the food. I closed my eyes and lay down on the soft sand before drifting off into a peaceful sleep.

Sometime later, a noise woke me. My heart began to hammer as the thought of wolveries or other nightstalkers filled my mind, but it wasn't a nightstalker at all. Dream was in the lake. The moon bounced off the glistening water, showing all the ripples of glitter where Dream swam. In a pile near me were his trousers and armor. On top of it all was his crown. It was the first time I'd ever seen him without it.

He was skinny dipping, just as I had earlier. Although his was voluntary, not forced upon him. Without moving, I watched him swim. How I could ever have thought he had drowned seemed silly now, as I watched how masterfully he cut through the water. He almost seemed to be enjoying himself. Another first. It occurred to me that I didn't know him at all. He kept so much of himself private, hidden, and yet he was someone who lived when the mood took him. I had a feeling that he'd have not been enjoying himself so much if he'd known I was watching. I kept my breathing quiet, not able to take my eyes off him. This wasn't the cold-hearted bastard I'd come to know and detest; this was a person who had to go through life alone. Whether it bothered him was a question I bet he'd never even asked himself. He just did his job because he had to. I wondered why that was.

My eyes never left him as he walked out of the water, and I couldn't help but suck in a breath as his whole body was revealed to me. I felt like a peeping tom, watching him, but he was so beautiful; it was hard to ignore the cut of his muscles, the way the moonlight bounced of the glittery water that clung to his body. And his cock. Oh my god!

I should have closed my eyes. I shouldn't be looking at him...no, perving at him, but I couldn't help it. I licked my lips before I realized what I was doing and brought my tongue back in my mouth where it should be. Sleeping girls don't lick their lips, and it would only take a brief glance my way for him to see he was being watched.

I pressed my lips together for fear I'd do something else involuntarily, like drool or wolf whistle. Ok, I wasn't going to do either of those things...probably, but just like before, my body was responding to the vision before me. My lips weren't the only things clamped together. I had my legs squashed together too. In fact, I didn't dare move a muscle. Any movement would give me away, and I wasn't ready to break this spell. He brought the towel I'd discarded earlier to his chest and began to towel himself down. I murmured quietly as he brushed it across his chest, then brought it lower.

Was it wrong to be jealous of a towel?

Bloody hell. I didn't even like the guy, so why was I watching him?

Because he has the body of a Greek god, the face of a sexy angel, and the cock of a horse. Cough

Fuck!

His eyes darted my way, and yet another part of me was then clamped together, This time my eyelids. I pulled in a breath then let it out slowly as though I was heavily asleep. All was quiet, and I wondered if he'd caught me watching him. I opened my eyes a sliver again to find him toweling off his feet with the bottom of the towel. His midriff, completely covered. There was a laviscious grin and a look of pure mischief on his face as he toweled between his toes. This time, I closed my eyes and really did try to get some sleep.

CHAPTER SIXTEEN

I awoke to the smell of cooking. Once again, it looked like weird monkey-rabbit was on the menu.

"How are you feeling?" Dream asked, slicing a sliver of meat from the bone and passing it to me.

I sat up and took the offering. "Better. My leg hurts less."

He nodded thoughtfully. "I'd like to check it before we set off. I think you should have a bit of a walk on the beach first to see how you cope before we start the walk through the woods."

"You care that I can walk?"

"Not particularly. I just don't want to have to carry you."

Great! I'd had a moment with him yesterday based on him grazing my leg and then me seeing him naked. I didn't know why I did this to myself. He might have been there when these moments were occurring, but he wasn't sharing them with me. He'd made it abundantly clear time and time again that I was merely a problem to him. Why was it that I continued to see affection that wasn't there? I guess it was a habit of a lifetime if David was anything to go by.

"I'll be fine!" I muttered, taking the rest of the animal and pulling the meat off it with my teeth.

We ate in stony silence, giving me time to reflect. I'd been in this crazy world for at least a month, and I'd yet to do anything, to see anything. And I was yet to find out what was happening to my mother.

Something told me that he wouldn't tell me if I asked. I was going to have to find out myself.

"I want to see what you see," I ventured, sucking the last of the meat from the bone.

He looked up, an eyebrow raised. "What do you mean?"

"The doors. I want to see what is beyond them." *And figure out what the freaking hell you are doing to people in there.*

"You know what lies beyond the doors. It is the dreams of your kind."

I nodded and threw the bone to the ground. "I get that, but knowing it's people's dreams and seeing it for myself are two different things. I want to know what you do."

He stood and crossed over to where I was sitting. Without asking, because when did he ever ask permission, he grabbed my arm and yanked me to my feet.

"Oy!" I yelled out, ripping my arm from his grip. "What are you doing?"

"I told you that we needed to test that leg of yours. I'm not starting the journey back to the doors if you can't walk. So come on..."

I stared at him, feeling the anger bubbling up again, but this time I was going to contain it. I didn't want to leave this beautiful place, but staying here wouldn't get me any closer to where I wanted to be. Just like Dream, I needed to get back to the doors too.

I took a hesitant step with my injured leg. Pain shot right up my thigh, but I kept my mouth shut. I needed him to think I was fine. I walked a small way, letting my muscles get some exercise. The pain abated slightly, the more I moved.

"Does it hurt?" Dream asked, standing next to me. He searched my face for the pain I felt, so I plastered on a smile.

"Nope. Not in the slightest. In fact, I'm ready to leave now if you are."

He pursed his lips, looking uncertain. It was like he could see through every lie I told him, and I hated him for it.

"Walk up and down the beach a few times."

Not a request. Another order, but I did as he said. He sat back down by the fire and watched me walk up and down past him. Feeling like a model on a runway, albeit a more self-conscious one, I kept my eyes forward and my legs moving. My muscles began to ease, and though they were still painful, walking was becoming easier. I even managed a twirl at the end before coming to a stop beside Dream.

"Ready to go?"

Without waiting for an answer, I stepped over his legs and headed into the forest.

Just being back in there reminded me of how spooky it really was. I'd been lulled into a false sense of security by the glittering beauty of the lake and mountains, but here where the moonlight barely reached, I was once again plunged into the strange blue darkness that reminded me of the wolveries and other strange

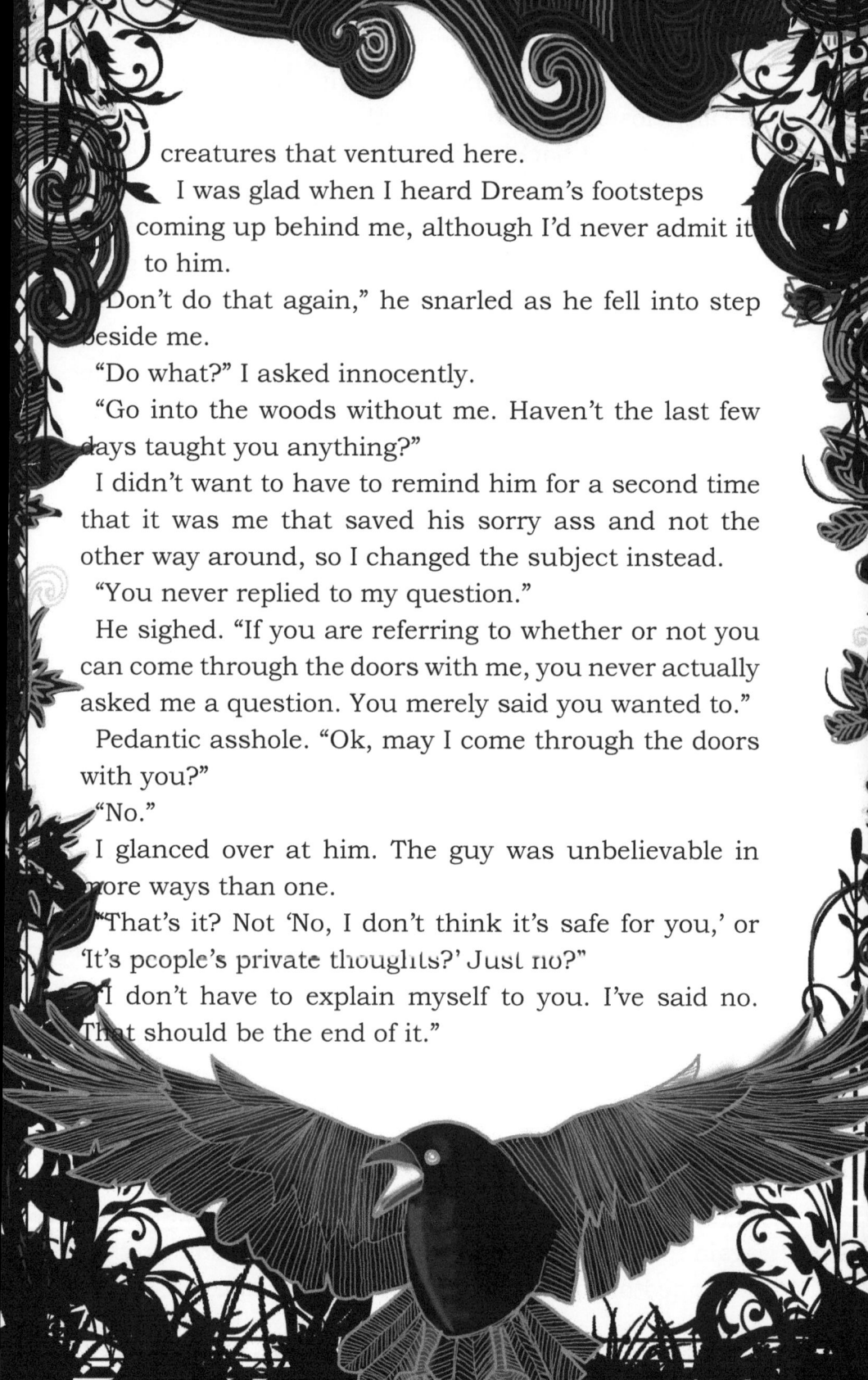

creatures that ventured here.

I was glad when I heard Dream's footsteps coming up behind me, although I'd never admit it to him.

"Don't do that again," he snarled as he fell into step beside me.

"Do what?" I asked innocently.

"Go into the woods without me. Haven't the last few days taught you anything?"

I didn't want to have to remind him for a second time that it was me that saved his sorry ass and not the other way around, so I changed the subject instead.

"You never replied to my question."

He sighed. "If you are referring to whether or not you can come through the doors with me, you never actually asked me a question. You merely said you wanted to."

Pedantic asshole. "Ok, may I come through the doors with you?"

"No."

I glanced over at him. The guy was unbelievable in more ways than one.

"That's it? Not 'No, I don't think it's safe for you,' or 'It's people's private thoughts?' Just no?"

"I don't have to explain myself to you. I've said no. That should be the end of it."

But it wasn't going to be the end of it. I hated being told no at the best of times, but to be told no without reason, even a bad reason, really irked me.

"Why not?"

He didn't answer. He'd reverted back into the silent brooding type again.

The journey back seemed to take forever, and though my muscles had eased up slightly on the beach, the initial relief hadn't lasted long.

Each step was torture, and I didn't even have anyone to talk to, to take my mind off it. Dream might as well not have been there with his lack of social intercourse, and Raven flew on ahead. Not that he could reply to anything I said to him anyway. I looked at Dream as we came to a standstill.

He looked around thoughtfully as though this was some mystical place, but to me, it looked like every other part of the forest. Dark.

"We camp here."

"Camp? I thought we were going back to the doors."

"And we are," he replied, sitting down and lighting one of his magic fires. "If you remember, we ran all the way to the beach. This time we are walking which takes a lot longer, and though you tell me you feel fine, the slight limp in your left leg tells me otherwise. You need to eat, and you need to sleep. Now sit down while I get you something."

We can't have been walking more than a couple of hours, but I had to admit, I needed the rest. My ankles had swollen up, and although no blood was seeping through the bandages, the cuts stung like a thousand bastard bees had held a party on my legs.

As Dream took off into the woods, I lay down on the crisp leaves that littered the forest floor. The same smell of flowers hit me. It was so strong I could almost close my eyes and imagine I was sitting in a beautiful meadow full of blooms instead of the dead wasteland of forest.

I wondered what time it was. Dream would know instinctively. My body clock was so messed up with the eternal darkness that it could have been midnight as easily as it could have been the middle of the day.

I heard, rather than saw, him sitting beside me. The rustle of the leaves beneath him, the crackle of the fire as he threw something on it. Something that didn't take long to smell delicious. I ignored him in much the same way he ignored me. I'd done my best to converse with him and given up with the constant stony silence he was so good at. If he wanted silence, he could have it. I'd eat whatever meat he'd found then sleep.

Then something caught me off balance. Like, seriously. If I'd been standing up, it would have knocked me to the ground. He was singing. It was a tune with words I didn't understand, but it was breathtaking. He not only had the body of an angel, he sang like one too. Was there no end to this man's talents?

How fucking irritating.

I didn't move as he filled the air with his lyrical voice, singing about goodness knew what. And then the song became more somber, and I imagined it to be a song about love and loss. It was like nothing I'd ever heard, but it spoke to my heart. I could almost feel the heartache of the person he was singing about.

When he went silent, I finally opened my eyes and pulled myself up into a sitting position. "That was beautiful," I conceded. "What was it?"

"It was a lullaby from when I was a child."

That wasn't what I expected. I couldn't imagine him ever being a young child.

"What was your childhood like?" I asked.

His face clouded over, and I waited for the inevitable silence, but he spoke. "I don't remember."

It was a lie. He could read me like a book. He'd had that uncanny and frankly annoying ability from the first day we met, but this time I'd read him. No one remembered a song like that and forgot the time it came from.

"Everyone remembers their childhood."

"Not me. You forget how old I am."

Actually," I reminded him. "You've never told me how old you are."

"I'm old."

And grumpy with it, I added silently. He said he was old, but he didn't look it. He was in the prime of his life. Maybe he was immortal. Nothing would surprise me when it came to him.

"You remembered that song. I can't imagine remembering a song and forgetting who sang it to me the first time."

He had a mother! The realization hit me that I'd previously thought of him as though he'd been born from nothing. But a mother would sing a song like that to a child.

"What about your childhood?" he asked, diverting attention from himself. Another tactic he liked to use.

I thought again about my own mother. How I'd wasted so much time away from her. How I'd not been there for her when she needed me the most.

"I was a crappy daughter." I started, picking at a leaf by my feet. Despite its deathly appearance, it was soft to the touch. This one had only just fallen from the tree.

above it. "I was born in Winnipeg... It's a city near..."

"I know where Winnipeg is. I have a vast knowledge of all your countries, cities, towns, and villages. I know the rivers and the mountains and the lakes."

Of course, he bloody did. Smartass.

"Well, anyway. I was born there. Just outside it, really, in a small rural town. I wanted to escape. My entire childhood, I wanted to escape.

"Your mother was bad to you?"

The way he looked at me told me he was actually interested in something I had to say. I wasn't sure if that was a good thing or a bad thing. I figured there was no point hiding anything. He'd seen all my sordid dreams. He probably knew my story better than I did.

"My mother was great. She was a perfect mother. She worked her ass off to bring my sister and me up. My sister is perfect too."

He cocked his head to the side. "So why did you want to escape such a perfect existence?"

"You know my dreams, don't you? You've seen everything I've dreamed since I was a baby. You remember it all?"

It was a sobering thought, but there was no denying it. I'd seen how his memory worked. Nine billion people on earth, and he knew each and every one of them intimately.

"I do."

"What do you make of my childhood?"

He shrugged. "It is not for me to say. Your dreams are private and yours only."

"A bit rich coming from someone who invades them every night."

"It doesn't make them mine. Nor does it give me the right to talk about them."

I mulled this over for precisely half a second.

"If I give you permission to talk about my dreams, then will you?"

He shrugged an acceptance or as close to an acceptance he was willing to give.

"So tell me, what did you think of my childhood?"

I don't even know why I was so bothered. His opinion of my early years hardly mattered, but I wanted to know.

"You had happy dreams. You dreamed of horses and puppies and rainbows on rainy days. You dreamed of laughter-filled snowball fights in the winter and swimming in the summer. Your mother featured heavily in them. Your sister too. All I ever saw were smiles."

It was like being punched in the gut. He was completely right. My childhood had been idyllic. Sure, we had barely two pennies to rub together, but we had each other. My mom, my older sister Arizona and me. And then I'd fucked it all up searching for something I'd never found. All I'd found was David and debt.

"It was never enough," I sighed. I had it all, and it wasn't enough.

"You had no father?" Dream asked, sticking the proverbial knife in further.

"I didn't need one. The lack of a father was never a problem. He left before I was even born. He was a total deadbeat by all accounts."

He mulled this over thoughtfully, his eyebrows knitting together. "You didn't know him? You've dreamed about him."

I shrugged my shoulders. "I met him a few times when I was about twelve. He didn't give a shit about me. Didn't want to know. I think he thought it would be better if my sister and I didn't exist. I told you he was a deadbeat, so no, I didn't know him."

Dream went quiet; his eyes drifted off into space until I waved my hands in front of them to bring him back. A muscle ticked in his cheek. His eyes slid into focus, though his expression remained stony. I'd thought I was breaking ground with him. Obviously not.

"So if it wasn't your father, or lack of one, what could you possibly have wanted that you didn't already have?"

Bile came into my throat. He was asking me questions that I'd spent years avoiding asking myself. And there was no answer. What I'd wanted at eighteen had been childish. I saw that now.

"I wanted more money. My mother practically lived in rags. My sister wore thrift store clothes, and I wore her hand-me-downs."

"I didn't see poverty in your childhood. If anything, I saw wealth. You had a house. You had a TV. You had a car."

Fuck! I stood up and folded my arms. "Alright! I had it all. I was hardly little orphan Annie. I guess you have seen poverty, real poverty. People in Africa or wherever that live on grains. I'm just a selfish bitch, alright. Yes, there was always food on the table, and yes, we lived in a nice house. It just wasn't nice enough. It wasn't big enough. Posh enough. My clothes never had the right labels. Our car was never flashy enough. It's pathetic, I know. And you know what. I left home to find fame and fortune and what I found was worse. I really did have to skip meals to survive. Sometimes in Vancouver, after David left, I could barely afford to think about food, let alone actually eat the stuff. But even before that, we were hardly rich. We lived in the shitty apartment you saw, and my car is held together with rust and wishes."

"So why didn't you go home?"

Anger flared in me. Not at him, at myself, but he was the only one there, so he got the brunt of it.

"I couldn't. I couldn't go home and admit how pathetic I was. I kept thinking just one more month, and I'd have life figured out. I'd be able to go home and share my riches with my mom and my sister. Fuck knows they deserve it. But I didn't have riches. I had letters from the bank with red stamps all over them informing me I'd gone over my overdraft limit."

Hot angry tears began to pour down my face, and there was nothing I could do to stop them.

I wanted to hide. To run into the forest so Dream wouldn't see what a complete fuck-up I was, but there was no point. He'd only chase me, which would make it even worse. So I turned my back to him. Foolish pride, once again taking over.

His arms wrapped around me, taking me off guard. He pulled me close to him, my back against his chest. I had no control over what happened next. I turned and buried myself in his chest, letting the tears fall as he held me tightly.

He didn't let go until I was completely spent.

Something had changed, in him, in me, in both of us. He was no longer my captor; he was a man. A man I couldn't take my eyes off. He still held that stern look that had occupied his face earlier, but now I saw something else in it. Confusion. My own battle raged within me. I shouldn't be enjoying him holding me. I certainly shouldn't be enjoying it with the way he was looking at me. It was like he'd never seen me before, although it felt to me that he'd known me his whole life. His gaze captured me in its intensity, and I couldn't look away. He searched my face, his eyes settling on my lips, and his hand moved up into my hair. I was completely trapped by him in a way that the magical bonds he'd previously used on me couldn't hope to do. I was consumed by his staggering beauty, by how perfect he was, and most of all, by how close we were. My heart thrummed in my ears, made all the louder by the silence of the forest. We were the only two people in the entire world, or at least, that was what it felt like in that moment. His eyes focused on my lips, and I saw desire in them and that painful stare as though kissing me would burn him. I could understand his conflict completely because I felt it myself. My emotions fought themselves as I strove to see sense. Kissing him would be awful. Worse than awful. He was holding my mother and hundreds of thousands of others against their will. I needed to keep that in mind, not get lost in the way his hands were running through my hair, or the desire to taste his lips, or how my body was responding to his.

It's only because he's beautiful, nothing more! I reasoned with myself. Ridiculously, overwhelmingly, devastatingly so. Anyone with eyes would respond this way to him. My body was only acting naturally. Anyone would feel the same. *Oh god, what am I doing?"*

He moved in closer so that our lips were nearly touching. Just one inch more, and I'd know what it was like to kiss Dream. My breath hitched, and my eyes closed as I bridged the gap between us.

I fell forward into air, no longer being held up by Dream. I opened my eyes to see him ragging his hands through his own hair, despair painting his features.

"I'm going for a walk. You should rest up. We've got a long walk tomorrow."

My mouth dropped open as he took off into the forest, almost as quick as he had when he'd been running away from the wolveries. Except that time, he'd been scared for me. This time, I wondered if he was scared of me.

CHAPTER SEVENTEEN

The next morning was like nothing had happened. And yet, as he packed up what little we had, I couldn't deny that something had. He was efficient, tramping down the fire that had kept us warm all night. Or at least it had kept me warm. I'd slept through the night and woken to find Dream already awake. God only knew if he'd slept at all. He didn't even look my way as he ordered me to eat an animal he'd overcooked on the fire.

My heart ached as I remembered last night. How I'd told him my life story. A life story that he already knew. And I'd still not told him about my mother being in a sleep-induced coma. He already knew about it, of course. He must have, but he didn't know how much it broke my heart. How I'd not visited her once since she'd been in the hospital, leaving all the emotional grunt work to my sister as I always had. He didn't know the shame I felt for that one. I'd unloaded enough shame-inducing shit on him already, and when he'd taken me in his arms, it was almost as if I could forget it all. And then he'd run away from me.

I looked up as he kicked over the campfire, then hid it beneath the leaves.

"It's best that the wolveries don't know we've been here," he explained. His tone was almost cold, his expression stony.

Whatever had happened between us last night had already faded, and he was back to business. He turned and called Raven, who flew from a tree branch to his shoulder. Without waiting for me, they took off into the forest. I had to run to keep up with them.

A warm breeze filtered through the trees, making the leaves rustle and fall down around our ears like confetti at a goth wedding. The light had changed slightly from the pale blue it normally was. It now had hints of pink, warming the forest slightly.

"You never did tell me who taught you that song," I began, wanting to see some reaction from him, anything to know that I didn't just dream the almost-kiss between us.

He scowled without even looking my way. A far cry from last night when he'd held me like we were the last two people in the whole world. A week or so ago, I'd have been surprised by this sudden change, but I was getting used to it. A weather reporter would have a field day reporting his ever-changing moods.

Icy with a touch of disinterest after last night's unexpected warmth. But don't get used to it folks, the weather around these parts is changeable. Ready yourself for an ice storm or burning heat...

Burning heat. What was I thinking? Last night had

been about comfort, nothing more. Sure, I'd spent the entire night in a state of unsatiated arousal, but that was only because I was hug-starved... and he was so bloody hot, it hurt. Damn. I didn't like the way my thoughts were leading...again.

A quick look at Dream made it clear he wasn't in the mood for talking. Above us, Raven flew through the branches, occasionally going higher above the trees then floating back down.

I envied his freedom. Sure, he had some inexplicable connection with Dream, but he could fly above it all.

It was hours before we got back to the doors and more hours still that we walked between the two parallel lines of them to get back to the red door. To Dream's home, if that's what you could call a small clearing in the forest.

"Did you get any meat?"

"Not likely," I answered too quickly before I realized he was referring to the charred animal he'd thrown at me hours earlier and not his dick slipped between my legs the night before.

I felt my cheeks redden at the way my mind worked. "It was too burnt. I had to throw it away," I mumbled.

"Sit down. I'll bring you some food."

I looked around the forest, suddenly nervous. It had been here that the wolveries had first attacked.

"Raven, keep an eye on her."

That was it? A bird was going to keep me safe? How in all that was holy, was a bird going to defend me from the monsters in the forest? It wasn't. But it was too late. Dream had already skipped through the red door. I could have chased him, but knowing my luck, I'd have ended up somewhere else. I didn't trust it not to spit me out in the middle of Antarctica or somewhere ala Monster's, Inc.

Dream came back, his arms laden with food.' Real food. It looked like he'd hijacked a fast-food restaurant, which he probably had. My stomach rumbled at the sight of it. I picked up a burger and shoved it into my mouth, not caring how ladylike I looked. Who wanted to look like a lady anyway when she could look like a ravenous beast, which is pretty close to how I was.

"It's ok?" Dream asked, not touching it. How he could keep from ramming the whole lot down his throat was beyond me. It smelled heavenly, salty, and a bit greasy like all good fast food should. To summarise, it was hard to resist, but Dream didn't seem to be affected. He was pretty good at resisting things, I thought wryly.

"For fuck's sake. Eat a bloody burger, will you? You're putting me right off my food staring at me like that."

His lips turned up at the corners, followed by his eyes. Glad to see my hunger was so amusing to him.

"The wolveries have nothing on you, do they?" he said. With that small quip, I knew he'd gone back to his normal self, whatever normal was for him. If last night bothered him, he'd gotten over it quickly enough. I'd have thrown a packet of fries at him if they weren't so damned good.

"Just eat," I ordered, ignoring the pit of sadness welling in my stomach, which was threatening to eject the french fries. Fuck, I didn't need this. I was heartbroken over David, Not Dream. Who gave a shit if he didn't want to kiss me? If I was so easy to get over, a man could do it before anything really started. It wasn't like I wanted anything to happen anyway. Our situations hadn't changed just because we'd both seen each other naked.

He gingerly took a French fry and looked at it as though it was going to leap out of his hand and eat him instead of the other way around.

"It's not poison, you know," I said curtly, pissed off that it bothered me so much. "It's potato."

He gave me a withering look and popped it into his mouth. I couldn't help the satisfaction I felt as his eyes closed in pure bliss, the way someone's eyes should behave after trying cheap French fries for the first time...or kissing someone for the first time. *Fuck. Get a grip, girl!*

"Told ya," I said, taking a handful of fries myself and cramming as many as humanly possible into my mouth. The salty goodness was all-consuming. Dream chewed on his one fry as I chomped mine all down and swallowed. He finally swallowed and licked the salt from his lips. A tightness spread across my stomach as he savored the taste on his tongue, and I imagined it somewhere else. I wondered what his expression would be after tasting me for the first time. The thought popped out of nowhere, just like all the other thoughts that threatened to take over me. I needed to concentrate. Back to the burger.

"Try this." I handed him the burger and watched as he ate it painfully slowly, taking small bites and savoring each one. I had to turn away to eat my own burger. Watching him was both excruciating and maddening.

After the meal, he stood up and collected the discarded wrappers and boxes and the two cups he'd brought that were now empty of cola. I imagined him conjuring up a bin to put them all into, but instead, he just made it all disappear. What I wouldn't give for his ability to make crap disappear from my own life.

"Stay here. I'm going to find someone to babysit you while I go back to work."

"Babysit me? I asked, affronted. "Am I a child to you?"

He stroked his chin, but as always, didn't dignify me with an answer. "I won't be long. Do. Not. Move."

Fat chance, I wanted to say, but I was too late. He'd already disappeared into the forest.

"I thought you were my babysitter?" I grunted at Raven, who flew down and landed on my knee to grab a fry I'd saved for him.

He squawked and then grabbed the fry straight from my hand.

Unlike his master, he had no trouble with wolfing down all the leftover food.

As he ate, I looked over to the doors. I'd never seen them still for so long. I wondered what happened to people's dreams if they didn't move. It would have been so easy to go and have another peek, or to step through the red door and see something that wasn't darkness. As long as I didn't go through it, surely there was no harm. I ached to see light and color again. Anything other than this never-ending darkness.

The itch was there, but I knew scratching it would

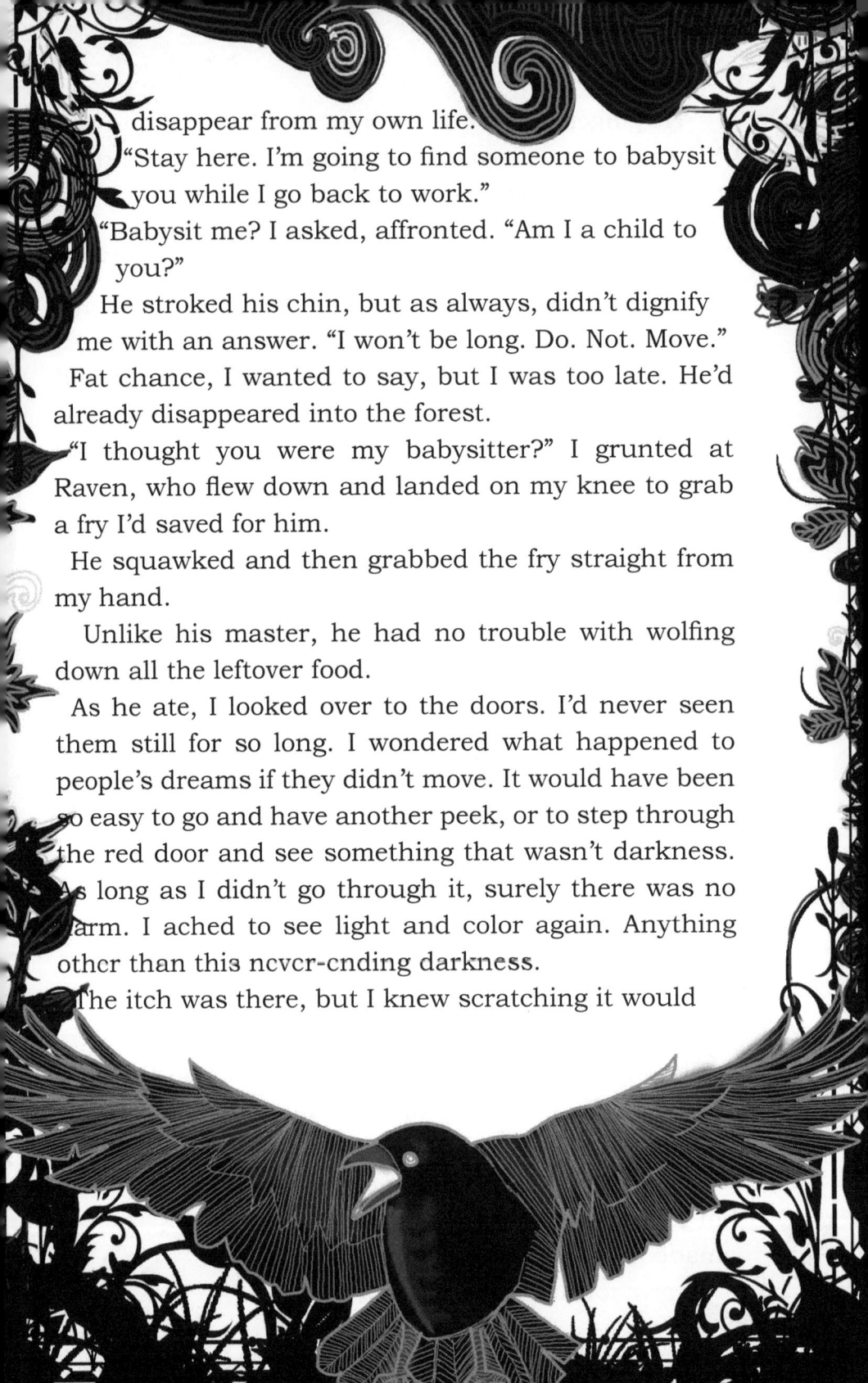

make it worse. If I saw the beauty of the world again, I knew I'd be tempted to go back there, and going back would put an end to everything. My mother would be lost to me for good. I'd fucked up with her so many times. Now was my chance to make it right.

"Hello again,"

I turned my head away from the doors to see Aethelu coming out of the forest, Dream at her side and Tour flying above their heads. Their beauty together was magnetizing. They were both stunning apart, but together, it was compounded so that they practically shone with it.

Ignoring the unjustified jealousy that was beginning to rear its ugly head, I stood up and greeted Aethelu. It wasn't her fault that she was the most divine creature I'd ever laid eyes on... except for the man beside her. And just because they looked incredible together didn't mean they were together.

"I'm guessing you are my babysitter?"

She laughed, her voice melodic... just like Dream's. What was it about these impossibly perfect people around here? Couldn't I meet just one ugly person... just to feel better about myself?

"I'm not here to be your babysitter. His Majesty asked if I would come and sit with you for a while as he works."

"Like a babysitter would," I countered.

I didn't know why I was being snappy with her. I actually liked the idea of getting to know her. There was something about her that made me trust her. It had been an awfully long time since I'd had any girl talk.

"Aethelu is just an extra pair of eyes in case there are more wolveries," Dream grunted. If there is trouble and I'm in one of the dreams, she can carry you to safety.

She can run as quickly as I do."

I wanted to point out that running quickly hadn't saved us the last time the wolveries had attacked, but I knew it was pointless. I'd saved us then. I could do it again...probably.

"My dress looks nice on you," Aethelu said as Dream headed to the doors.

I'd completely forgotten about the dress Dream had gotten for me. It was from Aethelu? Once again, I felt the bite of jealousy stab me in the ass. Why was it she was always nearby?

"Thank you for lending it to me. I was almost completely naked before Dream brought it to me."

She didn't seem like the giggling type, but her face softened into an expression of amusement. "I wonder what His Majesty made of that?"

"Not much, really," I said, trying not to sound too disappointed.

"Hmmm. Interesting."

Interesting? I'd had vague thoughts about Dream's love life, but for all intents and purposes, he didn't seem to have one. He didn't even have a relationship with his own right hand or hadn't while I'd been awake. No wonder the guy was so pent up all the time.

"What makes you say that?"

She shook her head slightly, and her cheeks colored, deepening from the pale grey to a slight pink, much like the sky had earlier, though it had gone back to the same blue hours earlier.

"Come on...What is it that you know? He's a weird kink freak? He's been married three times? He has a harem? Don't tell me he's gay?"

I refused to believe that. With all his indifference to my naked body, I had felt something the night before when he'd held me. Maybe I'd been reading too much into it.

"None of that."

"So what then?" I asked, impatient now.

"Literally none of that...or anything else. You have to remember I barely know him. I've seen him more in the last week than I have in months, years if you count talking to him. He is the King of the Dream Court. I am but a villager."

I turned this over in my mind. It looked like she was telling me the truth, but it was very convenient that she always happened to be around when she was needed.

"If you don't know him, why has he picked you to babysit? Why borrow your dress? I'm guessing there are other women in your village?"

She laughed. "Of course, there are. The day I met you for the first time, he made it very clear that I should keep your appearance here a secret. When he borrowed my dress, and just now, he summoned me."

"Summoned you?"

"Only he has the power to summon his people. I have no such power to...teleport, I think your word is. I can only come to him when he calls. I brought Tour with me because I don't like to leave her alone. She came to me quite recently, and I don't want her getting lost without me."

I raised an eyebrow. "You are telling me that he called you and you..what? Just appeared?" I'd wondered why she'd managed to get here so quickly. I wasn't sure I'd ever get used to the weird magic around here.

She nodded. "I heard him calling for me. Again. Telepathy isn't something I have the power to do, but I heard his voice as clear as day in my head. I heeded the call, both times." She paused. "But I came here for you more than for him. I wanted to make sure you were alright. Something about him tying you up doesn't sit right with me. He wouldn't explain why you are 'here, and until now, I've never heard of him being with anyone."

"What exactly are you saying?"

"I've never seen him with another woman. He is a painfully lonely man. I really think you are the first he's spent any amount of time with at all.

I swallowed hard, trying to comprehend what she was telling me. "You mean he's never had a girlfriend? Like ever?"

"I can't speak out of turn. He is my king, and I don't want to incur his wrath, but I've never heard of one. Of course, I'm by no means an expert on him. Nor do I follow what he does. I can only say with great certainty, he leads a lonely life."

Never had a girlfriend. It was a travesty that someone so hot could never have known intimacy...sex. "Oh, my god! He's a virgin?"

Dream rounded one of the doors as soon as I'd blurted it out. *Fuck! Had he heard?*

"Everything ok here?" he asked.

Both Aethelu and I nodded in unison, me blushing bright as a beet. He made no notice of having heard me, but then he made very little notice most of the time about anything. His being a virgin explained a lot. Like his general grumpy attitude.

He nodded, then retreated to go through another door. "No wonder he's such a miserable git. I've not had any for months, and I'm practically chomping at the bit for some."

Aethelu narrowed her eyes in confusion. For a polyglot or whatever it was that she called herself, she didn't understand me at all.

"Horny!" I clarified. "All the time."

Usually, I wouldn't admit that to a complete stranger, but I'd literally only had an emotionally stunted virgin and his pet bird to speak to for the last few weeks.

"I hear you, girl." she replied, surprising me with her candor. I expected her to change the subject. Then I realized she was using her translation skills on me and trying to speak my language.

"You mentioned the Dream Court before. What is it exactly?"

Her eyes darted toward the doors, and I knew what she was thinking. We'd almost been caught talking about things we shouldn't once already. And there was no telling how long he'd spend behind each door. Sometimes it was only minutes. Sometimes he was gone half an hour or longer.

She leaned into me, her long lilac hair brushing against my leg. "The Dream Court has stood empty for a long time. Longer than I remember. I am much younger than Dream. I only know stories of it. It is a place I have never ventured. They say it is overgrown now. Well, technically, this forest and my village are part of the Dream court, but the court itself is derelict."

"But what exactly is it?" A court? The only courts I knew were the ones on criminal investigation TV shows. I had a feeling that wasn't exactly what she meant.

"The Dream Court, of which Dream is king, covers a quarter of this land. Another quarter is taken by the Nightmare Court and half by the Dark Court."

She whispered the last two words as if saying them

out loud would somehow hurt her. She flicked her eyes back to the doors, but Dream was still gone,

"It is said that many years ago, the Dream Court was a happy place. Of course, it wasn't called the Dream Court then. That changed much later."

"Later than what?"

"Later than...I'm not sure I should tell you this. If His Majesty wants you to know, he'll tell you."

Wishful thinking. He never told me anything. "He's a vault of secrets, that one, and I don't have the key."

She shrugged. "Perhaps it's better that way. You probably don't want to know the state of our world. You'd never go to sleep again in yours if you knew.... talking of which, why don't you leave?" She nodded her head to the red door only feet from where we were sitting. The implication clear.

"I can't," I replied, knowing how pathetic it sounded. "It's not Stockholm Syndrome or anything like that," I added abruptly.

She cocked her head to the side. "I don't think I quite follow. Some words are lost in translation, I'm afraid."

"Stockholm Syndrome. It's named after some Swedish thing that happened a bazillion years ago when some guys took people hostage, and the hostages bonded with them. It means that the captive develops feelings for the captor and doesn't want to be let go."

She raised an eyebrow. "And you've not developed feelings such as these for the king?"

"No," I said way too quickly, a dead giveaway. However much I hated the thought of it and even more so having to admit it, I was horny for the guy. I wouldn't be a hot-blooded woman if I wasn't. I couldn't pretend to be blind to him. "Ok, He's hot," I finally admitted. "But that's all there is to it. "He's also an asshole and a jerk, and though asshole and jerk seem to be my type, I'm making changes. From now on, I'm only going to date sweet, sensitive types."

She nodded, though I could see that she wasn't convinced.

"So, why don't you go through the door then if you don't have feelings beyond a small crush?"

A small crush. It sounded weird. Whatever I felt for Dream was not a crush at all, but I couldn't explain that to her. I didn't have the words to even explain it to myself.

"He's not the reason I'm staying," I admitted.

"Surely it's not for the weather or scenery?" she joked, extending her hand around her.

I smirked. "No. I'm here because..." I hesitated. She knew Dream. Probably more than she let on. She was the one he had gone to when he wanted to bring me a dress. I couldn't imagine a King asking a commoner that he hardly knew for a dress, no matter what she'd told me. He'd ask a friend or a sister if he had any. He might even ask his mother. I was pretty sure he had one of those despite his quietness on the subject. I decided to tell her anyway, at least part of the story.

"My mother is sick. I think Dream has something to do with it."

She pursed her lips, and a strange expression I couldn't read descended on her face. "I've heard rumors," she said. "I don't think you are blaming the right person."

"What?"

"I've said too much." She stood. "I really can't stay here. I have things to do. If you are not going to run away, I think it will be fine to leave you here. Come on Tour." The bird flew down from its branch and rested on her shoulder.

"But what about the wolveries?" I moaned. "That's why you are here."

"I think we both know that's not why Dream asked me to babysit you. If the wolveries came here, they'd rip me limb from limb. I'm no stronger than you are."

Huh. She looked like some badass warrior. I'd have bet everything I owned, which, granted, was not a lot, that she could kick a wolveries ass.

So he was basically making sure I didn't run away. I wasn't surprised. Annoyed as fuck, but not surprised. If the wolveries did come again, I could run through any of the doors to escape in a way I couldn't last time because then I'd been tied up.

Aethelu headed back into the woods at the same time that the row of doors moved. Dream must have come out of one of them. I waited for him to stick his head around one of the doors and see me there alone, but he didn't. The sound of a door closing told me that he'd already gone in through another one.

I looked back and saw that Aethelu had already disappeared into the darkness and a sense of sadness took over me. I would miss her. She was the only person I could talk to in this weird place and a sort of ally against Dream. I'd never had a female friend before, and although she knew a lot more than she was letting on, she was fun to be around and despite her ethereal appearance, being around her felt like a small piece of normality.

A wave of anticipation made my fingers tingle. I was free. Dream was in one of the dream doors, Aethelu had left, and Raven was not really able to stop me from doing anything.

I tapped my fingers together, nervous energy running

through me. I'd made the decision not to go through the red door, but the others...the others were fair game as far as I could see. Maybe it was about time I stepped through one and saw what it was that Dream actually did in there.

I headed to the nearest door and slowly opened it.

CHAPTER EIGHTEEN

I saw the back of Dream first. A sliver of moonlight highlighted his crown. He didn't hear me as I crept toward him. Before him, there was only darkness, though as I moved closer, shapes began to take form.

At first, it was nothing but low light and a hint of color. But then the colors solidified into something horrific. Something I never expected when I walked through that door.

Dream stood stock still, his face glued to the image. I stood not far behind. If I reached out, I could have touched his shoulder, but I didn't. He still didn't know I was there, and if I kept my breathing low, he wouldn't have to know.

I should have left--gone back out to the relative safety of the forest, but something glued my feet to the ground.

There was a woman tied to a wooden chair, her wrists bound behind her with something...I couldn't tell what. Shoelaces, maybe? She looked to be in her early thirties, though it was difficult to tell with the mascara running down her cheeks and her lipstick smeared. A purple bruise was beginning to show on her cheek.

I couldn't hear anything, but I could tell she was begging. Pleading. The fear etched across her face said it all. A man stood before her, an ugly son of a bitch. He was younger than her, younger than me, even. Eighteen or nineteen, perhaps. He wore a white, sweat-covered vest stretched over his roping muscles. But none of that turned my stomach like the way he grinned at her. He was enjoying her fear--feeding off it.

She said something that made his grin falter. Then turn into something dreadful. Pure evil filled his stare as he seized her hair in his fist and slammed her head into the back of the chair. Part of me hoped she'd pass out, and this nightmare would end, but she didn't. Her scream cut through the air, and this time I heard it.

"Shut up, bitch," the man growled, his fingers still entangled in her hair. "Don't want the neighbors to hear, do we? They might come and spoil the fun we're about to have."

Every part of me wanted to run that son of a bitch down, but it wasn't real, and literally nothing I did would stop this sick scene from playing out. I already knew where this was going.

The man jerked her hips forward on the seat, eliciting another scream from her. This time it wasn't just fear. Her arms were still tied behind the seat back and were now at an angle that would be painful, if not excruciating.

"So what's it going to be, darling?" the man sneered. "Want to wrap that pretty mouth of yours around my dick?" He unzipped his pants, letting his dick fall out.

He wasn't even hard.

She clamped her lips shut tightly as he shoved his hand up her skirt. Her eyes followed her mouth, closing themselves against the invasion.

"She's nice and wet, boys."

Boys? My stomach clenched.

The scene panned out a little.

The two weren't alone.

Three more guys stood off to the side, all of them with predatory excitement in their eyes. None of them could be older than twenty, and none were as well built as the asshole, but they didn't need to be. Asshole was breaking her. All they had to do was follow. One of them, a skinny white guy, was already stroking his dick and practically salivating. The other two hadn't gotten that far yet, but they were close to it.

My eyes flicked to the man who towered over the bound woman. He still had one hand under the woman's skirt, but the other was rubbing his dick now, making himself hard. The woman's eyes were squeezed shut, tears seeping from beneath her lashes.

Bile rose in my throat as he pulled his hand away then grabbed her ass, bringing her whole body even closer to him. Someone screamed.

This time it was me.

"Stop it!" I screamed out, punching Dream on the back of his shoulder. "Why aren't you doing anything!"

He turned to face me, his eyes full of fire. I'd seen him angry plenty of times but never like this.

Terror filled me as I took a step backward. The sound of grunts and groans and screams rent the air as Dream grabbed my arm and dragged me outside, slamming the door behind him.

He didn't let go until we rounded the door. He threw me to the ground, disgust written across his every feature. I narrowed my eyes. He wasn't the only one disgusted. How could he just stand there and watch someone get raped and not do anything?

"What's the fuck is wrong with you?" I hollered at him.

His mouth curled down into a grimace. "Me? It is not I who act in such ways. Humans revolt me. I had begun to change my mind, but now I see how foolish I am."

"Don't lump me in with those monsters. You're the one who tied me up, remember?"

"I do remember, and I also remember why. Humans are the lowest of creatures. Always giving in to their base instincts."

I scrambled through the leaves until I found what I was looking for. Picking up a stone, I lobbed it right at him. It grazed the top of his head, sending his crown toppling to the ground.

I pulled myself up from the ground and faced him. "Don't you dare tell me what I am. I'm not the monster here. Maybe you should take a good long hard look at yourself in the mirror."

His hand darted out and seized my throat, tightening around it. He opened his mouth to speak, but instead, he let go of me. Reaching down, he picked up his crown and stormed into the forest, leaving me alone with my thoughts and Raven for company.

I watched with relief when the doors moved, and the one I'd just come out of moved past the red door. It was still there. It hadn't moved very far at all. Only a couple of feet, but somehow having it past the red door made it feel safer. I wondered if it meant the dream was over. I certainly hoped so. I'd never been attacked in the way that woman was, but I felt every ounce of her pain when I was in that room. It was going to take a long time to get over it.

My blood boiled as I went over and over the enco[unter] in my head. Nothing settled me, and with nothing [to] do, I stormed around the small clearing for hours, [as] vivid images of that atrocity spinning round and round in my head.

Raven had the good sense to keep his distance on a tree branch somewhere high above me. I was surprised he hadn't followed his master.

I didn't know what to do, which road to take. To stay here now would be madness. I'd let myself be fooled by a hot body and his gentleness when tending to my wounds. I'd told Aethelu that I didn't have Stockholm Syndrome, but clearly, I did. And more clearly, I was in denial about the whole thing. But leaving the brute now would mean abandoning my mother, which I couldn't do. It was the main reason I was here.

A strange kind of calm fell over me. I knew what I had to do.

I had to kill him. It was the only way, though the thought terrified me. If Dream were dead, whatever hold he had on my mother would be broken, and all those other people in the same situation would wake up too

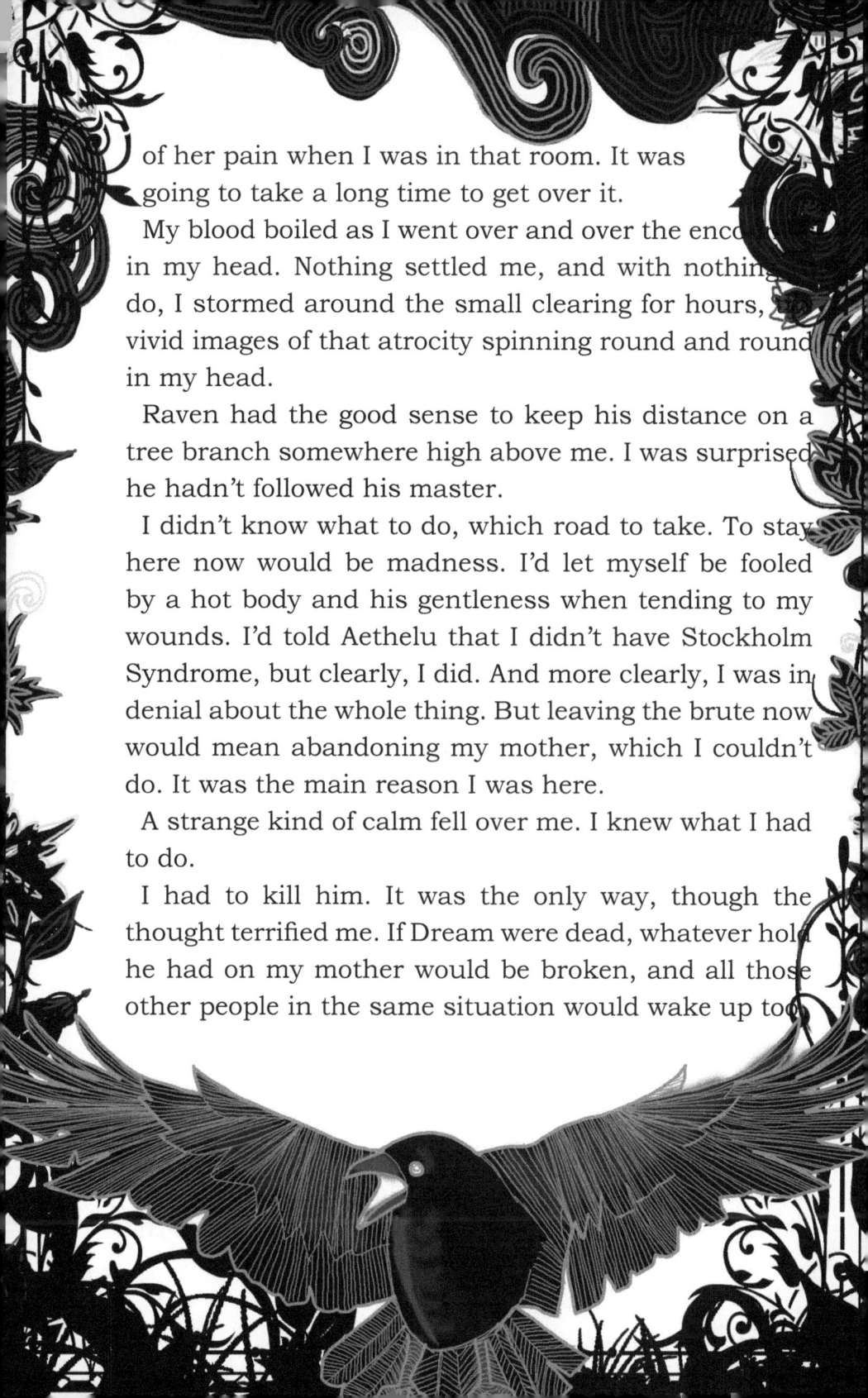

I'd been so wrong about him. So heart-achingly wrong. How pathetic I was to fall for a pretty face and the first hint of intimacy I'd had in months. Would I ever learn?

I couldn't fix my hopeless relationship woes, but at least I could fix *something*. For Mom, if not for me.

Once I made my mind up, I spent hours and hours coming up with ways to kill him, none of which were remotely possible. I was brought up in the country, and if I had a gun, there was a good chance I could put a bullet through his brain with my first shot, but I didn't have a gun, and I had no way of getting one in this creepy world with no shops. Hell, Dream couldn't even get me decent food here.

My idea of making a cross-bow and arrows stalled almost as soon as I had it, as I had no idea how. And the closest thing I had to a blade was a sharp twig. If I tried anything with that he'd laugh at me and then slit my throat with his own knife.

The red door sat there mocking me, urging me to go through it. Beyond it was my world with guns and crossbows and knives and a great many other things that could kill a man. But I knew I'd never get back. There was only one way for me to enter this world, and that was with Dream, and he was hardly about to let me go back to find something to kill him.

I heaved a sigh and gritted my teeth. This strange world had other inhabitants. Dream and Aethelu weren't the only ones. If there were people, then there had to be shops. It was just a matter of finding them.

Making sure Raven wasn't watching, I took off into the forest in roughly the direction of the stream. I found it quickly enough and stopped for a moment to drink.

A shudder skittered through me as a crack of a branch rang out through the forest. I hadn't realized how wound up I was, and it was only now that I remembered both Dream and Aethelu's caution of monsters in these woods. Nervous laughter bubbled up through my throat as I realized I was the one who'd cracked the dry branch beneath my knee.

I'd gotten lucky this time, but it would do me well to be more alert of my surroundings and not draw any attention to myself. And so it was that I walked quickly through the forest, careful to keep my steps light. My skin prickled with every noise, though noises were few and far between. Maybe monsters and beasts did roam these woods, but there was a distinct lack of prey for them. If any of them saw me, I was sure to be lunch.

It didn't help that every part of this damned forest looked like every other part. Dead and dark. I'd made sure to keep in a straight line, but it was impossible to know if I'd veered slightly. Keeping track of landmarks so I could get back to the doors was another impossibility. There were no landmarks. Every so often, I fancied that I saw a tree that looked slightly different from the rest, but in the end, they all jumbled together in my mind.

Ignoring my jangling nerves, I set my focus on what I had to do. I was on a shopping trip. Or so I told myself. Nothing to worry about.

After at least two hours of walking through the darkness, I began to wonder if hungry, vicious beasts weren't my biggest worry after all.

This whole place defied belief. What if there was no one else here in this hell hole? What if it was just Dream and Aethelu, and all this was some kind of game? He'd not tied me up again. Surely he'd know I'd run?

My stomach grumbled as if trying to convince me to turn round. If I did, my only option would be to go through the door and go home. I knew that now. I couldn't spend another second in Dream's company after what he did.

Ok, so he didn't partake in the assault...rape of that woman, but he was quite happy to watch. He didn't do anything to stop it. If he was the creator of dreams, then he was also the creator of nightmares. I hadn't seen his face when he was watching, but my mind filled in the blanks. It must be how he managed to go without sex for so long. His perverse mind conjured up horrifying acts and put them in people's heads.

It had been so real. The woman dreaming it must have already gone through the nightmare in real life and was playing it over and over in her dreams. I refused to believe any woman would be able to make that up with so much clarity. Though, that begged the question then—if Dream really didn't make it up, he'd still stood by and watched it. He could have turned around and let that door go at any time, but he didn't.

The bile that was threatening earlier came to the surface, and I threw up on the forest floor, retching up all my disgust and anger and frustration. I couldn't think about it anymore. Any of it. If I did, I'd only end up going mad with it all.

I was doing something about it. That's why I was here. There was nothing I could do for that poor woman, but I could stop the millions of nightmares like it that would come in the future.

As I wiped my mouth with a shaky hand, my eyes snagged on what I could only describe as a pathway beneath my feet. The fallen leaves had been flattened by the footsteps of many people...or beasts, it was hard to tell. Relief welled up in me. In that moment, I didn't care whoever—or whatever--flattened this pathway. A path means an end to the aimless walking. A destination. Perhaps that destination was the belly of a ginormous beast, but it was an end nonetheless. As I studied it, it became clear that one route curved around and would take me backward and to the left. The other way seemed more promising, so I took it, slowly this time.

The cloying darkness still surrounded me, but having a clear-cut path through the forest put me at ease slightly. Or at least it gave me purpose. With each step I took, I gazed at the path, trying to figure out whether it was shoes or hooves or claws that had carved it. Without any mud for prints, I couldn't be sure. Overhead, branches had been snapped off to clear the way, leaving almost a tunnel through them. By my estimate, whatever used this path was just under seven feet tall. Both Dream and Aethelu were well over six feet, so it could be human...or whatever they were. Of course, it could just be some freaking enormous monster with fangs sharp enough to rip my throat out.

Something sprinted through the woods right in front of me, nearly giving me an aneurism. It took a few seconds of my heart doing the samba around my ribcage to realize that it was a deer. Or at least deer-like. I supposed I couldn't call any creatures by the names of the animals they looked like in the real world. Besides, this dear had deep blue fur and glowing antlers and had disappeared through the trees before I'd managed to see much more of it than that.

It had acted like a deer, fast and skittish, and not out for my blood which was the only thing I could hope for in this place. And though it had moved so quickly I'd barely seen it, I hadn't noticed massive fangs anyway. Hopefully, it was an herbivore. It didn't take long before the trees began to thin out and the darkness began to clear. Or at least turn into a paler kind of darkness. The moon was bright, which made the trees almost luminous. I stepped out onto a grass verge with a dirt road running left to right. Directly ahead of me sat a small log cabin, the chimney puffing with smoke. My heart twinged with how cozy it looked, so much like the places I vacationed in as a child, the few times my mother could afford to take us anywhere. All that was missing was the snow.

To the right, the dirt road continued off into the distance, but to the left, there looked to be a small village.

I kept to the verge. Should anyone venture down the road, my plan was to hop back into the trees. I might be dressed like these people, but I sure didn't look like them. I was a foot too short for a start and had neither the ethereal beauty of Aethelu nor the unbridled gorgeousness of Dream. I had no idea what the plan was once I got to the village, but I was good at thinking on my feet.

As I neared the village, I realized that I couldn't use the forest as cover if I actually wanted to do anything. If I ever hoped to find a weapon, I was going to have to suck it up and go in. Taking a deep breath, I stepped out into the road and then along a path that I hoped would lead me into the village center.

The cobbles beneath my feet were a welcome change from the dry, dead leaves I'd been walking on for the past few weeks. They made sense somehow. Made it feel like I was in a real place instead of some dystopian nightmare. The houses helped too. Each was different, but all shared the same thatched cottage-style roof. Even in the darkness, I could see that these cottages were painted in bright colors. Muted now, though, in the moonlight, they were barely more than shades of blue. Why would these people bother to use bright colors in a place where there was barely any light? Perhaps that's why they had done it—anything to counteract the constant dusk.

So far, I hadn't seen a soul, which I reminded myself was a good thing. I would probably stand out as an outsider from a mile away. As soon as the thought slipped through my mind, I caught sight of someone.

I froze. I couldn't quite believe what my eyes were seeing.

CHAPTER NINETEEN

All my stress about standing out like a sore thumb melted away. The town square was filled with people of all shapes and sizes going about their business. They all looked human, or at least humanesque. Some were tall, some shorter than me. A lot had a similar skin tone to normal humans, though it was hard to tell in the low light. Some were pale blue, though they could just be so white that their skin appeared blue. Others had Aethelu's same grey skin tone. But they were all beautiful. It was like accidentally walking into a beauty pageant dressing room.

Thanks to Aethelu's dress I was still wearing, I stepped out into the square, safe in the knowledge that, though I didn't look like all of them, I wouldn't stand out as obviously human.

The buildings that surrounded the square were old-world, almost live a live museum or a movie set cobbled square was alive with the hustle and bustle of what appeared to be market day.

Stalls dotted the place, selling everything from live animals to food. My eyes widened. Exotic food, the likes of which I'd never seen before. One stall sold delicious-looking pastries, the other, bizarre fruits and vegetables. None, as far as I could see, sold weapons of any kind. The fear that had been dogging me for hours dropped away as the new sights and smells captured me. If it wasn't for the situation I was in, I could almost feel happy here. Maybe it was just the stark contrast to the forest that made me feel so.

A young woman with long hair and blue pointed ears peeking through accosted me, brandishing a leafy vegetable of some kind. "Want to buy some weedroot?"

Her voice matched her lip movement, but another voice hovered beneath it—talking in a language I didn't understand. It took me a few moments to realize this woman was a polyglot, too, though she wasn't as skilled as Aethelu, since I could still hear her original voice below the English.

I daren't speak back, knowing that if I could hear her original language, she'd almost certainly hear mine. I didn't think English was a common language around here, despite Dream speaking it. He knew it from the millions of dreams he'd been in.

I shook my head, hoping the gesture was universal enough to understand. She cocked her head at me for a moment, then moved away into the crowd. I blew out a shaky breath.

I could feel the eyes of the people on me as I walked through the square. Not everyone, but enough people staring at me a beat too long was enough to tell me that I wasn't as incognito as I'd hoped. My dress was dirty. Perhaps that was it. My bloody and bandaged legs were hidden beneath the length of material, so that wasn't the reason. I ignored the crawling sensation, hoping I was overthinking it and carried on my search of the market for anything that could be classified as a weapon.

In the far corner, a band played an upbeat tune. It was a far cry from the dimness of the low light and seemed as out of place as a pop band at a funeral.

My stomach jumped as I passed the cart full of baked goods. Different types of breads and cakes rested in symmetrical rows, and though I'd never seen anything like any of them before, the smell coming from the cart was delicious.

The urge to reach out my hand and take one was overwhelming, but the suspicious look the stall owner was giving me was enough to still my movement. I wasn't a thief, anyway. I never had been. Even when I couldn't afford to eat back home, I rode it out until my next paycheck and survived on ramen noodles.

"I don't recall ever seeing you around here before?"

I jumped as a middle-aged woman confronted me. Her skin was similar to that of Aethelu, but unlike Aethelu, the chalky white appearance overlaid a pale blue. On some of the other people I'd seen in town, this skin tone looked beautiful, but the wrinkles and liver spots on this woman only made her look old and drawn. Despite the casual comment, there was a mean look about her. Long blue straggly hair covered her shoulders, and a grey shawl hid just beneath it.

I couldn't speak. Saying anything would call me out as a foreigner immediately. This woman might not guess I was from the real world, but she'd know I wasn't from around here. I shook my head as I thought on my feet. My only option was to run, but to where? Back to the forest? I was no safer there than here.

"Cat got your tongue?" she drawled, her pale blue lips cracked as she extended a grim smile.

My mind ran at a hundred miles an hour as I thought about all I'd learned since arriving here. Aethelu hadn't known I was from the real world when I'd first spoken to her. She'd asked if I was from the Dream Court, the Nightmare Court, or the Dark Court. Neither of them sounded like places where people were to be messed with.

"I'm from the Dark Court," I announced, straightening my spine and fixing her with an imperious look. Her eyes widened, and she took a step backward as though I was made of lightning. She visibly shrunk before my eyes, and the scary old woman became a wreck right in front of me.

I was just about to hotfoot it away when a thickly-built young man clamped his hand on the woman's shoulder. "She's not from the Dark Court, mother. Look at her. No one from the Dark Court would dress like that."

"But what if she is?" the woman replied to her son, who was twice her size and twice as intimidating. Luckily, or unluckily as the case may be, having men try to intimidate me was something I was used to.

"Look at her hair."

My hair? My only play here was to keep bluffing like my life depended on it. Because it did. "I do not lie. Can you not hear it in my voice? The language

I speak? Now be out of my way, peasant." Oh, that good. Over the top maybe, but good, nonetheless. Better than calling him a bitch like I wanted to. I knew he would be able to hear my real voice in English underneath the strange translation over the top.

But the burly man didn't budge. "No one around these parts has heard the language of the Dark Court for years, which is suspicious in itself, but you are too short for the people of the Dark Court. You might have the hair, but you most certainly don't have the clothes. The Queen would not allow her subjects out of the Dark Court. She hasn't for scores of years, but if she did, she wouldn't let them dress like that." He looked me up and down, making me feel uncomfortable in Aethelu's beige dress.

What was it they meant about my hair? This place was totally screwy, although when I looked around, no one had hair the same color as mine. There was every shade of brown, from light, to almost black. Lots of blue, but no silver blonde.

"You don't have to believe me. What business is it of yours where I'm from anyway?" I made to shove past him, but the woman caught my arm. "No, you don't, Lassie. There's something strange about you. If you are not from the Dark Court, then where are you from? I think the elders would like to see you."

I tried to yank my arm away, but her grip was too strong. She was a lot stronger than she looked.

"Get off of me!"

By now, we were surrounded. Half the people in the marketplace had come to watch the spectacle. So much for being inconspicuous. I couldn't have done worse if I'd tied a billboard to my front reading 'Look at Me' and rang a bell.

The woman's son grabbed my other arm, and though his fist was a whole lot meatier than his mother's, it was no more or less tight.

"Get the fuck off of me!" Being nice hadn't helped my cause. Maybe shouting would.

The villagers began to jeer, reminding me of TV shows and movies about medieval times in Britain. I half expected a man on a white horse and armor to come to save me, but the only man I knew that wore armor was Dream, and he was the one I was here to buy weapons to kill. I'd never needed a man before, and I was sure as shit not going to wait around for one to rescue me now. I was going to rescue myself as I always had. I kicked out at the old woman's shins, sending her to the ground in pain. Her son's grasp weakened just enough for me to tear my arm away from him. Without looking back, I dashed through the crowd and to an archway between two shops, banging my elbow on the wall as I passed through.

The archway led to another street. Small houses and more stalls lined the busy dirt road. What was this? Market day? So many people were out and about that I had to weave my way through them, dodging the strange folk. A quick look over my shoulder was enough to let me know just what deep shit I was in. A whole pack of villagers was chasing after me. All that was missing was the pitchforks.

I was so busy looking backward that I didn't notice the arm out to grab me until it was too late.

CHAPTER TWENTY

"What did you think you were doing?" Aethelu demanded as she closed the door of the small house behind her. Her face was calm, but I could hear the anger in her voice.

"I was running away from a load of crazy idiots," I explained, though it was unnecessary. She'd seen enough herself. "I told them I was from the Dark Court."

Aethelu sucked in a breath and brought her hand to her mouth. "You didn't? Your hair...No wonder they believed you."

"They didn't believe me, and what the fuck has my hair to do with anything? They mentioned it too."

She narrowed her eyes. "The people from the Dark Court have not been seen for a great many years, but most of them are known to have hair of silver like yours. You really should not have told them that."

I rubbed my arm, pissed off that I'd managed to hurt it in the first place, and now it seemed I was about to be reprimanded for the whole load of inbred villagers chasing me.

"It's not my fault they are all crazy. Maybe the lack of light drives everyone to madness. I didn't even do anything."

Aethelu pursed her lips. "Sit down," she demanded, pointing at a chair in the corner.

I fucking hated being pushed around by anyone, but somehow with Aethelu, I didn't mind so much. She was my only ally in this place where seemingly everyone and everything was out to get me.

I did as she said and took the seat in the corner.

Aethelu paced the room in front of me, her mouth set in a grim line.

"Didn't you listen to me? Have you not listened to me at all? I've been quite clear that this isn't the place for you. I honestly thought when I left you earlier that you'd see sense and go back to your own world through the red door."

"I'm sorry, but..."

"Sorry?" she shouted, making my heart leap. I'd only ever heard her voice in soft lyrical tones. The harshness of it now made me more nervous than when the villagers were shouting at me.

"No need to be sorry to me. None of this will hurt me. The only person going to get hurt here is you. You came here like a lamb to the slaughter."

My muscles tightened in my jaw. "How was I to know the villagers would turn against me. It's hardly as though I was doing anything wrong."

"You just being here is wrong. Don't you think we have enough to worry about without humans coming into our world? It's so rare that most won't understand what you are, but they know you aren't from here. And if they think you are from the Dark Court..." she gave a shudder and trailed off.

"I still don't understand why it matters. So what if they think I'm from the Nightmare Court or the Dark Court or whatever court."

Aethelu sighed and rubbed her forehead.

"I'm going to make us some tea. Don't move a muscle until I'm back."

She hurried out through another door, leaving me with time to assess the room around me. In the corner, Tour sat on a perch, the beautiful coloring in her wings barely visible in the low light.

"Hey, Tour," I said to the bird. She clucked her beak and gave me a wink. Maybe Raven needed to take a leaf from this bird's book. The house was basic with drab brown walls, but Aethelu had adorned each wall with dozens of beautiful abstract paintings. Each had a range of blue hues, ranging from pale blue to almost black. Silver stars dotted each one like jewelry. It was like looking at the milky way. It was also odd that someone who only ever saw the night would decorate their house with paintings of it, but then again, this was all she knew. I wondered if she'd ever seen daylight. The strange tone of her skin told me that it had been a long time, if ever. I was saved from pondering it further by her bustling back in with two mugs of tea, one of which she handed to me.

I took a sip and almost spat it out.

"It gets better," Aethelu smiled, nodding to my mug. I'd been expecting tea. She'd said it was tea, but this was the strangest tea I'd ever drunk. I couldn't think of a single taste to compare it to, but as I let the liquid sit in my mouth, I got used to it. I swallowed and took another sip. The second sip tasted better than the first.

"This is..."

"I know your tastes may be different from ours."

"No..it's good. Really good, once you get used to it."

Her face relaxed a little.

"If you are serious about staying here, and for the life of me, I cannot understand why, then there are things you should know. Hopefully, if I tell them to you, you might be persuaded to leave for your own safety."

I sat back in the chair, excited to finally hear what all the madness was about.

"Over a thousand years ago, there was no Dream Court or Nightmare Court. Nor was there the Dark Court, although that came first. The people here have always been the creatures of the night, just not in the way you would expect." She paused and took a sip of her tea. "Our world shouldn't even exist. We only exist as an extension of yours. We came about hundreds of thousands of years ago when humans started to have dreams. At first, or so the story goes, we were nothing but an extension of those dreams. A place where human minds came together through sleep."

"So you are quite literally dreamed up?"

She nodded. "Succinctly put. In a manner of speaking, yes. That's why many of us look so different from humans, why our creatures resemble creatures in your world, but not quite the same. We were nothing but the collective imagination of human minds. However, as the population of your world grew, our world grew with it. A hundred thousand years ago, it took on a life of its own. Our people became real. Our lands solidified. It didn't take long before our realm was as real as yours is. People began to forget where we came from. Our humble beginnings became nothing but myth. Most people don't even believe in humans anymore."

I almost choked on my tea. "Don't believe in us? What do they think is behind all those doors in the forest?"

Aethelu smiled. "Listen to what I am about to tell you, and you'll understand. The royals knew that they were responsible for guarding the dreams of humans, even though the people began to forget. Those that didn't forget didn't care anymore. Humans were nothing to them. The royal palace kept everything running smoothly, and the knowledge of our past and the responsibility of the dreams of humans was passed down from generation to generation. For a long time, thousands of years, it worked. Even as your world grew and our world grew independently of it, the royals took an oath to protect your dreams.

"Protect?"

"Do you know what happens to humans when they don't dream?"

Finally - a question I could answer...sort of.

"Dreaming helps humans sort out their memories. It determines what to store for long-term memory and what to disregard from short-term memory. Imagine a giant filing cabinet, and dreams help us sort memories into the right files."

I was quoting one of McGee's favorite lines to potential customers, but I didn't care.

"And so what happens when the filing cabinet drawer is jammed?"

She waited for my answer. I didn't have one. "I don't know. I thought everyone dreamed."

"I don't know what happens either, but if your filing cabinet analogy is true, not dreaming could have catastrophic effects on humans, could it not?"

I shrugged. Despite working in a sleep clinic for over three years, I'd never really thought about it.

"So what happened?"

"A hundred or so years ago, a new queen came to power. Like all the other royals, she was brought up to keep order in our world in the knowledge that anything that happened here impacted your world. Her job was to keep the peace of our world while making sure the people of yours carried on dreaming. It was a symbiotic arrangement, really. Your world dreamed; our world survived.

"But this queen lost her parents while she was still very young. She was fifteen when she came into power and had not yet had all her training. Whether from grief or something else, she stopped listening to the royal advisors, some of whom had ancestors that had worked for her ancestors for generations. She began to listen to the naysayers. Those that thought that the human realm didn't exist, and those that believed it did exist, but that the humans were leeching from us. The truth was that the dreams of your people only enriched our world, but she started to believe otherwise.

"When she fell in love and married at the age of eighteen, she was already halfway to corruption and evil, but the man she married hammered the point home to her. I don't know his reasons, but he believed humans were scum. Having never been in the royal household, he was never privy to what they really did, nor the fact that human imagination was quite

literally keeping our world alive.

Sure, we were independent of you, but I don't think it would take long for our world to crash and burn if our connection was destroyed.

"He didn't believe any of it and made it very clear. His motivation was complete power over

everything and everyone. He hated to think that the humans had anything to do with his life at all.

Honestly, if he'd stopped to smell the coffee, he'd have realized that the human world didn't really affect him in any way. Maybe the shape our world took was molded by humans, but I believe that we were strong enough to be our own people, our own land.

"He was scared, and he passed that fear on to the queen. As I told you, she was already angry with the world. By the time they had children, twin boys, both the king and queen were done with the human world. The queen hadn't been doing her job. Humans were still dreaming, but not like they used to. The color of dreams had begun to fade. And as it did, the light in our world began to fade along with it. Gradually, our days got shorter and shorter and our nights longer and longer. And then the king was murdered by a human that had found a way into our realm. The boys were only ten years old. The queen was destroyed by grief, and the madness that had been threatening her for so long finally took over. She threw the boys out of the palace as the pair of them reminded her so much of her late husband.

"Oh, she told everyone that she was sending them out into the world to learn, but the truth was, her bitterness had consumed her. She had each of them a palace built in different parts of the land and gave them the job of keeping the dreams, not caring that they were only ten years old.

"Thus, our land was broken up into three parts. This is the Dream Court. To the east is the Nightmare Court, run by the king's brother, and to the north is the Court of Darkness, run by the queen. It's the biggest of all our lands and once the capital. Nowadays, no one goes there, and those that do never return. the villagers were scared because it is now known to be a place of evil."

I sat stock-still, taking this all in. In all my years of working in a sleep clinic, I had never known how insane our minds were and what they could achieve.

"And that's why it is dark now?"

She nodded. "It has been this way for fifty years. King Dream and his brother have been keeping the dreams going, but it is a burdensome task. In the Dark Court Palace, the royals had a staff of thousands doing the job. Now it is only the two.

There was something I didn't understand.

"What exactly is it that Dream does? I've been in those dreams with him, and he just stands there, watching. It's not like he conjures them."

"I cannot speak for him. His job is not something I

know about. The secret of it was protected by the royals for millennia, but I do know that without him doing it, the humans will fail to dream, and if that happens, our world will fail to thrive. If he gives up, we will all cease to exist."

I sat dumbfounded. The weight on Dream's shoulders was immense, and to have been doing it since he was ten years old. A job that had been performed by thousands.

What happened to his court? You said there was a palace?"

She shrugged. "It was his home for a long time, but it was a big place for a little boy. His subjects helped out as much as they could, but I don't think anyone really understood the burden that was placed on him. As the world got darker, he retreated in on himself and eventually gave up the court entirely. He moved to be alone in the woods. Just him and his raven."

It was a lot to digest.

"It certainly explains why he's a moody bastard."

Aethelu snorted. "He is a man of depth, but he has had no real contact in his life. I doubt very much he has spoken to either his mother or his twin since the day he left the royal palace. Everything I've told you I've found out through hearsay and myth. As I told you before, I barely know him. No one does, despite us all being part of his court. He comes to town only when he absolutely has to, and even then, he keeps to himself. Luckily, there are few problems here in the Dream Court. We usually go about our business without any problems.

"Until today," I said, rubbing my elbow again.

"Until today. I fear that the people knowing there is a human here will frighten them. You are nothing but a myth to them."

I sighed. "So what should I do? I can't pretend to be from another court. No one believed me. You saw what happened."

"You go home, Ana. Go home and forget any of this exists. You will still dream. His Majesty has many faults, but not doing his duty to humans is not one of them."

I sat up straight in my chair. "I'm not going home. I told you. My mother is asleep. Nobody can wake her up. She's not the only one. Thousands of people are in an unwakeable sleep just like her, and I know it has something to do with this place."

She seemed intrigued now. "Your world is failing too? I wonder if somewhere along the line, the symbiotic relationship between our worlds is fading. I thought it had only affected ours, but maybe it has affected yours too."

"It started a year ago. Did anything happen here a year ago? Our whole population fell asleep."

She shrugged her shoulders. "I don't know anything about it, but it sounds strange. Of course, I know little about the inner workings of dreams. I said right at the start that all my information was hearsay and years of listening to other people's thoughts on the matter. Only King Dream knows the truth, but there is a reason he spends his whole life out there alone. I believe he likes humans a lot more than you give him credit for."

"Right," I snorted. "He likes us like a hole in the head. He told me that humans revolted him. Maybe he just doesn't want to disappear like everyone else if he stops working."

Aethelu looked like she was thinking. "I don't believe that is the full truth. If he wanted to kill you, he would have done so already. You are the first person I've ever seen him with for more than five minutes. I'd say he likes you a lot."

"He made it very clear I was worth less than shit on his shoe the last time I saw him," I mumbled.

Aethelu stood. "Let me take you back to the doors. You'll be safe with me. If you decide to go home, then so be it, but if you decide to stay, I hope what I've told you today will help you understand why The King is the way he is. I also hope that you'll stay close to him. However much you think he hates you, you are safer with him than anywhere else in this world. Stay by his side and listen to him if you ever want to find out what is happening to your mother… assuming he even knows himself."

CHAPTER TWENTY-ONE

Aethelu let me wash and change in her house before we set off. The bathroom was just that—a bath that filled the whole room. I stripped down and stepped in to find that there were no taps.

"Is this one of those fill-with-a-bucket type of baths?" I shouted through the door to Aethelu. Immediately, I found myself knee-deep in hot water.

"It's one of those fill-with-magic type of baths," she replied with a chuckle. "Is it warm enough?"

I sat down and let the water go right up to my chin, savoring the heat. I'd never really been cold in this world, but I'd never really been warm either, just stuck perpetually between the two.

"Mmm," I groaned as the heat seeped into my bones. After the bath, Aethelu let me borrow more of her clothes, giving me a whole bundle of them, which I wasn't sure I'd ever use. Maybe Dream had a tragic back story, but at the end of the day, that didn't absolve him of the shit he'd laid on me. The red door was ever-present in my mind throughout the walk back to it. I was surprised to find the clearing empty.

"I'll be fine from here," I assured Aethelu.

She hesitated. "Are you sure you don't want me to stay with you until the king comes back?" Aethelu asked, always full of concern. "You never did tell me why you were running away from him again."

I shook my head. I needed to see him alone. If he hated me, then so be it, but I didn't hate him anymore. I wasn't sure how I felt about him. My emotions had become a rollercoaster that was threatening to get away from me. When Aethelu left, a heaviness pulled at my chest. She was my only friend in this place, but I couldn't predict how Dream would react to her being here without him knowing.

Not that I had to worry. He didn't come back that night, nor the next. I survived by drinking the water at the stream and foraging for what little food I could find. The threat of the wolveries was enough to ensure I didn't wander too far from the small camp. Even more noticeably absent was Raven. Wherever they both were, I hoped they were together. Just the thought of Dream being alone for so long was enough to pull at my already pulverized heart.

On the third night, I woke up to the sound of rustling leaves. I opened my eyes a slit to see a familiar figure sitting down across the campfire. The doors had started moving again. I didn't need to look, to know. The sound they made with each movement was enough.

I watched him through my eyelashes as he took a seat.

If ever there was a tortured man, this was it. He sat with his head in his hands, his hair a mess. I'd never seen him anything other than perfect before now. Sadness engulfed me at the sight of him. He looked exhausted, done with everything. Bereft, lost and haunted in quiet despair. This couldn't be the King of Dreams, the huge masculine hulk of a man who'd dragged me kicking and screaming into his world, then just as abruptly kicked me right back out of it. I resisted the urge to go over to him, to offer him comfort. He was looking the way he did because of me.

His eyes flicked over to me, and I clamped my own shut. My breathing increased, and I tried to pass it off as being in a deep sleep.

"Are you awake?"

His voice was unusually low, like a quiet hum. To answer him and give myself away would mean I'd have to have a conversation I wasn't sure I was ready for.

I chose to pretend sleep and worry about that conversation in the morning. As I was already breathing like I was asleep, the edges of my conscious began to darken. As I began to fall into real sleep, I was sure I heard him utter the words "I'm sorry."

I woke to him gone and the doors still again. For some reason, It had not bothered me the previous two nights. I'd always known he would come back, but now he had come back and then gone again. Fear crept into my soul and with it, the question of whether he'd ever come back again. He'd been keeping the world running for years. Both worlds. His and mine. Maybe I'd pissed him off to such an extent that he didn't care about either anymore and was leaving both to rot. But then that word he'd said last night. I could have sworn he'd said sorry, but then I could have dreamed it. Dreaming about Dream. The irony of it didn't escape me.

I stood and brushed myself down, letting the dirt from the ground fall from my dress. Maybe he was through one of the doors? I walked through the gaps to the rows of parallel doors.

It was impossible to know if they had just moved and Dream was inside one or if they had died, doomed to be still forever. I held out my hand to the closest door handle. As I did, a noise to my right startled me, and I pulled back my hand as though it had been electrocuted. Dream emerged from the red door, his arms full of food.

We both stood stock still, staring at each other. Like we were frozen in time. My heart pounded, and my body shook as Raven flew over my head and then settled on the nearest door frame.

"I was trying to see if you were inside," I said lamely, knowing I'd been caught doing the one thing that was bound to bring on more of Dream's wrath.

His expression didn't change much. There was no anger in it, not even quiet resignation.

"Are you hungry?" he asked, nodding to the food in his hands. I wasn't exactly sure what I'd been expecting him to say, but I ran with it.

"Starving," I answered truthfully. My stomach had gotten used to crappy forest food over these past weeks, but that didn't mean I liked it.

We sat back in the camp area. He passed me a plate on which was somebody's breakfast by the looks of it. The plate had an old-fashioned pattern around the edge of it, like ones my grandmother used to have or ones you might find in a thrift store.

Why was I focussing on the pattern on the chinaware instead of on the food? Oh, because things were weird between Dream and me, and I didn't know what to do or say. The last time I'd seen him, he'd blamed me for everything wrong with the world, and I'd stalked off with the intention of murdering the guy.

How things had changed. I shot him a glance as I picked up the cream cheese-covered bagel.

He was laying the rest of the food on the ground neatly and deliberately. Two bottles of coke, a bag of chips, some chocolate bars. My kind of meal—one full of delicious calories that I didn't have to cook.

He was deliberately not looking my way. Was this contrition? It was hard to tell. He kept his emotions in check pretty well. All except the bad ones. Those he was quite capable of showing.

"Why didn't you stop it?" I asked, knowing full well I was walking a thin line with him. I could have started with 'thanks for the bagel,' or "what a nice day we're having," but no, I had to go and start an argument. *What was it with me and my big mouth?*

He stopped what he was doing but didn't look up. His silence unnerved me, had my flight or fight instincts on full charge.

"I could no more stop them than you could," he finally said quietly.

The anger I'd felt toward him for so long evaporated, to be replaced by something else, something much worse. Sadness. I saw him as a small boy, left alone in a big palace. His father dead, his mother overcome with grief, having to do this ridiculous job alone. My heart broke for him.

"I saw Aethelu. She told me everything."

That was the point at which he looked up at me, his dark eyes filled with the reflection of the stars that shone through the forest canopy above his head.

"Aethelu doesn't know everything. Nobody knows everything, but me and…"

"Your brother?" I hazarded a guess. "She said he lives in the Nightmare Court. Does that mean he watches over nightmares while you watch over dreams?"

He licked his lips as though I'd said something distasteful. "In a manner of speaking. I don't want you to mention him to me again. I told you. Aethelu knows nothing. You take too much of her word, but I barely know her. She's one of my subjects. Nothing more."

Aethelu had said as much to me, but with a lack of anyone else in his life, Aethelu was probably the closest thing he had to a friend. Even if they didn't see each other very often.

"If your brother watches over the nightmares, and you watch over the dreams, why did that last one slip through? Why did you have to see it?"

He looked right at me, as though I already should know the answer. And then it dawned on me. It wasn't the woman playing back a memory in her mind. The dream had been that of the bastard that had raped her. It was a dream and not a nightmare because he'd enjoyed it. The thought made my stomach curdle.

"It was him."

Dream nodded. "It was him. I hate him. I hate a good many humans that are like him, and yet, I watch them night after night, month after month, year after year, I watch the hatred you all hold for your fellow humans, and it makes me wonder if my mother wasn't right in the first place."

"I hated it as much as you did," I objected. "It made

me sick to my stomach."

He nodded his head and spoke, his voice uncharacteristically quiet. "I know. As soon as I stormed off, I knew I was wrong about the whole thing, but when I returned, you'd gone. I couldn't find you. I thought you'd gone back through the red door. I hoped you had, and I hated that you had at the same time and...I don't know!"

He threw the last item to the ground - a chocolate bar and stood. This time when he made to stride off, I jumped up, knocking my bagel to the ground.

"Don't," I said, hurrying over to him.

He turned to face me, his eyes burning with both fear and anger. "Don't what?"

I took a deep breath. "Don't run away from me."

His eyes were steely. "You are one to talk about running away. You ran away from your world, and you've run away from me. Twice if I remember correctly."

I hung my head. He wasn't wrong. I'd spent my life running away. "Yeah, and look where it got me. A shitty apartment with peeling wallpaper and no money for food. Neither of us has to run away."

He was silent for a second, the brooding man-hulk that he was, but then he sat back down, picked up a bagel, and tore into it with his teeth.

"Aethelu told me about your mother," I started.

"Don't mention her to me again," he warned, and I could see that he meant it.

Not that I was surprised after what she had done to him. So his mother and his brother were both off the conversation menu, and I had a feeling bringing his father up wouldn't help matters either.

His eyes were fixed down at the ground in front of him. "It's time for you to go home, Ana."

"What? No!"

He looked up. There was anguish in his gaze.

"Why do you want to stay here? You've had plenty of opportunities to leave. I've...I've not treated you well. You have no reason to be here, and yet you stay. Why?"

I swallowed. Now was the time to tell him about my mother, but I couldn't because that wasn't really it. Not anymore. " I stayed because I was worried about you." *So help me god, it was the truth.* I hadn't gone through the red door these past two days because then he would be well and truly alone, and the thought tore me up.

He stood up, running his hands through his hair as he did. "No. This cannot be. You don't even know me. Why would you worry about me?" His voice was harsh. "No one worries about me. I'm not worth it."

I stood up and took his hand away from his hair. "I think you are."

"I wanted to kill you," he bit back.

I nodded. "True. I wanted to kill you too before...before I knew the truth."

He cleared his throat and shook his head, his mouth set in a grim line. "You don't know the truth. Aethelu doesn't know the truth. The truth is that you are not safe here. You've never been safe here. I don't want you here."

His words were enough to hurt me, but I had a feeling that was the intention. "I think you do...want me here."

He nodded, and though he didn't say as much in words, he accepted mine.

He pulled his hand free. A part of me thought he was about to take off into the woods again. That I'd misread him, but this time, he walked over to the row of doors.

He stood between two, his hand holding onto one of them as he turned toward me, a questioning look on his face.

"What?"

His eyes flicked to the door next to him, then back to me.

"You want me to come through the doors with you?" After what happened last time, I silently added.

"Only if you want to."

I jumped up and grabbed one of the chocolate bars, strangely excited by being allowed into the dreams again.

Dream took my hand in his, and together we walked through the door into darkness. "If I can't get you to leave my world, then you are not leaving my sight again."

CHAPTER TWENTY-TWO

The day went by in a haze of dreams, and so did many, many more days. Happy faces, happy memories, and, thankfully, nothing like the dream I'd first witnessed with Dream. "This is the second most common dream I see," Dream commented as a naked man stood in the middle of a supermarket and looked down. I giggled as shock spread over the poor man's face. One by one, the people surrounding him in the supermarket began to point and laugh. Their laughter only intensified mine, sending me into a fit of giggles as the poor man tried valiantly to cover his cock with a Pringles tube.

"People dream of putting Pringles tubes on their cocks?" I guffawed, trying to breathe between wracking sobs of mirth.

"Public nudity," Dream replied, his teeth gritted,

although I thought I saw a slight upturn at the corner of his mouth.

The guy dropped his tube, and I swear I couldn't take it anymore. Tears streamed down my face.

"Come on. Let's get you out of here. I think you've seen enough."

He caught my arm and half guided, half dragged me from the supermarket dream back into the forest.

"Sorry," I guffawed. How can you not find it funny?"

"Nothing is funny when you've seen it a hundred thousand times. A million times even. The scene you saw plays out hundreds of thousands of times a night. Most people have had that dream at some point in their lives. Young, old, male, female. Sometimes it's in a supermarket, sometimes a place of work. I once had someone dream they were naked on television. It grates after a while."

Only Dream could see something so hilarious and not crack a smile. He had a humor chip missing somewhere.

"What was the first?" I asked as the door slid away from us and another appeared in its place.

"First what?"

You said nudity in public was the second most common dream. What is the first?"

"People's teeth falling out," he answered as he opened another door.

I crumpled up my nose. "Yuck."

"I never said it was a nice dream. Are you coming?"

I followed him inside. Like every other dream I'd seen, this one started off dark. To my utter delight, a library formed around us. Libraries were my one saving grace back in Vancouver. Without any money for books, I spent what little spare time I had reading books from the local library. While this library didn't have the sheer size or style of the huge modern curved library in downtown Vancouver, it more than made up for it in coziness. And though it seemed smaller than the massive building, the rows of books shelves went on and on into the distance, giving me the thrill of my life.

"Oh, this is awesome!" I let out a squeal of delight and ran to the nearest bookshelf. On it were biographies of famous people, mostly from the seventies, though there were some more modern ones I knew. I looked for the occupant of the room. If someone was dreaming this, they had to be here somewhere.

"Jason!"

An old woman's voice rang out from behind me. She ran right past me and enveloped Dream in a hug as I watched on.

She kissed his cheek, leaving a smear of lipstick there. She grabbed a tissue from her pocket, licked it then dabbed it on the mark on his cheek in a caring manner.

"My, you've grown. I swear, you grow an inch taller every time I see you."

Her voice had a Scottish burr to it.

"Have you been eating properly?"

"Yes, mom."

My mouth dropped open in shock, and I did nothing to hide it. This was Dream's mom? This tiny old lady? She was human. In all my imaginings of Dream's origins, never once could I have come up with this particular scenario.

Him being spawned by the devil and born into hellfire, maybe, but this? Color me baffled as fuck.

"Let me find a good book for you. I know how lonely

it can be all alone in the forest..." Her eyes turned to me. "Although you aren't alone, are you? Got yourself a girlfriend? I must say it's about time, Jason. You've been alone a long time."

"You can see me?" I blustered, not understanding a jot of what was going on. In all the doors I'd been through, not once had a person been able to see either Dream or I. And Jason? Dream's name was Jason?"

What. The. Actual. Fuck?

She beamed at me through wrinkled eyes. "Of course, I can, child. Why ever would I not be able to see you?" She turned back to Dream. "She's a beautiful wee thing."

Dream nodded and grinned. Grinned. Like turned his mouth up at the edges and showed his teeth in a way that wasn't threatening. That was it. I was losing it.

"Oh, the book!" She held her hands up as though she'd just remembered. "I don't know if you'll need a book since now you've got a girl to keep you company at night, but I have so many. I'll be right back." My cheeks colored at the implication as she bustled off down one of the aisles.

"She saw you!" I whispered quickly, ignoring the fact she thought I was sleeping with...er...Jason, her son. *Fuck me!*

Dream murmured a light yes, though seemingly unperturbed by the insanity that was going on around us.

"But no one sees you." We'd been in enough people's dreams and fantasies now. I'd have noticed if they'd seen us.

He shrugged. "Some do."

He was so difficult to keep up with, with his two-word answers. I waited for him to elaborate, but he didn't. Of course, he didn't.

"Why do some people see you and others don't?"

"I don't always want to be seen," he replied simply, annoying the hell out of me as was his way.

"So why her? Why an old lady in a library? She's not seriously your mother, right? I mean, you cannot have come from someone as...nice as her."

He laughed. "I like the way her mind works. I like that her dreams are familiar and organized. Most people's are chaotic. and no, she is not my mother."

I tried wrapping my head around it all. "So why did she call you Jason?"

He certainly didn't look like a Jason. Jax maybe or something more exotic. Lucien or Castiel sprang to mind.

"Jason was her son. He died a few years ago of cancer. Since then, she's been dreaming of him."

"So she thinks you are her dead son?" She didn't look the type to have a son that wouldn't be out of place in a BDSM catalog.

"I appear to her as her heart's desire. Those that do see me, don't really. They see what they want to see. In this particular case, she sees her son."

Two conflicting feelings washed around in my gut. The first being that maybe I didn't see him as he was. No wonder everything about him had me in a puddle of lust if I'd conjured his appearance out of my own imagination. The thought made me feel ridiculous and shallow. I wondered if I'd have felt better if my brain had made him into someone more familiar, someone like an old boyfriend, someone comfortable like a favorite pair of old jeans.

I pushed worry about my own psyche away and concentrated on the other feeling fighting for dominance. The way he'd been with the old woman. How patient he'd been with her showed a softer side to him. One I wasn't sure had existed until now. I wasn't sure how I felt about that.

"Here it is," she said, pushing a book into Dream's hands. The cover of the book was a faded yellow without words or pictures on it.

"Thank you, Mom. I'll read it tonight.

"Mind you do. Oh!" Her hand went to her mouth. "I forgot a book for your lovely wee lassie here. Jason, could you be a love and go find one for her. She looks like a wolf shifter type of girl."

"You got me!" I said, holding my hands up. The last book I'd read was indeed a paranormal romance about a wolf shifter running amok in New York before finding his mate. The rest I barely remembered because I'd masturbated to all the sex scenes of which there were many. Not that I was going to admit to it in front of these two.

"Go on then," she said, shooing Dream off down an aisle.

When he was out of earshot, she turned back to me.

"So Dream has a girlfriend. Do you know what you're getting yourself into there, Lassie?"

My eyes widened. "You called him Dream?"

"That's what he is. Och, I know it's not my Jason. I've known for a long, long time. I may be advanced in age, but I'm not senile yet. I know my Jason is long gone; God rest his soul. Dream is a dear and pretends to be him for me, and I pretend to think he's my son, and the pair of us are a little less lonely for it."

Well, hot damn. There was something that lifted my

heart the way she spoke about him. She wasn't his mother, but perhaps she was the closest thing to one he'd had in a long time.

"He's a deep one, though, to be sure. Now don't get me wrong. I love that man as though he were my own flesh and blood, but I'm not sure he's boyfriend material. He's had a life of troubles, and things like that can make a man hard, and not in the good way if you know what I mean." She elbowed me playfully and grinned up at me.

"How long have you known him?" I asked, my curiosity getting the better of me.

Her face softened. "Since he was a wee boy, although I couldn't really speak to him until my Jason died. It was like a silkscreen came down between us. That night I wept in his arms, and he stayed with me for hours. The doctors told me I'd slept for so long because of the sedatives I'd been given, but I knew better." Her voice was wistful. "I see him often now. Once or twice a month at least. I've never seen him with a lassie, though, nor anyone else for that matter. He's a lone wolf; pardon the pun."

"Yeah, I get that."

She narrowed her eyes like she was inspecting me. "I dare say you'll be good for him, though. The boy needs a little light in his life. And it's undeniable, the attraction between the two of you."

I gulped. "There is?" This was news to me. We'd gone from pure hate to begrudging respect, but nothing more. The moment by the lake was long since past.

"Oh, yes, lassie. As I said earlier, I might be old, but my eyes work perfectly. The way he looks at you. It's just like the way my dear Fred used to look at me when we were courting."

I had no time to ponder this over because Dream was back, book in hand. It had a wolf and a title on the cover, but it was one I didn't recognize. When he passed the book over to me, I became all too aware of him. The old woman had tripped a switch in my mind, and I wasn't sure how I was going to be able to turn it off.

His fingertips brushed my fingers as I took the book, and his eyes rested on mine questioningly. He wanted to know if I liked the book he'd chosen. *What did that mean?*

The old lady was lovely, but little did she know she'd sent me into over-analysis hell. I was useless at this stuff. Flirting. It wasn't my thing. I had to have someone outright say they liked me or to literally throw me on their bed and rip my clothes off before I knew for sure. I was going to have analysis paralysis for weeks after this one, and it was something I sure as fuck didn't need.

Dream kissed the woman on her cheek and said his goodbye. The library was already starting to go fuzzy at the edges.

"You take care of each other and Lassie, come see me whenever you like. It will be nice to have some female company for a change."

We made it out of the door just before the woman disappeared entirely in a puff of darkness. The door moved down one place, almost the second Dream closed it behind him. A flutter of pink in the tree above us reflected my happy mood.

"That was Gladys."

I nodded, unsure what to say next. There were so many things swirling around in my brain, not the least of which was the part about Dream actually liking me. I decided to push that part down and start with another question. One that an answer to wouldn't completely fuck up my head.

"Why did she see you?"

He shrugged. "Everyone can see me in their dreams if I want them to. Very few see me when I don't want to be seen."

I strode around the door hoping Dream would follow me back to the camp. He did.

"And you wanted to be seen by Gladys?"

Dream laughed. It was a rare sight. It was nice to see him this way. Gladys must really have been something special to him. "Gladys has a force of will like no one else. She saw me on my very first night doing this job. I usually do not let anyone see me, even though I can. I'm not here to talk to people. That is not my job."

I crossed my legs and picked up a packet of chips we'd left behind. "Gladys told me that you see her quite often but how? There are nine billion people on the planet. It must take centuries to get through them all. How do people dream every night if you take ten minutes with each one?"

I'd not thought about it before, but the logistics of it were a nightmare.

"Time is not the same here as it is in your world. I see everybody's dreams every night. One night in your world is the same as centuries here."

I tried doing the math. It still didn't add up.

"But even if getting through nine billion people a night did take centuries, surely, even after all the time you have been doing this, you still wouldn't have made it through one night? Gladys says she sees you often."

"That is because of you."

Ok, now my mind really was fucked. "You see Gladys regularly because of me?"

"No. I've slowed down because of you. Usually, I work so fast that the doors would appear to be nothing but a blur to you. I cannot speed up or slow down time anywhere other than between the two rows of doors. Where we are here, the doors are still. They only move when I am between the rows. The speed at which they go is up to me. Just like time in your world and mine are different, time between the doors moves differently too."

"I've been here weeks now."

Dream shook his head. "To you, it seems like weeks have passed. If you stepped out of the red door, not a second of time will have elapsed in your world since you came through it."

"Show me. Show me how you make a full night go by in a second."

He smirked. "I cannot. Your body would not cope with the speed. Your frailness as a human would have you reduced to pulp barely seconds after we started."

"So let me sit here and watch you from the outside."

He mulled it over. "If I let a full night pass in your world, won't people worry about you going missing?"

I thought of all the people in my life. It was a depressingly short list. Only Chris would notice if I went missing for any amount of time, but one night. I could risk that.

"Not for one night."

"What about your boyfriend?"

Surprise flooded me. "David *was* my boyfriend. He left me for another woman. Did you not get that from my disaster wedding dreams?"

Urgh. Did I dream about David that often? I couldn't remember dreaming about him at all since coming here. In fact, my dreams had become increasingly taken up by Dream himself. Now that was a thread I didn't want to pick right now.

"I cannot see your dreams while you are in my world."

Thank fuck for that.

"And it is not mine to question what your dreams mean. I don't see nightmares, only dreams, so part of them must have been happy."

In no world was my dream about getting stood up at the altar happy. It had started that way before descending into misery. Maybe it wasn't misery after all and David showing up with Sophie was my brain's way of telling me to get over him. Maybe.

"Well, that dream you saw of mine meant that my scumbag ex dumped me and stole all my money."

"Why?" He seemed genuinely confused. A small part of me gleaned some satisfaction from that.

"She had money, and he's a whore," I replied, not bothering to keep the bitterness out of my voice.

I expected some kind of reaction to a statement like that, but he sat impassively as he usually did.

"Come with me." He stood up and held his hand out to me. A shiver of something ran through me as I reached out and took it. I'd held his hand before when we were running through the woods, but this time, it was different. There was no reason for us to be holding hands. We just were.

I followed him without question as he led me to the red door. My heart began to hammer as we walked right up to it and the thought that he was going to send me home filled my thoughts. But he veered slightly to the right and walked right past it.

I'd never gone beyond the red door. The movement of the doors implied that the dreams had already passed, that the people having them had already woken up.

The forest here was exactly the same as it was in front of the red door, but being behind it gave me the chills. The place felt forbidden somehow. Colder. The parallel rows of doors disappeared into the darkness, just as the ones in front of the red door did.

"Stand really still." Dream instructed, positioning me at equal distance between the two rows of doors.

The fear I'd felt at him making me go home was taken over by anticipation. He wrapped me up in his arms, pulling me close to him. One hand lay on the middle of my back, the other pulling my head down to his shoulder so that I was completely wrapped in him. I was so close to him that I could feel his heart beating beneath his chest, a percussion mixing with mine. There was something safe about his arms around me, as though he was about to protect me from something, but it was far from safe. Being this close to him was like jumping from the frying pan into the fire, and it was beginning to burn. A warm flush spread out through my body. If I'd have inclined my head slightly, I'd have been able to kiss him. As it was, my head was clamped to him, and I couldn't move, could barely breathe.

What the fuck was happening?

And just as a burn of heat threatened to take over my body completely, a ferocious gust of wind whistled past us, extinguishing the flames and nearly sending me into a catatonic state of fright. The wind was strong enough to tear down houses, and yet I was unmoving because of Dream. He withstood it with barely any movement at all. I tried to make sense of what I was seeing through my hair whipping around my eyes, but everything was a blur of speed. The roar was deafening, and it was all I could do to cling to him in the hope that he could withstand it because if he couldn't, the both of us would be dead.

It became painfully clear why Dream was holding me so tightly. If he let go, I'd fly away. If I held my arm out from the protection of his body, I was sure it would snap like a twig. And then it stopped, and the roaring quietened to the usual silence of the forest. My hair fell back down around my shoulders, and everything was back to normal. Dream loosened his grip on me, and with some reluctance, I pulled away from his embrace.

I looked around us. Nothing had changed. Everything was as it had been before the surge of wind just minutes before.

"What the fuck just happened," I murmured, breaking any kind of spell that had me thinking there'd been a moment between us. I was good at shit like that. Misreading signs and generally always second-guessing myself when it came to intimacy of any kind. Or mistaking almost dying in a weird as fuck windstorm as intimacy. Yep, I was *really* good at that.

He opened the nearest door and gestured for me to go inside. This was my first time in one of the doors that had gone past the red door, and the fact that he wanted me to go through first raised goosebumps on my flesh.

"What's in there?" I asked because I couldn't do anything without questioning it first.

He just smiled and nodded toward it again as he held open the door for me.

Inside it was black, exactly as I expected it to be.

"I thought that the people belonging to these dreams woke up after they went past the red door."

"They do," he confirmed. "Call this a playback."

Huh. "Why are we watching a dream you've already seen?"

"You'll see, look."

The darkness started to clear and a picture formed around me. This was not a dream I'd seen. We were standing in an apartment. A really nice apartment. Whoever lived here had money. The view from the window let me know I was looking at somewhere in Vancouver.

A door opened, and a woman in a smart dress appeared. Immediately my stomach lurched. I'd recognize that scraggly hair and bitch-face anywhere. It was Sophie. Why the fuck had Dream brought me to Sophie's apartment? What was he playing at? Less than a second later, David followed the woman, and my nightmare was complete. She was talking to him. It looked like she was giving him instructions as she was crossing items off a list. I studied David's face. He was not happy. He never did like being told what to do. I held my breath as their voices became loud enough for me to hear.

"I'm going to need you to pick up the flowers," Sophie ordered, "and I've got Mother coming round later to make sure that your outfit for the wedding is perfect. I don't trust you to get it right."

David nodded his head slowly, misery filling his features. "Okay."

Sophie checked it off her list. "Oh, and the caterers

want to come and have us taste some samples later. I'll need you here at 7:00 p.m."

"I'm going out tonight. I've got a game with the lads."

Sophie turned on her heel and glared at him. "No." That was it. Just one word. No discussion. She walked to another door and opened it. "I'll see you here at 7:00 p.m. Have a nice day, sweetheart."

She kissed the air between them.

"Have a nice day, sweetheart." David echoed back, but I could tell from his voice that he didn't mean it. He'd given up. I could see it in his face. There was no sense of happiness at all in him. He flopped down on the sofa and brought out his phone. It was one I hadn't seen before. The most recent iPhone. A definite upgrade from the crappy phone he had when he was with me. He used his thumb to turn it on and pressed the gallery button. The first picture was of a wedding cake, obviously part of the wedding plans. He quickly scrolled back. Going so quickly that every picture was a blur. I gasped when I saw where the pictures had come to a rest. It was the last picture he and I had taken together. A selfie near the waterfront less than two days before he left me. I remembered the day well. I'd felt hope then. The sun had been shining, and even though we couldn't afford it, we'd gone out for dinner. If this was a new phone, he'd purposely brought these photos across from his old phone. He used two of his fingers and pushed them away from each other, enlarging the picture so that it rested on my face. And then he stared. My heart went to my throat as I saw tears trickling down his face. David never cried. Not once in the three years that we had been together had I ever seen this kind of emotion on his face. I stood stock-still as he carried on scrolling through the pictures stopping at each one of us together. My heart almost stopped. The pain I felt was indescribable. He'd let me go, giving me up like an old shoe, and yet, he was no happier in his new life surrounded by fancy furniture and expensive gadgets.

"He misses me," I whispered.

The dream began to darken, telling me that it was almost over. Dream took my hand, but this time I didn't follow. I couldn't. I wanted to see more of what David was doing. I wanted to know that I had meant something to him.

Dream pulled gently on my hand. "We can't stay here. The dream is ended. It's over." He virtually had to drag me back out into the forest

"Why did you do that?" I screamed at him, my heart shattering into a thousand pieces. "Why did you bring me here?"

Dream took a step back. "I wanted to show you how much of an idiot David was. How wrong he got it. I wanted you to know that you are worth something."

That was fine for him to say. I'd never felt more worthless in my whole life. My breath was squeezed from me. I doubled over, not wanting to show so much emotion. Not wanting Dream to see how much that had affected me. Pain mixed with loathing took over my body as I descended into sobs. *Fucking fuck! I hated crying.* I was doing it again, letting the memory of the man I once loved take over. And that was the thing. I did love him once. But that was a long time ago. Things had changed. I had changed. This pain wasn't because I wanted David back. It was because he'd made a decision that had set us both on a course of misery. *Christ, it pissed me off!* I felt Dreams hand on my shoulder and looked up this time. When he embraced me, it had nothing to do with the moving doors. There was no roaring wind. Dream had brought me to the one dream he knew I needed to see. His fingers stroked through my hair as my body shook against his. I didn't even know why I was crying anymore. Angry as fuck tears, probably. It might have been David that started the tears. But I was crying for a past me. It was the realization that David was completely in my past. That had set me off. And the pain I was feeling, while intense, was a lot duller than it had been weeks before. Dream was soothing it away. I raised my head, and his eyes met mine.

"I don't love the cheating scumball anymore," I whispered.

It was almost as much of a shock to me to hear it said out loud as it was to him. He wiped my tears away with his thumb. My eyes focused on his lips, so close to mine. It was all I could do to breathe. And yet, I knew that if I didn't kiss him right there right then. I would regret it.

Because the grief I was feeling was not over David at all. It was the thought that I didn't belong here, that I had never belonged here. And that one day, I would have to go back through the red door. I'd have to go through it alone. There was no David on the other side for me even if I did want him, which I didn't. And there wasn't anyone on this side for me... except... Dream's hands were on each side of my face now. His lips so close to mine. Inches away. My body swirled in emotion. Not that long ago, I had wanted to kill him. Today I couldn't imagine a life without him. I leaned into it. Needed it, even though I knew I shouldn't. We were enemies, but I'd never wanted anybody so badly. Dream's hands moved down, and he pulled me toward him, and in that quick movement, his lips met mine. The doors once again roared past us, and my hair flew about us, but all I could feel was him holding me to him, taking over my senses as our lips crushed together. It was ferocious and fierce and wholly the best damn kiss I've ever experienced. If Dream hadn't kissed anyone before me, I couldn't tell. There was nothing measured or precise in his movements, but that was what made it all the more exciting. I didn't care about the wind whipping around my face, nor the dreams of a hundred thousand people literally flying past us with us caught up in the middle, a port in the storm. He was both the port and the storm and everything else, and I was windswept and horny and caught up in it all.

Just like that, the doors stopped. The forest was empty and silent, and everything was how it was before. And the moment was over before it had really begun. He pulled back, a manic look in his eyes. This was not the look of a man who had just had his first kiss. It was the face of a man who had leapt into danger and fallen into the abyss. He turned and stormed off past the red door and back to the clearing, leaving me completely alone, confused and with tingling lips and the memory of the hottest kiss of my life.

CHAPTER TWENTY-THREE

I didn't move. Uncertainty had me bolted to the ground. I could just about see Dream through the gap in between the doors. He was less than ten feet away from me, but walking the distance was proving difficult. We'd kissed. The thought filled me with horror. Horror because I'd wanted it. God help me, I shouldn't have. Dream was my enemy. Maybe we didn't want to kill each other anymore, but we were hardly friends, let alone more than that. But in the moment, I'd let the grief over David take over any common sense I had. And I recklessly leaned into the kiss. How stupid was I? Dream had never wanted to kiss me. He'd never shown any sign of being interested in me in that way at all. Quite the opposite. He'd only ever told me that me and my kind were terrible beings and like the idiot I was,

I'd fallen into him like a desperate woman, trying to get over an ex-boyfriend, which is exactly what I' was, but it hadn't just been my fault. He'd taken me back to David, even if it was only a dream. He was the one who put me in this emotional state. I'd been getting over my scummy ex. I'd been forgetting the bastard. What fucking right did Dream have to take me back to that place again? None at all. If I had developed feelings for the tortured bastard, it was his own fucking fault.

That was all well and good, but I had to walk back to him and sit opposite him around the campfire and act as though everything was normal and as though my whole life hadn't just been sent off-kilter by a kiss that had horrified him as much as it had blindsided me. I watched as he made a campfire for us, his face showing no sign of emotion at all.

Oh fuck. What if he was only trying to hold me to stop me from flying away in the wind, and I'd misread it and started kissing him. Mortification filled my soul until I ran it through in my mind. He'd definitely kissed me first, not the other way around. So why was it that his face looked like he'd been sucking on a lemon? Fine, if he could pretend nothing had happened between us, then I could too. I wiped away the last of my tears on my sleeve, took a deep breath, and pulled myself up straight.

He poked at the fire with a stick as I sat, purposely avoiding my gaze. I sat in my usual spot, waiting for him to look up at me. The silence was like a chasm between us, offset only by the slight rustling of the leaves above us as Raven shifted his position on a branch.

"Nice..."

"If you say nice weather we're having, I'm going to stand up and walk out of this clearing."

Right then, that's how it's going to be.

I cleared my throat, my gut tightening. "I was going to say nice fire, actually, but if we are going to be weird about what just happened, then I may as well say what I'm really thinking."

He stood up, his face taking on a decidedly sour look. "It can't happen. None of this can happen."

I took a breath, trying to steady the nerves that were threatening to overcome me. I'd not felt this shy since I asked out Kenny Henderson in eighth grade. At least when Kenny had turned me down, I only had to face the rest of our class giggling at me. I'd take that a million times over the mortification of where this conversation was going.

"Fine. Nothing happened. We didn't just kiss. You didn't just hold onto me like your life depended on it." I stood up and planted a hard stare on his face.

Dream couldn't look me in the eye. Where was the arrogant bully I'd met only a few weeks ago? "You should go back to your boyfriend. He obviously misses you."

My mouth fell open. "Are you fucking insane? In what fucked up world is it that someone would kiss you the way I kissed you and want to go back to a sleazeball ex?"

"It's my world, Ana." He said, his voice rising in anger. "My world that you are not a part of. A world you have no right to be in and one where you do not belong."

Anger tugged at me. If he could raise his voice, then so could I. It wasn't like anyone could hear us this far out in the forest anyway.

"I didn't ask to be here!" I yelled. "You brought me here."

His gaze finally landed on mine. The firelight danced

in the reflection of his eyes, giving him a manic look. "So go home. The door is right there."

I stood my ground, hands on hips. I didn't even know why I cared so much that he kissed me. I barely knew him, and the short time we'd been together, he'd kept me tied up for most of it. I should hate his sorry ass, and I did. I hated him with a passion, but that passion had a flip side, and the flip side was burning me up. "I'm not leaving. I told you. I'm only going through that door if you pick me up and throw me through it."

My voice echoed through the forest. Dream's eyes were full of hatred now. I'd not seen him look so cold at me since the first time I'd come through the door. My heart was ripping at the seams from the coldness of his stare. How had I misjudged this all so badly?

"Is that what you want? Because it can be arranged." he snapped.

I swallowed thickly. It wasn't what I wanted. None of this was what I wanted.

He walked right through the fire, which didn't seem to bother him in the slightest, and grabbed me roughly. My world shifted as he whisked me up into his arms. It would be romantic if his eyes weren't ablaze with anger.

I punched at his chest, which was absolutely fucking pointless. Like hitting a steel wall with a rubber duck. He barely noticed my fists as he carried me over to the red door.

This was it. He was going to throw me through the door, and all of this would be over. He kicked the door with his foot. It flew open to my shitty bedroom in my shitty apartment.

"You are a fucking coward," I yelled. "One kiss, and you are terrified. The wolveries never bothered you, even though they were maniacal killing beasts, but kissing me has you so scared you only know how to throw me away, just like you've thrown everyone else away. You know what. Throw me away like trash. See if I care. I'll go back to my shitty life, but even with no money and nothing, I'll still be richer than you stuck here in the darkness with only a fucking bird for company. Why is he even still here? You've just not bothered to discard him like every other fucker"

"Stop it!" he roared, twisting my insides further. "Shut the fuck up!"

In any other circumstance, I would have thought his choice of words amusing. Saying 'fuck' didn't suit him at all. He let me go, dropping me to the ground inches from the red door.

"Why do you do this to me, Ana? This is torture. I am alive because of you, and I am suffocating because of you."

"Me?" I exclaimed. "Me, torturing you? My mother is locked in her own mind because of you. Not just her, but hundreds of thousands of other people, and you have the gall to tell me I'm the torturer here. Why don't you take a long, hard look in a fucking mirror."

His eyes widened slightly then he lowered his eyelashes. Without saying another word, he turned and stalked away into the darkness.

My breath caught in my throat as I watched the darkness swallow him up. My heart was ripping in two, and I could barely catch my breath. Behind me, the light from my room shone through the red door, giving the forest a little color. It would be so easy to go back home. The sun was shining in through my bedroom window, and though my room was fairly bland, it was a riot of color compared to the forest. I inched closer to the door. One more footstep, and I'd be home. Back to a world where I could get a good burger and fries and not have to eat charbroiled monkeyrabbit in pitch blackness.

Why the fuck was it so hard to step through that door? It had everything this shit-hole didn't. Light, color, my job, my friends...ok, friend. Dream didn't want me. He'd made that perfectly clear, and what was also clear to me was that he was a fucked-up asshole who would never let my mother go. Years of being on his own had turned him into a monster. Maybe he'd always been one, and that was the reason he was on his own in the first place.

I put one foot through the door. Dream was wrong. There wasn't a chance in hell I was going to go back to David, but I was going to sort myself out. I owed it to my mom and my sister. I was going to give up the apartment, move back to Winnipeg and finally be the daughter my mother deserved.

Pain and grief overwhelmed me as I took the second step into my room. I was finally home...So why didn't it feel like it?

The red door began to close behind me. Once it closed fully, my only portal to the Realm of Night would be gone forever. I steeled myself against the grief, waiting for the click that would signal the door hitting the frame. I wasn't going to turn around and watch it. This was hard enough without seeing my pathway between worlds close.

A deep guttural scream filled the air.

CHAPTER TWENTY-FOUR

I whirled around, slipping my fingers through the half-inch gap between the door and the frame. Half a second longer and the door would have been closed. I slammed it open, almost falling back through it into the forest. Dream's screams were like something out of my worst nightmares. He'd not made a sound when the wolveries attacked, so what the hell could make him howl in pain now? Could he be feeling the same grief I was? Could his howls be . . . over me?

As soon as the idea surfaced, I dashed it. It was a fucking ridiculous notion that needed to be buried in my brain and never see the light of day again. His screams were way beyond emotional pain. Something was attacking him. Something worse than wolveries. I skidded around the gray door frames and came face to face with the most terrifying scene I'd ever witnessed.

Not even in my worst nightmare could I conjure a creature so terrifying. It made the wolveries look like cute puppies in comparison. It was all muscle and teeth and hair and horns and like nothing I'd ever seen before or ever wanted to see again. It was shaped almost like a man if you ignored the cat-like snout, glowing horns bristling down its back, and two blue eyes that shone eerily in the darkness. Although its body was very, very real, the parts that made it a monster, the parts that glowed, were see-through, almost ghostlike, as though a ripped human being was wearing clothes made from a glowing monster on top of it. Human or monster, it had Dream's leg clenched between its teeth and was already dragging him off into the forest.

I chased after them, struggling to catch my breath as they thundered through the trees.

Oh hell. What was it with everything in this place with superhuman strength and speed? I had no hope in hell of catching up to them, and yet I pushed through the dizziness and lack of breath, using muscles I'd forgotten I had, trying to keep them in sight. It didn't help that everywhere in the forest was darker than my ex's heart. Wherever the Nightwalker was taking Dream, it wasn't back to the Village. It wasn't to anywhere I had been before. The thickness of the Canopy above me increased, and the leaves blocked out the small glow of moonlight, leaving me almost blind.

But I could still hear them ahead. Dream's anguished screams as he was dragged across the forest floor sliced through the quiet of the night and filled me with panic.

"Mother fucker!" I panted as lower tree branches

whipped into my face. I was losing them. I didn't stop or slow down, but I could no longer hear Dream screaming, nor could I hear the sound of the Nightwalker dragging him through the forest. The silence deafened me, but stopping wasn't an option. I was in the middle of the woods all by myself in almost complete darkness, and fuck only knew where I was supposed to go next. I was well and truly lost.

"Dream!" I shouted out his name, hoping he would hear my voice and shout back, but my own voice echoed through the darkness. There was no reply.

My heart thundered in my chest as I bent to my knees to get my breath back.

I was in no fit state for this. Years of doing no exercise and eating, what was, quite frankly, a disgusting diet of greasy fast food, and in later months, not much at all, was not conducive to hauling ass through a forest after a motherfucking super-strength monster. If I got through this, I was going to have to take an exercise class or some such shit and maybe eat a vegetable or two.

"When," I corrected myself. *When* I got through this, not if. Because even though I couldn't see a bloody thing and the silence of the forest was thickly draped around me, I was still alive.

I closed my eyes. The same couldn't be said for Dream. At least, I had no way of knowing if he was still alive. I hadn't thought anything could rattle that man. Well, kissing me had rattled him, but the screams he'd produced when the Nightwalker had dragged him off through the forest were branded into my brain. Panic settled around my gut, adding to the overall sickness I felt at overdoing it. If Dream had died at the hands claws of the Nightwalker, then our world would eventually collapse. This world would collapse. *And Dream would no longer exist,* a small voice piped up in my mind. A strangled sob escaped my throat, amplified in the silence. Why the fuck did I even care? He wanted me gone. I should have gone. I almost had. Surely the people of this world could figure something out. What kind of weird-ass world would put so much responsibility on one person? Maybe everything Aethelu and Dream had told me was utter bullshit, and I'd fallen for it like a naive idiot.

I hated the thoughts that were spiraling through my mind, but anything was better than thinking about the predicament I currently found myself in. Lost in the darkest part of the forest with a bloodthirsty killing machine somewhere out there, not to mention the wolveries and fuck knew what else that might think I'd make a tasty snack. Going back, although an option, wasn't necessarily the best one. Maybe I couldn't save Dream. I certainly couldn't if I couldn't find him, which was looking more and more unlikely with each passing minute. But we'd twisted and turned so much that I doubted my ability to ever find the red door again. There was nowhere to go but forward.

I put one foot in front of the other and walked onwards, this time more slowly so I wouldn't add to the numerous cuts the branches had produced on my face. I hadn't walked far when my foot caught in something, sending me toppling to the ground.

"Fuck," I hissed, rubbing my knee where it had

hit the ground.

"Ana." The voice was faint, but it was unmistakable. Dream! I'd gone ass over tit over Dream's leg. I bent down and ran my hand up his chest, and when I brought it away, there was something sticky. I couldn't see what it was, but I didn't need to see to know that it was blood. "Dream, are you okay?" I asked frantically. "Use your healing magic!"

"Ana," he repeated quietly, his voice a hoarse whisper. He was not okay. Even in the dark, it was obvious, but what could I do? He'd carried me through the forest when the wolveries attacked, but he was much stronger than me. Much heavier. Much quicker. There was no way I could lift him. Nor would I know where to take him if I could. It was so dark I could barely see him. Clamping my hand against his chest to stem the flow of blood, I ripped off a layer of my dress, balled it up, and jammed it against where I thought the blood was coming from.

He groaned.

"Why aren't you healing?" I cried urgently. He had healing magic. Why wasn't he using it? "Come on! Do something." Panic laced my voice, but it was no use shouting at him. The guy was barely breathing. Whatever had attacked him had managed to bypass his healing magic. Or he'd been so badly injured that no magic could save him, and it was too late. A sob caught in my throat at the thought of it. "You'll be okay," I murmured through the tears falling down my face. "I won't let you die." The moment the words escaped my lips, I knew it was a lie. He probably wouldn't be okay. I couldn't help him. I didn't even know if the Nightwalker was still nearby. It was all I could do to sit next to him and try to stem the flow of blood escaping his chest.

The forest around us was eerily quiet. The Nightwalker was gone, for now at least, but who knew when it would come back to finish off its dinner? Reaching down, I rummaged around Dream's boot. His knife was still there. I pulled it out and gripped the handle tightly, ready for when the Nightwalker came back. I was no match for the monster, but I wasn't going to go down without a motherfucking fight. With my other hand, I clasped Dream's. It was cold. Dangerously so. His body was going into shock, and I had no idea what to do. Wasn't giving someone sweet tea a way to stop shock? The question was moot. I had no tea, sweet or otherwise. All I had was myself. Unlike Dream, I was hot and sweaty after the hours-long dash through the forest. At least I could share my body warmth with him.

I bent over him and wrapped my arms around his naked chest, shuffling as close to him as I could. He shivered beneath my touch but didn't speak. His breathing was labored, but at this point, I was just grateful he *was* breathing. His whole body quaked against mine, and his skin was like marble to the touch. Cold and hard.

"Ana," he mumbled, almost slurring my name.

"I'm here," I whispered back, but there was no more response from him. "Dream, can you hear me?" No answer. I put my hand on his chest, needing to feel it rising and falling to reassure myself. I left my arm draped across his chest, scared that if I took it off for a second, he would die, as if my arm could stop such a thing. I didn't want to lose him.

Fuck! I really didn't! Everyone's existence depended on him surviving. That was the reason... the only reason... Damnit, maybe it wasn't the only reason.

I closed my eyes and snuggled against him, wishing

that my small body could stop the quakes in his. I closed my eyes and let myself fall into an uneasy sleep.

I awoke with a start. Dream hadn't moved, but his shivering had subsided a little. There was no way of telling how much time had passed since we'd both fallen asleep. It seemed to be a bit lighter now, though that could be because my eyes had gotten used to the darkness. I narrowed them, squeezing them together to try and take in all the light possible so I could see where we were. All I could make out were the outlines of the trees. More infernal trees.

The nightwalker hadn't returned, and I didn't know why. It must have known that Dream would still be here. He was an easy target. I didn't even know why it hadn't killed him in the first place, though perhaps it thought it had. The thought made me shiver. It meant the beast was only out to kill Dream and not to eat him. Like everything else in this goddamned world, it was another question I'd have to put on the back burner for another time. *If* there was going to be another time. As it was, I was lost in the middle of a never-ending forest in almost pitch black with a man who was on the edge of death and wouldn't have been able to walk out of there if he was awake enough to want to...which he wasn't. I blinked a few times, trying to get used to the light, and checked Dream's chest. I could see it now. The ripped dress I used to cover his wound was saturated in blood, but it was dry, which gave me hope that his healing powers had kicked in. I felt his brow with the back of my hand and winced at how hot it was. I was no doctor, but hot was worse than cold. Hot meant an infection of some kind. Back home, I would have gone to a doctor or a pharmacy, but here there was nothing. I knew nothing about trees or leaves or medicinal herbs. Maybe Aethelu did. She seemed the type to know about that kind of thing, but I didn't know where Aethelu was, and I could no more have found my way back to the Village from here than I could find my way back to the red door.

I would have to find my way somewhere at some point, but for right now, I mopped up Dream's brow with the sleeve of my dress. More to give me something to do than to actually help him in any way. He needed water, but I'd not crossed a stream the whole time I'd been chasing after him. An idea dawned on me. There was the lake. I'd started running after Dream and the Nightwalker in the general direction of the lake. Granted, we'd twisted and turned a lot, but the lake was huge. If I kept on walking, I'd have to hit it at some point. Leaving Dream alone scared the hell out of me, but it was either that or we both die here in the darkness. I stood carefully, whispering to him in the darkness, "I'll be back. I promise."

He didn't respond—his shallow breathing was the only sign of life.

CHAPTER TWENTY-FIVE

I took it slowly, trying to remember every tree, memorizing the small details for the journey I would have to make back.

By some miracle, I hit the lake less than half an hour later. My senses had been right on the ball. I guess there was a first time for everything.

Just seeing the water was like a balm to my soul. If I could find my way here on my own, maybe, just maybe, I could get us both out of this mess. I pulled my dress over my head and flung it on the black sand, following it up with the long bloomers Aethelu had given me. I wasn't going to be winning any prizes for sexy underwear anytime soon, that was for sure. Cursing myself for even thinking it, I jumped in the warm water, letting it wash over me. I ducked under, taking a few gulps for good measure. There was magic in this water. Warmth flooded me, soothing my aching muscles. If I could bottle this stuff and take it through the red door, I'd be a millionaire in no time. No, a billionaire. The Kardashians would be kissing my rich-as-fuck ass. It was a nice thought, but I had bigger fish to fry; namely, he who hated my guts, bleeding out or dying of some weird infection.

I picked up the dry dress and, using Dream's knife, ripped another part of it off. If I wasn't careful, there'd be none left for me to wear. As it was, I looked like a Mary Quant model from the sixties with the ragged hem of the fabric now skirting my upper thigh. Reluctantly I pulled the bloomers on and, not for the first time, was glad that no one could see me.

I dipped the part of the dress I'd ripped off in the water, saturating it. This time I ran through the forest. I'd kept to a straight line as much as possible so that following it back wouldn't be so difficult.

Eventually, I slowed down until I was close, and it didn't take me long to find Dream from there. The balled-up fabric was only slightly damp by the time I got to him, but it would have to do. I wrung out what little water was still in it over his lips, wetting them and hoping it would have the same regenerative qualities that it had on me. I placed the wet rag upon Dream's burning brow. I could almost hear a sizzle as the cool lake water reacted with the heat he was giving off. It was unnatural and terrifying all in one. Had I had one, I could have cooked an egg on his forehead. I didn't know why I was surprised. He never did anything by halves. Why not have an infection that could boil water?

He murmured, and my heart jumped. *How the hell was he conscious with the heat he was giving off?*

"It's me," I whispered, finding my best soothing voice I usually only reserved for puppies and my local taco stallholder when I was angling for a free taco. "It's fine, I assured him. "I went to the lake. I got you some water."

"Go away," he mumbled back without even opening his eyes.

Motherfuckingfucker. Can't a girl tend to a supernatural dude without him being a bastard for once? It hadn't occurred to me that he wouldn't want my help, although I should have known, going by our past interactions. It was a bitter pill to swallow, that even half-dead, barely on the brink of consciousness, he still didn't want me around. *Way to go, Ana. You sure know how to push the boys away.*

"Go where?" I replied, my soothing tone slipping slightly. "I've just come back. I told you I went to the lake."

He shook his head, knocking the wet rag to the ground. I picked it back up and clamped it back on his forehead.

"Stay still," I demanded, just like an old matron.

"Go away," he mumbled again. "Not safe."

He was delirious and apparently wanted me to leave for *my* safety. I ignored the small leap of my heart when I realized he wasn't just pushing me away for the sake of it. I couldn't leave him. He must know that if I left him, he would die. Without someone taking care of him, he wasn't strong enough to go anywhere.

"You looked after me when the wolveries attacked me," I reminded him in the hope this wasn't going to turn into some kind of argument. "Now it's my turn to look after you."

He mumbled something, but this time it was incoherent. He was losing consciousness again. My courage bottomed out, and the small shred of hope I'd been clinging to flitted away like a dandelion clock on the breeze. It hit me then, just how fucked the pair of us were. Even if the nightwalker didn't come back, or if a wolvery didn't happen to cross our path, there was every chance Dream was going to die. My ministrations were making him more comfortable, but I doubted they were doing much more than that. The thought of Dream dying ran through my brain and my heart like a soul-obliterating steam train, annihilating any semblance of hope in its path.

I lay next to him, wishing I'd have thought to let my dress soak in the water before coming back. At least then, me lying next to him would cool him off rather than heat him up. The irrational fear that if I moved too far away from him, he'd die took over me again, like I was somehow tethering him to this mortal coil. Utter bullshit. I knew that, and yet the fear of letting him go, even for a second, filled my every pore. I was going to hold his mother fucking soul in his body as though my life depended on it...which it did...mine and literally everyone else's. If death came knocking, you could be sure I was going to stab its scary-ass eyes.

I lay with him for hours, and not once did he regain consciousness. His breathing evened out as the afternoon, or night or whatever it was, passed, and by some miracle, his temperature went from supernova to merely volcanic. At least the nightwalkers had not returned. Every second we were alone was an extra second that Dream was able to get stronger, and though our chances were slim, I was beginning to hope that maybe we would manage to get out of this after all. If I could only help Dream to the lake.

Its restorative powers had helped me; they would help him too. But we were a long way from that. Days at least. He was way too heavy for me to carry, being the great hulk of a brute he was, so I was stuck there with him.

I looked down upon his sleeping face. He had a beauty, even in sleep, that left me breathless. I wondered who it was that watched his dreams, or even if he dreamed at all.

When I slept, I slept next to him, and when I went foraging for berries, I never went too far. For all his strength, without me, he would die. What a fucking god-awful position to be in. I was pretty much the only thing that stood between the world surviving or the entire human race dying out if what Aethelu said was true. And McGee wouldn't even let me be in charge of the sleep clinic for one night. Well, screw you, McGee! The enormity of my situation didn't escape me, but for all the weight on my shoulders, it was only Dream that took up space in my head. I couldn't think beyond him dying. If that happened... Fuck. I needed to get a grip on myself. If he died, everyone in my world and this world would cease to exist. His personal part in his death shouldn't even play a part in my feelings. It wasn't about him...So why did my heart leap every time his eyes flickered slightly? Why did the thought of him dying create a deathly black hole in my heart bigger than this damn never-ending forest? Why the fuck did I kiss him at all? Because however much I hated to admit it, I was beginning to feel something for him. Something dangerous. He was a demon under the skin of an angel. I couldn't forget that. I couldn't let myself forget it.

The next day was exactly the same. I took another trip to the lake, but this time I soaked my whole dress so that when I lay next to him, the whole thing would cool him down. Laying beside him, my small body curved around his huge frame felt as natural as breathing, but I had to remind myself I was doing it for him, not for me. I did it on the first night to keep him warm, then on subsequent nights to cool his flaming skin. Throughout the days, he never woke, though he continued breathing. His chest still rose and fell, and with each rise, my hopes rose along with it that he would survive this thing, whatever it was.

On the third day, he finally began to stir. By now, my eyes had become so accustomed to the darkness that I could see his face perfectly. He was so beautiful, even in sickness. Seeing him so frail squeezed my heart. This wasn't how things were meant to be. He was the strongest man I'd ever met. He literally kept the world going. If anyone should be lying injured in the forest,

it should be me. Then I remembered it had been me.

Dream had taken care of me. Begrudgingly so, maybe, but I'd survived.

He called my name, and this time, his eyes opened.

I gave him a smile. "You're back in the land of the living."

"I should be dead," he responded, his voice empty of any emotion. For some reason, his words stung more than the thought of him dying.

"I saved you. You have an infection somewhere. You had a fever. I thought you were going to die."

He tried moving, but the pain in his face was obvious.

"Stay still," I demanded, holding my hand against his chest. He was too weak to even push against me.

"The savagara," he said, looking around him, his eyes assessing the forest.

"You mean the nightwalker? It isn't here," I replied. "We've been here three days, and I haven't seen it."

"Three days?" he croaked. We've been here three days?" Confusion painted his features. "Why did it not finish the job and kill me?"

I shrugged. I didn't know what to tell him. "I don't know. I just found you here unconscious. We are near the lake. It's about half an hour in that direction, so if you need water, I can get some for you. I've been going every day for the last three days."

He closed his eyes and rested his head against the floor, letting out a little breath.

"That was insanely stupid. You should have stayed back at the camp."

You're welcome, Asshat

"And let you die? Besides, being at the camp isn't any safer than it is here. Twice, nightwalkers have attacked, and twice, they've got us at the camp. If anything, the camp is the least safe place I've seen here in this world."

"Then you should have gone through the red 'door. You should have gone home."

I didn't want to tell him that it wasn't home anymore. This was my home now, but I couldn't because it sounded ridiculous even to my own ears. This couldn't be home. There was no color, no light. I couldn't even believe I was thinking it. But then a small voice in my head said no, not the world. Him

I brushed it off. Now was not the time for "I'm picking apart my insane, irrational feelings for Dream." We were both still in danger. And though I didn't understand why, I didn't need to.

"I can't leave you now. Not like this. The nightwalker—the savagara or whatever you called it might come back to finish what it started."

"That's exactly what worries me, Ana. You are in this world because of my own arrogance and stupidity. I cannot have your death on my hands. I don't think I would be able to bear it."

He wouldn't be able to bear me dying? Well, that was new. New and weird and vaguely exciting.

"You want me to go?" I bluffed. "I can go right now and leave you in this bloody mess. It's not like you can actually stand up or walk or anything. Leaving would be so easy right now."

It was an outrageous lie. Leaving him alone in the state he was in would destroy me.

He sighed. "That's not going to happen. I can't defend you against what's out there if you leave. From now on, you are not leaving my sight."

Nothing new there, buddy.

"You said the lake was half an hour away? Take me there."

I gritted my teeth. "You are a cocky bastard for someone who's been unconscious for the last three days. You're not fit to walk. You've lost a lot of blood. You need rest."

"Get me to the lake then," he insisted. "I will recuperate better there than here."

Every part of me screamed how dangerous it was and how unlikely it was that he would be able to make it to the lake, even with my help. But there was no stopping him. Even in the state he was in, he was stronger than I was, and pushing him down to the ground was having no effect. He merely pushed back harder.

"Goddammit. Will you stay where you are. Half your chest is missing. This is madness!" I huffed, using every bit of strength I had to fight him.

"Madness would be to stay here," he huffed. Each word ground on his breath, causing a sickening rattling sound from his lungs. "I didn't want to admit it, but now that my brother knows you are here, he will not stop."

His brother? What did his brother have to do with all this?

He grimaced in pain, and I let go of him after realizing I was making him worse. He groaned as he pulled himself upright, using a tree trunk to steady himself.

I hooked his arm over my shoulder, feeling his weight pushing me down, and the two of us began a sluggish pace toward the lake.

Neither of us spoke as we walked, but with every footstep, he grunted in pain.

The pain he was in must have been indescribable. What worried me the most was that the movement would start the bleeding again, and I didn't have anything to stem it. The bloodied makeshift bandage had been saturated with so much blood that I'd taken it off on the second night to get air to the wound. Not that the word wound came close to describing the pulverized mess of his chest. Part of me was glad for the eternal night because I couldn't see the full extent of his injury. It looked bad enough in the dark.

By the time we got to the lake, I was practically carrying him, a feat in itself. We both collapsed on the black sand beach, and once again, Dream fell into unconsciousness.

CHAPTER TWENTY-SIX

Fear washed over me at the sight of him. In the darkness, I'd not really seen how bad his chest was, but with the extra moonlight here on the beach, the enormity of his injuries hit me like a brick to the face. Teeth marks had ravaged his chest. From just below his neck to just above his stomach, there was no skin left, just ragged bits of wet flesh. Beneath that, bone poked through, and, *Christ Almighty*, I could see one of his lungs. I swallowed thickly to stop from throwing up on the beach at the sight of it. There was no way he should be alive. It wasn't possible, and yet the lung I could see was still moving up and down, in and out. Miracle didn't cover it. It brought it home to me just how strong he really was. A normal human would not have been able to survive injuries as extensive as this, let alone walk for half an hour. The real miracle was that his lung didn't just plop out en route. It was only his rib cage that kept it from doing just that.

I ripped off another part of my dress and dipped it in the lake water. I was basically wearing threads and not much more, but Dream needed the cloth more than I did. What was a little public nudity compared to keeping a vital organ in his body? I wrapped it gently around his chest, letting the water from it drip into his chest cavity. I was not going to be winning any nursing awards anytime soon, that was for sure, but I'd kept him alive so far...just about.

Beside me, Dream murmured, his eyes closed. There was no way he could do his job in this state, so what did that mean for the people of the world? Frustration settled in my belly. If only he'd told me things like how this world worked, but he hadn't. Not enough anyway. He'd forbidden me from leaving his side, but surely he wasn't in his right mind. I knew one thing. Without someone there to check the doors, they wouldn't move, and people...humans wouldn't dream. And then what? This world would die? How quickly would that happen? It had already been three days. Sure, there was some weird time difference in the parallel space between the doors, but I hadn't understood it when he'd told me any more than I understood it now. Anger surged through me as I realized I had no choice. Someone had to go back and watch those dreams, and the only someone around here that could walk was me. With great reluctance, I took one last look at Dream to check that he was still breathing then began the long journey back to the red door.

Anger and anger alone kept me going through the forest. I was sure that if I happened to come across a wolvery or a savagara, I'd break its bones out of sheer spite at this point. I was beyond fear. What was the point of constantly being in fear of the darkness and of the forest and its occupants? My life was worth nothing unless I could make it back to the doors. It was the thought that I might actually be doing something useful for the first time in twenty-seven years that kept me marching through the forest. Grit and determination were my only companions on the walk. Fear didn't get a look in. Not that I ended up needing the fear. No one and nothing bothered me the whole journey, and the familiar squawk of Raven greeted me as I came to the doors. He flew down and landed on my shoulder, where he jumped up and down excitedly. In all the stress, I'd completely forgotten about him. He'd lost us somewhere and obviously come back here in the hopes we'd somehow eventually return. That Dream would eventually return.

"He's by the lake," I said, in no doubt that the clever bird could understand every word I said to it. "He's unconscious, but I think he'll live. I came back to get the doors moving again, but you should go to him. He might wake up. I'll go back to him in a few hours."

Raven jumped impatiently up into the air and spread his wings. I expected him to fly off in the direction of the lake, but instead, he leapt onto the frame of the nearest door.

"You want me to go through this door?" I asked. He nodded his head and jumped up and down. It was the nearest door to the red one. There was nothing special about it, and I expected to find nothing special in it. Raven was just trying to help me.

I heaved a deep breath and turned the handle. The door opened, and I stepped inside.

I'd been through many of these doors now and knew that nothing inside could hurt me. There was nothing but the imagination of the person dreaming in there. Nothing tangible, and yet I felt nervous as the door closed behind me, leaving me in complete darkness.

The darkness gave way to a pale green meadow on a winter's day. A young girl of no more than five or six skipped happily through the meadow. She had a smile on her face, but it didn't quite reach her eyes. She slowed down and brought her finger to her lips. Her eyes darted around, looking for someone I couldn't see. Neither could she. Whoever it was, they weren't there...And then they were. The little girl beamed as a man, assumedly her father, ran into the scene and picked her up, spinning her around. She giggled, and the scene began to fade. Such a short dream and such a poignant one. I wondered if that girl often played in the meadow with her father or if he was somehow lost to her in real life. That was the rub. I had no way of knowing the truth to any of these stories I saw. They were the personal thoughts of the billions of people on the planet and truthfully bore little resemblance to reality. They were more the heart's desires of the people dreaming them than the truth. I left the room and watched as the door moved past the red door to the side where tonight's dreams had finished. Turning a hundred and eighty degrees, I opened the second door of the night, just as I had seen Dream do. I had no idea why there were two rows of doors facing each other, rather than one long row of doors, but Dream always alternated them and let both rows make their journey past the red door.

The second dream was of a young woman.

She stood at a lectern to tumultuous applause.

Just as the first one, this dream didn't last long. It was a happy dream of fulfillment, and yet, just like the first, I had no way of knowing whether the dream was a memory or a wish of the woman involved. Dream had seen billions and billions of these snippets of life, and yet, he had no idea what any of them really meant. Sadness crippled me as I stood in his shoes, going from dream to dream, not knowing what these people went on to do. It was like picking up a really good book right in the middle, reading a page, and then having that book ripped away, only to be replaced with another book. No wonder he was the way he was. Always being a part of people's lives but then having to leave, over and over and over again. Only a few, such as Gladys, even knew he existed.

I went through door after door for hours, watching people's lives flash by. Each one exhausted me further—even the happiest of dreams. I'd had happy dreams before where I'd been somewhere beautiful, the sun on my back, and yet I'd always woken up in my apartment, my fridge empty of food. This whole existence was pointless and fruitless. What a horrendous job to have. Deep down, I thought that maybe Dream knew it, but to abandon it would destroy literally everything. I was an emotional wreck by the time Raven hopped down from his place on one of the doorframes to my shoulder.

"Is that enough?" I asked, stroking his head. He bobbed his head which I took to mean yes. Another day of work done so both worlds could continue to exist. Except it wasn't a full day. What was hours of work for me was less than a flash for Earth. I'd exhausted myself for what was essentially less than the blink of an eye. It put McGee and his cheapness into perspective. He paid a fraction of what I was worth for eight hours of work, but this job paid nothing at all.

I made to step between the door frames to head back to the beach, but something stopped me.

The memory of the little girl in the meadow, the first dream I'd seen that night. It had reminded me of my mother.

Dream had controlled the doors so that I could see David's dreams. What if I could do that and go inside the head of my mother? It was possible that, just like Gladys, she'd see me. I'd make her see me. I needed to tell her I was sorry. Sorry for running away, sorry for not coming back. Sorry for not being as good a daughter as my sister.

"I just need to do something," I said, squeezing around the frame of the red door to the grey doors where dreams had passed.

Raven flew from my shoulder and landed on the red door's frame, where he hopped up and down, creating a racket.

"I'm only going to try it once. I need to see that my mother is ok."

Obviously, that wasn't what Raven wanted to hear, but as he was only a bird, there was little he could do to stop me. What could stop me was the fact that I didn't have the first clue as to how Dream had done it. How he'd maneuvered the doors so that David's appeared right in front of me? I'd been buried in his chest and missed out on the key detail as to how he started the process.

Looking around me showed me no knobs or levers. Nothing jumped out at me as a way to try. It had come from him. The magic or whatever it was to move the doors.

"How do you move the doors?" I shouted up at Raven.

The little git had the audacity to ruffle its feathers and turn away from me.

"Fine!" I shouted back petulantly. There had to be a way to do it. Maybe the magic was already here, and Dream somehow channeled it. My only knowledge of magic was the one Harry Potter movie I saw years ago, and they all had wands, but surely a wand was just a way of channeling magic that was already there, right? I had no idea, and it was only a work of fiction, but without anything else of much use to work with, I closed my eyes and tried to feel for any magic around me. I'd felt the vibrations of the magical bonds Dream had used to tie me up, so I knew what magic felt like. I tried pulling that toward me, to feel something in the atmosphere that would help me, but nothing did. There was no vibration. No low hum of magic. However Dream got his magic to move these doors, it was not coming freely to me. Maybe it was inside him after all.

Frustration bubbled up within me. My mother was here somewhere. Ok, not literally here, but the door to her dreams was, and yet, with over nine billion of these doors to check, there was no way I'd manage it without magic.

"I want to speak to my mother!" I screamed out, pounding my fist onto the frame of the nearest door. I'd barely gotten the words out of my mouth when a wind roared between the parallel rows of doors, knocking me from my feet. I would have been blown away entirely if it wasn't for me grabbing the frame of the red door and hanging on to it for dear life. The wind lifted my whole body from the ground until I was like a flag flying in the breeze. Dirt and dead leaves from the forest floor hit me in the face. The wind stopped, and I fell to the ground with a bump. I spat out the dirt I'd somehow managed to inhale and rubbed the grit from my eyes. Everything looked exactly as it had moments ago, except that one of the nearest doors to me was covered in thick vines.

"Is this my mother's door?" I asked, getting to my feet and looking up to where Raven had been moments before. He wasn't there. For a moment, a thrill of panic flew through me that I'd managed to blow him away, but then I saw him in a nearby tree. He wasn't stupid enough to get caught in the maelstrom of wind I'd managed to conjure.

"Is this door my mother's?" I asked Raven again. He flew to the door and landed on the frame.

It was times like these that I wished that he could talk. I wished he or I was a polyglot just like the other people here, but he wasn't. He could only speak raven, and I could only speak English, and that was that. I didn't need to understand his cawing to see that he was displeased by my actions. I ignored him and held my hand out to the door. I could barely see the grey behind the deep green vines that enshrouded it, wrapping their way, not only over the door but around the frame, too, making it impossible to open in the state it was in. Determination pulled at my guts as I brought Dream's knife from my boot and started hacking away at the vines. Each one was thick and sinuous, unlike any vine I'd ever seen before. Not that I saw many vines in Vancouver. I had to saw through each strand bit by bit, and when each came away, I threw it on a pile on the floor. My muscles burned with the effort, and a sheen of sweat beaded at my temple, but I kept going. Even as Raven's caws got louder and more intense, I carried on with my task, desperate to finally see my mother.

Dream hovered at the back of my mind. I should have gone back to him hours ago. He was incapacitated lying on a beach alone. The savagaras could come back at any second to finish him off, and he'd be defenseless against them. Two forces pulled me in opposite directions. I knew I needed to go back to Dream, but this might be my only chance to speak to my mother again.

Finally, I hacked through the largest of the vines, the only one left, and let it fall to my feet. The door was finally free. I pulled at the handle, afraid that it wouldn't open despite everything that I'd done to free it. I was almost surprised when the door opened as easily as all the others now that it no longer had the vines holding it.

I entered into the darkness, my stomach churning with anticipation. The door slammed shut behind me, echoing into the inky void. My mother's image appeared. She was stood against a wall, her fists hammering against it, her face stained with tears. My heart tore as I took in her appearance. She was so much older than I remembered her. She'd always had a youthful appearance, and despite our lack of wealth, was always dressed well. She never left the house with a hair out of place. In her dream, her hair was a tangle, her dress creased. Silently she hammered at the wall.

"Mom. It's me, Ana."

My voice sounded eerie and out of place in the silent dream. I knew the sound would come. It always did just after the vision, so somewhere deep in my heart, I'd hoped she'd hear my voice. But she didn't stop banging on the wall. Her eyes didn't even flicker as I called out to her.

I stepped up to her and touched my hand to her shoulder just as the noise finally began to kick in. Sound that drove deep into my soul. She was sobbing. She hammered on the wall again, and I thought I heard a faint thudding coming back in answer. Then a voice. It was faint, but it was a voice I knew well.

Arizona, my sister.

My mom held her head to the wall, trying to make sense of the sound. Arizona's voice was so faint that I had to copy my mother's actions. It sounded like she was reading a book. *Alice in Wonderland.* It had been both Arizona's and my favorite book as children, and we'd begged our mother to read it to us time and time again. Who would have thought that both my mother and I would have fallen down the rabbit hole ourselves?

I looked toward my mother. Tears were still streaming down her face, but she was no longer making any noise. If anything, she was holding her breath to hear my sister's voice.

She closed her eyes and just listened as Arizona read the words I knew so well.

My heart almost broke at the sight of her. This wall was what kept my mother locked in her mind. What stopped her from waking up. The voice she heard was my sister's real voice. Arizona was probably seated at her bedside in the hospital reading to her. All I needed to do was smash down this wall, and my mother would wake up. Probably.

I hammered at the wall in much the same way my mother had been doing moments before. The noise drowned out Arizona's voice, and yet my mother didn't react at all to me beating on the wall in front of her. She could neither hear nor see me. I should have been sitting at her bedside with Ari, not bashing at a wall in her dream. A wall that was not yielding to my fists at all.

Outside the door, Raven's cawing became more frantic. The more I hammered on the wall, the louder and faster he squawked. Everything seemed to be crashing around me. I needed my mother desperately, but I was no more than a ghost to her. Her tears were not over me but over Arizona. I could no more knock the wall between them down than I could get my mother to see I was standing right in front of her. Raven's squawking reached a fever pitch, and a rapping sound started at the door. It was thinner and more hollow than my pounding at the wall, but it was there and becoming more insistent. Raven!

"I'm coming!" I yelled toward the door. "One more minute!"

If only I could break the wall. Just an inch. I slammed my fists into the wall until they were bruised, but the wall remained solid.

Raven's squawking was now feverous as he bashed his beak at the outside of the door to get my attention.

"I've got to go, Mom," I whispered, kissing her cheek. I couldn't be sure if the taste of salt on my lips was her tears or mine. She didn't even open her eyes as I turned from her and headed back to the door. I pushed against it, but this time it didn't budge.

Something was stopping it. I pushed again, harder this time. Behind me, my mother's dream was fading into darkness as they always did. If I didn't get out in the next few seconds, I'd be swept away with the door and be lost forever.

CHAPTER TWENTY-SEVEN

A gap of light filtered through between the door and the frame. At the bottom, dark green strands were already creeping up. The vines were re-growing around the door and frame. Raven pecked at them from outside. I could just make out his feathery head bobbing away through the half-centimeter gap as he hammered his beak at the vine.

I pulled Dream's knife from my boots and held it between the frame and the door, ready to slice it through. "Step back!" I ordered Raven. His dark shadow, only a touch darker than the forest around him, disappeared, allowing me to push the knife through. My mother's dream was almost completely swallowed by blackness, and fuck knew what would happen when it petered out completely. It would move back to where it should be probably, taking me along with it, miles and miles away into the forest.

Adrenaline kicked in as I hacked at the vine, screaming in both determination and anguish. The vine finally snapped, and I fell through the door, landing with a bump on the ground. Almost immediately, the howling wind came, sending my mother's door away and me almost with it. Without warning, I was dragged along the ground, caught up in the current along with the debris that littered the forest floor. When the wind died down, I found that I hadn't moved as far as I worried I had. I could still see the red door in the distance, but my mother's door with the vines was no longer in sight. Raven flew over to me and landed on a door frame nearby. I could have sworn the little bastard was wearing an 'I told you so' expression.

"I'm sorry," I grumbled as I picked myself up. I was filthy, my clothes ripped in multiple places, and a bloom of blood was already showing where my brief journey along the forest floor had ripped at my skin. A quick check told me that all my grazes were superficial and probably wouldn't kill me, but that didn't stop them from hurting like a bitch.

"Ow!" I grimaced, twisting my mouth with the pain. I'd accomplished precisely nothing, and Dream was still at the beach by himself.

"Shit, come on, we've gotta go." Raven gladly hopped onto my shoulder, and the pair of us ran back through the forest to the lake, with me taking a minor detour to the clearing to pick up the other dresses that Aethelu had given me.

Dream was exactly where I'd left him. A knot of fear pulled at my stomach when I saw his body lying prone on the sand, but he was still breathing. I wondered if he'd woken at all since I'd been gone. It had been hours and hours—at least a full day. No footprints in the sand other than my own from when I'd gone to the lake's edge told me that he'd not woken, or at least he hadn't moved. I headed to the water's edge and filled my hands with water which I brought back to him. He didn't stir as I dribbled the soothing water between his dry, parched lips. The movement of his chest, what was left of it, told me he was still alive, but his face was serene as if in death, almost like a statue made of marble. A quick peek under the makeshift bandage told me that one of his lungs was still visible. Surely there was no coming back from that kind of injury?

If he died, who would take over his job? I couldn't do it. I'd done it for a few hours, and it had traumatized me. So many questions rolled around in my brain as I ripped up another dress to make a clean bandage for him. What would happen to this world? To my world? And the one question that was the loudest of all -- What would happen to me?

Raven sat diligently at his master's side, ignoring me as was his wont to do.

"I'm going for a swim!" I said at last to the bird. If I didn't get all the grazes covering most of my body clean, they would get infected, and I'd be in no better position than Dream. Without thinking, I pulled off what was left of my ragged dress and the horrible bloomers and ran to the water and jumped in. The pain stopped almost immediately, the water soothing all the places where my skin had been broken. It truly was magical stuff. I dived under the surface and swam until I couldn't hold my breath any longer, at which point I resurfaced. The feeling of freedom was palpable, and the cool water on my naked flesh thrilled me no end. Out here, I could forget about the doors, my mother, Dream, and the mess we were all in. There was nothing I could do, so instead, I floated on the water's still surface and turned my gaze to the heavens.

After half an hour or so had passed in the most glorious swim, I swam back to the shallows and stepped out onto the black sand of the beach. The water dripped off me, seeping into the soft sand beneath my feet. As I walked up the beach back to Dream, I saw that his outline had changed. He was no longer lying down. At some point during my swim, he'd awakened and sat up, and now he watched me in all my naked glory in front of him. I walked slowly toward him, stuck between the embarrassment of him seeing me and the desire for him to. His eyes took me in completely, looking me up and down. This time, there was no venom in them as there had been on many occasions, nor was it polite interest that had his eyes raking over me.

I swallowed my nerves, caught as I was in the headlights of his stare. He'd seen plenty of naked people before. I'd been there many times in dreams when people had taken their clothes off or found themselves without clothes. He'd shown such a decided lack of interest in all of them that it was almost scary to watch how intensely he looked at me. How powerfully his gaze was locked upon my skin so that I could almost feel the heat of it.

"Please pass my dress," I murmured, almost holding my breath. He hesitated slightly, then tore his gaze away from me. I saw the wince as he reached for my dress and handed it over.

I didn't take it. To do so would be to break the moment. He stared into my eyes, waiting for me to move toward him, but I was paralyzed. I wanted him to see me naked. I wanted him to continue to look at me the way he was doing. Maybe I had right from the start. He licked his lips, and I wondered how they tasted. How easy it would be to walk that one step toward him and find out for myself.

But he was still injured. Lust coated his face, but just beneath it was pain he was trying to mask. What the fuck was wrong with me. Half an hour before, I'd been wondering how long he had left, and now, all I could think about was touching him.

He was the sexiest man I'd ever laid eyes on, but if what Aethelu had told me was true, then he'd never been with a woman before. My emotions were a heady mix. To reach out and touch him would be madness, but that didn't stop me from wanting to. The pull of him was stronger than the current of any ocean, and yet, he was wounded in more ways than one. I reached forward and took the dress in my hands. My fingers grazed against his, making him flinch again. This time it wasn't pain that had caused the movement. He was scared. The big sexy brute was terrified, and he wasn't the only one.

I pulled the dress over my head and sat next to him, trying to keep any hint of desire inside. This was neither the time nor place. Heck, none of it was the right time or place. I was a human, he was a… well, I hadn't quite figured out exactly what he was, but he was the king of dreams, and without him, we'd all die. I needed to keep my lust in check and remember that small fact.

He could no more leave this place than I could stay here. Lusting after a hot dude who ruled this world of darkness was both stupid and irresponsible and totally and completely overwhelming.

I needed to get a grip.

"How are you feeling?" I asked, trying to dampen the conversation to boring levels.

"I hurt," he said with a small smile. "I need to get back to the doors."

"No need," I said nonchalantly. "I already went. I did your job for you today."

The smile on his face fell instantly, to be replaced by the thunder I was used to seeing. I guess the thrill of seeing me naked had worn off pretty quickly. Maybe I was reading into it too much anyway.

"I told you not to go into the forest alone," he roared. I feared that the effort was going to send his heart and lungs flying right out of his chest cavity with the force of it. Thank fuck I'd thought to retie his bandage because I'd be splattered in his organs if I hadn't.

"Yeah, and I also knew that if I didn't, your world would have come crashing down, followed very quickly by mine," I spat back. "You should be thanking me."

"Dammit, Ana! You should have woken me. You are not safe in these woods. How many times…"

I stood up. "You couldn't be woken. You were mauled by a savagara remember?" I pointed to the long ragged teeth marks in both his legs and the bloodstained cloth holding his chest together. "I've been gone hours, and you've only just woken up."

He slammed his hand into the sand, sending a plume of it up into the air. "What you did was incredibly stupid."

I brought my hands to my waist, anger seething inside

me. My voice raised an octave, and I was glad that the forest was so remote that no one would hear me shouting. "And what would you have me do? Let the world go to crap while you lay here

and died? Because that's what I thought might happen. I thought I would come back here and find you dead. I really thought you had died for a minute. It was only when I saw you breathing that I relaxed, but your chest is a mess. I don't even know how you are talking. It's only my ripped-up dress that's stopping you from falling apart." Hot angry tears fell down my face and the trauma of the last few days finally began pouring out of me. Seeing David's dream, followed quickly by the savagara attack. Then seeing my mother locked inside her own head. "And all there is in this god-forsaken hell hole is darkness, and I couldn't be here with you. I couldn't save my mother, I can't do anything for you and ..."

I was cut off by the crush of his lips against mine.

Shock was the first feeling that crashed into me, followed very swiftly by a need I'd barely registered before the last ten minutes.

Holy shit, this is hot! My hormones wreaked havoc on my body, and I didn't want it to stop. This messy violence of our two mouths crashing together violently in a maelstrom of emotion. The ferociousness as he pulled my body toward his savagely. This was like no kiss I'd ever encountered before. It was full of passion and intensity and disordered and impolite, and everything a kiss should be and everything a kiss shouldn't be at the same time. It was beautifully chaotic. I liked the chaos. His chaos sucking me right in. I found myself trapped in a maelstrom of desire and pain and hormones, and it was the most exhilarating experience I'd ever had.

My tongue touched his, and he flinched again, just like when I inadvertently touched his fingers a few minutes before. I wasn't the only one falling into something I didn't know how to handle. For some reason, his inexperience in this field excited me more. In all our actions together, he'd always been the one in charge, the one telling me what to do. Now I was the one leading him. And this time, there was no pulling away from it like he had done before. No hesitation, nothing that either of us could pass off as some kind of accidental meeting of mouths because his hands were everywhere, exploring my body as his tongue explored my mouth, and fuck, it was thrilling!

He pulled back, an almost crazed look in his eyes. He heaved a breath in then quickly breathed out. I thought it was the excitement of the moment we had just shared before his eyes rolled back into his head, and he collapsed onto the sand.

CHAPTER TWENTY-EIGHT

My head was a wreck. Everything I'd been keeping locked up was spilling out of me, and I didn't know what to do about any of it. I shouldn't have kissed Dream...Twice! Or at least I told myself that, ignoring the fact that it was him that had kissed me at first. I'd hardly been an unwilling participant in it. I'd reveled in his touch. I'd wanted it badly, and I hadn't been the one to step back. He had. Right before he slipped right back into unconsciousness.

What the fuck was I doing? This was all wrong. Everything about it was a bloody mess, including Dream himself, who was literally so.

"I shouldn't have kissed him," I murmured to Raven,

I'd come here to get my mother back, and instead, I was on a beach in perpetual night worrying if I'd done the wrong thing about kissing her captor. Except he wasn't her captor, someone else was... probably. None of it made sense, and it seemed that every move I'd made since stepping foot in this world had only served to make things worse.

My lips tingled with the bruising Dream had done to them. He was so utterly beautiful it took my breath away. Even unmoving with his eyes closed, it was everything I could do to stop myself from reaching down to kiss him again. Small beads of sweat appeared on his forehead. I felt it with the back of my hand. He was roasting. The fever was back. I pulled off my dress and soaked it in the lake before wiping his forehead with it. Then I gingerly unwrapped the makeshift bandages around his chest and cleaned the wound the best I could. What did it matter that I was once again without clothing? There was no one around to see me. I washed the dress in the lake and laid it out on a rock to dry.

I was exhausted, both physically and emotionally. I lay down on the sand next to Dream and let sleep take me away into its comforting hold.

My eyes flew open as something draped over me. It was only when I realized it was Dream's arm that my heart rate subsided a little. I'd thought the nightwalkers were back for a second. Then my heart rate increased again when I realized that *Dream's arm was wrapped around me*!!! His almost naked body spooned my back which, just so happened, was also naked. His face was nuzzled just behind my head, so close that I could feel his breath on my shoulder. His breathing was deep, as though he was still asleep, but without turning around to check, I couldn't be sure. His body was warm and comforting, and I found myself pressing my back into him further. All of it felt forbidden, but he was asleep, and he was the one who'd maneuvered himself into this position. The bulge of his dick beneath his pants sat right next to my ass, and he had one leg coiled around mine.

I didn't move. I couldn't even if I wanted to, which I didn't. Not in any way. If either of us was going to die here on this beach, this was the way I'd want to go. I closed my eyes and wiggled my ass a little. He moaned in his sleep, but I had a feeling it was no longer pain that was producing the moans. I let myself fall asleep again, but this time a little more content and safe within his arms.

I woke later to find him sitting down by the water's edge, facing away from me. Bizarrely I seemed to be covered in a thin layer of leaves. Above me, my dress fluttered in the gentle breeze hung over a tree branch. I'd not put it there, so Dream must have. I stood up and pulled it down from the tree. It had dried completely, so I lowered it over my head and let the folds of fabric cover my body.

"We need to get back," Dream shouted over to me. "I can't leave the doors any longer."

He stood and walked over to me. "I hung up your dress to dry. I hope you don't mind."

His behavior was odd, disconcerting. He had an almost detached cheeriness about him.

"I don't mind," I replied, going along with it. "How are you feeling today?" He looked better; that was for sure. He still had a ghostly pallor, but then again, he always did in this light, but the dark rings around his eyes had gone, and the sheen of sweat had vanished too.

"Don't you want me to check your bandages before we go?" I asked? I didn't see any fresh blood, but that didn't mean there wasn't any.

"They'll be fine. I'll go and see Aethelu when I get home to get something a bit cleaner and some new clothes for you. We can't seem to keep them clean, can we?"

He hummed as he stepped into the forest. Then he turned to me. "Are you coming?"

I was perplexed by the whole thing. He was being very un-Dreamlike. I wondered if the fever was making him this way, but the fever appeared to have broken.

"Stop!" I yelled out to him. He turned and eyed me curiously. "You can't go. I won't let you."

"You won't let me?" he asked, raising an eyebrow. "Since when do you get to decide to let me do anything?"

I stalked forward to where he was and grabbed his wrist. "Since you were given a hole in your chest and me looking after you is the only thing that's kept you from death, that's when. There's not a chance in hell I'm going to let you walk through those woods because we both know you'll never make it in the state you are in, superhuman or not. And if you think for one second I'm going to carry you back when you fall, you're even crazier than you make yourself out to be."

"The doors, Ana. I can't leave them for too long. You know that."

"I told you. I went to the doors. I've done them today exactly how you showed me."

His eyes narrowed in confusion. "Did you? I don't remember."

Like fuck he didn't. To acknowledge what I'd told him earlier, he'd also have to acknowledge the kiss between us.

"Yes. Now come back to the beach and let me look after you."

Surprisingly he let me lead him back. He sat on the sand, his back to me. I took a seat beside him and looked out at the small lapping waves. Neither of us spoke. I jiggled my knee up and down, uncomfortable with the silence.

Of course, I was the one to break it. "You kissed me."

He stared out into the distance, not even acknowledging my words.

"I said, you kissed me. Here on the beach."

His eyes continued to graze the horizon unblinking. "I don't recall. Maybe I was hallucinating and thought you were someone else. Or maybe you were hallucinating."

Ouch!

"Bullshit!" I pulled on his shoulder to make him turn to face me. "You. Kissed. Me. Not the other way around. Maybe the first time it happened, I could explain it away as an accident. I mean, you were protecting me from the wind, but not this time. You fucking meant it."

He opened his mouth to speak, then paused. "I can't. I can't do this."

I stood up. "Fuck you. Do you know how pathetic that sounds? You sound exactly like David did when I found out he was fucking his office bitch. I thought you were different. I thought you were better, but you're just the same as every other man. My father, David. You know I've heard all this shit before, right? 'I can't do this,' 'I wish things were different,' and the perennial favorite of shitty men everywhere, 'It's not you; it's me.' Christ, it's not only pathetic, it's a cliché. At least come up with something original. Although, props to you, blaming a loss of memory is a new one to me."

"Sit down." His voice was calm but firm. I'm glad someone's was because I was bordering on hysterical.

"The fuck I will. You stand up." I ignored the fact that standing would cause him more pain than me sitting down would, but I was all for that. The more pain, the better. He deserved to feel some of what I was feeling.

"Ana. Please sit down. I want to talk to you. You are right. I am pathetic, but there are a lot of things you don't know. I owe it to you to tell you about them."

My angry ass was ready to leave him there and hotfoot it back to the red door, but there was such sincerity in his voice that I did as he asked.

He sat agonizingly quietly, his eyes shuttered. I sat waiting for him to say something that would make me stay with him because I wanted to stay with him. I wanted it with every pore of my being, but I wanted him to want me to.

"I've not been honest with you, Ana."

No shit, Sherlock. "Go on."

He ran his hand across his forehead. "I didn't forget kissing you. How could I forget something so...so..."

"Hot?" I helped him out.

He uttered a small "heh," And continued. "Harrowingly, heart-achingly beautiful and painful and perfect and terrifying."

Woah! I held my breath, trying to take all those words in. He'd certainly expanded on David's and my father's vocabulary after all. "Why terrifying?"

He ran a hand down his face. "You came in here to my world, and I hated you. I wanted to destroy you, to cause you pain."

"We're kinda losing the moment here. You might

want to go back to the beautiful, heart-aching part," I quipped, my insides churning as I tried to work out exactly where he was going with this.

He laughed a low laugh again, rumbling in his chest. "All of this makes my heart ache, Ana. There's not one part of you being here that lets my heart rest. It hurts."

"You know, that might not be me because there's literally nothing but a bit of ripped-up, old dress holding it in your body."

"This pain I'm feeling has nothing to do with the injury the savagara inflicted on me. That is merely physical pain. I will heal, thanks to you."

"So what is it then?" I whispered.

"I wish I could tell you. It is pain like nothing else I've ever endured, and yet I crave it. I cannot imagine breathing without it. It is holding me together, and it is tearing me apart."

I sucked in a breath and brought my hand to the sand to steady myself.

"I don't understand."

He licked his lips and then ran a thumb over them. It was an incredibly sexy maneuver, and yet, he probably didn't notice the puddle of Jello I was descending into.

"I need to tell you everything and start at the beginning so you will understand."

I nodded. I needed to know what made Dream like he was.

"My father was killed by a human a long time ago. My mother threw us out of our own home."

I knew this. Aethelu had already told me the story of Dream and his brother.

"Nightmare," I said quietly.

He nodded lightly. "That is what he is now known by, yes. He is my twin. My best friend growing up. We were inseparable, and then my father died...was killed. No human had managed to come into our world. The man that killed my father was the first. The shock of my father's death sent my mother insane."

I lifted my hand and placed it on his. "It must have been a horrifying time. I'm so sorry."

"I cannot begin to tell you how bad it was. My whole world fell apart. My mother is the queen of the Dark Court. She used to be Queen of the whole realm before she broke it into three, sending my brother and me out to rule our own kingdoms. Our world has been fractured ever since. At first, my brother and I stayed in touch. We had help with our jobs from some staff my mother had deigned to send with us. They didn't know what to do. Neither did I. I was only a small boy, but I knew that if I didn't keep watching the dreams, both your world and mine would die."

"It must have been an awfully lonely existence." My heart ached for him. How anyone could send their ten-year-old sons out to rule a kingdom with barely any support beggared belief. I'd never met the woman, but I hated the queen. I hated her with a passion for everything she'd done and for everything she should have done but didn't.

"It was. Eventually, I left my palace and decided to live in the forest with Raven. My brother didn't understand. He thought I was weak. Maybe he was right, but watching an endless stream of nightmares had changed him. It wasn't long before we were bickering every time we saw each other. One day, we had an argument, and I've not seen him since. The nightwalkers are from the Nightmare Court. They belong to him. Both the wolveries and the savagaras."

My hand flew to my mouth. "Your brother did this to you?"

"In a manner of speaking, yes. The nightwalkers are his army. Wolveries and savagaras are just two types of shifter he has working for him. There are other nightwalkers. Some more monstrous than those."

I couldn't get my head around any of it. "The wolveries and savagaras are shifters? You mean that shit is real? I've read about shifters in books, but... well, it's PNR. They all wanted to fuck each other or fuck each other up by the end of every book. I thought they weren't real."

He shrugged. "They are very real, although I'd not heard the term shifter before you mentioned it that day in Gladys's library. Here, they are just called nightwalkers. Men who transform into monsters."

Something hit me then. "I killed a man. Two men." I thought back to the wolveries I'd killed. Bile filled my throat.

"It was them or you. Do not think on it. They are not men. Not in the way you think they are. I do not know about the shifters in your books, but even in their human form, they are bloodthirsty and more monster than man."

"I used to think the same way about you."

He sighed. "You might want to hear my full story before you change your judgment of me. In many ways, I am worse than any nightwalker my brother controls. They are savages, blood thirsty-monsters. They don't know how to be better, but I should, and in view of that, I am extremely ashamed."

I mulled this over. "So your brother wants to kill you?

You told me that he wanted to kill me, and that's why he sent the wolveries in the first place."

"That is what I thought, but then he came for me knowing that a wolvery wouldn't be able to kill me. I knew the second the savagara showed up, he'd turned his sights to me instead. They have a venom in their bite that not even I am immune to. That is why my healing magic is not working as it should. Thanks to you, I believe the venom is now out of my system. It was you that kept me alive, not magic."

I shuffled forward. "But why? What have you done to make him so angry?"

"I've made some stupid mistakes. You are the biggest of all, and yet, you are the one I regret the least.

You have become something to me that I never imagined in my wildest dreams. My brother has somehow found out about you. I do not know how. He must have realized what I feel for you, and for that reason, you should go back to your home. He will be back."

God, this was so intense and so confusing. Painful didn't cut it. It was excruciating.

"I can't go back. I can't leave you."

Dream groaned. "I don't know how to keep you safe, Ana."

"I'd rather be unsafe here in this world with you than safe in my bed alone back in Vancouver without you."

"This is torment. I wanted to kill you. I wanted you to feel pain. I wanted you to hurt, but in doing that, I've caused myself more pain than I can bear."

My voice lowered. "Why did you want to hurt me?"

"Ana," he brought his hand to my face and ran his fingers lightly through my hair. Just the touch of his fingertips had me burning. He was right. This was excruciating. "You are a human. You are everything

I was brought up to detest, and yet, you are nothing like I imagined a human to be. You are kind, and thoughtful, and funny, and so incredibly beautiful, I cannot keep my eyes away from you. I want to know everything about you, I want to touch every inch of you, I want to know what every part of you feels like under my fingertips, and most of all, I want to kiss you so bad it's tearing me apart. I can't function. I can't think. God help me, Ana, I can barely breathe when I'm with you."

My heart exploded with happiness. If his words were designed to make me feel bad, they were having the opposite effect. His fingers were still in my hair, his palm warming my cheek. I leaned into him and kissed him slowly. He didn't protest nor try to pull away. I moved slowly, giving him the time to pull back but hoping with every fiber of my being that he wouldn't. He didn't. He leaned into me, matching my movements. With a shock, I realized that this was his first-ever kiss. Ok, it was his third, but both of the first two were all angry passion. This was slow and deliberate and beautiful and…well, it was uncoordinated and jerky. His eyes were closed as I slowed down further still. His scent, the sweet smell of this earth coupled with the unique masculine scent of him, washed over me as he matched my movements with his lips. He groaned as I parted his lips with my tongue, and it was then that I closed my own eyes. I didn't need to see his beauty; I could feel it on me, in me, as his tongue hesitantly explored my mouth. The guy was a fast learner; I'd give him that. My body tingled in anticipation as he brought his hand lower, letting his fingers graze against my cheek and my neck, before lowering to the top of my dress. My touch-starved body pushed against his hand as heat flooded through me.

I became more insistent, and our slow, beautiful kiss turned into something more urgent. I moved slightly, not breaking the kiss at all, and brought my hands up to his body. One on his shoulder, the other to his chest, forgetting in my desire-addled mind, his chest, for all intents and purposes, wasn't there.

He cried out in pain and pulled back.

"Shit!" I murmured, my eyes opening in horror. I'd barely touched him, and yet obviously, I'd touched him more than I meant to. "I'm sorry."

"I am fine, Ana." He grinned through huffed out breaths. "Perhaps I was a little too enthusiastic."

"Maybe a touch," I grinned back. I couldn't help it. My mouth felt like it was pinned up at both ends. A maelstrom of desire was still echoing around my body, but getting him better had to come before…well, before I could. It was going to be a long, long few days. At least I hoped it would only take days now that his healing magic was kicking in. I didn't think I'd be able to wait any longer. "Let's get some more lake water on that chest of yours. It worked wonders on my own scrapes and cuts earlier. Look…" I pointed to my legs that were barely showing the mess I'd made of myself when I'd been dragged through the forest by the wind.

"Scrapes? How did you scrape yourself?" he ran his hand down my leg, and I shivered. This time not because of his touch. This time, because he wasn't the only one with a secret and now, it seemed, it was time to tell him mine.

CHAPTER TWENTY-NINE

I stood up, my nerves ragged at the admission I was about to make. "I might have made the doors move and gone to see my mother in her dream. I fell and was dragged along the ground with the wind. The lake water has cleared up most of the damage, though." I held my breath and waited for his anger, but it never came. In fact, he looked confused more than anything else.

"I'm surprised you were able to make the doors work in that way. I didn't think it was possible for a human to do so. And to survive the wind..."

"You aren't angry with me?"

He stood up to join me and took my hand in his. "I was angry when you first told me that you went to the doors, but that was because I was scared you'd get hurt.

There is no way I'm going to let you go there alone again, but I understand your wanting to see your mother. You've not seen her in a long time. I should have thought of it myself."

I arched a brow, two very distinct and separate forces fighting each other within me. It was his fault that my mother was locked in her own mind. At least, I thought it was. Aethelu told me not to blame him for it, but if not him, then who else? Still, his expression was not of a man who'd just been caught doing something wrong.

"My mother. She's..." I choked up, hardly daring to speak. If it turned out that it was Dream that had done this to her, I knew my whole world would collapse. I knew he was capable of awful things. Things I'd forgiven him for. Hurting my mother was not something I'd ever be able to forgive. "She's not woken up in over a year. I found vines keeping her door closed. I had to hack at them to be able to get in. I almost didn't make it out."

Dream sighed a long heavy sigh and closed his eyes. For an excruciatingly long second, I thought he'd slipped back into unconsciousness. "Everything I've done with you is wrong. Literally everything."

I opened my mouth in shock. "Is that an admission? Did you do this to her?" My heart pounded as I waited for him to answer. At least this time, it was mercifully quick.

"No," he shook his head strongly. "No. I didn't do that. I would never do that to her, nor to anyone else." He took my hand in his. It was surprisingly gentle. I wouldn't say comforting because whichever way I looked at it, my mother was still sleeping. "You saved me more times than I can count. You've looked after me while I've been incapacitated, and you kissed me, all the while thinking that I would do such a thing to your mother?"

"You were a monster. I didn't know what to think."

He sighed. "But you saved me. First from the wolveries, second from death at the hands of the savagara, and thirdly, from myself. Why would you do that to a man you thought was a monster?"

Tears began to form in the corner of my eye. I hated crying. It showed weakness. Mostly the only tears I cried were the angry kind, but I wasn't angry now. I didn't know how I felt at all. Confused mostly. "You were the most beautiful monster I'd ever met." Fuck, that sounded so shallow. And it was so wrong. It went way beyond how he looked. "I mean, I saw something in you that you keep so well hidden. I think for a long time you've been this monster you think you are. You certainly fooled me when I met you. It took me a while to see beyond the big angry man you show yourself to be, but I did see it. I see you now."

His expression looked pained. "I did not trap your mother in her own dreams, nor did I trap anyone else, but your mother is there because of me. It is my fault."

I pulled my hand back swiftly. Hadn't he literally just told me that he hadn't done it, and now he was confessing to the deed.

He shifted his position, and I saw a brief wince of pain pass over his features. "My brother's magic is what's causing those vines to spring up. There is nothing I can do to stop it, though it was I that started it."

"What? Why? How?" so many questions, I could barely get the words out.

He sat down and patted the sand next to him. "I know I told you that I haven't seen my brother in many years. That wasn't strictly true. About a year ago, he came to find me."

I nodded, understanding where this was going.

"It was a year ago my mother went to sleep. The whole world did."

He grimaced. "I know. He came to me out of the blue. I'd not seen him in so many years; I barely recognized him. He looked nothing like me, despite the fact we are identical twins. His hair was short and tidy, his clothes were refined. He was thicker around the waist than me from a life of eating well. I hoped that he'd changed, that maybe we could reconcile, but he was arrogant and sick in the head like my mother. He'd come to tell me that our mother was sick, possibly dying."

He laughed then, a soulless laugh that twisted my insides. "I didn't care. Why should I? She'd shown no interest in me for so many years. I told him I had no interest in seeing her. I don't know who was more surprised. Me at him for wanting to see her, or him at me not wanting to. Anyway, It didn't matter. He didn't stay long, and he went to visit our mother alone. At least I assumed he did. I've not seen him since. I don't even know if my mother got over her illness. I assume she did because the Dark Court is still running, but I don't know for sure, nor do I care."

"I still don't understand what this has to do with my mother."

He paused for a second. "It was a flippant remark. I told him that many years prior, I'd sought out and killed the man that killed our father. He was incensed. Not at me so much as at the entire human race. I think he was more upset that he hadn't gotten to the man and done the deed himself. I suspect he had wanted to kill him and hadn't been able to find him. Sheer pride in his own abilities led him down a dark path, one even darker than the one he'd already started. The very next day, vines sprouted up, stopping up every door. Every damned one."

I shook my head at the awfulness of it all. "You don't need to tell me anymore. It's barbaric."

He nodded, his face ashen. "Yes, it is, but you must know what happened next. Otherwise, you will only be left wondering."

"Fine," I conceded gruffly. My mother was in a hospital ward because some prick got his pride hurt. Maybe I should hear all the details, after all.

"I spent a week fighting my brother's magic," he continued. "He was much stronger than me, mainly because he'd spent years perfecting it in his palace. It took me seven days, but I was able to counteract some of it. Not all, though. There are hundreds of thousands of doors still shrouded in vines."

"My mother being one," I added.

Dream cast his eyes downward, but not before I saw the anguish in them. I followed his gaze, then let out a howl. Blood was seeping through his makeshift bandages.

"There's something I need..."

"Not right now," I shouted, jumping up. "Look at you. You need to get in that lake. Now!"

He didn't resist as I pulled on his hand. His face twisted in pain at the exertion, and he let out a groan as he got to his feet. He clutched his chest as I half helped, half dragged him to the water's edge. I didn't bother taking our clothes off. My dress and his trousers were soaked to the skin within seconds, but that didn't matter. What mattered was getting his chest submerged so the water could do its magic. We waded in until it was deep enough, and then he bent his knees and let himself fall into the water. He let out a whoosh of air as his injury was submerged. I had a second of panic that black water filling up the chest cavity might not be the best idea, but by the look of bliss on his face as he lifted his legs and began to float on the water's surface, he didn't seem to mind.

I leaned forward and kissed him lightly on the lips. A smile tugged at the corners of his mouth, and his eyes fluttered open.

"Feeling better?" I asked.

"When you are here, I always feel better. Something shuttered over his face, and his smile dropped. I recognized that look. I'd seen it once too often over the past few days. It was a precursor to him telling me I shouldn't kiss him or it was wrong, or, god forbid, "I can't do this."

I began to untie the bit of dress I'd used as a bandage. Partly to get him to shut up before he started, and partly because I wanted to see for myself what the water had done to heal him.

"I'm going to need you to stand up. I need to take a look at you."

He managed to upright himself without my help. Only the top half-inch of his trousers showed above the black water. He could almost be naked under there for all I could see beneath the inky depths. Naked and...

Focus!

Gingerly, I pulled the bandage from around him. I had to reach behind him to grab the other end resulting in my face brushing against his. My hands felt around his back, lingering on the unbroken skin there. He pulled in a sharp breath as I trailed my hand across his skin, making sure not to touch the damage at the front. He was way too wide for me to reach all the way around, so I had to let one end of the bandage go.

His breathing came fast now as I stood before him, hardly daring to look down at his chest.

My own breathing matched his as I took in the detail of his lips. Lips I'd tasted not ten minutes before. Lips I wanted to taste again. He put his hand to my cheek. Such a small thing, and my body responded effortlessly to his touch as a bolt of electricity traveled deliciously through my body to my core. I pressed my hips forward to find his. Beneath the layers of clothes, I felt his hardness. Somewhere in my lust-addled mind, I must have been aware of his chest because I leaned back ever so slightly so I wasn't touching that part of him. I found myself locked in his gaze of molten need and desire, echoing back the very thing I was feeling about him.

"Aren't you going to look?" He asked huskily, and my breath caught in my throat.

God, I wanted to. "Yes... oh, you mean your chest." I didn't blush easily, but I felt the heat rise to my cheeks as I realized my mistake. I gasped when I took in his chest. It was still a horrific mess, but it had begun to heal around the edges. The hole where I'd seen

inside him had closed up, and the skin around the injury was beginning to knit back together. He took my hand in his, and another jolt of electricity ran through me. He put my fingers to his chest where the skin had healed. "See. Getting better."

I looked up to find him gazing down at me. The lust in his eyes hadn't abated at all.

"We need to re-bandage that," I muttered.

croakily. He leaned forward and planted his lips on mine. This time, there were no unsure movements. He knew exactly what he was doing. I ground my hips against him, eliciting a groan from him. Without thinking, I let my breasts graze his chest. He jumped back in pain.

"I think maybe we should think about getting you healed before..." before what? Before he changed his mind or before he fucked me senseless?

I let the sentence drop and took his hand as we both walked back to the beach. He collapsed in the sand, his breathing deeper and slightly wheezy. His eyes fluttered shut.

"You still ok?" I asked, drying him as best I could with the last of Aethelu's dresses. I couldn't seem to keep the bloody things clean or dry.

He murmured and nodded slightly though he didn't speak. The accelerated healing process must have wiped him out. I ripped the dress into long strips and carefully bandaged him up. He moved when I needed him to and let me wrap the bandage around his chest, but by the time I finished, he was fast asleep, a light rumble of a snore escaping his lips. I stood up and pulled my wet dress over my head and threw it on the rock I'd used to dry my clothes last time.

"Hey," I said, nudging him awake gently with my toe. "You know I'm going back to do the doors again tomorrow, don't you? I'm going whether you tell me to or not. Just putting that out there."

He grabbed my ankle, causing me to topple over, then he grabbed me so I was caught in his arms. I fell asleep, my back half an inch from his chest and my ass pressed up against the front of his pants. His arm kept me warm as I drifted off.

CHAPTER THIRTY

I woke from a dream of angels to staring right up at one.

"Aethelu!" I cried out in surprise. She held her forefinger to her lips and nodded to the beach at the right of me, where Dream lay fast asleep. "What are you doing here?" I whispered.

"You might want to put this on while I tell you."

Oh yeah. I was naked! She handed me another one of her dresses, this time in a pale, pastel green. Thankfully, no bloomers were offered this time, so going commando, it was. I'd taken and ruined so many of her clothes that I'd never be able to repay her.

"The King requested my presence. I was summoned. From what I could tell from his message, you were being stubborn and not letting him go to the doors;

however, he didn't want you to go alone. I am to be your chaperone."

I looked to the side of me where Dream was still sleeping peacefully. I looked back at Aethelu doubtfully. "He requested you to come?

He's asleep."

"I'm not having you walking through that forest alone," Dream grumbled, lifting his dark lashes. So not asleep at all then.

"Not to be a party pooper here, but don't you think it's a bit shitty making Aethelu walk through a forest of potential killing beasts?" I pointed out.

Aethelu bowed her head down to Dream. "It is ok, Ana. It is my pleasure to help you and His Majesty out."

Something about the whole situation ticked me off. "No. I understand that Dream is the king and that you are not of royal descent, but you are my friend." I turned to Dream. "I will not have her used as a slave."

Dream sat up. I was pleasantly surprised to see no blood on the bandages. The water must have worked miracles. Despite that, I was spitting feathers at his casual use of his subjects.

"I didn't make any demand of Aethelu. I asked her if she would be interested in being a companion for you today. Just while I heal."

I held my finger up. "For one thing, I don't need a companion, and for another, can't you see that even though you asked nicely, Aethelu is not really in a position where she can refuse you? And she could die! What you are asking of her is ridiculous."

Dream's lips quirked at my anger. "No one will die today, least of all Aethelu and you. I have a connection to my subjects. I can send her to the doors and summon her back. She only has to feel a hint of danger, and I can summon her here.

If she is holding onto you, you will come with her."

"Oh." I'd forgotten about the weird telepathy and teleportation thing Dream and Aethelu had. A small streak of jealousy ran through me, but I batted it away quickly.

He scratched his chin. "Aethelu. I have no money to pay you for your service..."

She held her hand up. "I assure you, it's not necessary. I'm happy to help Ana."

I smirked. Despite her unusually simpering demeanor, she was still on my side.

"Please let me finish. You have done me a great many services since Ana came here, and as she so elegantly points out, I've used you without giving any thought to you. I want you to know that I am forever in your debt for your service. I will not forget your kindness. If you wish to leave, please do so and know there will be no consequences. I will not think badly of you."

It wasn't much. I'd have preferred that he at least paid her, but as he pointed out, he might be the king, but he didn't have a dime to his name. He lived in a forest, for fuck's sake.

"I'll walk with Ana. If you'll permit me, Ana?"

I guess I didn't have any choice in the matter. "Fine,

griped. "But I don't need an official chaperone. I do need a friend, though. Come on. Let's get this over with."

She took hold of my hand. Less than a second later, I felt the sensation of my body being squeezed through a toothpaste tube, just as when I stepped through the red door the first time.

"Thank you," I said as we appeared right in front of the red door. "You really didn't ha..."

"I don't want to be a... 'party pooper' as you put it, but I need to be the voice of reason. The last time I saw you, you were in so much trouble. You wanted to run away from the king. You told me that you didn't have er... Stockholm Syndrome."

"Stockholm. It's the capital of Sweden," I said pointlessly, suddenly feeling grim. I remembered exactly what I'd said to her the last time we met. I'd said that there was no danger of me falling for Dream. What a crock.

"The name doesn't matter, Ana. My dear Ana, I told you before. This world isn't for you. Do you want to spend your life being carried around the forest by servants? Because no matter what fairytale is going around in your head, things aren't going to change here."

I dropped to the floor and crossed my legs. "Things have changed," I replied tetchily. "He's not who I thought he was. He's not responsible for the things I thought he was."

Aethelu sat down beside me, crossing her legs in a much more elegant manner. "Ana, he is the man you see. Maybe he has changed since you've been here. Maybe all he needed was the love of a good woman."

"Love...No. It's not love. It's..." I couldn't love him. None of this could be love. I couldn't even explain it away as a great fuck, because we hadn't even done anything yet.

She put her hand on mine. "Your life is none of my business, but even if his majesty turned out to be the most wonderful man in this world, could you really live in the dark for the rest of your life, never seeing your friends and family again?"

Her words stuck like a claw in my throat. I hated every one of them because I knew they were true. I didn't want to hear any more, but she carried on as though her words were not breaking me apart. If I didn't like her, or if I thought she was wrong, I wouldn't have cared, but Aethelu had never spoken a word out of place since I'd met her.

"Look around you." She gestured to the trees and doors around us. "This is it. This is all he can offer you. There are no days off from his job. Look what happened when he became incapacitated. You had to take over."

I shook my head and ran a hand across my eyes. It was too fucking early to be having this conversation, and I hadn't even had my coffee yet. Never mind that I'd not had a cup of coffee in weeks. I damn-well needed one now.

"I can't leave him, Aethelu. You saw him. Did he tell you why he was bandaged that way? Or why we were on the beach in the first place?"

She looked at me with such pity that I wanted to scream. "It is not my position to ask, merely to serve."

I stood up. "I'm sick of all this bullshit. You are right. Dream's life fucking sucks, and my life here with him would fucking suck too, but what else do I have? I have just one friend in the real world." I held up a finger. "One, that's it, count 'em. And He's usually too busy cruising for guys to worry about what I'm doing, pissing my life away. I have a sister I've barely spoken to in years and, the last time I checked, only dust in my kitchen cupboards. At least here I have shitty berries and leaves."

She lowered her head. "I'm sorry. I did not know."

"Well, now you do," I snarled. I had no idea why I was angry at her. The world sucked, both of them, and neither was her fault. "Things could be better here. Dream has a court, right? His own palace somewhere? We could get married and live there. Maybe the fairytale is possible."

She looked up at me in shock. "You are talking of marriage now?"

My response stuck in my throat. What the fuck was I on? I'd never even slept with the guy, and here I was planning my wedding to him. *Jesus fucking christ, I was a mess*

"I...No, I..."

She stood up and took my hands again. This time when she looked into my eyes, I couldn't look away.

"I can't leave him. I know how insane it is. I know that this place is a mess. I know that every word you've said is true, but if I walk through that red door, I'll never see him again. And without me, who will watch the doors?" I added lamely.

She sighed. "The doors are not the problem of humans; however, I see by your expression, that is not the real issue. I understand the pain of love, for I have felt it myself a long time ago. It's a bitter sting when that love is lost, but that doesn't mean that it is right."

I fell into her arms. "Why does it feel so right then?"

She stroked my hair as she held me. "I don't know, my honey. The choice is yours whether to stay or go.

I think I already know in your heart which decision you've made. You were wrong when you said you had only one friend. You have two. I will stand by you. However, maybe it's time to think with your head rather than your heart."

It was easy for her to say. 'Bitter sting' didn't come close to the words that would describe how I would feel if I went home. Total devastation would be closer to the mark.

"I should go and check the doors," I said, pulling away from her.

She nodded. "I dare not go in with you. It is not my place, but I will be here outside, waiting."

Usually, when I went into people's dreams, I'd get a flutter of excitement every time. Each one was like a book waiting to be opened, with all kinds of stories inside. Today, my heart felt like lead, and I barely watched the dreams as they played out. Aethelu's words took up so much space in my mind that I didn't have the energy to bother to concentrate on what I was watching. I was glad when, after a few hours, Aethelu told me that Dream had requested that we both return to him.

Despite my irrational jealousy over the strange link Dream and Aethelu had, I couldn't deny that it was a handy tool.

Dream greeted us with a smile as we appeared right next to him on the beach. "Everything ok?"

I noticed Tour hopping around on the rock next to him. The bird must have figured out where Aethelu had gone and flown to her.

"Fine," I murmured as he kissed my cheek. It felt

forced and unnatural. Aethelu lowered her head slightly. Whether she was bowing down to Dream or merely didn't want to look at any form of intimacy between us, no matter how forced it was, I didn't know.

"Thank you, Aethelu. If there is anything I can do to repay you, please let me know." It wasn't just his kiss that was weird. He'd undergone a personality transplant in the few hours I'd been away.

"It's not necessary, Your Majesty. I enjoyed Ana's company. We had a nice girly chat." She gave me a pointed look, and my stomach flipped. We'd barely spoken the whole time we'd been near the doors. The only chat we'd had was when she warned me against falling for Dream.

Dream extended his hand, and just like that, Aethelu disappeared, back to her house I assumed, along with Tour, who had hopped up onto her shoulder.

"I'm glad you're back. I've had an idea." He was practically giddy. It was so unlike him. Where was the big brooding hunk I'd fallen for?

"What's going on?" I asked. May as well get right to the point. Maybe he had been eaten by another type of nightwalker that could shapeshift into looking like him. Nothing about this place would surprise me anymore.

He narrowed his eyes. "Nothing. what makes you say that?"

I sat on the rock where yesterday's dress had now dried. I pushed it to one side. "I don't know. I left Dream behind. I've come back to an over-excited puppy or a toddler. That kiss on the cheek, it felt so contrived. And the way you are speaking. It's not like you at all. Has the fever come back? Is that what's making you all weird?"

He sat on the sand near my feet and lowered his head. Maybe I'd gone a little too far. It wouldn't be the first time.

"I don't know how to be..." He looked up at me.

The silly grin had dropped from his face. Without it, he looked normal. Relief washed over me. Maybe I was overreacting. It had been a hard day.

"Be what?" I asked him, playing in the sand with my feet, letting my toes dip in and out of the black particles.

"Just be." He caught one of my feet and began to massage it. Holy hell, it felt so good after a day spent walking in and out of doors.

"I've had a lot of time to think today. About you, about us, and about the talk we had last night." He'd gone back to being his own serious self. I should have been happy, but I didn't like the way this talk was heading, despite the glorious feel of his fingers kneading my feet.

I leaned back and rested on my arms, letting my head fall back. If I looked up at the stars, it meant I wouldn't have to look at his face when he inevitably told me that we were wrong together. "Aethelu doesn't think we should be together." Figured I may as well get it in first. Get it over quickly like a band-aid being ripped off.

"Aethelu is very astute. There is a lot playing on my mind. It is paralyzing me. I've always done what is right. I've done my duty and never questioned it. I moved away from people so I didn't have to worry about them... and then you came along and showed me what a fool I was."

"There's nothing foolish about you," I murmured as he rubbed the fleshy part in the middle of my sole. If I concentrated on the touch of him. I wouldn't have to think about his words. I knew a precursor to a breakup when I heard one. This was no different from last night.

He might not be saying "It's not you,

it's me," in so many words, but he was saying it. The feel of his thumbs on my flesh did little to override the despair I felt in my heart. He was soothing my sole whilst shredding my soul.

He stopped, and immediately, the little salve I had was gone. "I am so very foolish, and yet I do not want to stop being so because my foolishness is what keeps me here with you."

"Is that meant to be a compliment?" I asked, pulling myself up so I could look at him.

"Yes, no. I don't know anymore. I told you. I don't know how to be. Before you, I knew exactly who I was. I'd already resigned myself to living out my days watching other people's lives and not having one myself. Before you, it didn't bother me. I had raven and the forest. I didn't need anything else."

I pulled my legs up and wrapped my arms around my knees. "And now you do?"

He closed his eyes. "I didn't know what need was. I never understood it, but now I'm filled with need, and it's tearing me apart. This need for you is tearing up my senses, and I don't want it to stop. I don't want it to end, and yet, I cannot bear it much longer. The touch of your skin is both the pain and the salve. You pulling away hurts more than the burn itself."

I'd pulled away? Yes. I'd pulled my legs up to my chest as a barrier to the pain I thought he was about to inflict on me, but the pain, it seemed, was all his.

I lowered my legs back down to the sand. "I'm scared you are using pretty words to tell me to go."

He took my foot again. "Heaven help me, Ana. I should, but I can't. This here is agony." He swept a finger up my calf while holding my foot in his other hand. I swallowed a moan. I couldn't be enjoying the feel of him while he was talking the way he was. He really had no idea just what he was doing to me, that his touch was sending prickles of desire through me, bringing goosebumps to my flesh.

He looked down at his finger, letting it come to a rest just below my knee. He was quiet as he circled my knee a couple of times, then brought his finger higher, where he joined it with his thumb.

I sucked in a breath as his hand moved higher up my thigh. He was watching with such intensity that I wondered what was going through his mind and if he had any idea just what he was doing to me.

He carried on his journey in silence, taking his own sweet time. His touch was measured, precise and he was taking it all in. I squirmed slightly, stifling a moan. Whatever he was doing, he needed it, and fucking hell, so did I. I was just more impatient than him. He stopped when he got to the hem of my dress and finally took his eyes from my leg.

I bit my lip, needing him to keep going. My insides were on fire, and it took every effort I had to keep from bringing my hips forward. He skirted the hem of my dress with his thumb, deep concentration on his face as though my thigh was the most fascinating thing in the world. It was excruciating torture, waiting for him to decide what to do next.

"There are many secrets between us. Many things that I want to tell you. Things that I've never told anyone before."

Was he fucking serious? He still wanted to converse with me? I was alight with need, and he wanted to have a fucking conversation about secrets?

I pulled the dress out from under his thumb and let him see a lot more thigh. "I think it's time for you to uncover another of my secrets," I murmured, hoping that the big goof would get the hint. He looked up at me, momentarily confused. He really was fresh. I took the hand on my thigh and guided it upwards, all the while my eyes locked onto his. His expression changed from confusion to one I'd seen on him only once before. Desire. And yet, he was hesitant. I was hardly playing it cool. Not that I could play anything cool while fire was ripping through my veins right to my core. I'd never felt so horny in my life, and I was pretty sure if I so much as sneezed, I'd come hard.

"What are you waiting for?" I breathed heavily. His thumb skirted my inner thigh inches from the top, and another wave of desire hit me. I gripped the dress I'd pushed aside on the rock, squeezing it into a fist, and bit my lip.

"Your permission, Ana."

Motherfucker! He was going to be the death of me.

"You have it!" I cried out, pulling my dress up further.

The wonderment on his face only grew as I was exposed in all my glory. "You are so beautiful," he said, his voice husky, his face flooding with arousal. About time! I was dying in my own sweet agony over here. I inched my hips forward again and lay back on the rock, letting the bunched-up dress I'd been gripping fall to the ground behind the rock. The dress I was still wearing was around my middle somewhere, and Dream's hand was still wavering. Finally, after agonizing seconds of waiting, he brought his hand up. Bingo! I arched my back at the feel of his fingers exploring me. Oh, what sweet torture it was. He moved agonizingly slowly, taking his own sweet time exploring me. This was so new to him, and he was pleasuring in the moment, but his unskilled hands were driving me wild without taking me over the edge. I bucked my hips, and he stopped again.

No!

My body tensed in overwhelming craving. I lifted my head, wondering what it was that had caused him to pause now, only to find his head dipping between my legs, and then his tongue was on me. His fingers might have been clumsy, but fuck, he knew how to use his tongue. I grabbed at his head and shifted his position slightly until his tongue found exactly where I needed it to be. I closed my eyes and gave in to the sensation.

Dream groaned as I pushed forward, grinding into his face, fistfuls of his hair in my hands. He found my entrance with his finger and slipped it inside, all the while sucking and licking me like a starving man at a banquet.

"You taste like manna from heaven itself," he groaned, his voice hoarse. Anticipation took hold as he moved back down to me, teasing and tasting with his tongue. My hips arched again, this time unintentionally, and I gasped as a thousand explosions took hold of me. My eyeballs rolled back in my head as the most glorious orgasm I'd ever had took over my body. My legs clamped around his ears as my body bucked around him. He held onto me, one hand firmly on my hip as he rode out my orgasm. But he didn't stop. In fact, he'd only gotten into his stride as his tongue moved faster, not letting me come down from the high of my first orgasm before a second hit me, this one more intense than the first.

"Fuck!" I heaved out as my body took over my mind and shattered around me, quaking with the intensity of my orgasm. When it was over, I let go of his hair and fell back on the rock, my body heavy as it relaxed into a coma of happy hormones and bliss. I let my breathing subside as I watched the sky above me. I'd not paid much attention to it before, but it was beautiful, with a multitude of stars pinpricking through the blackness.

Pulling myself up on my elbows, I found Dream, his hair in a mess around his face thanks to me grinding against it and pulling it as I came. There was a look of astonishment on his face that might have made me laugh in any other circumstance.

"Not seen an orgasm before?"

He shook his head slightly. "I have seen a great many things, but to feel you against me, to feel inside of you was beyond anything I have witnessed. It was extraordinary and beautiful."

"All thanks to you." I let out a long satisfied sigh. "You think that was good. Wait until you experience your own orgasm." I shifted to the edge of the rock and grabbed his pants by the waistline, pulling him toward me with my best come hither look. He was still as I slowly unbuttoned his pants, but when I made to pull them down, he grabbed my wrist.

"What?"

"You do not have to do anything for me. Your pleasure is mine also."

I narrowed my eyes. His pants were bulging, and I could see he was turned on.

"Mine doesn't have to be the only pleasure. There are other pleasures. I want to make you feel like I do right now."

He closed his eyes and let out a groan as I slipped my hands down the front of his pants and felt his cock. I let my hand feel the length of it and moved forward to kiss his chest, just above the top of his bandage.

He groaned again as I scattered kisses up his neck. I had to stand to reach higher. His breathing deepened as I kissed just below his ear, letting my hand work up and down his shaft. His cock twitched in my hand as I nibbled on his ear. With my other hand, I carefully eased his pants down, freeing both him and my hand.

I pulled back a little to see what I was doing. It seemed he was happy to let me lead, but when I saw the look on his face, I stopped. It was ashen.

"What's wrong?" Not his chest; please, don't let it be his injury.

He took both my hands in his, making me let go of his cock in the process.

"I've seen too many things," he said, his breathing coming faster. "Too much pain to inflict it on you."

"Pain?" I wondered if he was thinking of the rape dream we stumbled in on a couple of weeks ago. Again, with just snippets of life, he didn't know the full story of anything. "You will not hurt me," I encouraged, bringing his hand to my breast. He sucked in a fast breath as his palm covered my nipple. "I'm not a virgin. There is nothing painful in this. It is all pleasure."

I saw the torment in his face as he traced a line around my breast then rolled a thumb over my nipple, sending a fresh wave of shivers through my body.

"I want to believe the truth in your words, but I am scared of breaking you, of hurting you. I couldn't bear it if I ever brought pain to you."

I stepped back, taking him all in. Holy fuck, he was glorious, even with his pants halfway round his ankles.

The only blemish on his whole body was the ripped-up fabric wound around his chest. The rest of him was perfect in every way. He stood stock-still watching me as I watched him.

"Take off your pants," I murmured. He shuffled his feet, letting his pants fall to the ground. Now we were both naked. Lust and sadness coated his face, fighting for dominance. His cock, standing at attention, told me he wanted this as much as I did, and yet, he couldn't let go.

"Touch me," I whispered, taking the lead. This was as new to me as it was to him. I'd never had sex with a virgin before and especially one as overwhelmingly tortured and sexy as Dream. "You have my permission," I added. Subtlety wasn't exactly his strong suit, although how subtle a completely naked woman standing in front of a person could be, I wasn't sure. He needed it all spelled out.

He parted his lips a touch and reached out for me. This time I kept my hands to myself as he ran his up and down my body, discovering every inch. It was absolute torture having his hands on me and not being able to touch him, but I knew that would break whatever spell he was under. He kissed my neck as he ran both hands down the sides of my stomach. I cried out lightly as he brought his head to my nipple and sucked gently. The familiar beginnings of orgasm began to tug at me again, and still, I didn't move. I didn't let myself squirm against him as he brought his hand between my legs. Heat pooled there as he worked his finger against my clit. I had to grab ahold of him as my body shuddered against his, claiming me in yet another orgasm. I held on tightly, my arms around his neck for fear of collapsing in a puddle at his feet. He had me. In every way, he had me, and I didn't want to let go. Still gripping him, I brought him into a kiss. He kissed me back fervently as he grabbed my ass and pulled me closer to him. His cock was hard against my stomach as our tongues tangled in a clash of desire. There was no slowness about him now. He was in the middle of the flame that was consuming both of us.

"I cannot," he breathed between fervent kisses, but his body told a different story to his words. I moved my hips rhythmically up and down, letting my feet go on to their tip-toes, then back down to get some friction between our bodies. He groaned again, holding me tighter still with one hand still on my ass and the other gripping my hair.

"This is beautiful torture," he said, releasing me from his grip. "I cannot stand it. You feel sublime against me, but I cannot go any further. I cannot do this to you." His face was manic and tortured and intense and so utterly fucking beautiful, he could break me into a thousand pieces, and I'd still desire more.

"There are many things people can do with their bodies that feel good, that don't involve pain."

"I don't believe that."

God, the man was scared of hurting me. This wasn't a flippant thing with him. This was years of learning that sex was a bad thing, thanks to dreams like the one we'd seen. It was heartbreaking.

"I can give you pleasure without you being inside me." I moved forward slowly and ran my finger up his cock, feeling it twitch. His eyelids fluttered at my touch. I wanted to take him all in, to taste him, to have him fill me, but he needed something else.

took the girth of him in my hand and rubbed up and down slowly. He gripped my shoulder as I worked rhythmically, speeding up.

"This...Is..."

He didn't say another word as his breathing came in short sharp breaths. He held onto me as though if he didn't, he'd fall to the ground, and still, I worked my hand, getting quicker and quicker. His eyes were on mine the whole time, and I swear I could see the stars and infinity reflected in them. His body trembled, and his grip tightened on my shoulder as his cock thickened in my hand before he released himself, the mess of cum coating my stomach.

I waited for the euphoria to leave his face. He opened his eyes, then looked down in horror between us.

The revelation hit me hard. He'd never experienced that before. Not by his own hand nor by anyone else's. How was that even possible? He was a grown man. Jeez, no wonder he'd spent his life in a pent-up ball of anger.

"Don't even think about worrying about it," I said, seeing where his gaze had landed at the sticky mess on my stomach, dripping onto the sand. "We have our own private bath to wash it off in."

I took his hand and led him to the lake. We splashed

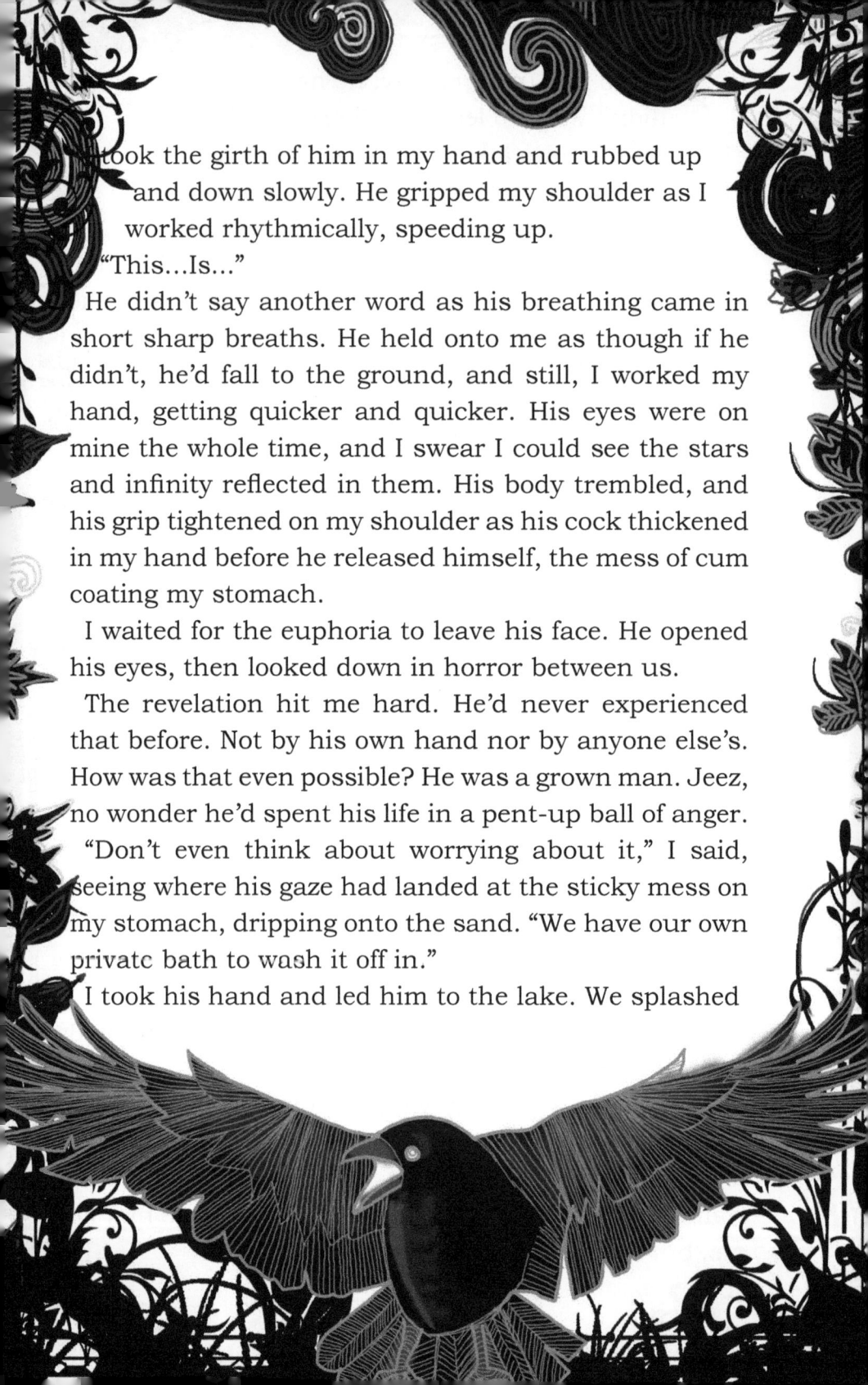

in up to our thighs, and he used his hands to wash me down. "That was... I don't know. I didn't know my body could feel things like this. And now it feels heavy and tired and tingly. I feel like I'm floating."

"Yeah, that's supposed to happen," I assured him. He pulled me toward him and kissed me again. It was sweet and soft.

"You know. I think we should take a look under those bandages. I didn't check them this morning."

"I feel great, Ana. More than great. I have never felt so good. I didn't know it was possible to feel like this."

I gave him a grin. "Nevertheless. I'm going to take a peek. I slowly unwound the ripped-up material from around his chest. When it came off completely. I gasped. While there was an unmistakable injury to him, it had healed far beyond my expectation. Skin had re-grown over what was essentially a wet mess just the day before. The ragged marks around the edge were smoothing out, and the flesh around them looked healthy.

"Think I'll live?" he asked

"You know, I think you just might survive this, after all." I jumped forward, playfully knocking him over. The pair of us fell into the water. He grabbed my waist and submerged me, but I swam down and knocked his footing out from beneath him.

"Nice try!" I laughed as we both came up for air. "You forget I'm a good swimmer."

"I'll never forget anything about you," he said, taking my hand in his and leading me back to the beach. "But now, I am exhausted. What you did to me shot me up into the heavens themselves, but my body is now betraying me and wants to do nothing at all but lie next to you on the sand and sleep.

CHAPTER THIRTY-ONE

I slept like a baby, cradled in Dreams arms, the warmth of the sand offering a warm bed beneath me and the quiet lapping of the lake nearby serving as a rhythmic backdrop.

I opened my eyes the next morning to find him already dressed, including his armor and crown.

"I brought you breakfast!" he said when he saw that I was awake. I wanted to be excited by the offering of berries, but I was getting sick of the same old thing. "No monkey-rabbit this morning?"

He knitted his eyebrows. "Monkey-rabbit?"

"You know. That little animal thing that you've cooked a few times."

He smiled. "Nope, sorry, I have no time for hunting. I've been away from the doors for too long. I need to get back. He handed me my dress, which I pulled over my head. The other dress and his bandages, he balled up and held onto.

"I really think that buying Aethelu a crapload of dresses might be a good way to repay her. I've lost count of the number of hers I've ruined."

He shrugged. "I have no money unless you want to learn to make it out of leaves," he said, gesturing to the trees around us.

"Some king you are," I joked. "Aren't you supposed to be dripping in gold and diamonds and furs?"

His face shuttered slightly. "Don't have any of those things anymore except for my crown, but I cannot give that to Aethelu."

I sensed that I'd said the wrong thing. He must have grown up in the lap of luxury, and even when he was sent away as a child, he had his own palace. For his own reasons, he chose to leave it all behind.

"Why do you still wear the crown?" I asked as we set off into the forest. Raven took off from the branch he'd perched himself on over the last couple of days and flew ahead of us.

"Because I am the king," he replied simply.

"Why don't you do that teleporting thing for us rather than having us walk everywhere?"

He laughed. "Still full of questions, I see. I suspect that part of you I'll never be able to satisfy."

I nudged his side playfully. "So why not then? Why is Aethelu so special that you can whisk her around the forest?"

He raised an eyebrow, a decidedly un-Dream-like smirk on his face. "Do I detect a hint of jealousy?"

"Don't get too cocky, mister. I just want to know.

No jealousy here. You can whizz all the girls in the neighborhood around the forest all you want.

I just want to know why I'm the one that has to get sore feet hauling my ass through these trees all the time."

"And miss out on this beautiful scenery?"

I groaned. "If I knew how corny me tugging on your tadger would make you. I'd have let you stick to your frustration."

"I honestly don't understand a word of that sentence, but I get the gist. If you must know, I was born with the ability to summon people to me. It is a trait brought down from hundreds of generations before me. I come from a long line of slackers who thought it was easier to summon servants rather than do anything themselves. I've lost the ability to some extent as I've gotten older. I can only summon those in my own court now."

I worked the words around in my mind. "So let me get this straight. You can get other people to come to you, but you can't teleport yourself to them?"

"I can't teleport myself anywhere. When I go anywhere, I walk, and before you say anything about me teleporting you, I cannot do that either. You are not from my court and have no magic in you."

I stopped in my tracks. "May I remind you that I made my mother's door come to me. If that isn't magic. I don't know what is!"

He gave me a quick kiss. "You have all the magic in the world inside you. Everything about you is magic. However, it's not the kind of magic that lets me send you off around the forest, so you'll have to walk just as I do."

"Nice save, buddy," I huffed.

Despite his uncharacteristic enthusiasm for life, which I suspected was more to do with him coming for the first time in his whole life rather than the long walk, he still kept his wits about him. He held my hand, his eyes darting about, looking for goodness only knew what. More nightwalkers, probably.

We got back to the clearing where Dream used his magic to set a fire.

"Want to come with me?" he asked, nodding to the doors. My legs hurt with the effort of walking, but there was no way I was going to sit by the fire without him. I think he knew that, too, because he didn't demand that I come with him, merely asked.

"Sure." I plastered a smile on my face. I'd done this before; I could do it again.

Once we were in one of the dreams, my feet forgot about the pain they were in, and my aching calves were salved by the excitement of watching other people's lives. I'd hated it when Dream wasn't here, but with him by my side, it was fun somehow. Yeah, I'm a voyeur; shoot me.

We watched a hundred lives, snippets of hopes and wishes and memories all drifting together, and yet, all I could see was Dream. I'd never noticed before the way he watched each dream with such intensity,

even the mundane ones. His eyes took in every detail of everything—the people, the places, the interactions. Neither of us spoke in any of the dreams. To do so would be to spoil them. I understood that now and I understood just how important these dreams were to Dream himself. Humans were the family he'd never had. He'd once told me that he hated all humans, but the truth was he loved us all. He loved us all, and it had destroyed him because while we were all he'd had from the time he was a child, he was never involved, never included, destined to live on the sidelines of other people's lives without having any kind of life himself. My mother had once told me that love and hate were different sides of the same coin. I thought at the time she was talking about my father, and she probably was, but that's how Dream was with the billions of people he saw. He loved us, and he hated us. As we went from dream to dream, I only saw love in his eyes. He was mesmerized by all of them.

"You've changed," I said, grinning as we came out of our tenth or so dream.

"You have changed me, Ana. I am who I am because of you."

Oh, he knew how to make my insides squirm with happiness. "When I first came in the dreams with you, you watched with indifference, eager to get away, but now you can't keep your eyes from the people. I'm practically dragging you away each time."

"I can't keep my eyes from you," he growled, pulling me to him and kissing me playfully. I closed my eyes and fell into it as the swoosh of doors sounded behind us. He was becoming so familiar to me now. His scent, the way he kissed. We'd fallen into a rhythm, and it was blissful.

After a quick lunch of sandwiches and a glass of wine each that Dream had procured from somewhere through the red door, we went back into the dreams. The first ten, twenty, thirty were similar to the ones we'd seen in the morning, but it was late in the day when one of the dreams stopped us both in our tracks.

Dream's hand tightened around mine as the darkness began to clear. There was a woman on a bed, completely naked, her face contorted in a silent scream. Her arms were being held above her head by a man. Another man positioned himself between her legs, his erection easy to see, even in the dim light. A third man knelt beside her, his head obscuring her chest.

"Come, I cannot subject you to this depravity again. We do not need to see this dream. Dream's hand tightened on mine, and he pulled me toward the door.

"Wait."

"What must we wait for?" Dream asked, his face dark with rage. "This dream won't end here. We cannot save her, Ana. I thought I made that clear the last time."

I pulled back on his hand. "Who's dreaming this? Is it one of the men, or is it her?"

Dream stopped, his hand on the door. I watched the rage in his expression drop, to be replaced with a hint of confusion. "It is her. The woman dreams this. Why would she dream about her own attack?"

"And there is no way that we can see nightmares here, right? They all go to your brother."

He furrowed his eyebrows. "Beyond the small ones of people losing their teeth and finding themselves naked in supermarkets which sometimes get mixed up, yes, it's impossible, but you can see it for yourself. We need to get out of here. Something is very wrong."

I glanced back at the scene playing out and allowed myself a small grin. "I think you need to turn around and look again."

Reluctantly, Dream turned. The positioning had changed slightly as we'd been speaking. Now the first man was running kisses down the woman's neck. The man that had been kneeling over her had one of his nipples in her mouth, and the third moved inside her in slow strokes. The scream on her face was not pain, but ecstasy.

"She is enjoying this?" Dream asked, incredulity filling his voice

I nodded my head. "I do believe she is."

The soundtrack kicked in. Her soft moans echoed around us as she was taken by the three men, each of them worshiping her. Her body writhed in pleasure as they kissed, stroked, licked, and nibbled at her body. My own body heated at the scene. I was so close to them I could reach out and touch them, and I couldn't take my eyes from them. From the beauty of it all. Something told me this was a memory rather than a wish. Each of the men moved in perfect choreography, knowing how to tease her, how to draw her pleasure out. It was fucking beautiful and was making me so fucking horny, I could barely stand it. I tore my eyes from them for a second to see Dream's reaction. He was taking it all in, watching it all hungrily. Now that he knew that it was consensual, it was affecting him in ways that turned me on even more. His lips parted slightly, and his breathing was more rapid. I wanted to reach out to him so badly, but I didn't want to break the spell he was under watching these people come together in their lovemaking. I was momentarily taken from the wonderment and arousal in Dream's face by the sound of the woman crying out. Her eyes shuttered closed, and her head fell back as her body trembled with orgasm. My own body began to ache with need at the sweet torture of watching this play out. I clamped my legs together as a surge of want and desire pulled together at my core.

"I think it's time to leave now," I whispered huskily, barely getting my words out. If I had to watch this any longer, I was going to come on the spot. My legs began to shake with the sheer intensity of need. Spending the day with Dream had been enough of an aphrodisiac in itself, but watching this with him had tipped me over the edge.

Dream didn't need asking twice. He drew me up into his arms and carried me through the door back into the forest. The last thing I heard as the door closed was the scream of another orgasm renting the night.

He carried me to the clearing and laid me down upon the leaves. Thankfully Raven had made himself scarce because what I was planning to do with his master would scar him for life.

"I never knew..." Dream groaned, his body held over mine by his straightened arms. He was so close to me, and yet, there was still a gap between us. His legs straddled mine, so I was completely trapped beneath him.

"Not the best time for a conversation here, buddy," I said, reaching down between us to unbutton his fly.

"I thought it was something horrible, something painful and insidious you humans did to each other, and yet, upon watching it, I feel..."

I licked my lips. desperate to feel him against me, desperate to sate this need that had been building in me for hours. "Feel what?" I urged, slipping his pants down over his hips, the tip of his erection skating my lower stomach. As his knees were on the outside of mine, the pants couldn't go very far. I shuffled into a sitting position, pushing him up so he was facing me, his legs still straddling mine. I dragged the dress I was wearing out from under me and pulled it over my head, throwing it to one side in a heap.

"What is it you feel?"

His eyes moved down to my chest where they held as

his breathing increased. He looked at me as one might gaze upon the Mona Lisa for the first, taking in every inch of me. My body throbbed in exquisite torment as he slowly drew his eyes up to mine.

"What do you feel?" I asked again, this time, my voice coming out in ragged breaths. If he didn't touch me soon, I was going to combust in flames.

"I feel that if I don't touch every part of you, I might die right here, right now, and that my entire life has been a lie that has brought me to this moment that I might finally know the truth of it all."

I took hold of his hand and laid it on my breast. His touch was agonizingly slow as he took it in. He ran his thumb over my nipple, and I bit on my lower lip to stifle a moan. Heat pooled between my legs as his cock twitched against my stomach. With anyone else, I would have ripped their pants off and demanded they take me on the spot, such was the ache of need, but Dream was taking his sweet time to explore, to discover, to set my body alight with a desperate longing of beautiful agony. He dipped his head and took my nipple in his mouth, causing the moan I'd stifled earlier to escape my lips. I reached out, wrapping my arms around his neck, pulling him closer while the need throbbed harder still. I fell back, and this time, he followed, finally kissing me. I felt the press of his cock against my stomach, jammed between us as he brought his full weight down on me. My body arched against him as he kissed me, driving his tongue into my mouth. I kissed back, matching his desire which had finally found the intensity of my own. He ground his hips against me, rubbing his cock against my stomach, making the ache within me unbearable.

"Stop!" I huffed, my breathing ragged. "We need to change position." I wriggled out slightly from underneath him and pulled my legs from between his. His eyes never left me as I drew my legs up, parting them in front of him. Awe filled his features as he gazed down at my core. He shifted himself so he was between them, his pants still halfway down his thighs as he knelt before me, as though he was worshiping at an altar. God, he was so utterly fucking stunning I could barely breathe.

He moved forward, so once again, he was hovering over me, his weight on his arms and his cock at my entrance. I bucked upwards, desperate to feel him inside of me, but he pulled back.

"I have to know that you want me to do this," he breathed, and in those words, I could see he was suffering too.

"*You* won't be doing it to me; *we* will be doing this to each other. This is not an act one person does to another. It's an act of two people working together."

He sucked in a breath. "This is like no work I've ever

participated in. It is transcendent of anything I have ever known."

"Keep your words for what comes next."

I reached down between us and grasped his cock, causing him to intake a short breath. Arching my hips again, I guided him to me. He hesitated a half-second of excruciating eternity before pushing forward. I gasped as he filled me. His mouth opened as his eyes filled with wonder. He let out a long shaky breath as I lowered my hips to the ground, pulling slightly backward, causing a delicious friction between us. He soon followed, filling me back up again deeply. It was his first time, but it was nothing like anything I'd ever known before. He moved back again and slowly thrust forward, getting into a rhythm. I pulled him toward me, one hand on his beautiful ass, the other wrapped around his neck as our mouths crashed together like the rest of us. He let out a groan as he tasted me, and he increased the speed in which he moved. I matched his speed, bucking beneath him in a frenzy of desire, holding onto him for dear life and dear release as the clench of orgasm began to take hold. I dropped my hand from around his neck, down his back, firmly resting it on his other ass check as I tightened around him.

"I'm hurting you!" Dream whispered, pausing his rhythm.

"Only if you stop now, " I heaved out, gripping my fingernails into his skin as a thin coat of sweat broke out all over my body. He thrust forward again, this time more deeply than before, and I shattered around him, crying out his name. He thrust harder now, taken by his own pleasure. I held on as a second orgasm crept up on me. My hands fell from him to the ground, and I clawed at the forest floor as bliss took me away somewhere to the heavens themselves.

"Oh, fuck!" I heaved out, my voice barely above a strangled whisper as my body trembled beneath his. He let out a long groan and shuddered as he came inside me, filling me with his warmth.

CHAPTER THIRTY-TWO

"That was...That was..."

"Fucking hot?" I helped him with his words as he held me in his arms, the pair of us coated in a sheen of mingled sweat and spent desire.

"I was going to say it was the most beautiful thing I have ever known, but fucking hot encapsulates my feelings well also."

I nuzzled against him, letting my head rest on his chest above where the scars from the nightwalker were still red and visible. "I don't know. I like your words too. they are much more poetic."

"Your poetry comes from more than mere words, Ana. It is in everything that you do."

I sighed, blissfully happy, and traced one of his scars

with my finger. The skin had knitted together really well, and the redness was beginning to dissipate. With the way he healed, he would be back to normal in a few days. "Flattery will get you everywhere."

"Is it always like that?" he asked, his voice low. I could tell it had been on his mind a while.

"Sex?" I thought back to all the lackluster sex and orgasms at my own hand with David and shook my head. "I can promise you that sex has never been like that for me before."

"No? Please tell me I didn't hurt you. I heard you screaming out, but you said not to stop and...I couldn't even if I wanted to."

I looked up and held my finger to his lips. "It was perfect."

He relaxed and brought his hand up to my hair which he ran his fingers through, only adding to my hormone overdosed, blissful, post-sex haze.

"If I thought I'd caused you pain, I would never forgive myself."

I sat up and recovered my dress from where I'd thrown it and pulled it over my head. He lay back, watching me with his hands under his head. " I love watching you dress. I love watching you undress even more."

I stopped. Love? It was a word I hadn't dared allow myself to say or to think. Not that he'd said that he loved me. He'd said that he loved how I dressed and undressed. That wasn't the same. Because he couldn't love me. And I couldn't love him because nothing good could come of it. I couldn't stay here, and he couldn't come to the real world, and I knew with every fiber of my being that I couldn't live without him, but I did love him. I loved him. *Oh, fuckety fuck! What had I done?*

A cawing above my head took me from my own thoughts.

"Raven." He flew down and landed on my shoulder, where he began to hop up and down.

"What is it?"

Dream jumped up and pulled his pants on quickly, just in time before Aethelu appeared through the trees, Tour on her shoulder.

She came to a stop when she saw Dream hurriedly getting dressed.

"I do apologize, Your Majesty," she said, falling into a bow. When she came back up, I saw a slight hint of color in her cheeks. "I only wished to see if you were better after your injury. I see I have come at a delicate time.

Dream grunted as he picked up his armor and crown from the forest floor. She caught my eye, and I swore there was a twinkle of mischief in hers. I couldn't help the grin that was plastered over my face. It didn't take a polyglot to figure out what had been happening here only ten minutes earlier.

"It's not a delicate time, Aethelu. I thank you for your concern. As you can see, I am fine now. Ana's been helping me." Despite his words, I could see he was flustered. It was very unlike him.

"I'll bet she has," Aethelu quipped. I let out a giggle, but it went right over Dream's head.

"Is there anything we can do for you, Aethelu?" I asked.

She shook her head. "No. I was in the forest anyway, and I thought I'd come and see how you are. Would you like to come for a walk with me, Ana?"

"Ana stays with me," Dream said abruptly. "The forest is not safe for her."

Annoyance rippled under my skin. He'd had sex with me once. Mind-blowing, out of this world sex, to be sure, but that didn't mean he owned me. "I'd love to come with you, Aethelu." I turned to Dream. "If Aethelu and I come across any problems, you can summon us back right. You have that telepathy thing."

Dream strode over to me and caught me by the arm, pulling me away from Aethelu. He spoke in harsh, hushed tones. "I've been doing a lot of thinking recently. I know you've made friends with her, but I'm beginning to suspect there is more to her than she lets on."

I glanced over his shoulder at Aethelu, who was waiting patiently for us. "In what way? You were perfectly fine letting me walk with her the other day. What's changed?"

He gritted his teeth. "Nothing has changed. It is merely a thought that has been going around in my mind for a while. It only just crystallized when I saw her just now. I'm not sure I can trust her with you. I need to know that you are safe at all times. I cannot and will not let anything happen to you."

I planted my hands on my hips. "What we did was unbelievably wonderful, but that doesn't make you my keeper. You tried that once, remember, keeping me chained up. Is that what you want?

A plaything? Because if you do, I'm not your girl."

He ran his hands through his hair in an aggrieved manner. "Of course, I don't want to keep you chained up."

"So let me go with Aethelu."

"No. I forbid it. I have stated my case. That is the end of it."

Like hell it is. "Are you fucking kidding me right now?" My voice was much louder than Dream's, and I knew Aethelu could hear every word I said. I didn't even give a crap. If he wanted this argument, he could have it, but I wasn't going to hide it. I was pissed off, pissed off being an understatement. "I'm going with Aethelu. You have two options. Either grow up and let me go with her or try to stop me. But let it be known. If you try to stop me, what we did earlier will never happen again, at least not with my consent."

He visibly blanched at my words. Consent in anything to do with sex was such a huge deal for him and yet he was blind to the concept in any other situation. He let my arm go.

"So be it. Go with your friend. I will not stop you."

"Too fucking right, you won't." Ok, I was probably being a little harsh, seeing as he'd backed down, but I was incensed and irritated. "Come on, Aethelu. Let's go."

I took Aethelu's hand and all but dragged her into the forest. Tour flew overhead, cawing at us.

"I think this is a mistake," Aethelu said as soon as we were out of earshot. "I didn't mean to upset the king."

"Yeah, well, the king's an idiot."

Aethelu groaned beside me. "I've told you before. You need to be careful, Ana."

I stopped and turned to her. Her beautiful face was cast in the shadows of the leaves above us. "He pretty much said the same thing about you. He told me that he doesn't trust you."

Confusion painted her face. "Why ever not? I would not hurt you, Ana. I cannot understand why His Majesty thinks I would."

I shrugged my shoulders. "I don't know what's gotten into him. He seemed fine when you were helping us. It was just something he came up with this morning. Hang on. He can't hear me through that weird telepathy thing you share, can he?"

"No. I know when he is in my head. He cannot come in without my permission. It's like he has to knock on a door before I let him in. You are free to speak your mind."

We walked a little further before I spoke again. "We had sex."

Aethelu snorted. "I don't need telepathy to know that. It's pretty obvious. That's why I wanted you to come with me for a walk. I want to make sure you are alright. I love you, Ana. I don't want you hurt."

"I love you too, but there is nothing to worry about. Dream treats me really well...most of the time."

It was weird how easy it was to hear the words I love you, from a friend and how easy it was to say them back. I did love Aethelu. It was nothing compared to the squeezing agony of feelings I felt for Dream, but it was a love of platonic friendship between women. Something I had always lacked in my real life.

"Your relationship with the king is not my business, and I don't want to interfere. If you say he treats you well, then who am I to get in the way. And while I don't understand his problem with me, I will give you both some distance. You know where I live if you should ever need me."

I was just about to tell her that I needed her right now. I needed some female company desperately, but I didn't get the chance to get the words out. A Savagara leapt out of the trees toward us, its weird blue ghostlike shimmer lighting up the forest around us.

"The king sends his regards," It rasped, extending its claws. It was a shock to hear it speak. I thought that it was nothing more than a beast despite the outline of a huge man beneath its ghostly surface. But that was nothing compared to the shock of it closing in on me, its teeth bared, and its glowing eyes fixed on me.

My mind spun. Dream had sent this thing? He had me going off with Aethelu so much that he'd kill the pair of us? I didn't want to believe it. He had a dark side, but this? After everything we'd done?

It leaped. I ducked out of its way, but I was too slow. Two huge paws crashed down on me, sending me to the ground. I cried out with pain as its full weight landed on top of me. "I've wanted a taste of you ever since I learned of your existence. My brother failed at killing your boyfriend, but I will not fail in killing you."

Above it, I could see Aethelu raining blows upon its back. Not that it even noticed. My mind whirled with its words. If Dream sent this thing, why was it now calling him my boyfriend? Nothing made sense. I kicked upwards, aiming for its balls, but when my foot hit the blue, glowing surface, it was like kicking a wall made of steel.

"Fuck!" I yelped as the pain rippled through me.

"Nice try, human, but there is no winning here. At least, not for you. I'm going to enjoy you for breakfast and then finish up with your friend for dessert."

Aethelu screamed and grabbed it by the horns. A quick twist of its head, and she was sent flying into the undergrowth. Tour landed on the monster's shoulder and began cawing in its ear.

"It's almost amusing how pitiful you both are. The human I can understand, but a Dreamlander. Well, that's just disappointing. I'm sure she'll be just as tasty as you, though." He lowered his head and opened his mouth. I closed my eyes as his tongue brushed against my cheek. It was more like the tongue of a large cat such as a lion or tiger than of a human. Fear and disgust settled in my stomach as I opened my eyes again. His hot breath made me recoil as he opened his mouth to swallow me whole.

Bang

A loud crack echoed through the forest. The savagara's eyes went wide before the life drained out of them. Its full weight landed on me, knocking the wind from my lungs. Seconds later, it lifted, and I sucked in a large lungful of air to combat the dizziness that was threatening to take over.

"Dream?" I croaked. He held out a hand to me to help me up. In his other hand, he held a gun.

"Are you ok? He didn't hurt you, did he?"

I shook my head as he pulled me to my feet. My emotions crashed down on top of me with more weight than the savagara.

"What is going on?" I asked as Dream pulled me to him and into his arms.

"I don't know, but I suspect she does."

I peeked out to see Aethelu sitting in the undergrowth, her hands up in the air as Dream held the gun out at her.

I pulled myself out of Dream's embrace. "Seriously. What is happening? Where did you get a gun? And why did you send that bastard thing to kill us?"

I looked down at the body of the savagara to make sure it was really dead. It wasn't breathing, which told me that I didn't need to worry about it anymore. I only had to worry about Dream and Aethelu, who were now both glaring at each other.

"I sent it? I think you'll find it was her." He indicated for Aethelu to stand up, which she did, her hands still above her head.

"Aethelu tried to save me from that

monster. She's not to blame here. The savagara told me you sent it."

Dream's eyes hadn't left Aethelu's the whole time he'd been here, but he tore them away to shoot a glance at me. He looked pissed. "Why would I send a savagara to kill you? I love you."

Oh fuck. There it was. Those three words at the most inappropriate moment ever.

"He said the king sent him."

Dream let out a quick breath that was almost a laugh. "There is more than one king in this realm. My brother sent this."

Oh shit. The King of Nightmares. I'd forgotten his title. I cast my eyes down, mortified at what I'd just said. I'd accused the only man I'd ever loved of trying to kill me. *Way to go, Ana!*

"Isn't that right, Aethelu?"

"Yes. The savagara no doubt was sent here by your brother, Your Majesty. I don't understand what this has to do with me, though. I've never even met the King of Nightmares, nor have I ever set foot in his court."

Dream's eyes narrowed, the hate in his features obvious. It was the same look he'd given me when I'd first stepped into this kingdom. The same look that said, 'I'm going to kill you.'

"Then why is it that whenever Ana and I are attacked, you are always around first. I didn't think of it before, but it's like someone is spying on us." He kept the gun steadily pointed at her but quickly moved his eyes to either side before they settled back on Aethelu.

"I don't see anyone else here. In fact, I've not seen anyone else in my forest for years before you happened to come along…just as Ana got here. Pretty coincidental

"No!" I shouted out as he readied his aim. "She tried to save me."

"Don't feel sorry for her, Ana. She'd see you dead in the blink of an eye. She is a spy for my brother. Why else would she lure you to this spot where the savagara was waiting?"

"I'm not a spy," Aethelu cried out, but I wasn't listening. Dream was right. How else could the savagara have known to meet us here? And all the other times we'd been attacked. Aethelu had known exactly where we were. Something clicked into place in my head. I calmly grabbed the gun from Dream's hand and shot the traitor right in the middle. She heaved a final breath and died in front of us.

CHAPTER THIRTY-THREE.

Aethelu stared at me wide-eyed, her mouth open in shock. I stood trembling and let the gun drop to the ground. Silence rained down on us as no one spoke. I couldn't speak. I could barely register my own thoughts. Tour's lifeless body lay at Aethelu's feet.

"Aethelu wasn't the only one who knew I was here," I croaked. "Aethelu, you told me Tour hadn't been with you for very long. When she landed on the savagara's shoulders and cawed into its ear, it didn't bat an eyelid. Surely, it would have attacked her unless…"

"Unless she was the one that had guided him here," Aethelu whispered, her voice cracking. "I'm sorry. I didn't know, but it all makes sense. She came to me not long before I met you." Her eyes widened, "She was out, and when she came back, she urged me to go for a walk with her. She was flying toward your clearing when you fell out of the tree."

"I saw her when we came out of Gladys's dream!" I exclaimed, remembering the flutter of pink I'd seen. I'd not thought much of it at the time. "Not long before the first savagara attacked you."

"How could I have been so wrong?" Dream said, eventually, picking up the gun from where I'd dropped it at my feet. "Nightmare always did like fancy things. The bird must have been watching me for months."

Aethelu nodded slightly, her face still registering the shock we all felt.

"I'm so sorry," she whispered, kicking its lifeless body away from her as though it might taint her if she stood close to it any longer. I ran to her and wrapped my arms around her as we both descended into sobs.

"I have been a fool," Dream said once we'd both wrung ourselves out. "Aethelu, please forgive me."

"There is nothing to forgive Your Majesty."

He walked over to us and took her hand. "Ana pointed out to me once that you feel that you have to do my bidding because of my position."

"I also pointed out that you are an ass," I reminded him.

"That too. I will not deny it. I offered you my gratefulness before, but if what Ana says is true and you fought a savagara to save her, then my gratitude will never be enough."

Aethelu, ever the lady, held her head high. "I assure you, I don't expect your gratitude or your forgiveness. Though if it makes you happy, Your Majesty, I will accept both."

Dream nodded slightly. "It is with that in mind that I'm making a formal request for you to

accompany Ana and me back to my palace and

be Ana's lady in waiting. If that doesn't suit you, you may come along as a confidant to her. Please be assured that the choice is entirely yours, and you should base it on your decision rather than my title."

"Palace?" I croaked.

Dream shifted his eyes to me. "I have been

thinking of going back home for a while now. I

have spent most of my life out in this forest. I

cannot ask you to do the same. I want more for you."

He took my hand in his. "I'm asking that you come with me and be by my side as I go back to my rightful position ruling the Dream Court. It is time I went back and did the job I was born to do. Just like I said to Aethlelu, the choice is yours. I only ever wanted the choice to be yours. I want you more than I ever thought it possible to want anything, but I will not force that life onto you. If you do not want to come with me with all your heart as I want you to come with me, then I will respect that."

"I do want it!" I said, falling into him. I wanted to be with Dream more than I wanted to draw breath. He held me tight, kissing my head with butterfly kisses. Once upon a time, I was a girl with no dreams. Now I was living a dream come true. I was going to live in a palace. It was a fucking fairytale.

Aethelu cleared her throat behind us. Dream opened his arm wider and brought her into the hug. I wasn't sure who was more surprised, her or me.

The three of us strolled slowly back to the clearing.

My heart had never felt so light, so alive.

"The palace will be a mess. I have not lived there for many years. We will need to bring in more staff to clean up."

"I can help with that, Your Majesty," Aethelu offered.

"No. I've offered you the place in the palace court as a lady, not as a servant. I cannot expect you to serve us. We will have staff to fulfill your needs. I only want you there as a friend to Ana. As a friend... to me."

I caught the flush in Aethelu's cheeks. "It is a great honor, Your Majesty, but I have always worked. I wouldn't know what to do with myself if I didn't."

"But it's not necessary," Dream continued.

"Actually, I think it's a great idea." I piped up between them. "You want Aethelu to come with us as an equal, right?"

Dream scratched his chin. "Yes. An equal. That's what I've been trying to say."

"Well, let her work. I'll be working. If you think that the pair of us will sit around all day doing nothing, then you are wrong. You said yourself that the palace will be a mess. Then let's clean it all up together. I have a feeling that Aethelu might like to paint something for the walls."

"I'd love it!" Aethelu grinned.

Dream looked like he was defeated. "Aethelu, how about I make you Artist in Residence?"

I'd never actually known what a swoon was, but I got a full grasp of its meaning as Aethelu did just that. She drew her hands up to her heart and pulled in a deep breath, grinning from ear to ear. I almost expected her to do a twirl on the spot and break into a song. I understood how she felt because I felt the same way. Dream had rescued both of us from our shitty lives, but we had rescued him too.

I was just daydreaming of how I'd look in a ball gown in the middle of a palace when Dream caught hold of my arm.

A swish of blue in my peripheral vision was my only clue as to what was going on. It all happened so fast. The blast of the gun, the sound of yelps and growling and teeth gnashing together. Dream ran so quickly with me that in a flash of black and blue and then red, it was all over.

We were in a dark room. Four walls, two red doors. The one we'd just flown through had slammed shut behind us. The one in front was open. It took me a moment to register what was through it.

My home. My shitty, crappy apartment where my hopes and dreams had long ago come to die.

"What's happening?" I screamed out, trying to catch my breath. "Savagaras. More of them. I counted at least five prowling the clearing. The only way I could get you away from them was to bring you through the red door, so that's what I did. This is a barrier between our worlds. The savagaras will not be able to get to us here."

"Aethelu!" I screamed, trying to run past him to get back to her. There was no fucking way I was leaving her behind. Dream caught hold of me, blocking my way.

"She's safe. I teleported her back to the village. I couldn't do that with you, so I brought you here."

Panic danced in my chest, but knowing Aethelu was safe calmed me a little. "So what now? We stay here until the savagaras go?

He wouldn't look me in the eye. His own eyes were downcast, shuttered. My chest tightened as I waited for him to respond, to say anything. When he did, his words cut me like a knife. "You will go through that red door. I'm taking you home."

"You mean you brought *us* home, right?" He had to mean that. There was no other option that wouldn't completely destroy me.

His voice was measured and dull like all the life had been sucked out of him in the last five minutes. "I have to go and sort out the savagaras. I don't think they'll attack me if they know you have gone. You have to go."

My mouth fell open. "Go? Go where? I'm not going anywhere without you!"

He looked crazed with grief, echoing the pain building up inside me. He couldn't be serious.

Anguish filled his voice. "You know why I can't go with you. My world would get darker and darker until there was nothing left."

"So let me stay with you in the Night Realm," I pleaded, my agony increasing with each moment, searing my heart. He shook his head, and in that small movement, my world shattered.

"I can't do that. My brother will kill you. I've tried keeping you safe. I thought I could, but I can't. I never meant any of this to happen..." He quientened for a second. I wanted to reach out to him. To grab hold of him like I did when he was sick. When I'd wanted to keep his soul inside his body. Except now, his soul was broken...destoyed.

"He isn't ever going to stop looking for you, and when he finds you, he will kill you."

Tears fell down my face as pain squeezed my chest.

"Why? Why does he hate me so much? He's never even met me."

I'd never seen him look so tortured, so desolate. Those black eyes of his no longer held stars; they held eons of pain. Pain that I could never hope to extinguish.

When he spoke, his voice was low and filled with torment. "Ana, it was your father that killed ours."

Shit. I couldn't believe what I was hearing. It explained everything. Why Dream had brought me here and why he had hated me so much at the beginning. It explained why his brother had set out to kill me and why my mother's door was one of those with vines on it. He hated me because of who my father was.

"I barely even remember my father." All of it made sense, and none of it made sense. "I'll go and talk to him. I'm not my father. I'll make him see…"

"See what, Ana? All he'll see is the daughter of the man that destroyed our world. You have to go back through the red door. "You'll come to me, though? You'll come and see me."

He didn't answer. He was a man as broken as I was. The pain was agonizing, and the longer I drew it out, the worse it was going to get.

I nodded slowly and stood. I needed him. I needed him so badly that kissing his cheek and knowing it was the last kiss between us hurt so much more than all the pain he put me through when we first met. This was the type of pain that would leave scars that would never fade.

He moved to kiss my lips, but I pulled back. I couldn't bear it. One more touch would slay me. I turned and walked to the red door, knowing that when I went through it, I'd never be coming back.

Every part of me screamed in agony as I took the step

through the door. It closed behind me, leaving me alone in my apartment. The time on my clock read ten' past two... only moments after I had left, and yet, it felt like a lifetime ago. I didn't need to turn around to know that the red door was already gone. I flung myself onto my bed and dissolved into howls of anguish. The grief like nothing I'd felt before. Not when my mother became ill, not when David left. All of that faded into nothing compared to the gaping wound in my heart left by Dream. I closed my eyes and pictured him as I left him. Alone, destroyed. It was heartbreaking, overwhelming. I closed my eyes and did everything I could to fall asleep so I could be with him once more.

EPILOGUE

The sound of urgent banging on my door woke me from sleep. I'd not dreamed about him, or at least, I couldn't remember the dream. Maybe that would come someday.

Dragging myself out of bed, I quickly pulled my robe around myself and answered the door, glad of the excuse not to think about Dream. It was already excrutiatingly painful enough.

"Oh, Em, gee. I thought you were dead. You look like shit, girl."

I rubbed the sleep from my eyes as Chris darted past me into my apartment.

"What are you doing here?" I asked blearily. The clock on the wall told me it was nearly seven am. I'd never seen Chris out of bed before midday, even on a nonwork day. "Shouldn't you be sleeping off last night?" He gave me a withering look. "It's hard to sleep when your phone is on fire. Look."

He passed his phone to me. It had thirty-three missed calls, all within the last two hours and all from one number. A number I recognized very well.

"My sister called you?"

"Er, yeah!" he said, grabbing his phone back from me. She told me that she'd been calling you non-stop, and you didn't answer. I told her that you were a lazy bitch and were probably asleep after getting fired, but she was having none of it. How did you get back here anyway? Your car is still in the parking lot at work."

"I was pulled into the body of one of the subjects," I whispered aloud, trying to remember back so long ago, although, to Chris, it had only been a few hours.

Chris shook his head dramatically. "Noooo. That's what I thought I saw, but obviously, I can't have because then we'd both be heading for the loony bin. Right?"

"Huh?" My brain was fuzzy with it all. "Oh, yeah, right. I ran out of the room and ran home after jumping on whatshisname. I knew McGee would fire me."

Chris eyed me curiously for a second. "Yea, that's what I thought. I need to take fewer party drugs. My mind was tripping. McGee did fire your ass by the way."

I didn't care. It was a stupid job anyway, made all the more pointless by the fact I now knew why the people weren't waking up, and no amount of money or sleep trials was going to change that.

"It doesn't matter. I'm going back home."

Chris scrunched up his nose as though I'd just told him I was going to live in a cow patty.

"You are going to Winnipeg?"

"It's not Winnipeg. It's a small town outside of

Winnipeg, and yes. That's where I'm going. I need to see my momma and sister. It's been too long."

"Yeah, maybe you should like...call her back."

I took the offered phone from Chris's hand and hit return call on one of my sister's billion phone calls.

My sister picked up on the first ring. "Chris, did you find her." I'd not heard her voice in months. Not since she'd called to chew me out for not visiting mom. My breath caught in my throat. It was so good to hear her voice. We might not have been the best of friends since I'd left, but I loved her with all my heart.

"Hey, Ari, it's me," I choked out.

I heard the long sigh down the phone. "Ana! Why didn't you answer my calls? I had to get your friend's number from your boss. He told me you were fired last night. What's going on?"

My eyes prickled with tears. This was all too much to deal with.

"Nothing," I lied. "I'm fine. What's happening with you? Why the urgency?"

"She's awake, Ana," Ari enthused. "She woke up last night."

My heart, already bruised from emotion, decided to do another lap around my chest. I let the tears fall as I took in the news.

"She's awake?" I croaked. "Is she ok?"

"It's a miracle. She's completely fine. She's been asleep for over a year, so the doctors will have to set up some physiotherapy for her. She's not used her muscles for a year, so she'll need to build them up. But apart from that, she's good. Really good. Hang on, she's just finishing up with her doctor. I'll put her on the line."

Dream had done it. I didn't know how, but he'd gotten my mother back for me.

My mom's voice came on the phone. "Hey, Ana, my darling."

"Mom!" my voice choked with emotion. It had been so long since I'd heard it. Tears flooded my eyes and fell down my cheeks.

"My mom's awake!" I mouthed to Chris, who was bouncing up and down with excitement. The grin that cut his face showed me just how much he cared for me.

"I'm here," my mom continued. "The doctors are telling me I was asleep for a while."

I snorted, sending both tears and snot flying toward Chris's clean t-shirt. "Yeah, just a while. I'm coming home, Mom. I'll be there as soon as I can pack my apartment up and get a flight."

"It will be good to see you again, baby girl. I've missed you so much. I even dreamed about you once. It's the only dream I remember. I was in a room and could hear your sister reading Alice in Wonderland. You were there beside me."

I nodded, unable to get any more words out. "I was Mom. I was with you. And from now on, I'll always be with you."

Chris pulled me into his arms and held me tight, and in the cool light of morning, I let myself surrender to the agony of grief and the thought that I was finally, after all these years, going home

The end

Carry on the story in...

Available on Amazon now!

OR

Find up what happened to Dream after Ana left in a free extra scene from Dream's point of view by signing up to my newsletter.
www.eliseknight.com/newsletter

OTHER BOOKS IN THE REALM OF NIGHT SERIES

Nightmare King
Queen of Darkness

BIOGRAPHY

Elise Knight is the secret pen name of a USA Today bestselling author. In this guise, she reads by candlelight while eating dark chocolate and wearing slippers. Her books contain fearless women and men you'll either want to kiss or kill (sometimes at the same time!)

You can find out more about her by checking out her Amazon page: https://amzn.to/36wUe1f

her Facebook page https://www.facebook.com/Eliseknightauthor

or signing up to her newsletter here https://www.eliseknight.com/newsletter

Lightning Source UK Ltd.
Milton Keynes UK
UKHW041221080222
398170UK00007B/110/J